Volume

Jack

Frank English

2QT Limited (Publishing)

First Edition published 2016

2QT Limited (Publishing)
Unit 5 Commercial Courtyard
Duke Street
Settle
North Yorkshire
BD24 9RH

Cover design: Charlotte Mouncey
Cover images: main photographs supplied by ©Frank English
Additional images from iStockhoto.com

Printed in the UK by Lightning Source UK Limited

ISBN 978-1-910077-98-6

For Featherstone Book Club

To Marion and George Holmes,

Mi Grandma and Granddad – Marion and Jud

with best wishes

Frank Gaylin

Chapter 1

"Hello, Jack," a silky female voice surrounded him on his way into town just after his eighteenth birthday.

He swung around, surprised, not expecting to meet anyone. His close friend Gordon Gittins was supposed to go with him, but a last-minute family event had stopped him.

"Hello," he answered politely. "But am I supposed to know you? I don't *think* we've met. You obviously know *my* name, but I don't have the pleasure of knowing yours."

"My name's Irene," she smiled, "your..."

"...Auntie Blanche's daughter," he continued. "We *have* met, but it was a long time ago. I wouldn't have recognised you."

"Yes," she went on, "it's been a while. I'm here on a flying visit really."

"You're a pilot then?" he chuckled. Well, at least *he* thought it was funny.

"Look," she said, allowing a friendly smile to creep into their conversation, "do you feel like a coffee somewhere? So we can have a chat?"

"Why?" he asked, in his usual pragmatic way. "Have you something to tell me that I need to know? Only, I have a lot to do today. I have to get a pair of new shoes with my birthday money."

"And?" she asked, waiting for the rest.

"And what?" he puzzled. "Isn't that enough for a Saturday morning in January?"

"Well," she grimaced, "it would be good to have a chat before I fly back to Oz."

"Oz?" he frowned. "Oh, of course. Australia."

"Tell you what," he offered, "seeing as we're closely related, and I haven't had the pleasure of getting to know you yet, why not come into town with me, help me to choose my shoes, and then come back to have a cup of tea at home. Me mam would love to meet you, I'm sure. Would that be OK?"

"Sounds like a plan," she agreed, linking his arm. "Come on, then. Shoes it is. I hear Dolcis is a good shop…"

-o-

"How lovely of you to bring my son home safely," Flo said, a slightly wicked smile creasing her face, "and with a pair of decent shoes, too. One thing I've not been able to do for years – is to get him to listen to the sense of buying decent shoes. Any chance you might come to live here, Irene?"

"I'm glad we met today," she answered, sipping at her huge mug of tea. "We've met before, Auntie Flo, but it was quite some time ago, and I think the last time I saw Jack, I was ten."

"I don't remember that at all," Jack said, scratching his spikes, and raising his eyebrows. "I must have been three or four, mustn't I? I don't like choosing shoes, or any other clothing for that matter. So I was glad of your help, Irene, and of your company."

"You're honoured, Irene," Flo said. "Our Jack doesn't usually do either social conversation or company."

"To go back to your question, Auntie Flo," Irene said with a smile, "I'm only going to be here another couple of days or so, before going back to Australia, otherwise I'd love

6

to spend more time with you. Mum's been poorly, you know. That's the reason I've been here. She's on the mend, but Dad has to keep an eye on her."

"I had heard - but none of us has been to visit, I'm afraid. Not an easy person to visit, your mum," Flo said. "You always were the adventurous one of Blanche's brood, and I always thought you'd do something daring. What is it you do out there?"

"I know. Things have never been easy since the breakdown between the triumvirate and Uncle Eric," Irene answered. "I'm a doctor now, in Adelaide."

"I don't know where that is," Flo said, "but I'm sure Mr Encyclopaedia here will find it as soon as you're gone."

They all laughed at the notion, as they finished their tea.

"Triumvirate?" Flo asked, puzzled.

"Rule of an organisation by three people," Jack explained. "The three here must be Auntie Blanche, Uncle Harold, and Uncle Allan. Dad always thought they were against him."

"Mmm," Flo answered, a flash of anger lighting her face, "and we all know why that is, don't we?"

"Mam," Jack urged quietly. "Irene doesn't need to be dragged into our skeleton cupboard."

"Of course not," Flo said, throwing her hands in the air. "Just got a bit carried away. Sorry, love."

"Don't worry," Irene said, soothingly. "I think I know all about it, Auntie Flo. I've heard nothing else for years. One of the reasons why I left for the other side of the world, really."

"Then," Jack said, trying to lighten the atmosphere, "Oz's gain was our loss."

"Fancy a sandwich or something before you go?" Flo asked as she put the pots in the sink.

"Don't want you to go to any…" Irene said.

"Well," Jack piped in, "*I'll* be needing something to stop me passing out before I walk you back home. So…"

"You don't have to do that," Irene protested with a smile. "I'm OK to…"

"I insist," Jack said. "Besides, it's not every day I get to spend time with my long-lost favourite cousin."

"I didn't think you had spent time with *any* of your cousins," she said quietly, a puzzled frown beginning to lower her brow.

"They're all a lot older than me," Jack protested. "They wouldn't really want to spend time with an eighteen-year-old, I don't suppose. Anyway, we're not too hot on family get-togethers, are we?"

"True," Irene laughed.

"I'm not about to lose you now, cousin," Jack insisted. "Besides, I like you. I have only one brother, and he lives a million miles away. Don't get to see him and my nephews and niece very often, so you're the closest I have to a sister."

"Welcome to my Jack," Flo laughed. "For everything he says, he has a sound reason. You can't shake his logic, ever. At least you know where you are with him."

−o−

"I don't think I even know where you live," Jack said as they walked along Wakefield Road towards town. He wheeled his bike in the gutter so that when he had delivered his cousin to his Auntie Blanche's, he would be able to cycle back home. He had been amazed, really, at how much they had found to talk about. He was a good talker, was Jack, but only when he wanted to be. He didn't see the point of nattering on for the sake of it. Talking for him wasn't a social nicety. It had to be used to some purpose, and in this people could become irritated with his insistence on accuracy and exactitude.

With Irene he had noticed a difference. He could chat to her without having to find out information, without its being to some purpose. He actually *liked* her company; the sort of company he would have enjoyed had she been his sister. It was with her that he was beginning to learn how to chat socially; to understand there didn't need to be an outcome. This was probably one of the most valuable lessons he would learn before he inflicted himself on the unsuspecting teacher training institution he would be starting at the beginning of the next academic year.

Depending to a certain extent on the marks he received for his A level exams, he had already been offered a provisional place at the City of Leeds College of Education.

Flo's pride and emotion at his achievement had overwhelmed her. She could never have imagined this day arriving: her strange, lovely little boy now a man. How could this have happened? It didn't seem five minutes since he was leaping into the big school at Woodhouse, with his letter from Miss Cordle. All mothers had talked about the milestones their youngsters had passed, most of which seemed to have happened at roughly the same time. Not her Jack. Nothing had ever been straight-forward with him.

And now look at him. A man in all but age.

"Did you say you had only a few days remaining before you went back?" Jack asked Irene as they stopped outside her parents' house.

"Three days, then I'll have to be away," she said. "Time's gone by very quickly, and I don't seem to have achieved anything … until now."

"How do you mean?" Jack puzzled, his social language still in its infancy. "Seen your mam, haven't you?"

"Yes," she added, "but I hadn't done anything much until I met you. I don't know why I didn't do it before."

"Then why didn't you?" he asked. "We've always been here."

"I know," she admitted, "but what with all the aggro between our three and your dad… Just listen to me, talking as if your dad were some sort of an alien."

"To us," Jack answered her slowly, choosing his words carefully, "he is. He's never acknowledged me as his son. So, for me, I can see where your three are coming from."

"Really?" she asked, shocked by what she was hearing. "Why? How could he think that? You're his *son*, for goodness' sake!"

"Not to him I'm not," Jack said quietly.

"You're joking me," she added. "That can't be right."

"Always been the case," Jack told her, "and I'm now OK with it. As long as we don't share the same space for too long, everything's fine. Will I get to see you again before you go back? Only - I've got a few days before I start school again, and I couldn't imagine a better way to spend them than chatting with you."

"Nothing I'd like better," she agreed. "Coffee in town tomorrow?"

"You bet," he agreed eagerly. "But it'll have to be the day after, because tomorrow's Sunday. See you at one on Monday at the Palm Beach coffee bar?"

Irene smiled, Flo's words about Jack's precise nature dropping into her mind. She could get on with this young man. She knew where he was coming from, and she felt she would understand his ways. Jack could be the brother she never had, but would have liked.

–o–

"It was very nice, wasn't it, love?" Flo said as she carried a tray of cups and her big flowery tea pot into the living room.

"Cup of tea, Mam," he retorted as he dragged his nose out of his book in his favourite chair. Flo had laid out and lit the fire earlier in the morning, as was usual for this time of year. The room would have been unliveable without it. "Any diges…?"

"How could you have tea without digestives, my son?" she laughed, anticipating his request. He loved his digestives with a cup of tea, did her Jack, but greater than his liking for digestives was his love of…

"…Chocolate digestives," he drooled. "Mam, thank you. There's only one thing I like more than a chocolate digestive, and that's…"

"…Two chocolate digestives," they chorused, laughing until tears rolled down their face.

"Irene being here, you mean, Mam?" Jack said once his first morsel of chocolate biscuit had slid down his throat. "Yes, it's a pity we hadn't met up before now. A first cousin I didn't know I had. I've always been a bit envious of folk at school who have either brothers or sisters whom they spend time with. I've had neither – until now."

My, those choccy biscuits were good. They were so good, he could have shut out the world with one or two of those and a cup of tea. However, his mam knew of and understood his love affair with them, and wouldn't let him become *too* involved at the expense of all else.

"I'm going to see her again on Monday," he carried on, "for a coffee and bun at Palm Beach Coffee Bar, round by the swimming baths. You know the one?" He often threw in a judicious question so he could indulge his twin passions.

"Yes, I do," she replied with a knowing smile. "But hark at you. A social drink? In a coffee bar? Is this *my* son I'm talking to? Come on, who's kidnapped my Jack?"

"Well," he started to explain, "I've never had anyone to just chat to before. It's quite fun. You get to know all sorts of stuff that will be useful at college next September. I wish she was staying in this country longer."

"Aye. Well, you never know," Flo said as she headed for the door laden with the tray and empty crockery. She was proud as anything for what her boy had achieved, but she felt that by going to college, he was entering the unknown. How would he cope with living on his own? Cooking for himself? Washing his own clothes?

"Oh, by the way," he said as he followed her into the kitchen, "I got a letter from the college today."

"Today?" she asked as she piled the pots on the draining board. "When? I didn't see it."

"Afternoon post," he explained. "I took it from the postman when I came back from taking Irene home."

"Well, go on, then," she insisted. "What did it say?"

"They've offered me a definite place," he began, "without the need for A levels, because my O level results were far above the average marks usually needed. The best part about it all, though, is that they say I can be a day student."

"Day student?" Flo asked, not really understanding the reference. "Do they have night students as well, then?"

"No," he laughed. "It means I don't have to live in, and I can travel to college every day, which means also I get to come home every afternoon. Bit like school really. I'll be staying with you evenings and weekends, so you won't have to miss me."

"And you'll have to eat my cooking, more like," she added, a huge smile on her face. "And have your washing done."

"Well," he said, a knowing grin beginning to spread as he hugged her, "there is that, I suppose. I wouldn't want you to forget how to do it, because the only one eating it would be mi dad."

"These exams, these A levels?" she asked, not quite understanding what he was on about. "Does it mean you won't have to take them, like?"

"Not really," he replied. "They aren't needed, as such, but I *will* sit them properly, like everyone else. I just don't need them. Matter of pride, really, I suppose."

"And your O level exams?" Flo asked "They were good?

12

You see, I never took exams, and…"

"You don't need exam results to tell folks you're the best mam in the world," he said quietly, obviously bursting with pride for *his* mam.

"Aw," she smiled, stroking his spiky head. "You're such a good boy, no matter what anybody else says."

"Thanks, Mam," he laughed. "Good to know that at least *you* love me."

-o-

"An' tha's off ter college then, is tha?" Jud said next day on Jack's regular Sunday visit. "So does that mean tha wayn't be allotmentin' wi me anymoower then?"

"Abaht same as now, Granddad, tha knows," Jack replied, "cos I'm goin' to be travellin' every day, does tha know, Owd Man. So I'll be livin' at 'ome. Weekends'll be all rayt though, si thi."

"'As tha got time today?" Jud said. "Onny, si thi, there's nowt much in t'plant line, but I've got some tidying up to do, and…"

"Course I can," Jack replied eagerly. "When?"

"Wheniver tha's ready," his granddad replied. "Tell thi what, I'll gerroff in a bit and I'll si thi yonder. If I get there first, I'll put a chalk mark on t'gate, and if thy gets there before-'and, thee rub it off. All rayt?"

"Aye, Granddad," Jack said, laughing. "I'd better get a shuffle on, then. Looks like we're in for a spot or two of rain later, but that won't worry us, will it? Si thi in a bit, up thiyer."

Jack kissed his grandma and winked at his granddad as he turned to go home to change and get his bike. It had been a while since he had been allotmenting with his granddad, what with his exams and his rugby, and now he was excited to be 'gerrin' 'is 'ands mucky' again, as the old man would always say. He loved his granddad. They shared a lot of exciting, happy and enjoyable history, and he wasn't about to let that go. His grandparents were still hale and hearty – a few twinges here and there, but nothing they couldn't cope with – but he worried about them. How would he feel if something happened to either one of them when he was away?

"Not much daylight left, Granddad," Jack pointed out as they were clearing stuff in the greenhouse.

"Aye," Jud agreed, a smile beginning to wax, "tha's rayt enough there."

"But," Jack puzzled, "what do we do if it drops dark? We won't be able to see what we're doing, will we?"

"Well," Jud said as he moved towards the back of the greenhouse, "then we do this."

With his last word, he reached under his staging, and an ominous click stopped Jack in his tracks. Slowly, a whirring sound began to grow, along with the light from several glowing glass orbs at the greenhouse's apex.

"Granddad!" Jack gasped, his eyes wide and unblinking. "Tha's a magician and no mistake. How did tha do that?"

"Ah, well, si thi," his granddad whispered, tapping the side of his nose with his forefinger, while a huge grin split his face, "that's a secret that…"

"Aw, Granddad!" Jack protested. "Tha can't do this to *me*. We've bin together, man and boy, for donkeys' years. You've *got* to tell me. Promise I won't let on to anybody – except me mam of course."

"All rayt then," Jud agreed, dropping to a low conspiratorial deep hum. "Ah've allus bin concerned abaht light and warmth particularly in winter, so I installed me own … machine, si thi."

He turned slowly to reveal a humming pile of rusty metal under the side staging for his tomatoes.

"What's that, Granddad?" Jack asked, unsure of what he

was seeing. "It looks like a huge … biscuit tin. Where'd you get it from? And, more to the point … what's it for?"

"Well, does tha know," Jud started, "it's a generator, like. It gives me enough electric to run three light bulbs and mi little heater ower yonder."

"I don't see any electric sockets hereabouts, Granddad," Jack puzzled. "So how does it function?"

"Ha ha," his granddad laughed. "Tha doesn't use electric to make 'electricity', tha knows. Tha uses a pint o' petrol at a time. Does thy know why tha uses onny a pint o' petrol?"

"No, Granddad," Jack grinned, "but I suppose tha's abaht to tell me."

"Aye, lad," Jud went on. "It's very technical. Under yon lid there's a reservoir for t'petrol, and yon reservoir holds … onny a pint."

They burst out laughing at Jud's funny, showing Jack what he had been missing by not being here with his granddad's sense of fun and good humour. He vowed he would never leave it so long again.

"Where'd you get that … machine from? Bottom o' t'quarry ower yonder?" Jack laughed, knowing full well his granddad could have picked it up anywhere.

"I got it from owd Isaac Tate's junk-yard, quite a while back now," he answered, looking into the distance, as he did whenever he was recalling anything. "Cost me two and a tanner, tha knows. But it were worth it."

"Isaac Tate?" Jack asked. "Johnny Tate's granddad?"

"Aye," Jud answered. "That's the one. Why, does tha know him?"

"Well, aye, Granddad," Jack said in triumph. "'E were in my class at Woodhouse. Went on to t'Modern School. Took up mechanicking I think. Works at Beddowes Garage on Wakefield Road, I believe."

"Tecks after 'is granddad then," Jud added. "'E were allus

into that sort of stuff. Tinkering. Strange world, dunt tha think?"

"Why's that, then?" Jack asked, puzzled at the reference.

"Why?" Jud echoed. "I were at school wi' 'is granddad. Owd Isaac were mi best pal, si thi. Allus had a fascination wi' owd metal. Used to collect bits of iron and steel and stuff, when *we* all collected stamps or conkers. Then when 'e were older 'e cashed it all in; made a lot o' brass … and t'rest is history."

"Does he still run the business, then?" Jack asked, genuinely interested.

"His two sons do all the day-to-day heavy stuff," Jud answered, "but Isaac's definitely the boss. He can't let go, si thi. His son, Johnny Tate, is your pal Johnny Tate's dad."

"So we can work through the night now, then, Granddad, wi' yon machine, eh?" Jack said, pulling his leg.

"Tha can work for as long as tha wants, Our Jack," Jud said with a great smile, "but I'm off for mi tea any time soon. Shall I leave t'keys wi thi?"

"No fear, Our Granddad," Jack protested. "I'm just as hungry as thee, si thi. Are we packing up, then?"

"We are that," Jud agreed, turning his magic machine off. "Thi grandma ordered me to bring thee back for meat and tatie pie. Is tha game? Happence tha might not like it?"

"Yeah, right, Our Granddad," Jack laughed. "It's onny mi favourite, tha knows. Game? I'm rayt in front of thee."

The natural light began to fade as they locked up and made for the path home, stomachs rumbling and mouths watering already at the thought of tea.

Chapter 2

Jack's last year at school disappeared as if it had never happened. Flo marvelled weekly how time was passing them all by. Before they realised it, Jack would be in college, with so much stuff in his head he would be lucky if it didn't burst.

Time was gathering pace as well for his grandparents. They enjoyed the time they spent together enormously, in the years since Jud's early retirement on ill-health, on holidays and generally in their home. Now *that* ill-health was beginning to catch up with him. A smoker since age ten and working in the mines, unprotected against coal and stone dust, his lungs were beginning to show the strain. Commonly known as Black Lung or Miners' Black Lung, pneumoconiosis, along with chronic emphysema, was the biggest killer after the mines themselves. Miners preferred to call it silicosis because it was easier to say and remember, and did not seem as threatening because it was a shorter word.

Although in its early stages, Jud's condition was beginning to have an effect on his life style. Breathlessness, and an inability to do the things he had always done with ease, gradually closed in the barriers of his physical world.

"Is thy all rayt?" his wife would say, as he stopped mid walk.

"Chest's a bit tight, that's all, Marion lass," he would reply, a slight air of concern knotting his still magnificent eyebrows.

One particular day, Marion knew things weren't right.

"Marion?" he said one Sunday morning as they were having breakfast. "I've made a decision."

"Has tha, lad?" she replied, sipping her tea. "Not feeling very well? Shall I call t'doctor?"

"Tha knows yon second allotment?" he went on, once he'd finished his bacon.

"Aye?" she said, puzzled as to why he was bringing this up now. "And which is yon second? Has thy got more than two?"

"Nay lass," he said patiently, "just the two. Well, one I 'ave mi greenhouses on and thi flowers. T'other … I grow us veg and stuff. 'As tha got it now?"

"Aye, lad," she replied, equally patiently, not too fussed about what he was saying. "I've got thee now."

"Well," he went on, "I've decided to give it up this coming winter. It's getting a bit too much; age and bones and all that. Tha knows 'ow it is."

Silence descended like a lead blanket.

"Marion?" he said turning towards her. "Is thy all rayt? Tha's gone quiet. Marion?"

"I'm flabbergasted, Jud Holmes," she gasped "May I ask why? Is thy poorly? Is this the beginning of the end?"

"Don't be so bloody daft or dramatic," he huffed. "Course not. Neither of them. Just felt it were time I spent more time wi' thee, si thi."

"Aw, you great lummox," she huffed back. "You don't have to do that for me. Are you sure about this?"

"Aye, lass," he assured her. "I've thowt it through, and once I've harvested this lot of veg, that's it."

"As long as tha's all rayt with it," Marion said, "then I'm glad. Time for a rest. Time for an 'oliday?"

"Well," he replied, "funny thy should mention it…"

"Hey up," a welcome voice rang around their kitchen, as the door burst open. "How are my favourite grandparents?"

"Hey up, Our Jack," Jud bellowed back. "Is thy all rayt?"

"Last time I counted," Marion interrupted their usual greeting routine, "we were your *only* grandparents."

"Oh, yes," Jack laughed, tapping his chin with his forefinger. "That's absolutely right. I'd forgotten"

"Not off to t'allotment today, tha knows, Our Jack," Jud said, once he'd sat down by the fire.

"I've not come about that, Granddad," he replied. "I just wanted to spend some time with you both before I start college."

"Oh aye?" his grandma said, looking round from her washing-up. "When's that, love?"

"A week on Wednesday," Jack said. "Got to catch the early train – very early. You *do* know I'm travelling every day, don't you? Bit like going to school, really, only a lot further away."

"Why's that, Our Jack?" his granddad asked, genuinely puzzled. "Wouldn't it be better to go away and stay?"

"Not really," he replied. "This way I get the best of both worlds."

"And your father?" Marion said, knowing Eric might not be best pleased. "Won't he be a … problem?"

"He doesn't bother me anymore, Grandma," Jack answered. "Anyway, we see little of him, and so it's … OK. I get a bit of grant money, which I'll give to mi mam for mi keep when I'm here."

"But what about when you're there?" Marion asked, ever the pragmatist.

"I get a dinner hall pass," he replied. "So I've no difficulty there. Besides, once I've finished mi day's work, I can come home. No problems."

"Got summat to tell thee, Our Jack," Jud said once Jack had joined them around the fire.

"Oh, aye?" he said, intrigued by what he might have to

say.

"Aye," Jud continued. "I'm giving up one of mi allotments."

The only interruption to the silence was the cracking and spitting of damp coal on the fire. Jack wasn't sure what to say next. He was convinced that, when his granddad gave up his allotments, either the end of the world was nigh, or there was something up with him.

"What is it, Owd Cock?" Jack said quietly, finally breaking the silence. "I allus thowt tha'd be *buried* in yon allotment."

"It's just an age thing," Jud said, not sure whether he would be able to convince this smart youngster.

"An age thing, Granddad?" Jack asked, puzzled at his evasive response. It wasn't like his granddad not to call a spade a spade. "And this 'age' thing? Could it be related to thee smoking when tha were ten?"

"How did tha work that one out?" Jud said, incredulous that he had been able to see straight through his subterfuge. He always was a smart young lad. He should have known better than to try to pull t'wool ower *his* eyes.

"Getting a bit short o' breath, si thi," he went on. "Got to stop now and again to catch up wi' missen, tha knows."

"Have you been to see Dr Twist by any chance?" Jack suggested. "Thy ought to, tha knows. He'll tell thee what's up wi' thee rayt enough."

"I *know* what's up wi' me," Jud said. "Probably Black Lung. Hazzard o' working down a black 'ole for all these years. Nowt to be done except for teckin' it a bit easier. More holidays in the warmth and sun. Be rayt."

"Then do it, Granddad," Jack advised. "I'm sure Grandma won't argue wi' thi. Eh, Grandma?"

"Too right I won't, Our Jack," she agreed. "Anyway, sixty-four is no age these days."

"Then it's a good call to pack in what you don't need," Jack said. "I know this is a silly question, but is there any chance in this world that somebody in this room might fancy a cup of strong tea?"

"And a digestive by any chance?" Marion smiled. "Ee, the number of times you asked if we knew where, why, when and how digestives came about, eh?"

They burst into fits of giggling at the picture conjured by this.

"I'll make it, Grandma," Jack offered.

"No, tha won't," she said firmly. "My teapot, my choice."

-o-

"Grandma and Granddad all right, love?" Flo asked her boy as she brought a cup of tea for them both into the front room for a sit.

"All right in the circumstances, I suppose," he replied, taking his tea and digestive with glee.

"And what's that supposed to mean?" Flo smiled. "Mysterious as ever, eh, Our Jack?"

"Well," he went on, "he's having trouble with his breathing, and I thought it might be to do with his smoking, you know, since he was a nipper."

"And?" she asked.

"I nipped into the branch library to check it out," he went on, "and…"

"Library? On a Sunday?" she puzzled.

"Aye," he answered, "it's open for an hour or so on Sunday mornings. Anyway, it seems like he might have either emphysema or pneumoconiosis; what miners call Black Lung."

"Newmanonny what?" Flo said, unable to get her tongue around the word. "What does that mean when it's at home?"

"Pneumoconiosis is a disease caused by breathing in coal dust," he started. "Silicosis is caused by stone dust, and emphysema can be a mixture of any of those, along with

21

nicotine. This obviously happens over a period of time, and is incurable. I'm not saying Granddad has any of these, because I'm not a doctor, but it remains a possibility."

"Does it mean he might … die?" Flo asked tentatively. "But he gave up smoking ages ago."

"We're all going to die, Mam, sooner or later," Jack laughed. "But I suppose it could shorten life in the worst cases, I guess. Forty-odd years though, Mam, is a long time to smoke. There are always consequences."

"Not good news," she muttered. "Not good news."

"Mam," Jack answered, warning her not to jump to conclusions that might not be right. "If you say anything, you might upset one or both of them. I'm sure Grandma will persuade him to go to the doctor. He's taken the first step by cutting down on his allotments."

"I suppose," she added.

"It means, as well, that mi dad might get it," Jack went on.

"No loss there then," she muttered, a smile greeting the possibility of peace at last.

"There was a young lady round here looking for you while you were out," Flo said, matter-of-fact, as she was sipping her tea.

"A young lady? For me?" Jack said, a puzzled look jumping into his face. "I don't know any young ladies."

"Oh yes you do," she smiled, amused at his discomfort that his mam thought he might have a girlfriend. "Remember Jenny?"

"Jenny?" he asked. "Jenny McDermot? William's sister-in-law? What did *she* want?"

"Well, she said she wanted to say 'hello'," Flo explained, "and that she would call in on the way back from her nana's. It's a day for visiting grandparents, eh? She's a lovely young thing now. Not been round for ages; not since just after the christening of William's third, I think."

"I wonder if it's anything to do with our William?" Jack puzzled. "Or…"

"Don't over-think it, Our Jack," Flo advised. "Probably just passing, realised she'd not seen us for a while, and decided she wanted to say hello."

"I might just nip out," he decided in a hurry. "Round to Gordon's for a while."

He'd always liked Jenny. She was fun to be with, and she was similar to him in many ways – only smarter, and much quicker on the uptake. He would, at times, have quite liked her to be his girlfriend, much like when they were at school. He often wished he had those times back again. They were much less difficult than now. You could be best friends with a girl then. Nothing was expected of you other than to be … there. Now it was much more … complicated, because there was an expectation on both sides, which Jack felt uncomfortable with. Perhaps his mam was right. Perhaps she wanted just to be … friends again. It would be good if she did.

"On consideration," he broke through his own thoughts, "I think you're right, Mam. It'll be nice to see her again."

"Good boy," Flo beamed. "Your mother always knows what's best for you."

–o–

"Not seen you for a while, Jenny," Jack said, a little uncomfortably as they walked past the Hark to Mopsey pub. The one thing that being at an all-boys school taught you was how *not* to interact comfortably with girls. Junior school had been a god-send for him, teaching him how to behave in many situations, and one of them was how to survive female company. "Why did you call?"

"Same old Jack, eh?" Jenny smiled.

He frowned, not quite sure what she meant, or how to react. Always sharp, she picked up on his quizzical look straight away.

"Straight to the point," she laughed. "No beating around the bush, eh?"

"Oh," he sighed. "Old habits die hard, although it's something I've been working on with my first cousin, Irene."

Still the funny little boy inside, she thought; the little boy she had liked so much as a child in school. "'Complicated'" everybody else said, but she always found him to be easy to understand and get along with. Truthful and honest to a fault, she liked him for how he was. The only thing to have changed, she could see, was his size.

"Don't change *too* much, Jack," she said quietly. "How you are intrinsically, inside, is something you shouldn't change too much because you'll lose the essence of … you."

"I take your point," he agreed, "but I've got to change enough so that people who matter can understand who and what I am. If I'm going to be a teacher, I need to be able to communicate and to make myself understood. I've got all sorts of stuff inside my head that other folks don't necessarily need to know about. I don't want to be a bore."

"You could never be that, Jack Ingles," she said, stopping to look into his face. "I can see you have a deep soul just by looking into your eyes."

"How on earth can you do that?" he smiled, uncomfortably again. Ever the pragmatist, he felt he had to be careful with stuff he didn't understand; stuff you couldn't prove or make solid, working assumptions about.

"I'm psychic you see," she answered, a mysterious smile crossing her face.

"And what does *that* mean?" he asked, flabbergasted by this deep stuff he had no idea about.

"It means that I can sense things I don't necessarily *know* about," she said. "Always been like it. One of the reasons – among many others – why I always liked you at junior school. You were deep, and I could sense it. Call it intuition if you like."

"Well," he said, after a bit of thought, "it could be mumbo jumbo for all I know. I can understand what I can see and think about, but this deep stuff is beyond me."

"I know, Jack," she laughed. "That's why I'm here. I've been sent, you see."

"Coffee somewhere?" he suggested. "Though I don't know where."

"There's a new one just opened," she said, "on Wakefield Road, opposite Johnny Chapman's barber shop."

"Oh, aye?" Jack replied. She might as well have been talking Chinese for all he knew. He wasn't into coffee shops and such like 'social' areas. He knew he would have to cultivate at least a knowledge of those sorts of places. Would Jenny help him with that? He liked Jenny. Always had. From their first meeting at school to having 'dates' with her in the playground.

"Why didn't we continue being friends, Jenny?" he asked, once they were sitting in the bow window of the One O Two coffee shop. "You know, like we used to be at Woodhouse?"

"Well," she said, looking into his deep green eyes from across the small intimate table, "the tiny thing of 'secondary' schooling, I suppose. We ended up in different buildings two hundred yards apart."

"I know all that," he agreed, "but there was time after school. I mean, I loved being with you at play times, and the odd times you called in on your way to your nana's."

"Oh, Jack," she teased, fluttering her eye lashes and smiling demurely. "Are you telling me you would like to see me more?"

"Well, yes, I suppose I am," he said honestly. "I don't

have many friends. Never felt the need. But you … you're different. I always felt *we* had a connection. Never was into *that* sort of stuff, but I felt it with you."

"'Ark at you," she laughed. "Jack Ingles being tender and soft."

Once Jack was on one of his trails, it was nigh on impossible to side-track him, but Jenny could do it at the flick of an eye lash, the toss of a curl … the twitch of the dimple at her mouth corner. She didn't as a child, although she knew instinctively she could, because she respected and liked his funny channelled ways. *Now* it was different. They were eighteen, and she liked him a lot. She wasn't sure yet how he would react to her flirting, but she would enjoy trying with him. She would *know* instinctively how he was affected, and so she would be able to judge how far she could take it. After all, she was eighteen, and most eighteen-year-old boys wouldn't stand a chance against her charms, but Jack was different. Always had been. He had always been an interesting and very deep youngster, who might just surprise her.

"Not really, Jenny," he answered her, pragmatic to the last. "Just wanting to be the person I ought to be, and…"

"You *are* the person you ought to be, Jack Ingles," she insisted again. "Trying to alter that artificially would change the essence of you for the worse. We all change throughout our lives, but that's only surface window dressing. The true, real you never changes - or at least *should* never change."

"One of the reasons I like you, Jenny McDermot," he said, taking hold of her hand in both his across the table, "is that I can trust you."

That rocked her back on her proverbial heels. She hadn't expected *that* reaction, which cast all her flirty plans through the door. She had never felt such strength, such depth, in a single touch before, which set her whole body on edge, on fire.

How was *she* going to cope with *this*?

Chapter 3

Railway stations and trains had always held a fascination for Jack, from the first time he had ridden one on his way to Bridlington aged eighteen months. Monstrous, black, fire and smoke belching dragons, carried Jack's *Dragon Riders* in their bellies to goodness knows what end. Riding the Dragon every week day for a year had become an unsought yet exciting bonus to travelling to college to become what he had always wanted to be.

The concerns he had had as a junior school child of eleven, transferring to secondary, now began to play around in his mind at eighteen. He had come this far by dint of hard work and determination, but how would he fare once in the new organisation? Would he succeed with what he wanted to do? *Would* he be good enough to become a teacher? If he *was* concerned, he never showed it. His mam *knew* he would be wary and unsure, but she also knew that he would handle the pressures, internalise them, and take them in his stride.

She felt for her little boy. Yet he had always coped with change and with all things new in his life, so there was no reason *this* new venture would be any different. She knew he had planned his first day as far as he was able, given the information he had been sent. She just *hoped* that it would all run to schedule, and there would be no chicanes to try to derail his plans.

"Big day today, Our Jack," Flo said as he sat down to eat his porridge. He may have been a little nervous, but nothing would put him off his porridge. It was a way of life. No porridge, no day. "Are you ready for it?"

"As ready as I'll ever be, I suppose," he replied, waiting for his cup of tea to be in place beside his porridge dish.

Flo knew what he was waiting for. Same routine every day. A routine he wasn't willing to change – unless of course he was on holiday where porridge wasn't provided. That would be hard. Manageable, but hard. It took her back to that first holiday in Blackpool with her mam and dad, when Jack was six. She couldn't believe it was twelve years ago. Such a lot had happened in those few long years.

"Time's your train, love?" she asked.

"Twenty-five minutes to nine," he replied, his last mouthful of his beloved porridge slipping down his throat. My, it was good, that porridge. The best porridge maker in the universe, his mam was. He wasn't sure yet whether he would like college refectory food, but he would have to suck it and see. Suck it and see? That was one of his mam's sayings, and one he had come to use a lot lately. Wonder why? She had a lot of sayings, his mam. 'Homey Lies' she called them. Like,

"What's meant for you won't go by you" and "Once bitten, twice bitten", because some folks never seemed to learn from their mistakes. He had never understood most of them until recently, and now they were beginning to make sense. Wise lady, his mam.

"Come on, then, love," Flo said as he was finishing off his tea. "It's five past eight, and you need to be off. I've put you a few bits of baking in your snap tin so you don't get too peckish. All you have to do is…"

"I know, Mam," he smiled. "Get a cup of tea. I will. Thank you. That'll be champion. Can't wait for mi snap time."

The crowded station was as Jack remembered it from the two times he had already been there. There was a ticket kiosk dating from late Edwardian times: one way in one way out. There were two exceedingly long through platforms: one north, one south. There were also two end bays: one north, one south. He couldn't wait to board his fire-breathing Dragon. Excitement began to build as the time for his train drew near.

Eight thirty.

No sign of his magically magnificent machine.

Eight thirty-two.

A train, which wasn't really a train at all, pulled into his platform. It was more like two single-decker buses fastened together. This one surely needed to move off urgently, or he would certainly be late.

"The train now standing at Platform One is the eight thirty-five to Leeds City, calling at Altofts, Methley, Woodlesford, Hunslet, and Leeds City," came the announcement.

"What?" Jack muttered. "Can't be. This isn't a … train."

Overcoming his huge disappointment, he managed to grab one of the last seats before the train pulled out, on its way to the city at last. His big adventure started here, being taken to his destination by a train that wasn't really a train at all.

The man he spoke to in Leeds about his problem, however, *did* assure him that this was the new generation of engineless diesel trains which were not only cleaner, but were much quicker too. Reluctantly, Jack had to accept and embrace the new progress, which was thrusting its way into everyone's lives quicker than many were comfortable with.

Leeds City railway station was an enormous building in transit. An amalgam of several other separately-owned stations, it had started an on-going massive redevelopment programme to take it into the next century. A high-vaulted hangar of a building, unfortunately it boasted scant purchasing outlets for the unhurried passenger with time to kill. At this stage in its evolution, it was simply … a railway station. Its access via the west side door poured out on to a dropping-off point a hundred yards long that ran down to Leeds' magnificent City Square, watched over and guarded by the bronze Black Prince on horseback.

This was all new and entirely overwhelming for Jack, as he had never seen such a place before. He thought Blackpool station was large, but *that* was sprawling, and in a different league from this. He had already memorised the directions the college had sent him so as not to appear too 'new' and … lost. He didn't like not knowing what he was doing or where he was going, so, preparation and never being late were key to him. He would rather be twenty minutes early than one minute late.

Fortunately, the stop for his bus to Headingley and beyond, for college, was only a walk of a minute or two down Bishopgate Street. The Number 1 Lawnswood bus would drop him off at the bottom of Church Wood Avenue, a tree-lined sub-urban street leading to the City of Leeds College of Education's main gates.

This was exciting stuff.

The next three years spent learning how to be what he'd always wanted to be was exciting but daunting, and more than a little frightening. How on earth was he going to justify his place there? In his usual pragmatic, orderly and no-nonsense way, that's how. Jack wouldn't be able to do it any other way. He was a dyed-in-the-wool Yorkshireman, and that's what a dyed-in-the-wool Yorkshireman did.

"I don't know whether I'll be able to travel to college every day, Mam," he had said to her a couple of weeks before he started his course there.

"And why's that, love?" Flo asked, puzzled at what he said.

"Well, it's five times the return train fare every week, and two times the bus fare every day," he said, trying to show her how grave the situation was financially.

"I'm sure they'll give you some money towards it, love," she tried to assure him.

"Who will?" he puzzled. "The college?"

"No," she smiled. "Yon folks who gave you the grant in the first place. You know, education at Wood Street in Wakefield? You've time before you start, so why don't you pop through and ask?"

She was magic, was his mam. Hit the nail right on the head. She always did. He had enough money in his grant, they had told him, and anything left over he could claim back at the end of the term. So, he wouldn't be out of pocket at all … Another worry ticked off.

The entrance to the grounds didn't seem to fit at all with the grandeur promised by the magnificence of the gates to them. Huge industrial dustbins, the back entrance to the kitchens, and a large modern refectory dominated the initial entrance either side of a long, sweeping narrow driveway. Once passed, the drive swooped round to the magnificent main building façade which would have graced any stately home. Two similar arms of buildings wandered almost into the distance, separated by a square green acre of land that was called 'The Acre'. All in all, a square horseshoe of several three-storey buildings dating from the early part of the twentieth century overwhelmed the onlooker.

Jack was awestruck. He stopped in his tracks as he rounded the last corner, never having seen anything as grand in his relatively short life. He had no trouble finding the main doors, approached as they were by a long, shallow flight of deep steps. Huge thick four-leaved oak doors of twelve feet or so in height – which were glass-panelled to halfway up - dominated the front of the building, leaving the visitor in no doubt as to where to start exploring the innards of this impressive edifice.

Quarter to ten. He had ten minutes or so to find the Great Hall, which he didn't think would be too difficult. Its name was a give-away to Jack. Probably just inside these double doors?

And there it was.

The Great Hall was immense.

Flanked by two identical enclosed quadrangles, it was part of an overall simple design based on rectangular interlinked corridors, punctuated by a grand marble stair-well either side of the Hall itself, that lead to the first of two upper floors. The downstairs main corridor housed the important administrative hub of the organisation – the admin offices, the bursar, the upper echelons of the management team – all of which had large windows giving on to the immediate Acre, the south wooded area of the Beckett estate beyond, and ultimately the River Aire, the Leeds-Liverpool Canal, and Kirkstall Abbey.

This could have been so overwhelming for anyone not having Jack's pragmatic approach to life, which allowed him to compartmentalise it all, to preserve his sanity. *This* day's business was, however, much simpler. It involved a meeting in the Great Hall at ten, to sort out grants, refectory passes, and timetables. Lunch was from midday, and then home on the half past three train ... Simple.

Would that all days were so easy, but he knew that lectures would start in earnest the day after, at ten o'clock sharp and finish at three. That wasn't a day's work, particularly when Wednesday was either a half day or *no* day at all. A twenty-three-hour working week wasn't at all impressive, Jack thought. Still, it would compensate for all that travelling, which had turned out to be something of a disappointment without the Fire-breathing Dragons on his run.

-o-

"How was your first day then, Our Jack?" Flo asked as they sat together at the kitchen table, a steaming mug of tea before each of them and a plate of … chocolate digestives that Jack had bought on his way home to celebrate.

"Underwhelming, I think, Mam," was his quick reply. "I hope we're going to have more to do tomorrow. Do you realise we finish…?"

His voice tailed away, as he regaled her with chapter and verse on his first session and the construct of each day until the end of the year. Jack was *so* precise, he just had to tell her his thoughts, and how he would have organised things better. He wanted to be a teacher like Mr Hardwick – he had for as long as he could remember – but he wasn't sure that *this* was how he wanted to go about it. Still, there was time to give it a chance, and to suck it and see.

"…And then we have to do a main subject for three years, a subsidiary for two, and a few basic ones for one year," he said as his voice faded back in again. "So there's a lot to think about."

"And have you decided what you're going to do with these … subjects?" Flo asked, finishing off. "I'm sure I've no idea what you're talking about, but as long as you choose the stuff *you're* happy with…"

"It's done, Mam," he said cheerily. "Did it this morning. French for three years, maths for two … and the others everybody has to do anyway. Sorted."

He smiled and sat back in his chair, satisfied with what he had achieved for the day. Perhaps things wouldn't turn out so badly after all. He would have to wait and see, wouldn't he?

-o-

Kirkstall Grange was an impressive building, constructed in the mid-eighteenth century for the industrialist Walter Wade, but acquired almost a hundred years later by the Beckett family. Detached and standing back from the main male halls of residence, it boasted its own driveway and car parking where once had luxuriated impressive gardens of velvet lawn, framed by azalea, lupin, forget-me-not, delphinium, and box.

This new college of education had been fashioned out of an older teacher training establishment and was the first of its kind in the country to offer the course Jack had wanted to sample. Paddy Hamilton, a former secondary school teacher, had been charged with the daunting task of establishing this new French department to train a new breed of teacher to take language teaching to primary school children by the 'direct method'.

As the new purpose-built department wouldn't be ready for another twelve months, the Grange had been chosen as their base until then. Although not fit for purpose, with its one room and one toilet to serve thirty mixed students aged from eighteen to forty-nine, it had to 'do' for at least another twelve months. The rest of Grange housed sixty or so male students during term time.

"And where are *you* from, Mr Ingles?" the lecturer asked in a getting-to-know-you sort of way. "I think I recognise the accent."

"I'm from Normanton in the West Riding, sir," Jack answered in his broad West Riding way, not understanding why he had asked him first. Surely it ought to have been an alphabetical thing, or logically and sequentially round the room?

"No need to call me 'sir'," Mr Hamilton said, "but you *can* call me 'My Lord' if you wish."

A polite titter crept through the gathering, which

Jack didn't share, because he didn't do polite responses if he thought they weren't necessary or funny. The room he found himself in was oppressively dark. The large leaded bay window threw daylight in, but it fell within two yards of the glass only, making the fluorescent light strips even more necessary throughout the day. The only problem with strip lights was that prolonged exposure could cause headache and nausea.

"Tell me," Mr Hamilton asked, "how do you find this place?"

"Easy. Train from Normanton, and bus from City Square," Jack replied, quick as a flash. "Here in no time."

The room erupted. Now that *was* funny.

The lecturer's fixed smile started to dither after a few moments of indecision and puzzlement. Mmm ... How was he going to handle *this* one? Seriously funny, or funnily serious?

"Perhaps we might have a look at the books you will need for the next few weeks of the course," as he re-joined his thoughts, "and then at the construction of this year's part of the course. I apologise for the lack of basic facilities here, but work on the new languages block should have started several weeks ago, and is now scheduled for opening Christmas next year. Anyway, the list contains..."

Jack already had all the books in the reading list he had been sent, otherwise, in his thinking, there would have been no point in sending the list in the first place. *This* session, then, would be a waste of time, because they would be going over what he - and no doubt Kay Taylor, Patti Levinson, Harry Hammersley, Terry Spencer, Tony Martin, and all the others in his motley group - knew already.

"And which part of the West Riding do you come from, Mr Ingles?" Miss Jones, a portly middle-aged English tutor asked in Jack's basic English course, during the session before lunch.

"How did you know I come from the West Riding?" Jack puzzled. "And it's Normanton, near…"

"…Wakefield. I know it well," she interrupted. "I used to teach at the Girls' High School…"

"…And I was at yon Grammar School for boys," he added similarly. "That…"

"…Was right next door," she added, smiling at his deliberate use of his vernacular. "I've only been here four years, so…"

"…You would have been there when *I* was," he added, in the parody of a double act.

"What a…" she said almost in an aside.

"…Coincidence," he said, finishing off her aside.

"Miss Jones?" he asked when everyone else had left at the end of the session.

"Yes, Mr Ingles," she replied. "What can I do for thee?"

"I appreciate your understanding my accent and all that," he said, a smile creeping in at her educated attempt at his dialect, "but is my accent *so* broad that I might have difficulty communicating with those who are not from my home area?"

"Regional dialect is important, Jack," she said. "*May* I call you Jack?"

"Course you may," he nodded, pleased that she was taking the time to explain.

"It just won't do if we all sound the same," she continued. "Diversity, identity and all that. So we *need* to preserve *all* dialects in this wonderful land of ours. Yet, there need to be certain times - certain circumstances - when we have to temper what we say so that those who don't live where *we* were brought up, can understand what we say. Do you understand what I'm saying?"

"Yes, I do, and this is my problem, you see," he answered. "I love my accent. I've spent a lot of time with mi granddad who was a coal miner, and we have an understanding that whenever we're together, we talk in our West Riding twang. Those have probably been the best times of my growing up, and I love where I live. Not loved *all* my life being the son of a coal miner and all that goes with it, but I've learned to cope so it doesn't bother me anymore."

"I'm not from the West Riding," she added, "but I do understand."

"Where are you from, if you don't mind me asking?" Jack asked, as polite as ever.

"Nottingham," she offered.

"Ah," he replied, "Robin Hood and all that. That's why you speak with a quiver in your voice."

"Quiver?" she said, a little puzzled. "Ah yes. I see what you mean. We've only just met, but do you know what I like about you, Jack Ingles?"

"My dashing good looks? My razor-sharp wit?" he said, smiling as he brought back Irene's social influence.

"More than that," she laughed. "It's your willingness to learn. You've no arrogance, and you *are* willing to learn - not like a lot of the students I have to deal with."

"I've allus wanted to learn how to be ... better," he confided, his earnest face trying to impress his thoughts on her. "I need order, structure and discipline in my life, and I feel uncomfortable if it's not there. Mi mam allus says that I have to be so precise that I'll be getting missen into trouble one of these days. I *am* getting better, but it's a hard road sometimes."

"There's nothing wrong with dialect," she explained with a smile, "but full dialect perhaps ought to be upheld and enjoyed where it might be understood properly. For those who might not appreciate its niceties and idiosyncrasies, a 'smoother', less 'direct' form might be used to better effect. For goodness' sake, don't lose it. Try to become an educated

West Ridinger."

"I understand," he nodded, "and I will. But please promise me when I get things wrong that you'll tell me? I need to be able to communicate with everyone, not just folk I know in the West Riding, so it's important to me to be able to use language grammatically correctly."

"From what I am hearing, Jack Ingles," Miss Jones finished, as she picked up her books and headed for the door, "your understanding and use of language are good. All you need to do is understand and embrace the use of words consciously, and you'll be fine."

"Thank you, Miss Jones," Jack said. "I'm grateful for your time. I hope I haven't made you late for your lunch."

"Oh my, young man," she exclaimed. "You are also one of the politest of people I have ever had the pleasure to encounter. Any time, Jack. Any time."

Chapter 4

"Mam?" Jack said in that lilting voice that told her there was something of great importance he was about to share.

"Yes, love," she said indulgently. "What's bothering you?"

"Well," he began to explain slowly, "I'm starting my second year in a couple of weeks, and college rules say that from next birthday I should become a resident student. How would you feel about me being away during the week, and coming to visit at weekends?"

"Then I should look forward to seeing you all the more, my lovely boy," she replied with pride. "Rules is rules, and you must obey them."

"Would you be all right though?" he asked, concerned she might think he was deserting her. "On your own, I mean?"

"I survived on my own before you were born," she assured him, "and I will do it again. Don't go thinking you *have* to visit *every* weekend. I'll be fine."

"Not sure," he said quietly, looking at her over the spectacles he had just bought from his local optician. "You wouldn't tell me if you weren't."

She smiled, getting on with her sock mending, remembering his confusion about her darning mushroom when he was little. Such a lot had happened in such a short time. He was almost a man now, but still there were things about which he was so naïve and needed to know before he entered adult life properly. She was sure things *would* be all right. Yet, it didn't stop her worrying, because that's what mothers did.

Her own health was beginning to trouble her a bit more of late, though she would never tell anyone about it. She knew that her Jack would only get himself into a state if she told him, so it would be her secret. She hoped beyond all hope he would be all right until he was off her hands, but health was a funny thing.

"They've already allocated me to a hostel and I've got my own room, so I'll only be travelling for one more term," he continued. "I *will* come to see you every weekend of course, and…"

"There's something else, isn't there?" she said pouring them both a cup of tea. "Something else that's nothing to do with yon college?"

Jack took a deep breath before he launched into his tale.

"You know that I travel to Leeds every day by train," he pointed out, obviously embarrassed by what he was trying to say.

"I *had* heard," she said with a smile, recognising his discomfort.

"Well," he went on, "I met…"

"…A girl?" she added quickly, trying hard not to steal his thunder.

"…a gir…eh?" he stuttered to a halt. "How did you know that? Did someone snitch?"

"No, sweet boy," she laughed, "but I *do* know *you*. Come on then. Tell me all about her."

"She's from Altofts and gets on the train there every day," he explained. "Lives up the Crescent off Church Road, just past Martin Frobisher Junior School."

"Yes," his mam replied indulgently, "I had rather gathered

that's what she'd do, but I have no idea where those places are. Never been to Altofts. What's she like?"

"We sit together if the train's not too crowded," he went on, "which usually it is, and on the bus from there. Her dad's a teacher. He teaches at Normanton Common Junior School, and that's what she wants to be too."

"You are very good, Our Jack, at stating the obvious," she laughed, "and telling me nothing."

"I don't know much about her missen," he said, scratching his spiky thatch, "save that she used to go to the High School, and she's called Wendy."

"I always thought you were good friends with Jenny?" Flo said, puzzled about his relationships.

"I am," he answered, trying hard to explain how he felt about girls. "But *she's* at uni now, like me at college, and I don't see her that often. Anyway, she has a boyfriend."

"I didn't know that," Flo said, reaching for the tea pot again as Jack beckoned her to refill his mug.

"How *could* you?" he said, taking a gulp. "She's not been round for an age, and…"

He was interrupted by a genteel knock at the back door.

"Woman's knock," Jack said, getting up to answer.

"You expecting anyone, Our Jack?" Flo asked as he strode into the passage on his way to the back door.

"I'll let you know when I get there," his muffled voice crawled back from the kitchen.

There was silence, broken only by brief mutterings Flo couldn't make out.

Jack's jaw dropped as he opened the door, not expecting to see the person standing on the top step. He simply stood there with his mouth open, not knowing what to say.

"Hello Jack," the silky smooth voice slid into his mind. "Not going to ask me in?"

"Jenny …" he gulped. "What on earth are *you* doing

here?"

"Same old Jack, I see," she smiled, sidling through the door. "How are your social lessons coming on?"

"Well enough to know when you are having a laugh," he smiled back. "What *are* you doing here?"

"Just on my way to see my nana," she answered, "and so I thought…"

"…and well enough to know when you're not telling the entire truth, Jenny McDermot," he said, a slightly admonishing grin creasing his face. "We have known each other for a long time; long enough to know when you're hiding something from me."

"Ooh, hark at you," she replied. "And *I* was supposed to be the psychic one."

"I don't need to be psychic to realise that you haven't been around for ages," he said, a little note of disappointment edging his words. "I know you're at uni, but you could have called. We *did* agree to keep in touch. Remember?"

"Same goes for you, Jack," she said, becoming defensive.

"I *have* called at yours," he insisted. "Several times. But you've been out with your … boyfriend."

"Ex-boyfriend," she corrected quietly.

"Is that why you've come to see *me*," he countered, "because you've now got some spare time?"

"Jack," Flo gasped from the passage doorway. "That's no way to speak to your friend. Come in, Jenny, through to the front room, while Our Jack gets us all a nice cup of tea."

"And one of those chocolate digestives," she shouted as they disappeared into the bowels of the house.

"…And I didn't call because of my ex," Jenny said, as Jack shouldered his way into the room with a tray. "It was because I felt guilty that I hadn't been around or kept in touch for a while."

"Try … twelve months," Jack protested as he put the tray

down on the sideboard. "We were supposed to be friends, Jenny, forever."

"That's enough now, young man," Flo insisted a little sharply. "Cup of tea time, please."

Jenny watched him as he poured the tea; that same Jack she had first known all those years before, with those same mannerisms and that same intensity. She *had* stayed away too long, and she felt sorry for that. It was no excuse that she had had a boyfriend, such as it was. She remembered their last meeting, when she had tried to flirt with him, and because he was having none of it, she had decided to look elsewhere. She had come to realise over time that his lack of response was not because he didn't care. It was because he hadn't understood. She should have known that *that* was her Jack. She had also come to realise that she felt more for him than she cared to admit.

"So, how's uni then?" Jack asked as he walked her back home, his bike by his side. He couldn't let her go on her own, because that was how he was: a gentleman and a gentle man. She knew that as well, and that was one of the reasons she liked him so much. He always thought about others first. "And when do you go back?"

"Why?" she teased. "Do you want to see me again?"

"Of course I do," he insisted, understanding what she was saying this time. "I *do* understand, Jenny. I may seem a bit slow in some instances, but where you are concerned, I'm not. Well, mostly not."

"I thought you might have forgotten about me," she said, chancing her arm, "what with me not calling."

"That's not fair, Jenny McDermot," he muttered, stung by her clever remark. "I *always* think about you. *I'm* always true to our friendship, and you of *all* people should know that."

"I'm sorry," she said quietly, sliding an arm through his

and squeezing his hand. "Things haven't been going so well for me lately, what with Barry and work."

"Barry eh?" he smiled. "Doesn't have the same ring as a … Jack, for example, does it?"

"Look," she offered, "can we start afresh? I mean, back to how we were before? The best of friends?"

"I never changed, Jenny," he said seriously. "You have always been *my* best friend."

"What about Gordon?" she puzzled. "You were *always* together."

"He lives down south now," he shrugged, "near to where he works, and near to his girlfriend."

"Down south?" she frowned, "I thought…"

"Between Castleford and Pontefract," Jack laughed, squeezing her hand back.

"Daft bugger," she giggled. "I like you, Jack Ingles. I always have."

"I know," he replied. "I know. It goes without saying what I think about you, Jenny McDermot."

They reached her front gate and he stopped.

"Coming in?" she offered, pulling him closer.

"No, I won't," he shook his head. "Fancy a walk in the park after dinner tomorrow? About one-ish?"

"I'd love to," she said, a grin of joy spreading across her face. "Thought you'd never ask."

As he turned to go, she did something she'd never done before. She leaned over and kissed him on the cheek, smiled and skipped towards her front door. She turned and caught sight of him pedalling furiously round the corner, waving as he went.

"You never finished telling me about your Altofts girlfriend," Flo said as Jack ambled through the kitchen door, a smile of satisfaction on his face. "Wendy, wasn't it? Why are you grinning? Lost a tanner and found a bob?"

"Happy, Mam," he answered. "That's all."

"I can see I'm not going to get any more out of you today," she laughed. "What do you fancy for tea?"

"Hows about if I get fish and chips from Colin Heald's Fish and Chip Emporium?" he offered loudly.

"You are funny, Jack Ingles," she smiled. "Fish and chips it is, then, and ... thank you."

"What is there to thank *me* about?" he protested good-humouredly. "What have *I* done to deserve *your* thanks?"

"You are such a good boy," she answered, kissing him on the cheek.

He took hold of her, his mam, and, kissing her on the top of her head, he said, "And I don't cost anything either."

"Don't cost anything?" she puzzled.

"Aye," he went on, suppressing a snigger. "I'm good for nothing."

"You daft beggar," she laughed, trying to ruffle his spikes.

–o–

"What happened with Barry, then?" Jack asked, looking into Jenny's deep green eyes, over a black coffee and a piece of Victoria sponge cake in the Majestic Cafe in the High Street.

"It was only a dalliance, really," she sighed. "Never going to last. He was fun at first but became boringly predictable."

"Well, I'm..." he began.

"You are predictably unpredictable, Jack," she answered him. "How you are, is ... comfortable. I've known you a long time, and you are my closest friend. We are, aren't we? Close friends, I mean?"

"I've liked you, Jenny, ever since the first time I met you," he replied honestly, "and I'm not about to change now."

"Anyway," she said, changing the subject. She knew she would get nowhere with flirting with him, so, friend it would have to be. Still, you never knew with Jack. "What's with the coffee? You were always a tea man."

"Got to try other things if you want to get on," he grimaced.

"But you don't really like it, do you?" she grinned. "I can tell by how your face moves when you put your lips to the cup."

"No, I don't," he agreed. "Can't seem to get the taste."

"Tea's cool, you know," she assured him. "Trust me, I know these things."

Jack had always been … different, ever since she had first encountered him as a six-year-old. You thought you knew where he was coming from, but could never be too sure, as he often surprised you with his cleverness and his unpredictable answers. She had grown to like him more as time had whizzed by during these relatively short periods between weeks away. Once she had gotten to know him again during those times, she didn't want to leave him. She wanted to hang on and shut the rest of the world out, because she knew he was the only person in the whole world she could count on. Unfortunately, however, she couldn't read him. She had no idea how he felt about her beyond friendship. If friendship was all it was going to be, then so be it. She would rather have him just as a close friend than not have him at all.

"Fancy taking that walk in the park?" he asked once he had finished the torture that went under the name of 'coffee'.

"I thought you weren't going to ask," she laughed. "I thought the coffee had stuck you to that chair."

He laughed. She always had been funny. She made him laugh a lot when they were little. She was clever, was Jenny, and they never were at a loss for things to say. He *knew* she was smarter than him - and perhaps a bit quicker too - but he was a deeper thinker, which made them good together.

"You never told me," he said as they sauntered through Haw Hill Park's great iron gates. It seemed pointless having such a huge ornate barrier, as there were no fences attached to them.

"Never told you what, Jack?" she said with a giggle. "You always the enigma, always saying the unexpected."

"When you were off back to uni," he reminded her. "I asked you yesterday."

"You and that memory of yours," she sighed. "Beginning of October. Why is it so important?"

"Because I have only a week left, and then I'll be back at college," he replied.

"And?" she asked, puzzled at his logic.

"Well, I'd like us to spend more time together," he explained, "because you'll be away studying for two or three months, and I won't get to see you. If it's OK with you, that is? Friends *should* spend more time together, don't you think?"

"I'd love that, Jack Ingles," she said quietly, a smile of contentment growing on her face as she drew closer to him, holding his arm more tightly than ever.

They walked for a while in silence, feeling the warm autumn breeze caressing their skin as they enjoyed the closeness of two young people wrapped in each other's company. Lovers, but not lovers. Close friends forever.

Chapter 5

Jack's final year at college was not the best year of his life. His mam's health was of serious concern to him, being in and out of hospital several times for what they called 'routine' check-ups. He had serious worries about her, and felt once or twice it was touch-and-go as to whether she would survive. She pulled through, however, with that dogged determination she had always shown.

He was very upset when he heard that Jenny - his life-long friend with whom he had vowed eternal closeness – had fallen pregnant after a drunken party in the halls of residence at university. *His* Jenny had gone off with someone else. That was something he would never have done, and something that he had not been able to talk to her about because she hadn't been near.

They were close friends for goodness' sake. Why wouldn't she want to *talk* to him at least? He had thought that his twenty-first birthday might have drawn her round, but he hadn't seen her since that last time in September the year before and a couple of fleeting times in passing during his second year at college. Nothing solid. Nothing tangible. Nothing to hold on to.

The brief relationship with Wendy, the girl from Altofts, fizzled out when he saw her coming out of another man's room in Fairfax Hall of Residence in college. It turned out that he had been someone she had always fancied, and because she couldn't have him totally she had settled for Jack as a stop-gap second best. He wasn't having that, so he dropped her pretty quickly.

This left him with thoughts of Jenny, the friend he considered he would keep for life. He couldn't understand why she hadn't been to see him. A year was a long time, even for friends. Her condition wouldn't have made any difference to him. Was she hiding from him?

"Cup of tea, Mam?" he asked Flo as she sat in the front room with her feet up.

"Yes please, love," she said, finding it difficult to catch her breath, "and a…"

"…Chocolate digestive?" he added, smiling as he tried to stay positive.

He filled the kettle and stood it on the single gas ring that was perched on the sink draining board, as, deep in thought, he watched the flames licking around its base. As the steam began to whistle the water's readiness to make his favourite drink, a light tap at the door brought him back to the kitchen's starkness. He mashed the tea and shuffled to the door.

"Hello, Jack," the voice said quietly. "It's been a long time."

"Jenny…" he replied, his voice not betraying his feelings at seeing her.

"Going to ask me in?" she said, a pleading look on her face.

"If that's what you'd like to do," he answered. "Cup of tea and a…?"

"…Chocolate digestive?" she added. "Yes, please."

"Just so as you are aware," he said as he stirred the tea pot. "Mi mam's not been too well, so please don't say anything that might upset her. OK?"

"Of course," she agreed. "I'm sorry to hear that."

"When we've had a cuppa, I'll walk you back," Jack suggested. "If that's all right."

"Hello, lass," Flo said with a smile as Jenny sat down beside her. "Long time no see, eh?"

"Pressure of studies, I'm afraid, Mrs Ingles," Jenny said, casting a furtive glance at Jack. "Still, not much longer to go, thank goodness, and then real life begins. Same for Jack, too, I should think."

"What will you do?" Flo asked. "Like, as in a job, when you've done? Anything exciting?"

Jenny would have liked to have told her, but Jack shook his head almost imperceptibly. That was enough for her. She had already let her faithful friend down by not coming to him in her need, and staying away for such a long time. She always seemed to do this when away, and she always felt guilty when she saw him again. She had *that* feeling now, more than ever before. It pained her to know that she might have hurt him in any way. Why did she do this? Self-destruct in case Jack didn't want her? She remembered their last few hours of togetherness vividly, and the feelings for him that welled up inside. Oh, how she wished she had said something to him then. She knew what he was like, and perhaps she should have taken this particular bull by its proverbial horns.

"I don't know yet," Jenny answered Flo's question. "I've not looked to see what's out there waiting for me."

"Have you heard from your sister recently?" Flo asked. "Any idea how they are getting on?"

Jack knew only too well why his mam was asking this. She hadn't heard from her elder son, his wife, and their three children for months. Jack accepted they had busy lives, but William at least should have written. He *knew* how important it was to his mam, and so he should have made the effort. Jack couldn't tell his brother so because he didn't know his address, and he wouldn't ask Jenny for obvious reasons.

"Not for a while, really," she replied, careful what she said. She knew instinctively, intuitively, why Jack had raised his eyebrows slightly. She could read his dear little face. She knew him so well. Then why did she treat him as if he didn't exist when she was away? She thought about him constantly, but didn't feel she could share her innermost feelings, her innermost shame. "I think they might be coming up sometime around Easter time ... school holidays and all that. The youngsters will be growing up so quickly, I should think."

"You OK, Mam?" Jack said, concerned, noticing that ashen look growing in her face. "Can I *do* anything for you?"

"No love," she sighed. "Just a bit tired, that's all."

"I'll walk Jenny back home, then," he said, "if you'll be all right for an hour or so."

"I'll be fine, love. You go," she urged. "Your grandma will be up in five. So go on, and be careful."

–o–

"Your mam's not well, is she?" Jenny said, as they turned the corner on the way to the Hark to Mopsey.

"Why, Jenny?" he said, ignoring her attempted pleasantry. "Why didn't *you* tell me about your situation? Why haven't you been to see me? It's over a year, for God's sake."

"Don't know," she said quietly, looking at the floor as they walked. "Guilt I suppose. Felt guilty that I didn't tell you what I'd done, and guilty that I hadn't been. It's a mess, Jack."

Tears began to well in her eyes as he took hold of her hand and kissed it tenderly.

"I've always been here, Jenny," he assured her quietly. "You know that, and I always will be. I could have, and still would, look after you and ... yon bairn, if that's what you

51

need. What do you think?"

"You'd do all that for me?" she said, overwhelmed by what she was hearing. "And for a child that's not your own?"

"I've known you for a long time," he continued, "and I suppose I've known that you have always been more than a good friend. I suppose I've always … loved you, but was never able to admit it to myself."

"Oh, Jack," she gasped, bursting into tears, and flinging her arms about his neck. "If you'd only told me that on that last night we were together."

"Well, I'm telling you now," he said calmly. "What about it? You and me?"

"I can't," she sobbed. "The father's asked me to marry him, and I've agreed. That's what I came round to tell you."

Jack was stunned. He didn't know what to say. He couldn't understand why. She should have *known* he would have stood by her, and yet, here she was about to move off in an entirely different direction to marry a complete stranger … from where he might never see her again.

"Then," he muttered, "I may never see you again. After all this time, this might be the last time I walk you home. Do you love him? Truly love him?"

"I … don't … know," she sobbed. "If I do, it's nothing like with you. With you, there's always been something … more. Something special that I've never felt with anyone else."

"When's the wedding?" he said flatly, and without either emotion or real interest.

"Don't know yet," she mumbled, numbed by the prospect of living with somebody whom she didn't really love … who wasn't Jack.

"And the baby?" he asked.

"I'm three months," she replied. "So sometime after Christmas. If it's any consolation, I intend to call it Jack or Jackie."

"And I'm supposed to be flattered?" Jack said, eyes flashing. "It's no consolation at all, Jenny. How could it ever be? It would be better if you didn't use either of those names. Better for both of us."

"Coming in for a cuppa?" she asked hopefully, as they stopped by her front gate.

"Better not," he said with an air of finality. "I should get back to me mam. I hope everything turns out all right for you, Jenny. See you around perhaps … sometime?"

Then he was on his bike and away, pedalling like a demented piston, around the corner and out on to Wakefield Road without either a goodbye wave or a glance. As he disappeared Jenny burst into uncontrollable sobs of despair. Life with her best friend that she had loved and enjoyed, finished there.

-o-

Wednesday fourth of January 1967 was a date he would never forget. Not only was it the day he became an adult officially, but a week the following Monday would see the start of his final teaching practice. Crunch time. Would he cut the mustard? His other two school placements had been three and four weeks respectively, whereas this one – make or break – would last until Easter; almost a whole term.

His final placement was to be in a large junior school in Swarcliffe in North Leeds, where he had been drafted in to continue with the French teaching to nine- and ten-year-olds, that had been started by their teacher Mrs Bentley. He had visited already, so he was aware of the school's expectations in *all* his teaching areas. This, of course, as far as Jack was concerned, was a two-way process, where *his* expectations of the school were equally high.

Apart from his mam and grandma, the two main women in his life wouldn't be around to share in his low-key celebrations. Irene was still in Australia and would be for some time, and of Jenny's whereabouts he didn't have any idea. The last time he had seen her, tears were streaming down her face, and he had cycled away from her obviously extreme distress. How could he have allowed *that* to happen? He was supposed to be a caring and compassionate young man, yet he ran away from his closest and oldest friend at her time of greatest need, and now he had lost her entirely. Would he see her again, the woman he would love forever? Probably not, which caused him a great deal of pain.

"Nervous, Our Jack?" his mam asked.

"What about, Mam?" he replied. "Getting old, or starting my last term but one – or my final teaching practice?"

"You always were old before your time, love," she laughed. "Your last spell in school before you finish your course."

"Yes and no, really," he said, shrugging his shoulders. "When it's over, at Easter, I'll be home to celebrate. Dinner will be on me."

"Oh aye?" she smiled. "You taking me to yon swanky restaurant then?"

"Course I am," he laughed back. "Colin Heald's Fish and Chip Emporium."

They laughed together as he threw his arms about her and almost hugged the life out of her.

"Not seen mi father for ages," he said. "Is he working?"

"I've not seen him either," she replied. "I think he's gone."

"Gone?" he puzzled. "As in … gone?"

"Think so," she added. "Is that a problem for you? Do you *want* him to be here?"

"It's just that I need him to countersign my grant form for the last time," Jack said, "and I've not seen him for months."

"Can I sign it for you?" Flo asked with a smile. "I *can* write, you know."

"We'll be able to get round it I think," he replied. "So no

worries, really."

"Anyway, happy birthday, love," she said, hugging him. "I know you're not bothered, but *I'm* here and I've baked you this."

She turned towards the pantry and, pulling out a huge cake tin, she thrust it into his eager hands. Although never one to lay any store by birthday celebrations, even from an early age, his eyes bulged at what he saw inside.

"Mam," he whooped. "I can always depend on you to come up trumps. My favourite spice cake an' all."

He put an arm around her shoulders whilst keeping a careful eye on the fantastic cake balancing precariously on his outstretched and dithering other hand. He put the cake down carefully onto the table, and hugged his mam with both arms.

"This is the best," he added. "You know I'm not one for presents and stuff. I've had only one birthday, and I see…"

"…No reason to celebrate what doesn't exist," she laughed. "I know, love. You've told me before – twenty *other* times."

"Am I *that* predictable, Mam?" he said predictably.

"Yes, love," she smiled again, "but it's part of what you are. You're my Jack, and I wouldn't change you for the world."

"What are you going to do today, then," she continued, "now that you're finally a man?"

"Well," he said, hesitating in an affected sort of a way, "I think I'll nip into town in a manly sort of a way, and pop in to say 'hello' to Joyce in the library, to see if she notices that I've finally become an adult. She'll probably laugh and say that it's never going to happen."

"Joyce?" Flo queried. "Another girlfriend I know nothing about?"

"She's just a friend, Mam," he sighed, "so don't get excited. She's the librarian and she became an 'adult' a couple of months ago. Known her since I was seven, really. She was in my class at junior school. You remember? I sat next to her. Joyce Jones? Her mother's…"

"…Dotty French," Flo interrupted quickly. "I know. Least said about her, soonest mended, I think, Our Jack."

-o-

"Twenty-one, eh, Jack?" Joyce said over a coffee in the café next door to the library. "I've got my twenty minutes break so we can have a gab. Never thought you'd get there at one time."

"When was that, Joyce?" Jack answered, tucking into a large piece of chocolate cake.

"Trouble with your dad and my mum," she said, sipping her steaming coffee. "It was touch-and-go on a few occasions."

"Mmm," he mumbled. "Suppose it was. There was never any real danger, you know. Me granddad would have flattened him had he tried anything. Besides, I would never have let it get out of hand at any time. Master of becoming invisible, me, you know."

"Any movement on the romantic horizon?" she asked, changing the subject quickly.

"You mean apart from my on-going liaison with Marilyn Munroe?" he smiled.

"Daft bugger," she laughed. "I take it that that's a 'no' then?"

"You know all I ever wanted was you, Joyce Jones," he bantered.

"I think my Kevin might have a word to say about that one," she replied, a smile dancing around her mouth corners. "We're getting engaged soon."

"You're a shifty beggar," he gasped. "Kept that one secret, didn't you? Are you sure?"

"Sure about what?" she said, not understanding where this might be leading. "The clue is in the word 'engaged', don't you think?"

"I'm sorry, Joyce, but I'm just looking out for you," Jack answered quietly. "It's just that…"

"…You're concerned about that spot of bother Kevin got himself into last year?" Joyce suggested. "All in the past, Jack, my son. Trust me."

"Well, if you say so," he added, taking another bite out of his cake. "Will I be invited to the wedding? I'll have to buy a new flowery hat, you realise."

"Ha ha!" she burst out. "You *are* funny, Jack Ingles. Of course you'll be invited. Why wouldn't you be? You can be godfather to my children too, if you would like."

"Now that *would* be an honour," he said quietly, "and an awesome responsibility. Do you still live with your dad?"

"No," she said. "I've got rooms not far from where we sit. Just off Princess Street."

"'Ark at you," he said in mock shock. "Posh."

"Not really," she replied. "Bedroom, bath, kitchen and lounge, but it's enough for me. When we get hitched, we want to get our own home – none of this council renting stuff. We'd like a place down Ash Gap Lane, or High Green Road in Altofts. Somewhere … nice."

"Good for you, Our Joyce," Jack smiled. "You always were the sensible one in our class. I'm sure it'll happen."

"What about you, Jack?" she asked, looking into his deep green pools. "Where do you want to be when you've finished colleging?"

"Already got my eye on a nice little school in South Leeds," he assured her. "A rayt grand little stepping stone."

"Stepping stone?" she puzzled. "How does that work then?"

"Use the first school to get experience, and then move

on when a suitable post becomes available elsewhere," he explained.

"Got it all worked out, eh, Jack?" she said, a glint of pride in here eye that this ambitious young man counted her as a close friend. "You always did have, even at seven. I remember…"

Her voice tailed off, and was gradually swallowed by the surrounding shushing chatter as the black finger of the café clock clicked inexorably round.

"…And the teacher was astounded by how much you knew about coal mining," her voice shrugged its way out of the babble again. "God, is it that time already? Got to go, Jack."

"Same time next week?" he called as she bustled towards the door, a cheeky grin on his face.

"Love to, Jack," she said, "but I'm on duty, and you'll be back in college."

They both guffawed as they hugged and parted.

Her voice drifted back to him as she scampered up the steps to her library.

"Don't forget me when you're on your stepping stones!"

A wave, a blown kiss as she pushed through the huge door, and then … swallowed up by the hissing silence of that most mystical of buildings.

Jack smiled fondly, remembering the days he shared with her as a nipper, and the juvenile plans they made for their future. Joyce had always been his friend and always would be, despite her Kevin's misdemeanour the year before, which hadn't been serious anyway. He *knew* she would be fine. She was an undemanding realist, was Joyce, and whatever came her way, she would handle without complaint, fuss or panic.

Jack, too, was never fazed by anything he was convinced was right. Yet, the approaching final test of his skill as a trainee teacher was stalking through his thoughts a little.

There seemed to be something at the back of his mind niggling away; something intangible but important that was causing him to be nervous and uneasy. He couldn't - wouldn't - let that distract him from his chosen path, because this was too important to the rest of his life to allow intrusions of any sort. No. When he entered those school gates, that first classroom on that first day, he would need to be focused. No room for error. No mistakes. The best he could be.

Chapter 6

"*Comment t'appelles-tu, Sally?*" Jack asked, part way through his French lesson with a class of ten year olds.

Sally looked perturbed as she thought about her answer. She wasn't sure about this new teacher and his sense of humour.

"*Je m'appelle … Sally, meshur,*" she uttered finally, her face reddening around the cheeks.

"*Monsieur,*" he corrected. "*Encore une fois, Sally.*"

"*Monsieur,*" she repeated, dutifully deliberate.

"*Maintenant, mes amis, c'est la fin de la leçon,*" Jack launched into his finale. "*Levez-vous, et au revoir.*"

"*Au revoir Monsieur Ingles!*" they chorused.

At his "*Allez-vous en!*" they trooped out of the classroom to playtime – all except for one little boy.

"Mr Ingles?" he drawled deliberately.

"Yes, Jack," he said, knowing what was coming next.

"Next lesson," the boy continued, "may we play…?"

"I just gave you my answer Jack," Jack said as he played along.

The boy was a little puzzled, until someone switched the light on in his head.

"You were going to ask if we might play *Jacques a dit'*. I know that," Jack said, a smile growing. "So, I said yes before you could ask."

"Aw, Mr Ingles," Jack laughed at their shared joke. "I'll hold you to your promise, do you know?"

"Yes, I do, Jacques," Jack said, eyes glinting.

"You did it again," the boy whooped, clapping his hands in glee.

"A bientôt, Jacques," Jack said.

"A bientôt, Monsieur Ingles," Jack replied. *"Merci."*

"Tu es bien gentil, Jacques," Jack said as Jack skipped out of the room.

"You are a natural, Mr Ingles," Mrs Bentley said once Jack had left the room, "and the class adores you."

"Please call me Jack," he replied. "Everybody else does. But thank you. It's a delight to spend time with them, and they are a credit to *you*. After all, *you've* done all the hard work with them, and all I do is get the benefit of what you've done before. It's a lot of fun."

"I agree with Mrs Bentley, Jack," Philip Archer, the deputy head, chipped in. "You have a definite flair for working with children. They know where they are with you, and they respect your discipline … and your sense of humour. We would love you to have a job here, but unfortunately there's room for only one French teacher, and I don't think Joan here is going anywhere any time soon."

He flicked a wicked glance at her, but, true to form, she didn't react, knowing *his* sense of humour of old.

"How's your mum?" Mr Archer asked as they ambled towards the staffroom for a cup of break-time tea.

"I'm a bit concerned, Mr Archer," Jack confided. "She's been taken in to hospital again. St James's over Harehills way."

"Please call me Pip," the deputy said. "Mightn't it be the best place for her if there's something of concern?"

"Not sure," Jack replied, unconvinced. "We'll have to see. I've been to see her once or twice, and I've telephoned each lunchtime, but there's been no change, and they don't seem to be doing anything constructive."

"You've no transport, have you?" Pip observed. "That must be a tremendous drain on your emotions and on your resources. In to town from Headingley and then up to Burmantofts is a long way."

"She's all I've got, Pip," he said gently. "She's mi mam. I can't let her down and leave her alone. Family's in Normanton, and that's even further away. By train and bus, it's almost an hour and three quarters. No matter how long it takes, it's the least I can do."

Jack's eyes began to drift, but he drew himself back, not wishing to betray how he truly felt. He *was* upset and felt his pain keenly, but nobody else was to know. *That* was how he had lived his life to date, and that's how it would always have to be.

"If there's anything else I can do to help, Jack," Pip returned, an understanding hand on his shoulder, "don't hesitate."

Blue ribbons of cigarette smoke drifted across the staffroom, intermingled with the steam from the boiling water urn, and sickly smell of simmering full-fat milk, that had been pan-heated for coffee. He took a cup of tea and wandered over to the giant picture window that overlooked the playground, wistfully gazing out over the energy-filled yard, bursting with youthful games and screeching children.

What if she had to stay in hospital? What if she didn't get better? What if she ... died? The last question he couldn't cope with at all. *His* mam couldn't leave him. Not now. She wouldn't let it happen. She had come through such a lot in her relatively short life, what with her rheumatics, and all the trouble wi'*'is* father. She was only fifty-three, for goodness' sake. She couldn't die.

"Mr Ingles?" a gentle voice cut into his subconscious

meanderings. "Mr Ingles. Break's over. Time for class."

Jack turned to face Mrs Bentley, a puzzled and almost vacant look on his face.

"Class?" he said vaguely. "Oh, God. I'm sorry. I'll get there straight away."

Although he did his classes as he was supposed to do, the rest of the day passed in a blur, until early evening found him at his mam's bedside in St James' Hospital. Trying not to wake her, he took her hand gently as he sat quietly by her bed, his eyes never leaving her sunken lids, as if searching for - willing there to be - any signs of waking. How could he not have been aware she was so ill? How come this … this curse had taken her so quickly? It was only the weekend before last that she had been at home, seemingly well and on good form. He had visited her later that week, as she had settled into her hospital bed, and she had been awake and alert, if a little tired. Then, why…?

That was it. He hadn't been to see her last weekend, because he had had to prepare for his assessment lesson for Monday that week. Why had he been so wrapped up in his own important little world that he hadn't seen this coming? Her hand, cupped in both his, was so painfully thin, her skin almost transparent, and dreadfully, searchingly cold.

"Nurse?" he called softly, as he tried desperately to warm her hand, searching her face for the vaguest flicker of an eyelid, the slightest flaring of a nostril, the tell-tale sign of a breath that told him there was still the glimmer of life in her precious body. None came to support his hope that all this was a dreadful mistake, and that his mam would wake up to greet him in her usual way. "Nurse."

"Mr Ingles?" the nurse said quietly from the foot of the bed.

"Why are mi mam's hands so cold?" he pleaded. "Is there any way we can get them warm? Gloves? Hot water bottle?"

"I'm afraid it's her condition, Mr Ingles," the nurse replied dispassionately. "There's nothing else we can do until her new medication starts to take effect. We're trying her with some new water tablets."

"Jack," a soft little voice interrupted. "Is that you, Our Jack?"

He turned sharply back to the bed to catch the weak smile on his mam's face, her eyes desperately trying to find his.

"I'm here, Mam," he assured her quietly as he smoothed the fine hairs on the back of her hand, relieved she was still with him. Tears began to well in his eye corners as he tried to engage without tiring her. "You feeling any better?"

"Now that you're here, love," she sighed, trying to hutch herself into a sitting position, which the nurse helped her with. "I need you to go home and collect something for me. At the back of the top drawer in my bedroom dressing table, you'll find an old handbag. Would you bring it to me when you've got the time?"

"Course I will, Mam," he replied quietly, not asking why. "Today's Thursday, so Saturday OK?"

"Yes love," she sighed weakly. "Just be careful with it. Is that all right?"

"How are you?" he asked again, holding on to her hand. "Feeling any better?"

"Better from what, I'd like to know?" she sighed, seemingly resigned to not knowing why she was here. "I just feel ... tired all the time."

"That young nurse yonder says they're trying you on new medication," he tried to reassure her, all the while feeling unconfident of what he was saying. "Though I don't understand why."

"That makes two of us, then," she agreed, eyes flashing like the Flo of old. Memories of a past life eh?

"Seen anybody else, you know, from home?" he asked, concerned she would be on her own unless he came.

"Your grandma and granddad came at the weekend," she said, finding it difficult to breathe properly. "They stayed over in a hotel so they could come both days. The hospital's been very good letting them stay as long as they wanted because of the distance from home."

"I had my teaching class assessment to prepare for," he said, "otherwise I'd have been here. Wish I had now."

He lapsed into deep thought, wondering if there'd be any end to her suffering, his mind wafting back to the snapshots of events in his past life.

"Would it be all right if I had a sleep now, Our Jack?" Flo asked, a sigh betraying her desperate tiredness.

"Of course it would, Mam," Jack replied, unsure what his next step ought to be. "I'll go now, and be back tomorrow, if that's all right?"

"What day is it tomorrow?" she asked drowsily. "I lose track in here. Every day could be a Monday for all I know."

"Friday tomorrow, Mam," he answered with a smile. "March the third."

He leaned over to kiss her good night, and, finding she was asleep, was careful not to wake her.

"Sweet dreams, my beauty," he muttered, pain rising in his throat to see her in this precarious state. "Rest peacefully until we meet again."

"Nurse?" he said softly as he stopped at her night desk. "I know mi mam's struggling, and I understand that you aren't able to give preference to one over another, but would it be possible for someone to phone me at these numbers – day or night – if anything untoward happens? It would mean a lot."

"Yes, Mr Ingles," the nurse replied, making a note. "I'll make sure Sister knows about your request."

He turned once again to say his mental 'good night' to

his mam, as strong feelings of disquiet and foreboding were growing slowly inside.

The evening air was cool but pleasant, banishing immediately that cloyingly warm, sticky feeling from the ward. That sanitised disinfectant smell particular to all hospitals, clung to the inside of his nostrils, loath to let go, as he waited for his bus. A myriad aimless and pointless conversations rattled around the bus shelter, playing out fears, hopes, and simple observations as folk passed the time until they started the next phase of their journey home.

By the time Jack had reached the top of Church Wood Avenue, it was eight o'clock, the refectory was in darkness, and dinner time was an unfulfilled dream. Fish and chips it would have to be then, from the chippy next to the Dutton's Arms, a five-minute walk across the park. It wasn't ideal, but very necessary, as he hadn't eaten since midday.

Jack slept fitfully that night, which his mam would have put down to eating a fish and six and scraps too late. Images of her in her hospital bed gave way to the panic and despair of losing her and tramping corridors in some indeterminate building, trying unsuccessfully to find her; opening doors onto more doors. Fleeting flashes of Bridlington, and Blackpool's Punch and Judy woke him as dawn stretched her chilly fingers into this dull and drizzly day.

The coach waiting to take the respective students to their schools was warm as its engine idled on the roadway between The Acre and the steps to Main Block. Usually filled with bustle and banter, the coach today was unnaturally quiet and low-key, with only a slight buzz of muttered conversations, which were often around the importance of what they were doing. Jack sat on his own, gazing out of the window as the trees and buildings along the Outer Ring Road blurred past, taking neither notice nor part in this gentle, sleepy banter. His numb mind could register only his mam's peaceful face and those emaciated, cold hands. How he wished he could have warmed those poor hands. Why wasn't he able to do that? Surely…

"Jack…" a friendly voice shuffled into his deep and painful thoughts. "Jack? You OK? Jack…?"

"Sorry? What?" he said, turning towards this intruder. "Chrissie? What…?"

"We're here," she smiled. "School. Had a bad night?"

"Yeah," he said quietly, flinging his bag over his shoulder once he was on the pavement. "Something like that."

"Not many weeks to go now," she chatted, linking his arm down the school's drive. "I'm going to…"

Her voice trailed away as he shut out all external sound and returned to the pain of the evening before. Lunchtime couldn't come soon enough for him so he might telephone the hospital as usual.

"…So, do you fancy…?" Chrissie's voice fought its way back into his consciousness.

"Sorry?" he said, a look of puzzlement invading his face. "Fancy what?"

"I swear, Jack Ingles, that you don't listen to a word I say," she laughed. "Tonight then?"

"Yeah," he agreed, vaguely, not really hearing her. "Whatever you say…"

-o-

"Mr Ingles?" a little voice crept up on him at the start of morning break.

"Yes, Jessica?" Jack answered, turning to face the little girl. "What can I do for you today?"

"Why are you so sad?" she asked disarmingly. "Can I call you Jack?"

"I tell you what," he replied with a smile, "why don't you call me … Mr Ingles?"

"OK," she agreed, unabashed, "but back to my first question?"

"Which was?" he said mischievously.

"Oh, Ja … Mr Ingles," she sighed, hands on hips like a little old washerwoman. "You are having me on, aren't you?"

"Yes, I am," Jack said, a mighty guffaw lifting his spirits. "I'm not sad, Jessica, just feeling a bit … under the weather. I'm probably starting with a cold. There's a lot about. Anyway, how could I be sad with you lot to keep me happy?"

"Tell you what," Jack began again. "How about if I called *you* Miss Barker?"

She thought for a moment or two, then shook her head sagely.

"No," she said, an old head on young shoulders. "It wouldn't be the same. Jessica – or even Jess – it should be."

Jack found it hard to suppress a laugh. These youngsters were *so* good for adults. Everyone should have a Jessica about the place when they were feeling a bit low.

"Mr Ingles?" her little voice piped up again.

"Yes, Jess. What do you want to know this time?" Jack smiled, a steaming cup of tea in his hand.

"Are you a real teacher?" she asked. "I mean, will you be staying here with us?"

"No and no," he replied honestly. "I'm *learning* to be a proper teacher - but unfortunately, I won't be staying, much as I'd like to."

"I think you are at least as good as all the proper teachers in this school," Jessica said with finality, "and *we* would like you to stay."

"Thank you for your very kind words, Miss Barker," Jack said, bowing in gratitude, "but the school already has all the real teachers it can take."

"Then it's not fair," she pronounced to the accompaniment of the end-of-break bell.

"Well, Jess Barker, I thank you for your most entertaining company," Jack added. "Now, *I* think we need to go to class. Don't you?"

-o-

"Good afternoon Jack," the deputy's cheery voice accosted him as he opened the office door. "How are things today?"

"Been quite a good morning I think, Mr Arch ... Pip," he answered good- humouredly. "I'm just about to phone the hospital to see how mi mam is, if that's OK? I *will* pay for the call, naturally."

"Phone's free," Pip said. "I'll be in my office if you need me."

"Hello?" Jack said once he'd gotten through. "Is that St James'?"

An unclear disembodied voice crackled at the other end of the line.

"Would you put me through to Ward 4 please?" he asked politely. "I just wanted to find out how mi mam is today. She's called Florence May Ingles."

There descended a few moments of uncomfortable silence before the voice replied.

"Hold the line a moment, please," it said eventually, leaving a faintly unreal void buzzing gently in his ear.

"Hello? Mr Ingles?" Different voice. "I understand you're calling about your mother, Florence May Ingles?"

"Yes, I am." Hadn't he just said that? Why repeat it? Unless...

"Well," the voice went on, "I'm very sorry to tell you that she passed away ... passed away ... passed away..."

Passed away? That can't be true. Not *his* mam. Must be some mistake.

"There must be some mistake..." he said, finding it difficult to drag the words out of his mouth "...I only saw her yesterday evening. She can't be ... *gone*. She's ... mi mam. She's all I have left."

No. It couldn't be true. His mam, the one constant in his little life; the only person to love him unconditionally – if only because he was her son. No.

He stood, rooted to the floor, unable to move, the phone locked to the side of his head, as the room began to fade and darken and the happy screeching children's voices slowly dropped to a hushing, hissing silence.

"Mr Ingles?" the Voice insisted. "Are you still there? Are you all right? Very sadly, she passed away quietly at four o'clock this morning. Her husband was at her side. I'm very sorry for your loss."

That was it? She was gone? Husband? Did he hear right? What was *he* doing there? How on earth did *he* know? No matter now. Knowing about his whereabouts wouldn't lift this incomprehensible weight of loss, dread, and ... guilt from his still young shoulders. How was he going to manage without his ... mam, the most important person in his life?

"Would it be possible to come and ... see her, please?" he stumbled, not being able to think of anything else he might do.

"Today?" the voice asked quietly, not really understanding his unbelievably crushing pain. "I'll arrange it for three o'clock."

The Voice faded, ushered down that little hole that was the modern telephone system, back into its void until summoned again to deliver its unconscionably devastating dose of pain to some other unsuspecting, unprepared creature.

Jack stood, numb, the phone still against his ear, loath to put it down in case it came to life again to tell him it was all a ghastly mistake, and that his mam was just finishing her jam roly poly, ready to see him at five.

"Jack?" Pip Archer's voice brought him back to *this* world.

"Anything the matter?"

"Mi mam died at four o'clock this morning," he said quietly, still keeping the tears from washing over him, as Pip took the receiver and put it back on its cradle. He turned to his deputy head, and with a look of utter anguish, walked slowly towards the door. Pip took hold of his arm and guided him gently towards his office, where they could talk.

"What can I say, Jack?" Pip said quietly, as he tried to comfort this extraordinarily brave young man. "I am so sorry you had to find out like that. I can't imagine how you must be feeling."

"A bit shocked and surprised, really," Jack replied, wishing he was on his own somewhere quiet to deal with this horror in his own way. "Would it be all right if I took this afternoon off to go down to St James' to pay my respects?"

"Of course it would," Pip replied. "Would you like me to take you in my car?"

"No, really," Jack said, preferring to travel alone in his own time. "I should like to take the bus to give me time to prepare myself for what I might see. But thank you for the offer."

"Take as long as you need, Jack," the deputy offered.

"I'll be back mid-week, as soon as I know what the arrangements are going to be," he said quite firmly. "If I go now I'll be able to catch the quarter past one into town, if that's all right. I should be grateful if you would pass on my apologies to the teachers whose classes I would have been working with. I don't like to let people down."

"Think nothing of it, dear boy. Everyone will be sorry to hear about your loss," Pip assured him. "We'll see you whenever we see you."

-o-

The world had never seemed to be a lonelier place as Jack strode up the drive towards the road and the graffiti-covered bus shelter. A chilly keen breeze whistled about his ears, obliging him to draw his overcoat collar closer around his neck. The shelter was unsurprisingly empty and stark, with the stink of urine and stale beer making it a place not to tarry in. The Number 49 couldn't come quickly enough for him, although he didn't know what to expect when it delivered him finally to his uncertain destination.

Apart from the thrum of the engine, it was quiet, with individual passengers dotted about the lower deck, travelling alone, due no doubt to the time of day and the frequency of the service. Although a pragmatic and logical young man, Jack found extreme difficulty rationalising the last eight hours' sequence of events. The inevitable questions of 'Why *his* mam?' and 'What did *she* do to deserve this?' crashed about in his head, knowing the answers but not accepting them. She *was* poorly, he accepted that, but couldn't she have been allowed to stay just a *bit* longer, until he had finished college at least? His anger subsided as the bus juddered to a halt.

"St James' Hospital," the conductress's clear voice rang out, urging a swift disembarkation for those who needed to be off. The bus pulled away slowly, leaving Jack perplexed as to where, in this monolith, he might find someone who knew where his mam might be. Overwhelmed with sadness, he fought back the tears which told him he was on his way to one of the last times he would see her physically on this earth.

Chapter 7

"Excuse me, please," Jack said to the tall uniformed man behind the hospital's reception desk. "My name's Jack Ingles, and I…"

"Ah, yes," the man interrupted quietly and without fuss. "Mr Ingles. Come this way if you please. Your mother is waiting for you."

As natural as anything. As if she was sitting in the next room ready to greet him. If the man's demeanour seemed to be flippant, it was anything but. Deferential, compassionate, with a solemn but pleasant manner, he put Jack at ease straight away.

"She's in here, Mr Ingles," he said, opening one half of an immense double oak door. "Please take your time. There is no rush."

Jack wasn't prepared for what met his gaze when the door clicked shut behind him. As he turned, he gasped, and, overwhelmed suddenly by emotion, tears rushed to his eyes, and his hands hung limply at the ends of useless arms.

Although relatively small and dimly lit, the room exuded a deep spirituality he had not experienced before. A small vaulted stained glass window cast its watery light on to a raised catafalque at the centre of the wall opposite the door, upon which lay Flo Ingles, dressed and covered.

"Mam," he croaked almost inaudibly. "Ee lass. What are

you doin' 'ere, eh? You look so peaceful on yon nice comfy bed. Shall we 'ave a little chat then eh, an' you can tell me what you've been up to?"

He stumbled across the room and sat down next to her, as the quiet strains of the Intermezzo from Cavalleria Rusticana oozed over them both.

"I see they're a bit chilly again," he sobbed as he took her hand in both of his, rubbing gently as if trying to restore a little warmth. "Come on, love. This won't do."

Her naturally wavy hair had been done, and a touch of make-up had been applied tastefully here and there, neither of which she had ever had done in her life, to Jack's knowledge.

"Ee, you look rayt grand, mi owd love," he continued, his emotions now under control. "Do you remember that time in Blackpool when I were six, and I thought we had to climb the Tower on the outside?"

He smiled as he dropped into his considerable store of happy memories, glancing into his recent past as easily as looking into a mirror. He sat there for a quarter of an hour, a smile on his face, as if sharing more memories quietly with his mam. Periodically, his bottom lip quivered as he looked again mournfully at her peaceful, almost serenely smiling face. He wanted to go; to put all of this behind him. Yet, he found it very hard to draw himself away from *his* mam, whom he would never see again on this earth.

–o–

"Thank you for your kindness and patience," Jack said to the receptionist as he made his way out after half an hour.

"You are more than welcome," he replied, the reassuring smile still on his face. "I am so sorry for your loss, although she *is* in a happier and more restful place now."

The overriding feeling as he trod the walkway outside

was one of complete emptiness after his overwhelming sense of loss and grief. He made his way to the bus stop without a backward glance. He had said his tearful goodbyes, and would now be looking forward, as his mam would have wanted him to. His next ordeal would be the wake, traditionally held over the open coffin in the front room, followed by the interment itself.

He had already decided that he wouldn't attend the bun-fight after the service, which was always held in the Majestic Café at the top of High Street in his home town. The burial would be hard enough to cope with without the shenanigans which would undoubtedly take place there. His mam wouldn't have wanted to be party to any of this money-wasting nonsense, particularly if her 'husband' had anything to do with it.

He still had two buses to ride to get back to college where, no doubt, he would be able to have a leisurely tea for a change, and a sit in his own room afterwards to have a think and a cup of tea.

Chrissie was the first to greet him in the refectory queue. She rushed up to him, threw her arms about his neck, and hugged him, mumbling her distress in his ear as they stood.

"It was a surprise, I can tell you Chrissie love," Jack said, once he had disentangled himself. She was a loving and compassionate lass, was our Chrissie, and he appreciated her thoughts.

"So what's next?" she asked, genuinely concerned for his welfare.

"I don't want anyone else here to know," he said, raising his brows as he looked into her face. "Can we keep this between you and me? I trust you and love you to bits, Chrissie. Please?"

She smiled, and, nodding agreement, she squeezed his hand as they waited for tea. Her Fred would understand.

They both loved this strange Yorkshire lad who had squeezed himself into their lives almost unnoticed.

"Funeral will most likely be Saturday," he continued, "because that's when they always have 'em round our way, and I'm not looking forward to it one little bit."

"It'll soon be over, my lovely," she said, soothingly. "So … best be looking forward to beyond. When will you be back at school?"

"Probably Wednesday," he said quietly, "when I've had time to find out about the arrangements."

"Don't you think that's a bit soon?" she asked, a little surprised.

"Got to get back on with it, Chrissie," he answered, pragmatic to the end. "Mi mam wouldn't have wanted me to mope. She was a doer, and so am I. Now then … which of these culinary wonders is going to tickle my palate this fine evening?"

Chrissie smiled as they inched along this gastronomic line of delights. 'He'll be all right, will our Jack,' she thought. 'Tough these Yorkshire lads.'

–o–

True to his word, Jack was back at school Wednesday first thing, ready to pick up where he had left off the Friday before. Surprised to see him, everyone he encountered expressed their sorrow, and best wished for the day.

"What are *you* doing here, young man?" Pip Archer's voice stopped him in his tracks. "You shouldn't be back because…"

"I couldn't stay away any more, Pip," Jack replied almost apologetically. "I couldn't have rationalised letting people down any longer. Besides, mi mam wouldn't have been comfortable with it either."

"Then you have to do as your mam tells you," Pip laughed,

slapping him on the back as they shouldered their way into the staffroom. "Thank you for being here. Oh, by the way … your tutor, Mr Matthews, is coming in today to watch Chrissie Mattinson's lesson. He'll be surprised to see *you*."

"Then he'll be able to kill two birds with one stone," Jack smiled. "He can come and watch me teaching French to Class Five."

-o-

"Mr Ingles," a deeply bass voice oozed over him as he waited for the break time kettle to boil. "What are *you* doing here?"

"Mr Matthews … hello," Jack replied with a smile. "Good to see you."

"Should you *be* here?" the tutor said over a cup of steaming tea. "I mean … you *are* allowed time off to grieve, you know."

"I know," Jack said wistfully, "but people rely on me to be there, and I can't in all conscience let them down. I've already had *two* days off I could have done without. I can do nothing about mi mam. I've said my goodbyes, and my head and my heart are where she will live on. Not looking forward to the funeral, but that will soon be over. Are you coming in to see my French lesson?"

"You are unbelievable, Jack Ingles," Mr Matthews said, with a shrug and a smile. "I don't know of anybody who would rationalise pragmatically such an emotionally charged event like you have. Most folks would have taken the week off, or even longer, but not Jack Ingles. I should love to see your French lesson, though you probably know far more about it than I do."

"Well, let's go then," Jack said. *"Suivez-moi, monsieur. La classe nous attend."*

Chapter 8

Saturday 11th of March 1967 was undoubtedly the worst day of Jack's twenty-one years. He had been devastated when he had seen his mam on her last day, and when he had sat with her in the chapel of rest. Yet, the wake, the funeral, and interment took his despair and pain to a whole new depth.

The wake was an experience he vowed never to put himself through ever again. His granddad called it 'The Circling of Vultures', where family and friends were supposed to gather in the front room around the open coffin to extol the life of the departed. This particular Circling descended into a female free-for-all in double quick time. The only male in a gaggle of ageing gabbing females, he sat quietly in a corner out of the way, minding his own business as he looked at his mam's serene but cold face. Once their conversations turned to 'women's things' and their furtive glances and nods towards Jack were obviously marked, he became uncomfortable enough to decide this was no place for a sane, intelligent young man. So, he beat a slow but dignified retreat. The vultures had claimed their prey once again, but not before he had tucked the favourite woollen scarf he had bought her around his Mam's neck to keep her warm.

Stepping over several handbags in the doorway, he

was reminded of some of his mother's last words to him. Rummaging in the drawer in her bedroom as she had urged, he drew out the old handbag she had described. Thrusting it into his ruck sack, he thought no more about it until later when he would discover no doubt her urgency over its return to her.

Brother William was there, but his wife was not. Their three children were too young to be left, and they had no one else with whom they might stay. He had arrived early and would be leaving shortly after the service because of the distance he had to travel.

"Well, Our Jack," William said, hugging his brother. "This *is* a pretty pickle and no mistake."

Why hadn't you been to see her? Why hadn't you brought the children? Why hadn't you involved her in your life? These were all questions that needed to be asked. But not today. Recrimination and bitterness were for another time. Today was for the solemn and upsetting act of laying his – their - mam to rest, following protocol and tradition. No more, no less.

The black hearse and the one funeral limousine parked outside the house that Flo and co had lived in for fifteen years, had silenced the whole street, as if the Devil himself had brought his chariots to carry away another unfortunate. The members of every household who had known Flo stood respectfully outside their respective gates, heads uncovered and eyes downcast, as the coffin was carried out.

True to himself and to his years of avoiding his father's direct company, Jack squeezed into the funeral car between his brother and the corner of the back seat. His father occupied the corner seat at the opposite side, and Grandma and Granddad were in the front. The only time he had been in a car, since the time Mr Lee had taken them to the station when he was a nipper at the start of their adventure to Blackpool, just had to be in these circumstances.

No one spoke as the cortége set off at walking pace for the cemetery, neighbours bowing their heads in sorrow and silent tribute as it passed.

Houses and people and other cars ambled past as the cortege left the estate behind, turning left on to Dalefield Road past the one lone red sentinel telephone box, and taking his mam away for the last time. Jack knew, too, that he wouldn't return to live in the house they shared together. He understood in his heart that once his beloved mother had made her last journey, then so had he. *She* would have wanted him to move on with his life in the direction of his choosing, and he *shared* those feelings as they had shared all else in the short years they had been together.

The coffin's slow descent into that black, seemingly bottomless hole, dragged his heart and his soul with it, and it was then he felt that last, deepest despair that she was gone.

"...and we commit her body to the ground; earth to earth, ashes to ashes, dust to dust..."

Finally, in a last desperate act of acknowledgement, tears welled into his eyes, and rolled down his cheeks in silent homage to her passing.

Chapter 9

Jack Ingles' first recollections of his initial teaching appointment were the interview and the subsequent visit to his first school. He had applied to the local authority's pool of staff, theoretically, if he was successful, to take up appointment in any of the sector's schools should a vacancy arise. Because his initial teacher training had given him skills in teaching French to eight year olds, he hoped this would give him a head start. The first Leeds school to follow this route was run by a head teacher called Moore, and he had been the first teacher in the country to start up this initiative. Jack had had the temerity to write to Mr Moore to let him know he might be available to fill a vacancy for a French teacher in his school were he to be successful at the Education Office interview. Although Mr Moore couldn't make any offer himself, he had wished him good luck. Fortunately, also, the interviewer was the inspector for Modern Foreign Languages in the city. This interview was Jack's chance to circumvent due process, and provide himself with an advantage ... or so he thought.

"And how do you feel your college course, er, served you?" started the interview at the Education Offices. "My name by the way is Atkinson, subject specialist for modern foreign languages, er, and you said – ah yes … It's got to – … Now Mr er um, said he was willing to have you should you fulfil our criteria. Are you, er? … So that's settled then … Good day Mr Er, er … You'll be hearing from us in due course…"

Just three minutes: he hadn't said a word, and he was in. The interviewer hadn't said so, of course, in so many words, but the signs were there, unmistakably. Atkinson the Astute had scored again. He would be now recovering from the ordeal with a glass of scotch and water and a cigarette.

Jack made his way out of this holy of holies – grand edifice of bureaucracy, fount of educational ideologies – with something of a feeling of lack of fulfilment and of being strangely unsatisfied, as if he had had some forbidden fruit dangled before his nose, had taken a bite … and had missed.

So this is what it felt like to be a fully-fledged, qualified (if probationary) member of the teaching fraternity. He could now hold his head up in the world, no longer a mere student scorned by staffs, and tolerated by tutors. He was now a teacher, a respected member of society.

The school he had requested, was an early Victorian pile of black stone held together by invisible mortar, with an enormous iron fence where rust had been allowed to grow, no doubt, in an attempt to cover its ghastly khaki paint. Two parts of the school crept out in to the playground like welcoming arms, which, once inside, threatened to stifle the breath out of your body.

With heart pounding, and mouth dry with apprehension, he climbed the three hallowed stone steps to the matching gate. It was locked. There seemed to be no other way in so how would he enter? Shout? No, that was no good. He couldn't be seen to be making a spectacle of himself – not so early on anyway. Pick the lock? He couldn't have picked a worse one. No, there was only one thing for it – climb over. Couldn't be late for his first fact-finding visit.

"'Ello, 'ello, 'ello," came the tones of authority someway below his left ear. It was the gently encouraging shape of the caretaker, a Mr Harrison. A small, leery, shifty-looking character with a loud voice and no sense of delicacy or style, he was - as Jack was to find out later to his cost - the most important person in the school. With him behind you, anything could be achieved.

"Learning to climb, are we?" he asked sarcastically. "Or are we getting a little exercise?"

"Er, well, no, actually. Er no," Jack replied, a little nonplussed from his perch atop the gate. He had to stay there for a while because he had, in fact, caught his trouser behind on one of those infuriatingly small and inaccessible pieces of protruding metal that can neither be seen beforehand, nor found afterwards, and he was ... stuck. He could, of course, have come down minus trousers and covered in embarrassment, but he elected to wait.

"Actually, I have an appointment ... to see Mr Moore," he explained. "I'm the new teacher, you know, and I couldn't find the way in because this gate is ... er, locked."

"Oh aye?" he said, leaning on a king-sized brush, which didn't seem to show any signs of wear. "Finding it difficult to get in, are yer?"

"Er, yes, well," Jack stammered. "I say, could you give me a hand down from this ... perch?"

"Do you know who I am?" the caretaker growled, leaning closer to the gate.

"No idea. Cleaner or something?" was Jack's swift reply.

"Caretaker, lad, caretaker," he barked back. "Not allowed to work above 'ead 'eight. Union rule 28. You'll have to get yerself down."

This didn't give him much leeway, because he couldn't have been much more than five feet four. With his last words, he turned on his brightly polished heels, and shuffled off across the playground. Halfway to what Jack guessed to be the boiler house, he turned and shouted, "By the way, yon lock's been broken for many a month. It opens easily. You only 'ave to push," and, with a malicious chuckle, he disappeared into the school.

Eventually, Jack managed to disengage his rear quarters from his point of contact with the gate, without too much damage either to himself or his clothes. He dusted off his one and only suit, pulled himself up to his full five feet nine inches, and made his way into the school. That was his second mistake. The front of the school was like a comedy of errors. It looked as if the builder had, at a number of points, run out of stone temporarily, and - so as not to interrupt the flow of work - had built a door at each point instead. These doors, of course, had to lead somewhere, or hide something, if only dustbins. One of them hid the only direct front entrance into school … but, unfortunately, Jack had not chosen that one. He did, however, manage his first close-hand inspection of the boys' toilets.

He found his way out of that torture chamber in very quick time, and ran full tilt into what he thought must have been a character straight out of Dickens. Tall, close-browed, with a mass of slick, iron-grey wavy hair, this he felt sure must have been someone in authority. The face was stern, eyes close-set, and above the almost invisible, twisted mouth snaked a thin pencil line of bristles balancing precariously on the top lip. He had on a well-worn tweedy sports jacket with one shoulder larger than the other, and he spoke with a deep and clipped, nasal tone, exuding the intelligence and *savoir faire* of a half-educated chimpanzee.

"And 'oo might you be?" he glowered.

"I have an appointment to see Mr Moore," Jack returned. "I take up a post in September."

"The H-eadmarster is busy right now," the character's

reply came back, as gentle and musical as a circular saw missing a few teeth. "You would be Mr Ingels?"

"Ingles *is* the name, yes," Jack countered.

That correction was another mistake, for he brought his non-too-handsome face close to Jack's, and uttered in a tone which could only be construed as threatening.

"The name's Sparks," he hissed, "and I'm the Deputy H-eadmarster. You remember that."

He led Jack towards another door, which was identical with the one he had already encountered, and through into a dimly lit and narrow corridor. It was more like a tunnel really; square in section, painted dark red and green, and smelled rather damp. Later he discovered that this was the staff entrance, and was, he also found later, identical in every respect, with the other two – boys' and girls' entrances – around the other side. There were no windows or doors along this dungeon-like corridor, and so the only daylight to be seen was quite severe, at either end.

They had just seen the one end, and the other led into an assembly hall with a high, vaulted ceiling and small leaded windows near the top. The walls bowed outwards slightly, because of age and weight, and were kept from falling outwards by steel tension bars running across the hall, some ten feet up, and continuing through the walls to the outside. These were fastened and stabilised by heavy-duty iron plates on the outside. The wooden floor wore a highly polished top coat, but the walls, clean only to about head height, were peeling, in urgent need of repainting, and seemed to have been stitched together at the top corners by huge dusty cobwebs.

Along one of the longer walls ran a wooden platform, forming a stage, and along the other, ran banks of stacked wooden chairs. Two great dungeon-like wooden doors, one either side of a large cupboard/bookshelf, led to hidden chambers in the end wall of the room. The other end supported a glass-panelled door only, giving on to what he guessed to be a classroom. Just outside this door, was the inevitable but somewhat ancient upright piano and matching stool.

They passed the first of the twin doors, and made for the other. This, Jack assumed, must be the head's office. His escort hammered rather unceremoniously, and shuffled his way in. Jack made to follow, but had the door closed in his face none too gently. After a few moments, the deputy emerged and ushered him in.

It was rather a small room where the walls were fortunately lined with cupboards and glass-fronted bookcases to cover the peeling paint. In the middle of the floor, and slightly off to the back of the room, grew an enormous desk, that was completely clear of everything other than a desk diary, an over-sized blotter pad, and an inkstand, which, along with the school, must have dated to late Victorian times. In the opposite corner cowered a much smaller desk with typewriter set neatly to one side, destined, no doubt, for a secretary, but who was nowhere in evidence. Behind the larger desk sat a small, grey haired, mild-looking man, in a dark blue serge suit. A pair of old, tortoise-shell NHS spectacles nestled in front of two grey, slightly naïve and bemused-looking eyes.

"Well, now, er … Mr Ingles isn't it?" he began in a softly spoken voice, taking a deep breath. "Do take a seat. You've met our Mr Sparks, I see. Good.

At this point he seemed to lose momentum a little, and lapsed into a few moments' silence before picking up his thread again.

"This is an old school, as you see, but a happy one, as you will no doubt find out. We'll have a little chat first, and then I'll take you around."

This general 'little chat' about inconsequentialities, lasted around ten minutes and then they emerged to examine the seat of learning. Broughton County Junior and Infants School was the old type of junior school catering for children from a very working class, almost downtown-but-not-quite area of Leeds. The children, it turned out, were well cared for by their parents in the main, but had none of the refinements held in high esteem by their contemporaries to the north of the city. On the whole, they were good children. The school had a strong reputation in that area, and, indeed, many of the parents of present children had themselves been pupils at the school, taught, it might be said, by some of the teachers still in there. By some standards, it was a medium-sized school of perhaps two hundred or so pupils. By others, however, it was thought it should have been levelled many years before.

Their tour of the school showed it to be a veritable rabbit warren of subterranean corridors, little doors, and umpteen corners full of lots of material which came under the wide term 'equipment'. The other main feature, he discovered, was another hall that was parallel with, and almost identical to the one just met, and this one doubled as part classroom and part PE hall, for use when the weather did not allow outside activity.

It took just seventeen and a half minutes to complete the tour of inspection, and to meet all the staff who were available. In fact, Jack met all but one, and he was out on the field with a class of budding ten-year-old athletes. He was a tall, curly headed, rather pale individual, with a lively (or perhaps restless might be more accurate) nature, who was always ready to try anything new. He was the self-styled Physical Education expert/scientist/mathematician/drama producer of the staff, even though his teaching experience totalled only around eighteen months. He turned out to be a somewhat enigmatic if friendly character, who was inching towards his late twenties on account of his four years in industry.

Once the last classroom had been left behind, they headed again for Mr Moore's room.

"It will soon be time for the kiddies to go out to play," he said as they entered, "and when they do, we'll go and have coffee with the staff. It will give you chance to chat to them a little more, you know. Most valuable time."

He coughed nervously, looked at his watch, moved towards his desk, hesitated halfway and came back, picking up an imaginary something from the floor. As he was straightening up, a strident bell heralded the end of his discomfiture and the start of morning playtime for the children.

"Right," Mr Moore burst out, becoming vaguely animated for the first time. "Let's go along to the staffroom and have coffee. It should be about ready now, and afterwards we will discuss the matter of your start in September."

-o-

The staff room was hiding behind the door that was twin to the headmaster's, and proved to be identical in size and shape to it. It was, however, not quite as well furnished or as tidy as the other, and it possessed two startling mod-cons - a sink and a gas tap. It had the same high-vaulted ceiling as the others in the school, and the one large window was caged on the outside, (because of the rear playground) and dirty on the inside. Wall cupboards kept the paint clean along one wall, and on the others, a film of grey dirt protected the paint from the caretaker's cloth. Seven easy chairs – four wicker and three cushioned – formed an L shape under the cupboards and the window, all of which looked to have been there since the school opened. The one outstanding feature in an otherwise uninteresting place, was a very large, ancient, curved bentwood hat and umbrella stand by the door.

Mr Moore beckoned Jack to take one of the steaming cups of coffee, which were lined neatly on the sink's draining board. There was no sign of their author, so he took one and sat down in one of the easy chairs. Mr Moore took his, and, muttering something about an important phone call, hurried out of the staffroom, as its usual inmates were filtering in. The seats filled up quickly, until there was one person left by the sink, stirring her coffee.

She was quite magnificent. Like a battleship in full sail, she looked as if she was built to last. Slowly, she turned on her heels, and fixed Jack with the most terrifying basilisk stare he had experienced, silently daring him to remain in that seat. He began to wilt almost immediately under her gaze, and the rest of the staff stopped whatever they were doing, turning towards him to add weight to the battleship's broadside. In face of these reinforcements, he could do nothing but capitulate, and, asking very lamely her pardon, he relinquished the chair and ambled towards the door. The last he saw of her, was a vast billowy shape filling all the space he had occupied, and spilling out on to others also, with an enormously enraptured look of triumph glowing in her face.

Pushing his straight, dark spiky hair from his deep green eyes, he managed to slink into the hall to reform and regroup his scattered wits … when he was joined from the room by the multifarious expert. He proffered a large, flat hand, and introduced himself.

"David Aston's the name," he offered. "Ingles, isn't it?"

"Yes," Jack returned, "pleased to see a friendly face. I'm afraid I haven't made the best of starts, have I? Name's Jack, by the way."

"Shouldn't worry, if I were you, Jack," he advised, with a grin on his face. "Nobody - but nobody - gets one over on old Vanessa. One thing you must learn in this place, is that everybody has his rank, and as long as you stick to it, you'll be OK. The older ones on the staff, for instance, have their own chairs. Even if they are not in the room, it doesn't do to sit there. On *my* first visit, I fared even worse than you. I spilled coffee down her neck – an accident, you understand – and it took her a full fortnight to forgive me. She's never forgotten it though, and never will. She has an elevated status. Plays the Joanna."

"Been here long, has she?" asked Jack.

"Over twenty years," he replied with a grimace. "Can you imagine that? All that time in the one place. She no longer just works here, she's *part* of the place. Wears it like an old shoe. She's the one who calls the tune, if you'll pardon the pun. Take old Sparks too. Been here even longer, they say. Doesn't do to ask him how long though. He's a rum sort; thick as two short planks, but the people hereabouts respect him - or perhaps fear might be closer to the mark. Came into the job quite late from goodness knows where else, and now he swans around not doing an awful lot.

"Now, what I was saying was … these two have been on the staff here together for the best part of twenty years, and do you know what? They still call each other by their surnames. 'Yes, Mr Sparks …' 'No, Miss Page …' Three bags full to the both of you." With that he blew a raspberry, and made a sign.

"Mr Moore seems a decent sort, though," Jack ventured, after a few moments silence.

"He's OK, I suppose," Aston replied, "in a quiet sort of a way. His trouble is that he's not strong enough, particularly to handle the likes of Sparks. He will do almost anything for a quiet life. He hasn't got long to go now anyway. No, what this place needs is knocking down, rebuilding, and a strong head to take over. Now, I …"

He wasn't allowed to finish. He was cut off in mid-flow

by the end-of-break bell. The duty teacher was letting the hordes flood back in after letting off enough steam to ensure reasonable quiet for the rest of the morning.

"Ah well," David went on, "must get back to the grind. Are you staying for lunch?"

"Well, I hadn't planned to," Jack returned. "Would it be hard to arrange?"

"Tell Old Moore you want to stop to chat over some things with me, and I'll see you then," he advised. He then turned on his heels and disappeared along another corridor. Where it led, Jack had no idea.

He ambled back to the Head's office to finish off their earlier discussion, and to find out the sorts of things he would need to know to ensure a smooth start to the new term. He knocked, and was greeted by a hurried "Come in". As Jack slipped around the door, he caught a brief glimpse of what could only have been a newspaper disappearing into a side drawer of the desk.

"Ah, yes, well, Mr Ingles," he stammered. "Had a profitable and enjoyable break time, I trust? Have you met all the staff again? We are very lucky to have a pleasant, friendly and co-operative staff at Broughton …" There was a distinct pause, which Jack filled in his mind with the word 'sometimes'. Clearly, Mr Moore couldn't handle *all* the staff, and obviously he wished he could. Therefore, he tried to exert his authority in other ways, particularly with the younger teachers.

"Sit down, Mr Ingles," he said, as he beckoned Jack to an armchair across the desk from his. "Have you any questions you would like me to answer?"

"Yes," he continued, "I would like some idea of what to teach when we start in September. I have lots of ideas myself, of course, but I was wondering if you have a formal set of schemes I could use."

"Ah, well, you see," he started stammering again, "the others were so out of date when I took over here, that I've had to redo, and have them retyped. They'll be ready sometime this term. You see, I've only been here a short time myself, and in many ways I haven't yet got things as I would like. I can let you have some of the old ones as an example, but I wouldn't stick too closely to them. You will, by the way, have one of our two second year classes, and you will have the room you saw at the end of the second hall. The other second year class is under our Miss Page – a fine teacher. She'll show you the ropes."

"Miss P ...? But ..." he muttered aghast, but didn't continue with what he was thinking. No argument. He would have to grin and make the best of what he had been given.

"It might be a good idea," Moore went on, "if you popped down to see her now. She should be with her class."

It was with a certain degree of apprehension that Jack left the Head's room, and made for the other end of school. The staffroom door was open, and, as he passed, he could see the Deputy Head very busily sitting down, obviously trying to do a newspaper crossword, completely oblivious to the kettle boiling away somewhere close to his left ear.

The trek along the second corridor seemed to take a year. He knew then just what the prisoners being taken in the tumbrils must have felt on their way to the Sharp Lady. He had another sharp lady waiting for him at the other end, and he wasn't sure whether he would keep *his* head. As he opened the door, sound burst upon him like an exploding cannon, and the scene into which he had unwittingly stolen was pure children's hour. The cacophony was overwhelming, and he had to sit at the side amongst pegs and pump bags until it had ebbed and flowed away.

It was a music lesson. It was not obvious not from the

sounds he had witnessed, for similar sounds could have been experienced on any building site. No, the diversity of musical instrument and the zeal with which they were 'played' were the deciding factors. Miss was sitting at another – older – piano, banging away on the keys for all she was worth, accompanied by xylophones, cymbals, triangles, drums, recorders … – in fact a veritable Broughton Symphony Orchestra. There was the odd violin or two (and very odd some of them looked), screeching out their pained protests. All participants were totally oblivious to Jack's existence at that moment. One little boy, behind the piano and away from the gaze of Miss Page, was beating time with his violin bow on the already vibrating head of the boy in front, who, being closest to the source of authority, couldn't take retaliatory action – yet.

The teacher reached her final crescendo of sound, and finished several lengths ahead of everyone else - who, gradually, in their own time, came to their own private finales also.

"All right," she said, "quite good for a twenty-second attempt, and Jeremy, don't hit Simon with your bow again – you'll break the hair on it. Now, pack away your instruments – that's not the intended use of a recorder, Jonathan. You don't stuff bits of paper in the big end and shoot them out at the girls – and settle down to some arithmetic."

At this point, Jack got up and ambled as nonchalantly as he could, across the hall, to her desk. She had her back to the class, while writing on the board, and so she didn't see him. His first words seemed to have a somewhat startling effect on her, for she spun around, the board ruler still in her hand, and had he not ducked, he would have been the first headless teacher this side of the Wash.

"Mr Ingles," she said cheerily, as if nothing had happened. "You have come, I doubt it not, to talk to me about next year's work."

"You're absolutely right," he answered. "You see, Mr Moore …"

"… Hasn't yet managed to give you any schemes of work," she interrupted.

"How did you know?" he ventured.

"My dear young man," she went on, "it is a well-known fact, in this school, that in the main you are left very much to your own devices. I have been waiting, during the years he has been here, for a set of new schemes, and still they are in process of being prepared, and I haven't seen them. Anyway, I don't think we really need *his* ideas here. We have been working perfectly well for the past twenty years."

"Well, I've got quite a few ideas for some subjects – history, geography, and so on – but English and arithmetic need a structured approach, don't they?" he returned.

"Never worry," she replied. "Our two classes are supposed to be parallel, so what would be easier than to follow one scheme of work – mine."

"Suits me," he said, rather relieved.

They stayed there talking over points of relevance for quite some time - almost until lunchtime, in fact – and all the while, her class was becoming progressively noisier and more unruly. Miss Page, however, was completely oblivious to it all.

–o–

Eventually, Jack decided not to stay for lunch. He would eat almost anything edible, but Spam salad, or whatever, somehow did not appeal to his stomach's sense of well-being. He did, however, seek out David Aston to take his leave. He was in the canteen, supervising entry of the hordes, with hands on hips in almost hopeless resignation.

"Going? Can't stand the pace, eh?" he asked, with a grin

on his face.

"Can't stand the smell," Jack replied, wrinkling his nose. "See you in seven weeks. Don't work too hard."

As he turned, swimming against a tide of flailing bodies to regain the door to sanity, he noticed Mr Moore at a corner table, oblivious to the mayhem around him, tucking in to his Spam and egg pie, as if he was in the condemned cell.

Outside, the fresh air of a fine summer's day began quickly to lift his sagging spirits, tasting amazingly sweet after that ordeal of the canteen. How his heart raced with the excited thoughts of Cook's culinary concoctions only seven short weeks away.

Chapter 10

Jack's first year at Broughton was rather an interesting time on the whole; interesting but devoid of much of the educational experience he would need to build up a store upon which to draw for the future, and it was stifling also for his promotion prospects. An intensely ambitious person, he found his outlets for self-advancement very slowly being drained away, and sealed off. He was the lowest of all teaching staff there. Holding no trump cards, the deck was in exactly the order it had been shuffled and dealt ten years before, and the picture cards had all the sway.

Each person had to wait his turn, irrespective of ability or expertise, and when his turn came, he would be duly rewarded with a promotion point, and a pat on the head, for his loyalty. These promotion points, of course, meant extra money, and so this redistribution of wealth was keenly contested by all interested parties on the staff.

Jack knew that his only chance of promotion lay outside, in some other similar school perhaps. It was, however, both amusing and interesting to watch teacher antics, posturing and jostling for pole position in the run-up to the awarding of these precious promotion points. This school was so small with regard to promotions that they didn't become available very often. Usually it happened when some holder had either died or left the school for another. Should any post thrust itself to the fore, there were eight other hopefuls in the queue before Jack, so he had to be content with the side-show's entertainment value.

The job he had taken on had been relinquished by a man wanting to move nearer to his home, some twenty miles away, and he had had his point for looking after the school's menagerie (tortoise, rabbit, gerbil etc), or so it seemed. It was quite obvious to Jack, a near outsider, that there was a number of candidates with an equal chance of running away with the loot. There was Brenda Peterson, a spinster with ailing parents, who deserved the point on her merits as a fine dedicated teacher. She would work lunchtimes and break times in an endeavour to bring reading to those less able to receive it, but she spoiled her chances somewhat because she was very outspoken. David, of course, was in the running simply because of all the 'necessary' extras he did out of school – sport, drama etc. He was, however, perhaps a little young. Miss Page should have had it as an extra for the excellent way in which she played the piano (and because she was the oldest).

Then, there was Stanley Awad. What could you say about Stanley? He was one of those people who tried to convince you that, financially, he did not need the post, and that professionally, he was above it all.

He was the one who produced and directed all the drama extravaganzas for public display, and everything he did was window dressing as a means of achieving his one secret aim – promotion. He would have denied this most strenuously, but to climb the ladder was his goal.

Had it been left to Sparks, the choice would have been obvious, but the final decision was the Head's. In many respects, Mr Moore was brow-beaten by the bullying tactics of Sparks, who had pulled out all the stops to get for Miss Page what *he* considered was her due. However, there were a few areas where Mr Moore enjoyed standing against Sparks, and this was one. *He* would jolly well decide where the point was to go, Sparks or no Sparks.

The staff never got to know officially just where the post came to rest, neither from the Head nor from the person concerned. Speculation was rife, however, that Stanley had carried off the prize, though he wouldn't admit it, and nobody would ask. His general attitude, however, became rather more superior than his usual superciliousness, and, obviously to celebrate, he decided to put on 'something special' that year. His panto, or what he more grandiosely called his 'dramatic extravaganza' was to be *"Scheherazade – 1001 Nights"*, where the sheer opulence and extravagance of production and performance would outdo any forerunner.

"Getting ambitious in his old age, isn't he?" Jack observed to David Aston one grey, foggy and uninteresting November morning. It was one of those sorts of days when the mist lifted momentarily to give a brief glimpse of the cloud above.

"Who do you mean?" David replied, not taking too much notice of what he was saying. His attention was taken up by his drawing a moustache and glasses on the face of some personage whose poster was on the staffroom wall. They were the only ones there at that time, having one of those rare moments of freedom whilst Sparks was treating the school to one of his fatherly pieces of advice, and giving gentle warnings about something someone had done wrong at a break time two weeks before, or something else equally trivial.

"You know, old Zeffirelli," he returned. "He's gone just about mad, what with costumes, make-up, scenery – now that might be his stumbling block – and they're doing it all by themselves. Mind you, it ought to be well done, because he's given himself plenty of time. The show doesn't go on until March next year. You could get a monkey to learn a part in that length of time. I think it's ridiculous spending so much time – in lessons too – on something which has only a limited value, and ..."

"*We* are putting on this valueless extravaganza," he interrupted, quite dispassionately. "I'm helping."

"Well, I think you're barmy," Jack returned, quite honestly. "Who do you think will get *all* the kudos? You? Don't you believe it. It will be put down to our friend, Stanley, and probably you'll do more than half the work."

"Don't worry," David answered. "I'll make sure I'm mentioned in dispatches. Besides, it's all good experience, and it'll go down on my brag sheet when I apply for other jobs. Anyway, it gives me something to do during the lunch hour."

David tried to make Jack party to this dramatic fiasco, but he was impervious to all entreaties, and refused. Besides, he had better things to do at lunchtime. He was just telling him so in very round terms, when the great man himself came in. Bloated with his own self-importance, he made an entrance (the only expression to describe that usually simple action), and stood by the cupboard in typically theatrical pose.

Stanley was one of those ageless types, whose exact time of life was difficult to tie down. You would put him down as fortyish, which could make him anywhere from thirty-five to fifty. At a little less than medium height, he didn't cut any great dash for size, but what he lacked in stature he more than made up for in sartorial elegance. Every day he came with a different shirt, and he wore shoes that most would use for funerals, weddings, or other special occasions. The jackets to his many suits were, however, amply cut to cover a slightly 'comfortable' midriff. He was a very pale, pasty-faced individual, with carefully tailored wisps of hair immaculately arranged to allow maximum coverage. Although a northerner by birth, his very cut-glass accent heavily disguised this, putting him somewhere in middle England by heritage. On one hand he had a sixth finger which, when out of lessons, he sucked on incessantly, sharing his distasteful habit with all around him. Here surely was the complete success story? At the top of his career in industry (or so he would have all believe), he changed to teaching because of its creativity, and was now heading for the top in his new career. That, surely, showed a remarkable degree of diversification and rare ability, didn't it?

"That does it," he burst out, seeing that nobody was about to give him a lead in. "It's all off."

"What's the matter, Stan?" David queried, as he was putting the finishing touches to his portrait. "Have they finally given you the sack? I was just telling Jack here that you were too good for such humble company."

"Stop messing about, David," Stanley snapped, rather crossly. "The play's off. I'm not doing another stroke at it."

"Off?" hooted Aston. "You can't call it off now. Everything's planned. The scenery is well under way … not ready for a long time, but well under way. What's put you out?"

"They won't let me have the time I require," he returned loftily. "Both the Head and Deputy - though I suspect that Sparks is behind it - say children can't be withdrawn from lessons, and I can't have any free time either. We directors must have time to get the best out of our performers, you know."

Jack was ready to smile, but had to suppress it quickly. As he glanced at David and Stanley in rapid succession, he noticed that they were both in deadly earnest.

"The only thing we can do," said David, after a moment's

thought, "is to forget about the extra time in school, and produce something really special from our own time."

"But the children …," interrupted Stanley.

"Lunchtime and after school," David added quickly. "It will make our efforts seem all the more creditable."

"I'm not after credit," Stanley protested in mock indignation.

"Yes, you are," replied his friend; "just like the rest of us in this game."

"Perhaps you're right," he agreed. "OK, we'll start extra curricula rehearsals tomorrow."

And that, abruptly, was that. They went out together, discussing some minor point of detail, quite satisfied with themselves, leaving Jack with his mouth half-sagging and not knowing what their next moves might be. Their unusually noisy duet left a void of quietness, that was almost tangible, and very welcome. A short while later, noises of shuffling feet and scraping chairs told him the great debate had ended, and the children were on their way back to class. That was his cue also to head in the same direction, being the end of his entertainment - for a while anyway.

Shortly, there was to be a lunchtime staff meeting called by Mr Moore "to outline certain points which needed clarification". That was his pompous and authoritative way of trying to add importance to his light-weight words. This activity usually added a bit of spice and variety to an otherwise mundane and uninteresting period.

Mr Moore always called staff meetings at lunchtime because he said it would be an incentive to finish within the time set out. This was really a euphemism for his not wanting to stay beyond afternoon school, of course. They usually tended to be something of a pantomime, with his not really knowing what to say after about five minutes, and with the Deputy trying hard to discredit him by asking awkward questions. This one, however, was important within the currency of the school. It was the one time when Sparks knew what he was talking about.

It was tied up very much with a trust established by an old boy of the school, who had gone off to the antipodes, made sack loads of money and had bought himself into favour by donating several thousand pounds to his alma mater. It was to "provide rewards for good hard-working children, that they would not normally receive through usual school channels". Mr Sparks had taken it upon himself to keep alive the ceremony in perpetuity.

Anyone, given the number of years he had seen it through, could have done the job equally well. Year after year he had said the same things, followed the same lines, and spoken of the rewards in sound educational terms. Year after year, there had been the same arguments, the same travesties of justice, giving the prizes to the ablest and usually the least deserving. This was because the older sitting members virtually decided who was getting what without recourse to the rest of the staff. David Aston had decided that this year was going to be different, and Jack had offered to support him if he could. However, normally at these sorts of gatherings he was content to sit on the side-lines, observe, and daydream, being the 'baby' of the team.

At one o'clock, with lunchtime over, the teachers returned to the staffroom to take up battle stations. With cups replenished with tea, and cigarettes at the ready, they sat in silent expectancy, waiting for Sparks to start. Mr Moore slid round the door, then Miss Page and the others filed in as slowly as they were able. They knew that if they delayed, it would have to be finished some other time. This was not to be, however, as the Deputy burst through the door with an enormous tome under his arm.

"Beg pardon for being a little late," he smiled, "but I have to bring my book of words here."

"What on earth's it for?" asked Mrs Josephs from the other side of the hat stand. She, too, was new to this particular game, but, unlike Jack, was not in her first year of teaching.

"It's my bible," he said, tucking it even closer under his armpit, and patting it like a much loved dog. "In here, there is every record that was ever made for the Prize Giving. It goes back thirty-five years or more, as far as I can see, and most of the records *I* have had the pleasure in keeping."

The clouds outside drew Jack's attention through the murk on the window. They were gathering like so many black ravens densely flocking over the roost, and it looked as if the earlier promise of rain was about to be fulfilled.

"Now, our first task," Sparks droned on in that interminable monotone, "is to acquaint the newer members of staff with the idea of the ceremony, its history, and the procedures.

"Many years ago, an old pupil of the school decided to give a sum of money to buy items most in need, and which the authority didn't provide, like sports shirts and such. Instead of spending all the money at one go, it was decided to put it in trust, and to spend only the interest each year, so giving benefit *every* year. It was also decided to make a prize-giving ceremony for those children of the fourth year who had achieved a certain standard of work by their own efforts ..."

... The rain began to splash across the windows, leaving great gashes in the dirt on the outside glass, like some ethereal window cleaner. The surrounding walls and outbuildings also began to show signs of the onset ...

"... It is our job, then, to choose boys and girls who we think are fit to receive such prizes as we decide upon ..."

... The grey slate slabs of the 1930s terraces and back-to-backs on one side of the road took on a newly washed look, mirroring the sky in their highly polished wetness. The rain reduced everything to that same even colour, neither favouring one thing nor neglecting others …

"… And we then choose prizes according to the designation of the award, and how much money we have. It is an honour to be chosen, and the standards must be high so …"

… It could have been monsoon rain, bouncing high off wall and roof, except that there were no tropical forests, and this *was* South Leeds. It wasn't difficult, however, to use the imagination. Roads became rivers, and the traffic islands were small boats butting through the rapids, as water swirled and eddied around cats' eyes and bollards. Great war canoes thrust their way through the stream, ready to stop at some of the many staging posts to disgorge their human contents onto the banks that were already awash…

"… ask for nominations? The categories are as follows: H-andwriting, Industry, Behaviour, Leadership, Improvement. I think they are all self-explanatory, and so we shouldn't have too much trouble there. Perhaps people might like to consider their choices, and we will have another meeting at the same time next week …"

The children were like drenched rabbits pouring back into the warren after spending too long in the rain. Nothing seemed to get those children down, not even the weather. They would jostle back to the classroom, to shuffle through the enormous pile of comics, collected over the last ten years for just such a purpose as this, and sit happily, if noisily, for the next quarter of an hour or so.

"If we could meet earlier next time as we'll have a lot to talk about…"

Here, he finished his monologue, and the pause injected a much-needed and refreshing breath of silence into the room. The meeting broke up amidst grumblings, mutterings, and feelings of apathy amongst the staff who thought the whole process ought to have been scrapped years ago. The only really enthusiastic supporters were the stalwarts – Sparks and Page – who were the executive members of the syndicate.

"Three minutes left," grumbled David Aston, "and not even time for a cup of tea."

"You and Stanley are going to get just a little wet," Jack smiled, drawing their attention to the weather, "when you have to swim across to your huts." He was thankful that his classroom was inside - even though he did have a cracked window, which let some of the rain in.

There were to be two more meetings before any decisions were taken about either prizes or prize-winners. In the meantime, another piece of news put the award excitement into the shade; the fact that the school was to get a new teacher. It wasn't so much a new teacher as a swap for one of their existing ones.

"Have you heard about the new body we're getting?" David asked Jack one Thursday morning during their school-assembly-broadcast free period.

"No. First I've heard," he said, showing no real sign of interest. He carried on piecing together a jigsaw of a picture he wanted for display later that morning.

"Alan Simmons has landed this year's exchange in Canada starting after Christmas," Aston went on. "Lucky so-and-so. I didn't even know he'd applied."

He paused for a while to try to light his pipe for the sixth time.

"He's getting all costs paid, fare to and from Canada, living expenses, *and* what's more, a supplementary allowance to take in the difference in cost of living."

"Can't be bad," Jack returned, rather irritated that he would persist in talking inconsequentialities, when he wanted to concentrate. He never liked Alan Simmons much anyway. He was one of those sorts who always wanted you to agree with his point of view even when yours was obviously the right one. Boorish and uninteresting is how Stanley had described him, and for once Jack had had to agree.

"Who's his replacement? Do you know?" he returned, trying to muster some interest.

"Yes," he returned. "A woman – young and unattached."

Jack lifted his head and looked at Aston.

"Hum," David added. "I thought that would get your attention. Quite true, though."

"Are you sure?" he asked.

"Of course I am," he said. "Would I lie to you about a thing like that?"

"Yes, of course you would," came Jack's sharp reply. "Details?"

"Twenty-four years old; five feet six tall, slim, blue eyes, and six legs," he went on without a pause.

"Not so much of the mickey-taking, David," Jack said good-humouredly. "Well now, things could be looking up for a change. The hunting grounds have been barren for too long, and there's not much sport around these haunts."

"Yes, you need the change," Aston went on, joking. "I've been worried about you just lately. You need a further interest in life."

"Oh, shut up," Jack said, digging him in the ribs, and taking a playful swipe at his head with his roll of sugar paper. "Seriously though, have you seen her?"

"I'm usually in the habit of popping over to Canada for the odd quick weekend, you know," he mocked. "No, my dear chap, she's not yet hit terra firma in this fair and sceptred land. Doesn't come until the beginning of the New Year."

"Oh, yes," Jack said, thoughtfully, "I hadn't thought of that."

"The description's right though," David went on, "except that I lied about the legs. I happened to see the information sheet on the boss's desk the other day, as I was 'looking' for some cartridge paper. The sheet fell on to the floor accidentally - must have been a draught blowing from somewhere – and, of course, I picked it up to replace it."

That news gave Jack a great deal of food for thought, all of which had to be consigned to the back of his mind for the time being. For now, they were entering into the run-up to Christmas. Trimmings were hung once again, and had their own piles of dust blown away (only to land somewhere else, of course). It took just half an hour in Jack's room, as there were many willing and industrious hands just itching to help. Their motives were, however, tinged with a little self-interest, in that if they were helping their teacher, they couldn't possibly be doing lessons. This was the only reason the volunteer force for any job during lessons was grossly over-subscribed.

The school couldn't afford, or at any least the Head *wouldn't* afford a specimen Christmas tree or trimmings, so each class either made its own in the case of trimmings, and asked one of the children to lend a tree (usually artificial) and wassail cups and general baubles to decorate it. Decorations were not the sole excitement. There was the usual matter of class parties, which aroused a great deal of interest and speculation as to who was going to keep away from whom in the dances. Partners had already been chosen, just in case. Excitement was high, and teachers had to dampen the enthusiasm of several budding Romeos. Just a steady and gentle run-up to the events was what was needed.

It was quite usual at this time of year, two weeks before the end of term, to play the 'Squeezing Petty Cash Out of the Head' game, to pay for prizes and presents. Most of the time, so Jack gathered from older teachers, this game was won handsomely by Mr Moore. He would hum and har first of all, making out that there was no such thing as petty cash. This was followed, upon insistence, by his assertion that there was none left. Finally, in the face of persistent badgering, he would loosen the purse strings slightly to allow a few shillings to tumble out.

Because of Mr Moore's reluctance to part with the cash, many of the teachers were obliged to pay for these prizes out of their own pockets. Most, that is, except for Jack Ingles. The others, he thought, were well able to afford it, but he would have had to go without weekend lunches for two weeks to pay for it out of his meagre salary. The pay rise awarded two months before was very much overdue in coming through for him. The others on the staff had received theirs - with back pay - the month before, but those new to the authority had to wait for the December advice.

Jack paid three visits in all to see Mr Moore, each time encouraged to return by David Aston.

"He's just fobbing you off," he said. "Go back and ask again. Tell him it would be a shame to disappoint the children, and you can't afford it. If he refuses again, tell him they will then have to do without this year. That usually gets him to cough up the money..."

"... You understand," explained Mr Moore, "that it will have to be a special case just this once. You spend what you want, and then bring me the receipt. That way, we'll know just how much we need to give you."

Not to be outdone, Jack's response was quick.

"I already know exactly how much I want," he replied. "Thirty-six prizes at one and elevenpence a dozen is five and ninepence. I'll bring you the receipt when I come back."

"Five and ... Oh, well, all right," said Mr Moore, who was as near to bursting a blood vessel as he could be. He shuffled over to the large oak cupboard behind his desk, and took out an enormous bunch of keys. He fiddled and sorted through this bunch for some moments before trying the lock of the one he had chosen. The door creaked open upon rusty, hardly-used hinges, to reveal another door, fastened by a different type of lock. Again, the same ceremony spawned a different key. The door again opened, silently this time, to reveal a small, squat, dark grey safe with an enormous handle and lock to the front. Key after key was tried in the lock, but without success, until he had gone through the whole bunch to no avail. He stood there, scratching his head, not knowing what to do next.

He turned to Jack and, with a smile of apology, said, "Sorry, Mr Ingles, I don't seem to have the key. I think we had better look another time."

With that, he pulled on the golden guard chain across the front of his waistcoat, and fished out a rather old, shiny gold watch, and there, hanging from the fob at the top of the watch, was a … key.

"Could that be the one you are looking for, Mr Moore?" Jack said, pointing at the key in triumph, barely able to suppress a victorious smile.

"Ah! … Well … Yes," said the Head, his face falling as he spoke. "Yes, I think you may well be right. Well now, let's see."

The key fitted perfectly, and opened the safe with a resounding clang. Mr Moore heaved open the door, for indeed it was very thick and heavy, and inside could be seen only one thing – a metal box, roughly a foot square by about six inches deep. Very carefully, he lifted it out, and fumbled in his other waistcoat pocket for its key. He opened the box swiftly and with the minimum of fuss. Jack had expected to see pound notes spilling over the top, but all he could see inside were four compartments, each containing a different denomination of coin. The sum in total amounted to something in the region of two pounds ten shillings. Quite a haul for some enterprising burglar.

Chapter 11

Christmas was a wonderful time in school. During the last week, the children were so excited that work was impossible, so formal lessons had to be suspended, even though Mr Moore didn't wholly approve. There were plans to finalise for parties, hats and decorations to finish, games to decide upon, and a thousand and one other things to attend to. Lessons, break times, and lunchtimes were completely filled with things to sort out, and with an atmosphere of happy excitement.

In each party, to be held on the last four afternoons, the two classes in each age group were to combine. They would play games, sing songs, and dance for the first half, and then have their food until the end of the day. Four half days, therefore, were taken up in this way, with the food being provided by the children. They were encouraged to bring cakes, buns, jellies (for preparation at school), sandwiches, and all the other necessities for bloating them to nausea by the end of the party. The school provided the orange juice. From the beginning of the week, children had been seen pouring in to school laden with all types of goodies to eat, and the problem had been finding storage space.

The parties were usually a great success, and this year was no exception. Mr Moore kept well out of the way; that is until the food and drink were uncovered. Then, quite miraculously, his engagements fulfilled, he joined the fun, sampling food and generally circulating amongst the tables.

Many of the children were either on the point of bursting or bringing back what they had stuffed down their throats, they had eaten so much, and yet, there was still a deal left to be taken away, or eaten the next day. At the end of each party, a horde of cheerfully full children could be seen leaving the school premises, making their noisy if happy way home. On the other hand, the staffroom was almost the last resting place of the exhausted party staff, who collapsed into easy chairs, shoes thrown off, and eyes half-closed, each gasping that it would be the last time.

The party for the Second Years had been the best of all, and had 'happened' on the last afternoon but one. It had been so good and so well enjoyed because of the merriment of the piano played by Miss Page. She couldn't read music, but she could bring the instrument to life. After the 'happening', Jack Ingles was sitting on the table in the staffroom, swinging his legs, and trying to muster the energy to take himself off home.

Home to him was a reasonably sized room in the posh north area of the town. His North Park Avenue bedsitter was the only home he now knew, as his mam had died nine months earlier, and his father had remarried his on-off lover Dottie French, and his only other relatives were a female cousin who lived abroad, his brother, William, and his grandparents, Marion and Jud. They weren't well enough to have him stay with them over the festive period, and he didn't have the money to travel to them and to pay his way. His was the prospect, therefore, of going to a cold room from a cold, dark late December day.

"You're far away," came a voice from his right. It was David.

"Yes," Jack returned. "I'm just trying to gather enough

enthusiasm and strength for moving off."

"Anything special on tonight?" asked David.

"No, just the usual," replied Jack. "Tea, listen to the radio, and early to bed."

"Feel like coming down to my place for a meal and drink afterwards?" David asked. "I don't want you to think you have to, mind. Only … Mother asked me if I'd like to bring you down. Nothing special you understand, just steak and chips."

"Nothing special," he gasped. "Strewth. It sounds like a feast. I'd be delighted. You've no idea. Not met your parents before."

"Mother, actually," David said, quietly. "Father died a few months ago. Before you came here."

"Oh, I'm sorry," Jack apologised. "I didn't know."

"It's OK," David began. "It was a bit hard at first, especially for Mother after thirty years of marriage, but we're gradually picking up the pieces and getting over it. She won't get over it completely, but- … Hey! Why are we so glum? It's nearly Christmas, the end of another delightful term. Come on. Let's eat."

The blue-dark of dusk ambushed them noiselessly, and the filaments were beginning to wax in the orange sodium lights along the main road. Most of the children had long since disappeared, and there remained only a few mothers waiting for their offspring to find some misplaced article of clothing. It was that quiet, in between time of early evening when children had long since disappeared, leaving the streets uncannily deserted. And yet the evening rush wouldn't start for another half-hour or so,

Developers were gradually sweeping away the Victorian terraces of the other side of the road and replacing them with modern town and semi-detached houses. It wasn't long between the demolition teams moving out and the builders moving in to a site. Here and there a solitary island building grew out of a sea of fallen and crushed bricks. The only one left butting this particular sea of rubble on David's side of the road was the Ship Inn. It had been said that there had been a mass migration of rats when certain terraces were razed. They would obviously find new lodgings quite easily, and would move on until the demolition was complete. Some of the sites were to remain empty, due to the proposed widening of the road, which meant that the grass, rose bay willow herb, and other plants would flourish and repopulate as weeds where they were once Victorian cultivated flowers.

David lived off the main road, along quite an attractive street of pre-war semis. The front boundaries were a mixture of open-work stone, privet and trellis, and the gardens were equally varied, ranging from neat and well-tended, to open prairie. It was a small street, rather like a quiet backwater off the main river flow. David's parents had been lucky with the size of their plot of land, for not only had they a sizeable piece at the back, but the side was almost half as wide again as the house itself. On the whole, the building was beginning to show its age, but it was in reasonable shape, with its tiny, individually leaded diamond panes on the main windows, a small tiled canopy over the front door, and a roof-high bay to the front. Tell-tale signs of damp staining down the tiles on the bay, moss and algae growing on the roof, and those unmistakably pre-war flat, roof tiles, were a give-away to its age. The garden to the rear was the traditional mixture of lawn, herbaceous border, and vegetable plot across the back, and from what Jack could glean in the dusk, it was reasonably well-tended. They negotiated the uneven driveway as they made their way around to the kitchen door.

"Nice garden," Jack ventured politely, although he knew next to nothing about gardening.

"Yes," replied David. "Father was the gardener of the family. He could turn a swamp into a lush area in no time.

I took over as a matter of courtesy to Mother, and I must admit that I rather enjoy it now. I'm no great Percy Thrower, like father *was*, but I'm gradually picking up the rudiments. And although I may say so myself, I'm making my usual brilliant job of it."

"That's the thing I like about you, David," said Jack. "You are so modest."

They shouldered their way into the kitchen to the tantalising smell of steak braising in the oven; a smell that Jack hadn't experienced for a long time. The kitchen was small but tidily kept, and all the while he looked around, thoughts of that food invaded his mind and stimulated his stomach into action. David's mother wasn't there, and all was quiet, except for the intermittent click of something away above them.

"We're here, Mother," shouted David at the hall doorway. "The hunters have returned and are ravenously hungry."

There was no reply except for the swish and quiet step of someone on the stairs. A petite, slim figure of about fifty or so appeared in the doorway, a smile already decorating her face.

"Hello, dear," she said, reaching up to kiss her son on the cheek. David put his arms around her, and picked her up quite effortlessly. She smiled at his show of affection, and ruffled his hair.

"How's my young lady today?" he said, with smiling eyes. "Not been too busy I hope."

"Put me down you great big oaf," she smiled. "The dinner will spoil."

As he did so, her short, wavy auburn hair bounced slightly, but fell back into place quickly. Her eyes were bright and sparkling, and the touch of sadness at the corners made them all the more attractive. Her face was still quite youthful, and had only a few lines across the forehead and around her

115

mouth.

"Aren't you going to introduce me to your friend?" she asked, looking across at Jack.

"Oh, yes. Sorry," he apologised. "This is Jack Ingles. Jack, this is my mother."

"Very pleased to meet you, Jack," she said, shaking his hand. "I *can* call you that, can't I?"

"Yes, by all means," he replied. "The pleasure's entirely mine"

"David has told me a lot about you," she went on. "So I wanted him to bring you home so I could meet you. You are very welcome to come any time you have a mind. David doesn't bring his friends home half often enough. I've said many times that it's about time he thought about settling down with someone nice …"

"Oh, Mother," David butted in, flushing scarlet, "you don't have to go on. Jack's come for an evening out, not for a potted history of either the family or my amorous misadventures. Shall we go and wash, Jack? I believe tea won't be long."

"Yes," Mrs Aston replied unabashed, "it's almost ready. You two men must be ravenous. Pour yourselves a drink when you're ready."

The last was a parting shot as they climbed the stairs.

"Nice house you have here, David," Jack ventured as they neared the top of the stairs. "Been here long?"

"Yes," came the reply from the bathroom. "I was born here. I didn't go to Broughton, though. I went to Cross Farthing Street, which was even worse than Broughton. It's a warehouse now. Best thing for it, if you ask me."

–o–

The meal was the best Jack had tasted for a long time, and was far superior to his own cordon noir efforts. Cordon noir was in fact cordon bleu, but usually burnt.

They were sitting quietly digesting their meal and finishing off cheese and coffee, when in the distance could be heard the faint warble of the nightly seasonal singers, doing their rounds.

"Listen," said Mrs Aston. "Carol singers. We haven't had any round here yet this season, surprisingly. Are you going away for Christmas, Jack? To stay with your parents'?"

"Afraid not," Jack replied quietly. "My mother died in March and my father remarried suddenly. There is still a feeling of emptiness …"

"Yes, we know," she replied, taking hold of her son's hand. "I'm sorry. So you'll be alone this year?"

"Yes," he returned. "I usually am."

"Why not spend it with us?" said David.

"Yes," joined in his mother. "That's a splendid idea. We have a couple of spare beds. You could stay with us over the Christmas period. We have no other family, you know. You would be more than welcome."

The idea had taken Jack quite by surprise, but he liked the images it conjured and the memories it rekindled, of quiet family celebrations, warm fireside togetherness, and comfortable slippered evenings. How those far-gone days crowded his thoughts…

"But that would be absolutely marvellous," was Jack's prompt reply, and "Thank you very much" was all he could offer in the way of gratitude. It wouldn't be the same as in times past with his mam even though they weren't great on celebrations, but at least he would be sharing happiness with others.

Jack and David insisted that they should do the washing up, and when it was over, they all settled to make plans for the forthcoming event. The Astons, very reluctantly, acceded to Jack's one provision – that he should be allowed to share in the expense of the festivities. He would have it no other way. This visit, and this evening spent with the Astons was to be the first of many happy occasions, they hoped.

-o-

The last day produced many presents from the children; chocolates, after shave, a tie … and one which Jack treasured for many years afterwards. It was from a little boy who, up to that time, had been rather aggressive, resentful of authority, and sullen. They hadn't got on very well, and Jack was about to write him off as one of his failures.

At the very end of the day James, for so the boy was named, hung back, waiting for the room to clear. Jack realised that something was afoot, as the boy was usually the first out, so he didn't press him to move along. James shuffled around, silently cursing the dawdlers who had either remained to talk to Jack, or who had taken their time looking for a lost item. His air gradually became more sullen as time went on as he stood by the nature table, his head slightly bowed and his hands thrust deep into his pockets.

At last … the final straggler had left. James seized his opportunity, and before anyone else could return, he hurried up to Jack, thrust a small package into his hand which he had dredged from the depths of his pocket, and before Jack could utter anything he had muttered a low "Merry Christmas" and had made a dash for the exit. He was through the outside door, and half way across the yard before Jack had had the time to draw breath.

Jack looked at the package, which was wrapped in crumpled Christmas paper, and tied with a knot of dirty string. Carefully, he unfastened the knot and removed the paper to reveal a largish matchbox, which was slightly damp and so was difficult to open without crushing whatever was inside. Jack took out his penknife and carefully cut around

118

the top to release the contents. He inched off the lid, to find inside a small model of Father Christmas fashioned from an acorn nut and its inverted cup, a scrap of red felt, cotton wool, and a smudge of paint.

All the other children had either bought their gifts or, more usually, had had them bought by grateful parents. Although theirs had been the product of kind thoughts, James' gift meant a little more to Jack as it was the only one to have been made personally. With a slight lump in his throat, and a fixed smile on his face, Jack sought the comfort of the staffroom.

"Had a strange incident this afternoon," David said to Jack as he entered. "You know that sullen boy in your class? James Watkins I believe his name is. Never could get on with him. The strangest thing happened towards the end of lunch. I saw him in the yard scrabbling about under that large oak near the canteen, like a sow snuffling for truffles, he was. Anyway, I saw no more of him until this afternoon, about half past two."

"Yes," Jack butted in, "he went to the toilet."

"Well", David carried on, "I was in my classroom, when I heard the door open. Took no notice as my lot were in and out much of the time, until someone grabbed my arm from behind, and thrust a package into my hand, and then ran off. It was young James Watkins, and this is what he left. I haven't opened it yet; only just remembered about it a short while ago."

"Aren't you going to open it?" Jack asked, wanting to know what was inside. He had a vague idea what they might see.

"Sure," replied David, tearing away the crumpled Christmas wrapping and knot of string. Under all that was a matchbox, sellotaped at each end to protect its precious cargo. After a disproportionate struggle, David managed to get inside, to draw out the exact twin Father Christmas to the one Jack had. At the same time Jack had pulled out *his* present from his pocket, and held it next to the one in David's hand.

"Snap!" they both guffawed, and collapsed into their chairs in fits of bubbling laughter.

"Well, at least we must be getting through to him," laughed David. "Of all the people on the staff of this school, the two to occupy bottom places in his league, I should have thought, would have been us two."

As usual the rest of the staff had departed very soon after the bell had stopped vibrating, at the unusually early time of three thirty. This seemed to be quite a concession for the head, as the normal time was not a second before ten to four. As it turned out, it wasn't a concession to the festive season at all. It was simply because he wanted to call at the barber's for a trim and be home by his usual time. David and Jack, however, were in no hurry to depart, and so decided to stay for a chat and a cup of coffee. David's meal wouldn't be ready for another hour or so, as his mother had a hairdresser's appointment for a set for Christmas. Jack also had nothing better to do other than go back to his chilly bed-sit to a slap-up meal of beans on toast.

"Been a long term," David broke the silence finally, sipping his coffee, and easing his feet on to the table.

"Yes," Jack replied. "Feels at least as if it should be Easter."

"I have an urge for something a bit stronger," said David, "you know, to go with this coffee?"

"They don't open for another hour or two yet," returned Jack, "and besides, I can't afford it."

"I didn't mean to go to the pub," David said. "I meant this."

He sprang to his feet, knocking over a chair in the process, and leaped across to his locker. He drew out a long, thin, slightly tapered package wrapped in blue tissue paper. He came back across to his seat with a sly smile on his face, and with a flourish, he whipped off the wrapping to reveal a bottle of whisky.

"*Voilá monsieur*, as they say in Spain," he said, holding up the prize for Jack's eager gaze.

"Where did you get that from?" Jack asked, on the edge of his seat. "You know 'intoxicating liquors are explicitly forbidden to be consumed on Education Department premises at all times', or so the regulation goes."

"True," said David, unfastening the bottle, "but it is the end of the year, and there's nobody here but us. 'Arrison t'caretaker's not 'ere. Gone into town, so he has, leaving the school our oyster. Besides, what do you think all those nobs up at the Office will be doing now? Drinking sherry and making free in the typing pool, I don't doubt… There are some glasses, I think, in that cupboard over there. If there aren't, we can use those glass science beakers in the science cupboard. This dratted cork's taking some moving …"

Jack rummaged around in the cupboard but to no avail, so after a few minutes, he gave up.

"Need to ask for a free period to sort that lot out," he said in a muffled voice, his head inside the science cupboard. "We'll have to use science equipment." He emerged triumphant, two glass beakers in his hands, but with an amount of dirt on his face.

"These need a rinse," he muttered.

"Yes," continued David, "and so does your face. I think we really ought to put in a requisition for some decent whisky glasses:

'Drinking, for the purpose of'."

"Don't forget to make it out in triplicate," returned Jack as he dried his face, "and put on pink socks, write in green ink, and tender the form on the fifth Thursday of the fourth month of the Chinese New Year. Then you might even get the Old Man to glance at it before he puts it in the bin."

"My word, you are learning quickly," jibed David. "You've only been here a term and you've got *him* weighed up already."

"Doesn't take much doing," said Jack. "He's like an open book. Pages are getting a little worn now, and it could do with a reprint, but it's readable nonetheless. Where's that drink?"

He held out his beaker which had been duly scraped clean of all traces of grime and chemistry experiments, and received a generous measure from David who, by this time, had managed to coax and cajole the cork out of the bottle.

"You never did say where it came from," Jack reflected, staring into the bottom of the beaker as slowly he swished the last golden drops around the glass.

"Present from Joanie Pallister in my class," he replied. "Father's in the wine and spirits business. All I did was let it be known that I am partial to a wee dram of the hard stuff, and Presto – Christmas present. Stanley drops the odd hint when it's his birthday, and is usually inundated with stuff. I wouldn't go that far, you understand, but I'm not averse to a little something at Christmas time. Another?"

"I shouldn't really," Jack answered. "I've had four already, and I've got to get home yet. Wass the time?"

"Just after half four. Time for another coupladrinks to straighten the road," he slurred.

There was a distinct haze forming around both of them, and things certainly began to take on a much rosier hue. The staffroom had changed in the last half Ihour, and had become the comeliest and most comfortable place in the universe. Both sat back with their feet up, enjoying their end-of-term celebration.

Trouble was, if they didn't get a move on they would be locked in for the night. Old 'Arrison was just doing his rounds, having got back from town a short while before. His first consideration was to lock up as quickly as possible so he could start *his* celebrations. The cleaning of the school could wait. There was plenty of time to do that later; two whole weeks in fact. He cursed all those teachers who didn't close their windows and doors; those who made his job all the more difficult. He made his way along the labyrinthine passageways to the main hall, pausing for a moment outside the staffroom door, thinking he had heard something. Shrugging his shoulders, he put his hand around the door jamb, turned off the light, and pulled the door shut on its Yale lock. He would tidy up the mess in the morning.

-o-

David woke up first. His mouth like a tram driver's glove, and he felt decidedly cold and clammy. At first he didn't know where he was, until suddenly the realisation stabbed his brain.

"Oh my God!" he blurted out almost in panic. He scrutinised his watch closely, which had a luminous dial: half past eight. He scrambled to his feet, knocking over the chair he was using as a foot stool. His left leg was numb. He couldn't feel it because of the cold and the fact that he had been resting the other across it. Trying to put weight on it, he collapsed to the floor, unable to walk as it seemed to be made out of Plasticine. The clatter of the chair and his uncontrollable body hitting the floor brought a startled "What the hell ...?" from Jack.

"Here, Old Man," David whispered. "You know what's happened? We're bloody well locked in."

"Oh! My head is just about ready to fall off and roll away," Jack complained. "How on earth do we get out of this one?"

"Think. Must think," muttered David, whose head by now was swimming and whose mind wouldn't latch on to their situation. It kept wandering back to that warm euphoric state of total intoxication.

"Can we get out of one of the windows?" asked Jack.

"Don't think so," replied David. "All the large ones were nailed up some time ago because of the difficulty we had in keeping them closed. No, that's not the way."

"Just a minute," Jack butted in. "There *is* a way out. Why didn't I think of it before? In the library, there's one of those large inward-opening half-moon windows that hasn't been nailed up. In fact, it won't stay shut. I spoke to Mr Moore about it only a week ago. He said he would put in an order for repair. Come on let's go. It's at the back of the school, so we won't be seen."

They stumbled out of the room somewhat unsteadily at first until their circulation had returned. It was rather chilly in school, and the effects of the Scotch had worn off, leaving that cold, clammy and empty feeling. They felt their way along corridors and walls, not daring to turn on any lights, and hoping there would be no obstacles to their progress. Fortunately, they had both taken their outdoor clothing along to the staffroom at the end of school, and so they were quite tightly clad.

"Ouch!" Jack muttered as quietly as he could. "Who's left that flaming article, here of all places?" That 'flaming article' turned out to be the folded climbing frame that had been stored along that stretch of corridor for more than three years. They managed to reach the library without further injury to find that the door was … locked.

"Now what?" asked Jack, a note of desperation creeping in to his voice.

"Worry ye not," answered David quite jovially. "Sir has the wherewithal for getting clear of this situation."

"What the hell are you *blathering* about?" Jack hissed.

"I have an internal master key," David replied with glee,

"and what is more, it is an illicit key. It is illegal, immoral and it makes you fat. Nobody knows I have this key, you see. I copied Moore's some time ago; one of the few times he let it out of his sight for more than five seconds. It allows me to enter places I wouldn't otherwise be able to visit."

There was a barely audible click as David's passe-partout turned the tumblers in their barrier.

"A barrier no more," he crowed as he opened the door wide with a final flourish. "And now for that window ... Which one did you say it was?"

The moon slithered through their glass obligingly, giving them little trouble finding their means of escape. Like two frightened squirrels with a cat on their tails, they squeezed through the gap left by the window sash. Once outside, the rest was plain sailing.

"What's your mother going to say?" asked Jack. "Will you tell her the truth?"

"Of course I will," answered David. "I never lie to Mother. Anyway, she'd know."

As they rounded the last buttress of the old building, Jack was jolted into greater action by the sight of his last bus making ready to pull away.

"See you day after tomorrow," he yelled, breaking into as fast a sprint as his aching limbs would allow. "Don't drink too much in the meantime."

He assumed the speed and agility of a graceful gazelle in flight as he lurched for the safety rail at the rear of the open-ended bus. He managed to catch hold – just, and the last David saw of him that night was a trailing foot being hauled on board, and an overcoat belt waving frantically behind in the cold night air.

Chapter 12

Christmas Day that year fell on a Monday, which was doubly difficult, mostly because Christmas Eve arrived on Sunday when the shops were closed. The up side of this was that most retail staffs were able to celebrate for four days without a break. But the considerable down side was that the rest of the population had to wait until Wednesday to get fresh produce. It was the bane of most people's lives.

Jack's feelings for Christmas never matched anyone else's, largely because in his childhood household, Christmas had been an everyday sort of a day. Because Christmas knocked on his birthday door, it had always been a 'double' celebration, with his getting only half of what everyone else got. Consequently, his growing feelings for its being something special had only just begun to develop. His beloved mam's untimely death had put a huge dent in all of that.

His brother, William, lived so far away, that it was nigh on impossible for them to meet at any time during the year. He had the demands of three growing children and a full-time job to juggle, along with sharing everything in his life with a wife for whom working as a teacher was equally important. They were happy, but busy.

Consequently, Christmas usually was a mundane and lonely time. He missed his mam. He missed her dreadfully. She had been the rock upon which he had built his castle, and she was the safe haven when the stormy winds blew. He had loved her with all his being, as she had him, and her untimely departure had been a serious blow to his life. That she was taken from him before she had been able to see him qualified as a teacher; the ambition she had always helped to nurture in him, was doubly crushing. Yet, she would have wished him to carry on, unswerving, towards that future life he so wanted.

That's what he was doing now, in her memory, from his heart.

His only other close relative was his first cousin, Irene, his Auntie Blanche's daughter. They had only become reasonably close since their meeting on his eighteenth birthday. A chance meeting on his way to buy shoes in his town had thrown them together, and from there they had become like brother and sister. She had been an enormous comfort to him during that period of his great sorrow, but had only communicated sporadically since.

She was several years older than him and lived in Australia, where she worked as a doctor. He would have loved to share Christmas with his grandparents, but they were not in a position to entertain or accommodate him. He would visit them for a day at sometime early in the new year, but meetings with them were now difficult, consisting mainly of his grandma haranguing everyone he knew. He couldn't cope with that, because she made not only *his* life difficult, but his granddad so obviously wasn't either comfortable with it or able to cope with it physically. So he had taken the difficult decision to write to them regularly instead, with an occasional day's visit.

After his mam's death, Jack had become intensely anti-religion, perhaps as a retaliatory reaction. He understood his grandma's feelings about God, but he realised that his mam wouldn't have wanted her death to become a cross he would want to bear. Those feelings passed, with Irene's help, and he returned once again to his spirituality.

His relationship with David and *his* mum were a lifeline for him which he hoped would develop, and through it he was looking forward to this season with suppressed and tingling delight. The presents he had bought for the Astons were not extravagant, because he didn't have the money, but they were an expression of his gratitude and esteem. He had bought a small gift for his cousin as he had done over the last year or two, but had forgotten to post it in time. He would send it, with his profuse apologies, after the event to avoid the inevitable backlog of mail and the possibility of its becoming lost. He knew she would understand. He *had* written to her, however, to tell her of his arrangements, determined this year to let nothing intrude on his enjoyment.

He had eaten very frugally during those few days before and hadn't been out for a drink at all, in an attempt to be able to share the cost of Christmas with the Astons. Fortunately, he had been blessed by the good fortune of receiving his back pay from the annual rise in pay. *That* ten pounds would go a long way.

–o–

He was up and about early on Christmas Eve, excited that he was about not to be alone again on that day. He had packed his bag with a few essentials the day before, so preparation for this day was at a minimum. Although his stomach told him it was time to eat, breakfast and lunch he ignored, in anticipation of what was to come.

The buses ran only every hour, so he had to make sure he didn't miss his chosen one. At half past two, he slipped the latch to the front door and hurried down the winding path to North Park Avenue. A keen northerly wind forced him to huddle under his overcoat and tip his face downwards to avoid the pellets of snow from stinging his eyes.

"Hello, Jack," a familiar voice halted him at the gate. "Lucky to catch you I see."

"Irene!" he gasped, throwing his arms about his cousin, and picking her from her feet. "How wonderful. What are *you* doing here, and why are you not enjoying the sunshine of the antipodes? Not seen you for ages."

"Put me down you great silly," she gasped. "You'll break my ribs."

He set her gently upright again, and slid his arm around her shoulders.

"How long are you here for?" he asked. "A long while, I hope."

"For good this time, I'm afraid," she replied.

"But," he went on, puzzled, "I thought your contract had another three years to run?"

"It does," she added. "But I couldn't stand the place, the people, and above all the job any longer, so I quit. Now don't give me any of that useless nonsense about opportunities and so on. They just weren't there. Far greater chances and scope for improvement here in good old Blighty. Hey, are we going to spend the whole of Christmas out here? Aren't you going to let me in?"

"Oh, Lord," he uttered loudly. "I'd forgotten about that. You see, I have been asked to stay over the Christmas period with a colleague, and I was on my way to the bus when you popped up. Have you got anywhere to stay?"

"I am just as you see me, my lord," she said, taking a very low bow. "No, I've got nowhere to go. I had rather hoped I could stay with you until I can get myself fixed up, both with a job and accommodation."

"Well, I can't leave you here, that's for sure," he puzzled, scratching his spikes. "I know. Just hang on a tick."

He fumbled with the lock again and disappeared into

the foyer of the house. She could hear the sound of banging and rummaging, and the occasional curse.

"Come on," he said once outside. "We pass a telephone box on the way to the bus stop. I'll give David – my colleague – a ring, and tell him the situation. Where's your luggage?"

"At the station in safe deposit," she replied, puzzled at first. "Why?"

"Well, if we are going to stay together," he said, "you may need some stuff."

The cold and intermittent flecks of snow forced them to huddle together until they reached the phone box. Breath spurted from their nostrils, hanging in the air like vaporised icicles. Irene had said she didn't feel the cold, but Jack noticed a slight tinge of purple forming around her mouth and cheeks. This made the telephone box a welcome shelter for them both from the biting wind.

The familiar clicks heralded Jack's call to his friend had been heard.

"David?" Jack shouted. "Yes, I'm on my way. Unfortunately, I've a slight problem. My cousin has arrived unexpectedly from Australia, and she's nowhere to …. Yes, of course. That would be excellent … You sure? Fantastic. We'll be there shortly. Yes. Ha ha! I *will* stop calling you shortly."

"Sorted," Jack assured his cousin.

"What does that mean?" she asked, unsure what was going to happen next.

"It means, my dear cousin, that your Christmas is assured," Jack said, a great grin spreading across his frozen face. "We will be spending it with my friend David and his lovely mum."

"But how can they accommodate me as well?" she asked, unsure. "Have they enough room for both of us? I don't mind…"

"Well I do," he assured her, pulling her closer to him

as they squeezed out of the box. "Where I go, you go. OK? Come on. I can see the bus."

"Staying over?" she asked. "Are you sure it's going to be all right? And what about night clothes and things?"

"You can borrow some of mine," he said, a deadpan look not betraying his sense of humour.

"I don't think so…" she told him, an unsure look invading her face, as she looked at him from under lowering lids.

"Only kidding," he laughed. "We'll stop off at the station and get your stuff. Don't worry. Everything's going to be fine. We're going on an adventure that we're all going to love."

"Are you sure they're all right with taking in someone they haven't yet met?" she asked, quite surprised still with all this.

"The difference between you and anybody else, is that not everybody else is my favourite cousin whom I adore," Jack added. "Don't worry. Just relax and enjoy."

"Didn't get many letters from you whilst you were in Australia," Jack said as they were crossing the road to the station's left luggage.

"Well, I sent plenty," she replied indignantly. "I answered almost all of yours, and wrote just a short while ago, telling you when I'd be in this country, but you weren't there to meet me."

"Answer's simple, really," he said, making a sweeping gesture with his arm. "I didn't receive it. The last I heard from you was two months ago when you told me how happy and settled you were."

David had anticipated the bus they would take, and he was standing sentry on his top step, ready to greet his new guests.

"Greetings and felicitations, O favoured ones," he warbled as they approached. "And this must be Irene. Come in please. You must be frozen."

The house was comfortably warm and very inviting, with trimmings and holly everywhere. David's mother had come in from the kitchen to welcome the new arrivals.

"Hello Jack," she said, greeting him with a hug and a kiss, eyes sparkling as usual. "Aren't you going to introduce me to your cousin?"

"Yes, of course," he replied, ready to share her with the world. "Irene is my first cousin on my father's side, and she's arrived very recently from sunny Australia."

He wasn't too comfortable with formal introductions, finding them pretty tedious. He preferred to let people discover and get used to each other gradually.

"Come into the lounge, my dear," she cooed. "You must be tired and cold after your journey. Shall we have a chat and cup of tea after you settle into your room? David, show Jack to his room would you? And I'll do the same with Irene, and do stop drooling, dear."

David's mother always radiated enthusiasm and kindness to everyone she met; an enthusiasm that seemed to envelope whomever she was with, and which set them completely at ease. Irene had been apprehensive at first, not knowing what to expect, coming as she had from her trials and problems in another world. She had planned to spend a few days with her cousin hopefully to get things sorted out, but to hare off to stay with someone she didn't even know existed was a bit of a stretch.

Mrs Aston led Irene off to her room, linking arms as if she had known her all her life, and chatting easily all the way. David in the meantime had joined Jack back in the lounge where he was warming his broad muscular frame in front of the blazing and crackling hearth, and was deep in thought.

"You didn't tell me you had a cousin," David said, as he finally broke the quiet.

"You never asked me," Jack returned. "Besides, I've not seen Irene for over a year, and then only fleetingly, on one of those hop-in/hop-out trips which are so quick they give you indigestion, and make you forget which way you are heading."

"Come on, man. Don't be so close," David urged with a wink and a nod. "Details?"

"Her statistics I don't know," Jack said with a knowing smile. "Hair auburn, eyes brown, slim, pretty, medium height. All those you can see. She spent the last few years, since qualifying, doctoring in Australia where I thought she would stay. Conscientious career girl, not too inclined towards romance.

"That's about the best I can offer, I'm afraid. We were never close as children, and in fact we only met properly on my eighteenth birthday on my way into town to buy shoes, would you believe. This visit is as much a puzzle to me as it is a surprise to you. No doubt we will find out the reason in due time."

The rattling of crockery in the dining room drew their attention, and then they caught the sight of Irene standing in the doorway. Neither of them had heard her enter, but David's gaze was immediately and completely riveted by what he saw. A very pretty and attractive woman, she had changed into one of the new-style figure-hugging black dresses which highlighted her colouring perfectly. Her normally jaw-length hair was swept back at the sides revealing attractive cheek dimples, and petite ears adorned by small pearl button earrings.

Jack became slightly embarrassed by the unashamed intensity of silent attention David was paying her, but Irene obviously didn't share Jack's feelings. In the fleeting time they had seen each other there seemed to have been set up a bond of understanding between their minds. This moment of brief euphoria was broken by Mrs Aston calling them to dinner.

–o–

Good food and company in convivial surroundings relaxed the atmosphere even more. Jack of course had spent several delightfully easy evenings with the Astons, but for Irene this was a completely new experience. She had read and heard of the warm welcome and hospitality of Northern folk, but never had she experienced it first-hand. She might now have been Mrs Aston's daughter for the way she had been accepted by the older woman, and far from being jealous of Irene's youthful good looks, her own attractions as a mature woman were heightened and complimented by her. David's attraction to Irene was obvious and well felt by this beautiful young lady.

She luxuriated in that day more than she had done for many a year, yet there was still that intangible, barely noticeable reserve; that touch of sadness around her eyes which hinted that not all was well.

"How wonderful it is to have young people in the house again," David's mother said when the table had been cleared and the two men consigned to the kitchen to do the washing up. "I can see you're not entirely happy, my dear. If you have something on your mind you would like to share, I'm here, anytime."

"You are very astute, Mrs Aston," she replied, "but it's something I must keep to myself, for now. I have no wish to burden anyone, let alone the friends you and David have become, although I've known you both only a short while."

"Any time you need me - us," Mrs Aston said, "you know where we are."

"Thank you for your kindness," Irene returned. "I am grateful."

"Anyway," David's mum said, raising her glass "I need to propose a toast. Where *are* those young men?"

By now everything was quiet in the kitchen, a sign that either all was well and clear, or something had gone amiss.

Mrs Aston sidled into the room to see where they were and what they were doing. As she entered, her eyes widened in surprise at what met her gaze. The pots had been done and tidied away, and everything was spotless and shining. There were no breakages that she could see, but neither could she see Jack and David.

In their place, in the middle of the floor, stood a box. It was threatening, dark and mysterious, leaving barely enough space to squeeze past. The top of one side was dominated by a large red, oval label resembling a bloodshot staring eye. Menacing in its enormity, the label read simply "From a well-wisher".

"Irene," she shouted through to the lounge. "Come and look at this."

Irene was there in an instant, sensing some urgency. "Where are the men?" she asked.

"Behind you," came a gruff but clear voice. It was Jack.

Mrs Aston started a little at the surprise, but soon overcame her nervousness. "Where've you two been?"

"Just for a … Good Lord," David gasped. "What's *that*?"

"You mean you've no idea either?" Mrs Aston asked, a sense of mystery weaving itself around her as fear and excitement began to grow in equal measures.

David approached the unknown object cautiously, looking to all intents and purposes as if he were dealing with an alien, and would expect at any time to be asked to take it to his leader.

"Only one thing for it," Jack said decisively striding forward penknife in hand, his renowned pragmatism taking over. "Come on David, let's open it."

When David had seen that Jack was still in one piece after the first cut, he joined in. Once the end flaps had been sliced away and had released the outer packaging, it cleverly fell away, taking them all by surprise.

The clever construction inside drew gasps and ahs! from them all, as they marvelled at what they saw. Two shelves, one above the other, seemed to hang magically, floating without obvious support, and bearing gifts for the occasion. The lower shelf bore a plucked and dressed turkey that had assumed the proportions of a small ostrich, and the one above boasted a piece of meat - presumably pork - which was so large it might have been, at one time, the back end of a hippopotamus. As if this wasn't enough, the base of this mobile meat pantry held a magnificent hamper laden with enough Christmastide provisions to sustain celebrations for the whole of the holiday for the largest of families. The *pièce de rèsistance*, according to David, was the crate of fine wines hiding behind it all.

They simply stood, eyes unbelieving what they were witnessing.

"Wow!" was all Jack could utter, his gruff voice almost unable to mouth this most unprepossessing of exclamations.

Mrs Aston shook her head in disbelief, muttering almost inaudibly, "I don't believe it. I simply don't believe it."

"Have you some fairy godmother up there smiling down on you?" Jack asked David with a chuckle, whilst rubbing his hands together in glee.

"Well, if I have," David replied quickly, "she must have access to the quietest helicopter in existence!"

"And a goodly slice of insight and intuition," Jack added.

"How do you mean?" Mrs Aston asked, unable yet to take her eyes from the 'happening'. "I don't understand."

"Well," David went on, "this is the reason we weren't in. Mr Tate, the poultry man, called just as we were finishing the pots, to tell us that he couldn't guarantee our turkey for tomorrow. There seems to have been a hitch, and his birds are held up in Castleford ten miles away."

"Well, then," Mrs Aston smiled, "we've no need to worry

now. We've more than enough."

"For the whole Christmas period," Jack laughed.

"But you don't seem to understand," David tried to explain. "We have no idea where this lot came from, or even how it got here."

All this time, Irene had remained silent, an impassive observer, a slight smile decorating her face throughout, watching with interest her companions' antics around the package, like so many primitives dancing around the totem to the Great God Gluttony. An idea had begun to germinate in her mind concerning the origin of their gift from heaven. Yet, she decided not to share her theory, just yet for fear of spoiling the sentiment.

-o-

It took them all of a quarter of an hour to extricate all the goodies from their protective packaging, and to agree on suitable storage for it all. Jack's usual pragmatism and concern for the disposal of the packaging turned out to be unfounded, for it seemed to have eventually folded itself into a bundle small enough to push down any mouse hole!

Within twenty minutes, they were all sitting in the lounge enjoying a post prandial brandy or glass of wine, discussing inconsequentialities.

"Old Moore's due to retire any time soon, you know," David observed as he blew smoke rings from his pipe.

"Didn't think he'd reached his personal Eldorado yet. How old is he?" asked Jack. "He's got a Stanley face, don't you think? Can't tell how old. I suppose you could cut him across the middle and count the rings."

"Sixty-three," David replied

"What? Rings?" Jack chipped in.

"No, idiot. Years," David laughed, nearly spilling his drink into his top pocket.

"Interested in his job, Jack?" Irene asked playfully.

"No, I'm too intelligent," he returned quickly. "Still, the salary would be handy."

He was interrupted by a loud banging on the door, which sounded and felt as if an enormous gorilla had taken the house by its guttering and given it a good shaking. A few seconds later, the inevitably tuneless drone of 'Away in a Manger...' invaded the house.

"Oh no," David moaned, slapping his forehead in exasperation.

"What's the matter?" Jack asked drily. "Recognise the murderer of that once beautiful tune?"

"Too true," David admitted reluctantly. "Jason Darren Sutcliffe is his excuse of a name. He promised to slither round this week to bend our ears, and I promised him that if he did, I should bend his skull – around the nearest holly bush. I'd better go and have a quiet word with him before the aforesaid ears curl up and wither away."

He was gone just one minute, during which time there were deep rumblings to be heard at the door. Silence descended for a few moments. And then there was a slam which rattled not only the light shades, but also Jack's teeth.

"Did you send him away with a flea in his ear?" Jack smiled as David shuffled into the room, hands in pockets.

"Yes. Well, in a way," he said quietly, a slight flush of embarrassment suffusing his face. "I was set to give him a piece of my mind, when I noticed he wasn't alone. He had brought his family along – all nineteen of them. Amongst them was the gorilla who had shaken the house; at least eight feet tall, with arms the size of tree trunks. Anyway, in view of the season, I thought for once I'd be charitable – good will to others and all that you know – so I put five shillings in their collection box, which at one stage threatened to claim my nose as interest."

138

They burst out laughing at the image this conjured, and settled back to enjoy the rest of the evening in each other's welcome company.

-o-

That night Jack slept the sleep of the dead.

For David, however, sleep was elusive. Too many thoughts crowded his already overactive mind, with this new dimension to his life. He had to have it for his own, of that he was sure, and would not rest until it was achieved.

Irene slept uneasily and fitfully. Her subconscious took her time and time again through her recent past, woven around by this new thread. She was like a dancer performing an intricate pattern of movements, when suddenly the pace quickened until she was caught up in a headlong chase after a point that constantly eluded her. She reached a crescendo, and then her pace dropped away suddenly, and dramatically slackened, leaving her limp and exhausted, only to be taken up again shortly after in another direction.

Chapter 13

Once Christmas had been enjoyed and consigned to a memory, they entered into that barren time of the year which heralded the long, slow uphill struggle towards summer. Life in general at this time entered a dormant phase, with little to entertain or excite; a period just to exist, huddled around an inadequate source of heat. Days were short, pale and watery, simply hanging out in the cold air, as if trying to attract substance.

Irene and Jack spent several days together, generally enjoying her new-found peace and tranquillity. Gradually he had fitted together many of the links in her life in Australia, but as yet she had not revealed her main reasons for leaving. It was three more days to school's start to the new year, which they spent flat and job hunting. Probably the wrong time of year to find the right sort of job in medicine, but she was prepared to take on anything as a stop-gap until the right job sauntered by.

Flat-finding was much easier. She had managed to bring out enough ready cash to furnish suitable rented accommodation, which she found almost overnight. Standards were much higher in the UK than those she had been used to, and there was so much more choice.

"I couldn't go back, you know," Irene said over a cup of coffee in their local café, the morning they had found her new pad.

"I didn't suppose you'd want to," Jack replied pragmatically.

"No, I didn't mean like that," she shook her head in resigned frustration. "You don't understand. I couldn't go back even if I wanted to. I'm an undesirable now."

"Good heavens ... Why?" asked Jack, somewhat puzzled, and more than a little surprised.

"It all started shortly after I arrived there," she recalled with obvious discomfort. "I'll not bore you with the details, but, as medical officer for an area, I came into contact with every imaginable type of person. Well, in my area folks of many ethnic backgrounds were lumped together, in absolute poverty of an appalling level. Talk about country of equal opportunities! They neither had the resource to buy food and medical supplies, nor the wherewithal to obtain them. Anyway, the long and short of it was that I found it quite easy to 'obtain' funds to help those people."

"But how?" Jack asked incredulously. "Local businesses? The rich?"

"No way," she snorted. "They didn't want to know. No. I found a way of short-circuiting some of the local medical region's funds, so that I could re-channel them to help those poor unfortunates."

A stunned silence began to build around them, as Jack didn't really know what to say, what with his entirely honest and unblemished approach to life. The Robin Hood principle was all very noble, but it was entirely dishonest, and Jack found that hard to rationalise. Irene carried on after a slight pause.

"I'm shocking you, obviously," she observed.

"No, not really," he answered. "Carry on please. I just find it a little difficult to take it all in, that's all."

"Anyway," she went on unabashed, "I got away with it for a few years, until they began to realise that all their funds weren't getting to where they should have been. I had been very clever, you see. I creamed off only what I considered to be surplus, and never from the same place twice. They eventually traced the discrepancies, and this led straight to me. There was such an incredible overflow of public sympathy and support when the authorities wanted to send me to prison, that they decided upon deportation as an expedient. Fortunately, I was able to send all my money to England, so I can support myself for quite a while until I have sorted things out.

"Shall we look at the flat today, do you think, Jack?"

The change in her was abrupt, and totally at odds with the story she had been telling him. Although he knew she was incorrigibly unashamed of what she had done, a slight smile creased the corners of his mouth. In a way, he was proud of her noble stand against such an uncaring organisation, but he would not be dwelling on the dishonesty of it all.

"You amaze me, Rene," he gasped. "You really do. Here am I barely able to make ends meet from day to day, and you deal in what must amount to thousands of pounds."

"Hundreds of thousands," she corrected. "I have it all written down and itemised in precise detail. Anyway, I'm bored with talking about trivia, so let's get down to something important. What are we going to do today?"

Jack didn't understand at all her hierarchy of importance, so he changed the subject.

"What do you think about the Astons?" he asked.

"Mrs Aston is a dear," she replied with a crinkled smile at her eye corners. "A very perceptive lady, who knows much more than she lets on, I think."

"David has a very high regard for you, you know," Jack explained.

"Yes, I know," she replied, a slight smile tiptoeing around her mouth. "He's asked if he can see me again."

"And have you...?" Jack asked tentatively, raising his eyebrows.

"Oh yes, of course," came her instant reply. "He's a poppet, and I feel quite at home with him. I'm beginning to – oh I don't know – feel there is a 'bond' between us already. I know it sounds so silly when you say it, but it's the best way I can describe it. I feel as if I've known David Aston a long time, and he makes me feel as if I have roots. Besides, he makes me laugh."

She stopped talking suddenly, as a far-off wistful look hijacked her eyes. She thought about her parents who had both passed away whilst she was at the other side of the world, and her eyes filled with tears at the rawness and grief which were too near to the surface for comfort.

"You're thinking about your mam and dad, aren't you?" Jack said, slipping his arm under hers. He of all people understood the pain she was feeling; a pain he had had to bear alone, without anyone to share the burden. *His* mam had gone only months before, leaving an enormous, unfillable void in his once perfect life. How could she have done that to him? How could she - his one constant, his one rock throughout his life - have deserted him so abruptly? He felt deeply that he had been robbed - had had her taken from him so unnecessarily, so much before her time. She was a good, compassionate and loving mother for whom nothing was too much trouble for both her sons. Yet, *she* was *his* mam with whom he had shared so much ... so much pain, and so much joy.

"I didn't know them for long," he said, "but they wouldn't have wanted you to dwell on them with sadness, you know. Tell you what; let's go see your new home."

After the comfortable warmth of the café and the glowing heat of coffee down their throats, the cold outside was a shock to the system. Frost and the occasional peppering of snow pellets forced involuntary intermittent gasps from their rapidly chilling bodies, forcing them to brace together against the cold. Fortunately, Irene's new flat which was part of a small purpose-built block, wasn't far away from Jack's bed-sit.

Their return was rapid. The cold had begun to seep through Jack's inadequate coat, turning his mouth a paler shade of blue and his ears deep red. The inner hallway of Number 36 was chilly, but much warmer than the outside. There was a letter waiting for them on the little table, from the afternoon post, which Irene reached for while Jack struggled to shut out what had by now become a raging blizzard. They hurried up to his room to retreat and hibernate for a while. They had quite a lot to talk about, and didn't want to waste a moment as Jack's school was beckoning him back within the next few days.

Irene reached for the gas tap to turn on the inadequate gas heater, only to be greeted by a mean ever-decreasing flame which disappeared finally like a pathetic fart.

"Jack," she said, a resigned sigh escaping her lips, "the heater seems to have decided not to be with us anymore. Do you have any more coins?"

"There's a vase by the hearth with a few tanners in it," he replied. "At least, I hope there are some tanners in it."

"'Fraid not," she replied, putting down the vase after giving it a silent shake, "and *I* haven't any."

"Neither have I," he added, "and the land lady is out."

"Cold comfort then," Irene observed.

"Not quite," he said, his eyes twinkling with mischief. "There's still one unfailing way – for emergencies only you understand?"

He knelt by the fire, feeling gently around its sharp exterior, as if looking for a particular spot. He stood up with a smile on his face, took a swing with his right boot, and hit the meter close to the grill. The result was startling, and even a little magical, as the fire burst into life once again, the flames leaping higher than if he'd dropped a shilling into its slot.

"That should last us a bit longer," he said defiantly. "The gas meter is too expensive anyway."

"I'll get the tea," Irene offered, a warming smile lighting her face. She recognised the conflict inside Jack's head; dichotomy between honesty and deceit. The judgement came down – marginally – on the side of ... pragmatism. She knew he would pay it back later, without fail.

"I wonder whom I know in Liverpool," he muttered as he sliced open the envelope. The only two things he could make out because of the fold in the paper, were the date and the heading.

'*Littlewoo....*' he read subconsciously, but stopped mid-word.

"Oh my God," he gasped. "It's the pools. I think I must have won the bloomin' pools."

Irene spun round with a big grin on her face. "You mean we don't have to work after all? Come on ... How much have we won?"

"We?" he grinned. "Since when has this become a 'we'? You read. If it's what I hope it is, I need you to break it to me gently."

"South of France," he mused, eyes spinning with excitement and anticipation, "and no more kowtowing to authority. Just think…"

"You are the lucky winner of…" she interrupted, "… twelve and sixpence. Here's the cheque."

They looked at each other quite seriously at first, then dissolved into uncontrollable fits of laughter.

–o–

The spring term blew in amidst a heavy downfall of snow. Threatening skies had gathered and deepened throughout the night, promising chaos the following morning. That chaos arrived as Jack was leaving for school. One minute the ground was clear. The next an inch of white had appeared from nowhere.

The bus shelter was a welcome refuge from the onslaught, and it seemed like the social place to be, as twenty or so people tried desperately to squeeze into its tiny interior out of the blizzard. The tennis courts and all the gardens along North Park Avenue dazzled as the coating deepened, maintaining its pristine blanket because there were no takers for tennis or gardening on that day.

Eventually the bus arrived and swallowed up its passengers with ease, allowing them a twenty minutes' respite before disgorging them again to struggle their way through town to respective places of work and shelter.

This particular bus gathered a wide cross section of folks mostly from the three stops before Jack's; people he had seen most days during last term, whom he recognised in passing. There was the old man in the corner seat, trying desperately to turn the pages of his newspaper without digging his elbow into the ample side of the moustachioed lady next to him, and the two high school girls trying vainly to show off their French language skills, much to the amusement of the fat lady behind them.

The conductor was a cheery soul, jollying along his passengers, flitting from customer to customer collecting his dues. He was a one-man variety show, singing, whistling, dancing, and climbing like a monkey up and down the stairs to the top deck. By the time the bus had warned them of the approach of town and their work places, they were loath to leave this travelling vaudeville show. Although the performance was almost the same every day, with a surprise

146

element as an encore, Jack wouldn't have missed it for the world. The last view Jack had of this particular performance was the conductor trying vainly to push a rather stout lady up the narrow staircase to the upper saloon.

Town seemed to have escaped the worst of the storm, although the sky following them was gathering in an angry mass. Unfortunately for Jack, however, his connecting bus was beginning to gather pace ... with him still several yards adrift of its open rear end. One almighty lunge would have to be enough for him to catch it. Or he *would* catch it ... from the deputy head for being late.

His ride to school from town was very short, and boring, because it didn't give him time to think. However, *this* day was different because of the snow and the fun youngsters were having in it as his carrier struggled along. By the time his terminus stop had loomed, the snow storm had overtaken and passed them, and left a two-inch-deep calling card for them all to deal with.

Looking across at the icing-topped building that was his work place, he could see the children sliding skilfully down the sloping playground, with whoops and screams of joy ringing through the clear sharp air, as those not performing pirouettes flung snow at each other with unbridled glee.

"Excuse me," a strange voice tapped him on the shoulder from behind his flapping scarf. Jack turned quickly, almost knocking over its owner, who leaped back to avoid a catastrophic collision.

"I'm terribly sorry!" he apologised, steadying her. "You startled me."

"It's OK," she replied, a smile on her face. "No problem, but could you tell me the way to ... B-r-o-w-t-o-n Junior School?"

"Don't know that one, I'm afr ... Hang on a sec," he said. "That's not an English accent, is it?"

"No," she replied. "I'm Canadian."

"Then, you want Br*ough*ton Junior School," he smiled again. "Yes. I can do more than that. I can *show* you. If you would kindly follow me, I'm *going* there."

"Do you have a post there?" she asked as they crossed the icy waste that was the road, and struggled up the drive, trying valiantly to avoid dozens of flailing bodies.

"You might say that," he said, with a slight if frozen smile. "Have you come to see someone?" he added. "To visit?"

"In a manner of speaking," she drawled.

They shouldered their way in, glad to be out of the biting cold and wetting snow. Although chilly in normal terms, the corridor felt warm enough for them to disrobe before reaching the staffroom.

"My, how quaint," she gasped as they emerged from the tunnel into the hall. "Old, isn't it?"

"Yes," he replied, "last century. And that's when it should have been pulled down. I'll just take you to see the Head."

Jack knocked on his door where, after a quiet "Come in", he showed the young lady into the room. He retreated, leaving them exchanging pleasantries as he hurried to the staffroom for a much-needed cup of coffee. Stark, bare, depressingly dull and cheerless were the words springing into his mind as he shouldered his way through the door. It looked totally unfamiliar, as if he had never been there before. It had become alien and unwelcoming.

After wishing "Good morning" to the three inmates in the room, and with a steaming cup of coffee in his hand, things began slowly to take on a distinctly more civilised aspect.

"Top of the morning to one and all," a loud and cheery greeting forced its way through the door as David Aston breezed in. Forgetting himself after a long holiday away from the staff room, he slammed the door to be covered in

148

loose floating off-white flakes of paint from the wall above the door frame.

"Dandruff bad today, David?" Jack quipped as he sipped his still-hot and steaming coffee. "Your trouble is that you've had too long a holiday, my friend."

"How'd you like a handful of powdered paint down your ear?" David grinned, unabashed, as he removed the offending objects from his neatly brushed curls.

"You really are trying your best to help the place on its way to demolition, aren't you, Mr Aston?" came Miss Page's voice from the corner.

"I'm doing my little bit," he muttered through a mouthful of coffee. "Soon have a new school for you all."

Most people by this time had filtered into the staffroom, covered in snow, and very thick clothing. With only a quarter of an hour to letting in the hordes, Mr Moore stuttered into the room, with a strikingly pretty young woman in tow.

"Well, now … Here we are my dear," he said, seemingly a little embarrassed. "Ladies and gentlemen, this is Miss Lee Genet, our exchange for Mr Simmons."

"Exchange for the better, if you ask me," David quipped.

When the laughter had subsided, a red-faced Mr Moore went on,

"She's with us right until next Christmas; for a year in fact, and I have given her Mr Simmons' third year class. So, I should be obliged if Mr Marchant would show her the ropes."

With that he rushed out to the relative safety of his office.

Stanley moved slowly forward, beaming magnanimously, revelling in the situation. If there was anything Stanley liked more than public adulation, it was more public adulation … and giving advice. Perfect partnership.

"Well now, Miss Genet," he started.

"Sakes, call me Lee," she interrupted as she was taking

off her coat and scarf.

"That'll give the Old Man something to think about," David muttered to Jack, nodding towards her bright green trousers.

"All right then, Lee," Stanley went on, as he led her out the door, "let's go over to my classroom, and I'll show you what we are about."

A few seconds later, she dashed around the door, grabbed her outdoor clothes, and disappeared again as quickly as she had entered.

"She'll learn a lot from Stan," Jack said to David with a wink and a grin. He would have carried on but for the cracked clang of the bell, heralding the start of morning school. Duty teachers Page and Sparks ushered in hordes of cold, wet children towards pegs in cloakrooms, in an attempt to restart the learning process, but a stray 'accidental' snowball cracked into the wall above Mr Sparks' head, causing him to turn sharply, fury printed on his face, and smack the nearest boy to him. That this one was not the culprit was completely irrelevant. It had been important to make a show of his authority. Punishment by proxy was not unknown in this school.

"The boy who threw that snowball ought to be punished," David said, with tongue in cheek.

"...For missing," Jack whispered to him as they marched on to class, their suppressed amusement hard to contain as they tried to talk to their children en route.

The school seemed depressingly bare and empty. Walls had been stripped of all traces of the pre-Christmas festivities on the day they broke up. All hanging trimmings had been un-hung, except for the one or two stubborn tab ends that had refused to let go of the ceiling, that had left one or two twelve inch awkward pieces of tinsel dangling in the warm air that swirled about at the top of the school, where they would stay while ever the school remained standing.

Register almost taken and dinner money collected for the week, Jack realised that Jeremy was missing.

"Still on holiday?" he enquired of his nearest friend.

"No, Sir," he replied. "His hamster died yesterday, and today is its funeral. He'll be back in tomorrow."

"Is he, er, very sad?" Jack asked, attempting to show genuine concern, whilst all the while trying to suppress bubbles of mirth.

"Not really," the little boy said, looking at Jack as if he was a little unhinged. "He'll be getting another tonight."

End of conversation. After half an hour in that room, it seemed as if he had never been away from the place, even if he *was* more refreshed now than at the end of the previous term. That stretch from September had been the longest and, in Jack's words, the draggiest in the entire academic year. It was a commonly held view that most of your year's work needed to be achieved during that period because of shorter terms, parents' evenings, open days, public performances, and a million and one other distractions that could take away the onus from 'work'.

–o–

Jack's one and only 'free' lesson in the week, apart from the head's Thursday morning BBC broadcast for the whole school, was on Wednesday, and fortunately he shared that precious half hour with David Aston. This was the time when Miss Page took his class for singing. Glad for another coffee break, Jack shouldered his way into the staffroom, only to have to duck sharpish to avoid being hit by cascading lumps of wall plaster and flaking paint. He scuttled in smartly to be greeted by David's wicked chuckle of delight from the opposite side of the room, feet on Miss Page's chair, from where he was bouncing a size three football against the wall over the door.

"I'll manage it one of these days," he chuckled, and with a wicked wink he hurled his demolition equipment again at the wall.

"What happens if the Old Man comes in?" Jack asked, becoming a bit agitated by all this, as he was stirring his coffee and putting *his* feet on *Mr Sparks'* chair.

"Being somewhat simple and naïve," David replied, "he'll think *he* did it opening the door, and then perhaps something might get done around here. I haven't yet managed to catch him in a 'shower', but we've had one or two near misses. He *must* catch it sooner or later, and I'd rather it was sooner."

"He'd probably try to mend the wall himself, if I know him," Jack said, cynically, "just as he goes around picking up litter when there are any bigwigs due to visit, or just as he descends to his knees when he is talking on the phone to anyone from the education office at county hall. How are things between you and Irene now that she's in the flat?"

"Blossoming, my dear chap," David replied, well pleased with himself. "We're going out again tonight. Care to join us?"

"No, thanks," Jack said, with a grimace. "I'm not the right shape or colour for a gooseberry."

"Bring Lee along," David suggested. "She seems like a nice sort."

"Haven't seen much of her lately," Jack added, "and besides, she wouldn't come out with the likes of me."

"Asked her, have you?" David said pointedly.

"Well, not really," Jack stammered. "Haven't really had the time, and anyway…"

At that moment, Lee pushed her way through the door.

"Greetings to our Commonwealth brethren," chirruped David. "You will come out with Jack and his cousin and me tonight, won't you Lee? Dinner and a drink?"

She smiled demurely.

"There you are, old man," David said triumphantly. "Told you she would."

"Will you?" Jack ventured rather shyly. "I'm sorry for my friend's forwardness."

"Yes, Jack," she replied with a grin. "I'd be delighted. Don't worry about David. I've learned even in this short time to take what he says with a pinch of salt."

"That's told me what to do with my big mouth," David said, drawing an imaginary zip shut across his lips.

"Pick you up at half sevenish?" David ventured. "In my car?"

"Yes. That would be great," she answered.

When she had gone, Jack turned to David and said incredulously,

"But … your car's tiny. Won't we be cramped?"

"That's the general idea, my boy," David said, glee smeared over his face. "Nice and cosy, you see."

He was about to launch his missile again, when the door opened and in shuffled Mr Moore.

"Must order some more of these," David said to Jack with a wicked twinkle in his eye, staying his throw, and spinning the ball on his finger. "Expensive but good quality, don't you think, Jack?"

Although he gave no indication he had heard David's conversation, Mr Moore turned on his shiny heels immediately, and hurried out of the room without mentioning what brought him in in the first place.

"Knew that would get rid of him," David laughed again. "The mere *mention* of money never fails. Should be a good night tonight, don't you think? Dinner at the Griffin in Leeds and drinks afterwards with two beautiful young ladies. What more could you want?"

Over again for another week, no other half hour had ever

achieved so much. Jack's liking for Lee had grown over the weeks she had been here, and he had been on the verge of asking her out for a while, but at the last minute had bottled out. And now? Taken out of his hands by his mate's mouth. David was a good friend, who could be counted upon to do the right thing for his friends in need. College girls were … well, college girls. Yet here was Lee, a beautiful and experienced woman with whom he might be able to enjoy – dare he say it – a loving relationship. The only time he had ever had such a relationship was with his mam, and she wasn't here to see him anymore. She *had* to go and leave him at an important stage in his development, which he was finding hard to get over, but she would have been proud of what he'd achieved so far in his little life.

Double art and single PE would take care of any stray thoughts of what this evening might bring. Unfortunately, the white shirt he wore so proudly, was the only one he had clean for tonight, and he couldn't guarantee it would remain clean by the end of the afternoon. His shoes, too, might be susceptible to some staining and regular little circles of grey clay sticking to their undersides.

He had had to admit that perhaps it might have been something of an error of judgement agreeing to do clay modelling with a class of eight-year-old inco-ordinates. Their concept of faces, houses, and animals was seriously underdeveloped as far as reality was concerned. They were still in the comic cartoon strip caricature stage, and so most of the clay, to the caretaker's chagrin, had ended up as small flattened discs scattered across the floor. Lucie, the class toady, had had two saucer-like pieces of clay stuck over her eyes by a perceptive and intelligent boy called Michael Jay. When he was questioned about his reasoning for doing this to her, he said he thought she looked better as a toad. Jack had to agree, but not to the boy.

That evening's entertainment cost Jack twenty-five shillings, but he felt it was well worthwhile to have to tighten his budget – and belt – for a week or two. Everything went off perfectly – Lee looked fabulous, the company was convivial, and the meal was outstanding. Joy of all joys … they were all invited back to Irene's new flat for coffee and brandy, to finish off a very enjoyable evening.

"What a delightful apartment," Lee remarked, genuinely impressed by what she saw. "You've worked wonders, really. It hardly seems possible you've been here only a few weeks."

"Nothing else to do during the day," her answer floated in from the kitchen, as she brought through a tray of steaming coffee mugs. "I've enjoyed every minute of it."

"That dinner was unbelievable," David said, patting his midriff.

"Nearly as good as school dinners?" Jack joked.

"No talking shop please," Irene admonished. "You promised."

"Sorry," Jack apologised, holding his hands above his head in supplication. "I forgot."

Settled in front of the fire, drinks in hand, soft music blurring the edges of the rage from outside, and even softer lighting taking away the sharpness of the room's dark corners.

"Anyway," Irene continued, "I had to get a move on, because I'm back in business from next week."

"You've got a job?" Jack said, rather surprised. "When? You never let on."

"I only got to know today," she replied. "It's nothing grand, you understand, but it's in medicine, and that's got to be worth something."

"Hospital?" David asked.

"St Michael's," she said. "In casualty to start with. I can move up from there at some time."

"Well done, you," David congratulated her as she sat

back next to him.

The fire had shrunk to a sullen dark red, casting vague shadows across the room whilst bodies relaxed and settled into the fabric of the room. They were so comfortable in each other's company that conversation mostly was unnecessary and irrelevant.

"Heck!" Jack exclaimed, after what must have been an hour of relaxed bonhomie. "Look at the time. It's almost half one. Got to go. Work in the morning."

They were all loath to break up such a happily comfortable society, but all had good reason.

"How can I get to my place from here, Irene?" Lee asked.

"I know the way," Jack ventured. "I'll walk with you, if you like? I can't offer you the sort of luxury that David has to offer, but it's only a five-minute stroll from here."

"Brisk walk I should think," Lee smiled, wrapping up as she made for the door. "Still very cold out there."

"I'll stay ten minutes longer if I may?" David said, looking for agreement from Irene. "There's something I'd like to talk to you about."

Jack and Lee left, shrouded in a cocoon of heavy clothing, arms linked and bodies close to hold on to their shared heat. Breath spurted from their nostrils, the concentrated droplets forming a curtain before their faces. At this time in the morning, few people were abroad, except for those on shift work, scurrying on their way. It was at times like this that he realised how little he knew about her, apart from the occasional snippet about her home and family, which she dropped almost casually into the conversations they had had.

He would have liked to get to know her better by taking her out more, but he was too shy and inexperienced to take the plunge. She was a very charming, open, and attractive woman, which made matters even worse for him. He had just about plucked up enough courage to ask her if he might see her again, as they approached her home, when she opened their now dormant conversation.

"We enjoy a good deal of weather of this sort, of course, back home," she started.

"You'll be used to it then, I should think," Jack added.

"Yes," she continued. "James always says that this is the weather that suits me best."

"James your brother?" he asked in passing.

"Sakes, no," she smiled, as they reached the steps to her front door. "I have no family. No, he's my fiancé, but we…"

The rest of her words didn't enter his head. Fiancé! The word rang in his mind, and all communication was killed, all links severed, all light extinguished, and all enthusiasm squashed. He would no longer need that bolstered courage, as he looked at Lee, not registering her smiling face.

"…before I came here," she had continued, not realising that Jack had heard not a word. "Jack? Are you all right?"

"Pardon? Oh, yes, of course," he stammered. "Well, I think I had better be going. It's late. Bye, Lee. Thank you for coming. See you at school tomorrow."

There hovered a look of puzzled surprise around her eyes as he turned and marched away. She had sensed the sudden change in his outward attitude towards her, which made her wonder if she had said something to put him off. She muttered her farewell as she watched his broad back receding in the gloom. She would perhaps find out at school - if not from Jack, then from David.

Jack, on the other hand, shut out the incident completely. The relationship between a man and a woman was nothing to do with him. He had had that a plenty when he was little, and it didn't appeal to him at all. As far as he was concerned Lee belonged to someone else, and that was a line he was not prepared to cross. He was disappointed; of course he was, but he knew he had to push his feelings in this case to the back of his mind. On reaching home, bed was uppermost in his thoughts, bearing in mind school was only a few short hours away. Lee now was no more than a valued colleague.

Chapter 14

The annual parent/teacher meeting for Jack was a new phenomenon, which David called the annual 'moan' evening.

How anyone could say what they had to say in a five-minute conversation with parents, where situations could become difficult through heated exchanges, nobody ever knew. It was more akin to putting on a show than providing in-depth usable feedback on the year's performance. Most parents turned out because they were expected to, and ended the evening in the pub across the road anyway, where they would have been had the discussion evening not gotten in the way.

Each five-minute session almost always ended with the fatherly advice 'Don't be afraid to belt him one if you need to'. This was advice no one ever heeded, or needed to heed. Had teachers heeded or needed to heed such a heads up, the Head would have needed to heed parental complaints. Mr Moore would then have needed heads on a platter to placate them. Unfortunately, most parents heard what the staff had to say about little Johnnie or tiny Jillie, but never *listened* to their advice. Consequently, most interviews lasted not much more than two or three minutes. Even so, with a class of thirty some children, the evening's session could last anywhere between an hour and an hour and a half.

In the main, Jack's class reports were reasonably positive, as most of his youngsters had responded to his teaching style. However, there was one grey spot. Jessie Brown was pleasant enough, he supposed, in a perverse sort of a way. If you kept your eyes on her all the time, she could be well-behaved. Unfortunately, she was usually a shrew of a little girl who preferred to lie her way out of most situations rather than be up front about her misdemeanours. Plausible and prim on the outside, unless she was watched closely and evidence produced to show she had done wrong, she would swear she had done nothing to warrant admonishment. The problem? Which teacher could afford the time to do nothing but watch the antics of Jessie Brown?

Her father, however, had been taught at some stage in another school by Mr Moore, whose favour he had courted ever since Jessie had attended the Infant school, which was just a dozen or so yards from the Junior's doors. A large, bluff character who had a fat, red face and incongruously small piggy and shifty eyes set under enormously bushy and sprouting eyebrows, he had occasionally managed to offer Jack a little advice about handling his daughter. No doubt, the head had whispered in his ear that Mr Ingles was an inexperienced young teacher who would benefit from a certain amount of guidance on child management. Mr Moore feared, however, that Jack would give the full unadulterated chapter and verse on Jessie's dishonesty, and how she was untruthful in the extreme. He hoped he wouldn't, but how do you stay the honesty and forthrightness of youth, which he knew Jack possessed in abundance, and wouldn't hesitate to use?

Other teachers hadn't been so fortunate in either their children's progress or how their parents would be likely to receive the report. Once, for example, Mr Sparks had been having rather a hard time trying to lick his eleven-plus class into shape on the run-up to their exam for transfer to secondary schooling. The deputy head had been delivering a particularly scathing verbal attack on Joey Osmond, the youngest of five brothers whose dad was a rag and bone man. Not too enamoured that he was about to lay into him with his slipper for insolence and laziness, Joey decided that enough was enough. He grabbed his exercise book from Sparks' desk, where it was being marked, threw it at the teacher's head and legged it out of the classroom, dragging displays from the walls as he flew past.

This took Sparks by surprise, but not so much that he didn't have the wit to give chase as fast as he could. Across the hall, through the corridors, and through the back gate the chase careered, with the boy only just in front. The chase led them up the steps at the back, down the slope, and across the muddy field, which was still recovering from a snow fall, towards the road and escape. The boy's terror at being caught added wings to his feet as he glided gazelle-like over puddles and mire. Sparks wasn't so lucky, though. He was trying to negotiate the second mud slick, when, his direction not too sure, he misjudged his footing and took off in a spectacularly gyrating leap, only to land, face down, in the middle of the slick.

Most of the school had followed cautiously, witnessing the spectacle at a safe distance. By this time Joey was away across the road, and out of sight down one of the side streets on the opposite side. Mr Sparks picked his sorry mud-dripping frame slowly out of the mire, and, shaking a fist and muttering dark threats at the absent boy, he turned towards the school to be greeted by suppressed sniggers and guffaws.

His muddy roar at the children to get back inside rang around the school. Although he fought hard to re-establish his authority, his credibility never really recovered.

He obviously couldn't continue in school in such a state,

so, after washing his face, he hurried home to change into something more comfortable. Fortunately for Mr Moore - for he was the only teacher free to take the unsupervised class - Mr Sparks lived close by, so the agony of 'class-sitting' lasted only a short time. His spectacular acrobatic escapade provided lively conversation for a long time, and David's comments about mud packs and beauty treatments were only to be expected. Joey Osmond, however, was so terrified of recrimination that his mother had to move him to another school, where his role in all this became legendary.

For once, morning break saw Jack standing quietly by himself, stirring his coffee by the sink. He had decided to spend the minimum of time in the staffroom because of what had happened the night before, in case he had to engage Lee in uncomfortable conversation. As he turned to leave, she bustled in and, smiling demurely at him, stopped to chat. *He* passed the time of day briefly, and without pausing, hurried out of the room. Puzzled by this, she watched him disappear into the gloom of the linking corridor. She had wanted to talk to him and to arrange the next time they might go out together, but clearly *he* didn't. She felt sure he would want to ask her out again, but she was obviously mistaken. Was it something she'd said?

"Now then my bonny lass," a cheery voice tapped her on the shoulder. "How are you after last night?"

"Fine, just fine," she replied outwardly cheerful. She would wait a while longer to see if Jack's attitude towards her might change.

It didn't. It got worse. Jack stayed out of the staffroom increasingly, until he went there for morning coffee and afternoon tea only. Unsure of what she had said to put him off her so comprehensively, she had no idea what to do next. David noticed there was something not right with both his friends, so in his usual delicate way, he decided to find out what was causing them so much distress.

"How are things between you and Jack?" he asked one lunchtime when they were alone in her classroom. He had dropped in to leave materials for his history lesson with her class after lunch.

"What things?" she said, looking out of the window.

"Well, I thought…" he said, rather surprised and taken aback.

"There isn't anything between Jack and me," she replied flatly. "I don't know what I've done wrong, but ever since that night out of ours, we've hardly spoken."

"I've seen very little of him lately," David went on, rubbing his chin thoughtfully, "but I put that down to the work he was doing on his social studies project. Now you mention it, he's hardly been in the staffroom at all over the last couple of weeks. I'll have a word and see what's up."

He jumped down from the cupboard he had been sitting on, and strode through the open door and across the hall to Jack's room. David could see through his open door that Jack was busy mounting diagrams and pictures around the room. He was alone.

"Haven't seen you for some time, Old Man," David began. "Been busy?"

"Yes," was the quiet reply. "I've had to get this display ready for next week's social studies."

He carried on with what he was doing, as David walked around looking at his displays.

"Hey!" he exclaimed. "This is great. What's the method?"

"The kids will be working mainly on programmed learning, self-help methods," Jack replied, "with the last resort to me in case of arriving at a dead end. Should be fun."

"How are things with Lee?" David asked quite pointedly. "Matters taken off yet?"

Jack stiffened visibly, but didn't stop what he was doing.

"Why? Should they have?" he said as he finished pinning up a chart, and turning on the inquisitor.

"Just wondered," David replied casually. "I thought you might be taking her out more since our last evening out."

"Can't imagine what gave you that idea," Jack said, turning away from his friend.

"Hang on a bit," David insisted. "OK. If you can't take a hint, I'll be blunt. I've just seen Lee, and she feels that you're avoiding her for some reason, and…"

"I think that's my business," Jack snapped, interrupting his flow. "I don't want to have to tell you to keep your nose out of my affairs, but…"

"Now, just wait a minute, old chap," David butted in, rather indignantly. "I'm only trying to be helpful."

"OK," Jack snapped back. "You've poked your nose in, so I'll tell you. She's engaged. To be married. You understand the implications of that? Hmm? Back in Canada, see? I don't want any part of that sort of an arrangement."

"Look, I'm sure there must be some sort of an explanation," David said a little more quietly than before. "You could at least go and see her, talk to her. I think she's quite upset by your not speaking."

"If you've finished now?" said Jack, still rather sharply. "I've rather a lot of work yet to do."

As Jack turned away ostensibly to complete his jobs, David shrugged his shoulders, and bounced out of the room, slamming the door. Jack resented David's intrusion, interference, and insistence at his supposed treatment of Lee. Yet, was *his* intransigence the stumbling block to understanding? Should he, perhaps, make the effort to speak to her? Didn't he owe her that much at least? His musings were vanquished by the intrusion of the bell. Within two minutes the great unwashed burst through his door and, on seeing Jack – the breakwater upon which this almighty flood was about to burst – they slowed to a shuffle and turned the volume to a whisper. Within minutes, they were in, seated, with faces upturned in eager anticipation.

-o-

A loud bang at the door jerked heads upwards momentarily from reading books, until the children were beckoned to resume their reading. Lee shouted a cheery "Come in", not knowing who was about to bestow a presence upon her classroom. A small neatly-dressed girl entered, a plain brown envelope in her hand. Her pert little face smiled as she handed over the prize without saying anything. She then turned smartly and retreated with dignity.

Intrigued, Lee flipped it over several times to find a name which, outwardly, might hint at the sender, but there was none. Slicing it open with her silver-handled letter opener, she removed the single, folded sheet of paper, upon which she could see a scrawl she recognised immediately. It said simply

Coffee after school?
Jack

Her note was swift in reply, suggesting her place.

They didn't say much in her car on the way, other than to share pleasantries: the weather, the odd item about the children. The journey, fortunately, didn't last very long as the rush hour was more than an hour away.

Although not furnished to her taste, Lee's flat was clean, well-kept, and functional. The main feature of the lounge was a large Draylon settee, into which Jack settled with a sigh. Deeply cushioned and comfortable in front of the gas fire, it held the sitter loath to move.

"You stay there whilst I make the coffee," Lee told him

165

as they took off their outdoor clothes.

"Anything I can do?" he shouted to her in the kitchen.

"Not really," came her reply. "Won't be long."

Days were drawing out a little each week, and so the tail end of daylight seemed reluctant to let go.

"Why have you been avoiding me lately, Jack?" Lee asked as she sat in the easy chair opposite him. He sipped his coffee, and thought for a while, trying not to be put off guard by her forthright manner.

"I haven't been avoiding you, exactly," he countered, "more not seeing you as much as I could have, you might say."

"I thought our friendship was beginning to flower after that night out of ours," she went on, "and I had hoped for many more."

"I *was* attracted to you as soon as I saw you, I have to admit," Jack added, taking his courage in both hands. "However, something you said as we went back to yours set me back on my heels."

"Oh yes? Tell me what that was," she said, leaning forward eagerly, "please?"

"Your fiancé," he blurted out, flushing pink at the same time.

She sat in silence for a few moments, looking directly into Jack's deep green eyes.

"My relationship with James," she began again slowly, "is reaching its end. That was one of the reasons I came over here on this exchange, to have the time to myself to think. I had decided by the end of the flight to break off with him, so seeing you had nothing to do with it. We had been engaged for two years, but I realised over time that we had agreed to be married for all the wrong reasons. He wasn't the type of husband I wanted and needed. I don't know what I want yet, and that's why I need space and time to think."

Jack sat quietly, dazed by what he had heard, understanding perfectly where she was coming from. Had his mother taken her time with *her* choice of husband, perhaps *she* might have lived longer, and enjoyed life more. Was all this true, he wondered? Yet, he had no reason to doubt what she was saying. Why should she not be telling the truth? She wore no ring. *That* he had noticed from their first meeting.

"I ... I'm sorry," he said quietly, looking into her face.

"No need to be," she answered softly. They now understood each other fully.

"Will you come out with me again?" he asked. "I'll understand if you say no after my rudeness."

She smiled and moved across to his side. Taking hold of his big square hand, she suggested that they might not need to go out.

"Why don't we make an evening of it here?" she said. "Stay for supper and a drink or two?"

Jack's face lit up, giving her his unspoken answer. This evening would be the best he had ever had, and it would be the only date he had ever had ... on his own with a woman he desperately wanted to be with.

-o-

"Well?" David urged, looking around to make sure nobody was eavesdropping his conversation with his friend. He had seen Jack crossing from the bus and had deliberately headed him off as he approached the hutted classrooms.

"Yes, it is a nice day, isn't it?" Jack replied, evading the obvious point to David's question with a sly glint in his eye.

"Come on," David said impatiently. "How did it go?"

"How did what go?" Jack replied, quietly amused at his friend's urgency.

"You know full well," said David, catching the sense of Jack's amusement. "You're having a laugh, and enjoying

167

keeping me guessing. Did you sort things out last night?"

"OK," Jack chuckled, as they walked across the hall to his classroom. "I'll put you out of your misery. Yes, we sorted it all out, and I'm seeing her again tomorrow night, to finish off where we started last night."

"Finish off where…?" David whispered. "Well, you old dog … I bet you…"

"Down boy," Jack warned grinning at his leap into the unknown. "Just friends, old boy. Just good friends."

"Good show, old chap," David sighed shaking Jack's hand vigorously enough to pull his arm out. "That's a relief. You need a steadying hand, my boy,"

Sticking his thumbs under his lapels, he struck a mock fatherly pose, as they dissolved into hoots of mirth on the way to the staffroom. Only a short step away, February half term would allow them all time to indulge their passions and develop their romantic friendships to the full.

"Fancy a foursome for a few days away at half term?" David suggested hopefully. "It would allow us chance to spend time getting to know each other better, you know, and…"

"Steady, gigolo, steady," Jack laughed. "I know *your* game."

"The girls could share rooms, and…" David said, ignoring Jack's attempted humour.

"Share a room? With you?" Jack guffawed. "Now that's taking friendship a bit too far, don't you think?"

"I had thought the Lake District, perhaps? If you can stop sniggering for long enough," David laughed back as they were pushing their way into the staffroom.

Four others were occupied in the room: Miss Page talking to Miss Peterson, Mr Sparks reading yesterday's newspaper, and Mrs Josephs crammed into her usual corner, knitting. Stan Awad would make his entry at precisely eight minutes to nine, to achieve maximum impact. Unfortunately for him, the Head burst through the door first, in as near a state of agitation for him as he could summon.

"Er, I've had a phone call from Miss Genet's landlady," he blurted out in a breathless rush. "She's ill, and won't be in today."

David raised his eyebrows and looked across at Jack, who simply shrugged his shoulders, and shook his head, a look of concern invading his face. Lee had been fine the night before, and so Jack was at a loss as to why.

"That means you'll have to take her class, Mr Moore," a low raucous voice from behind the paper reminded him of his responsibility to the children in the school. "We haven't any spare teachers."

"Er … Ah, well now," he spluttered, "that's the snag there, you see. I have a number of very important phone calls to make, and then there are the visitors. No, well, I mean, I'm afraid we will have to split the class and give four or five to each teacher here," and after a slight hesitation before he reached the door, he added, "I'll leave the details to you Mr Sparks."

Sparks slammed down the paper, and with barely suppressed annoyance and anger, he stomped out of the room to find the class attendance registers.

"The elusive Moore does it again," whistled David through a wry smile. "You've got to hand it to the old boy. He certainly knows how to wind up Mr Sparks, and get out of facing children in the classroom. He'll be in there now, 'Engaged' sign on the door, reading his newspaper."

At that precise moment, seven minutes to nine, Stanley entered with a flounce and a flourish. The only thing lacking was a fanfare of trumpets and a supporting drum roll.

"You're late," Jack said, straight faced.

"What are you talking about?" Stanley retorted, crossly indignant at the insolence of it all.

"Can't have this," David joined in, keeping the game moving. "We'll report you to the Head."

"What? To that ... charlatan?" he said, barely keeping his temper and voice under control whilst his face turned a chameleon dark red.

David and Jack could hold their mirth no longer, and immediately bust into fits of uncontrollable laughter at Stanley's expense.

"Oh, you two are incorrigible!" Stanley spluttered, realising at last that they were taking the mickey. "I'll pay you back one of these days."

The strident sound of the bell for the start of morning school interrupted Stan's discomfiture, allowing him to glower at the 'Two Stooges' as he made his way to his den.

"Will you see how Lee is tonight, on your way home?" David asked.

"I should imagine so," Jack replied, "but I think I'd better take Irene with me, to be on the safe side."

"Give me a ring, would you, when you find out anything?" David suggested as they reached the corridor crossroads by the second hall.

Already there were children everywhere, crawling around like ants wearing duffle coats and school bags. There was the half-booted variety hopping about trying to remove a difficult welly, the semi-cloaked type rushing about - coat tied securely at the neck and nowhere else, flapping out behind, and the partially capped sort, head-gear firmly pulled over ears. Jack's ear was close to being flattened by an over-sized boot which someone was brandishing whilst chasing the thief of its partner. Order was eventually brought to the battlefield, and cohorts marched off to their barracks in a semi-orderly fashion. Such was the chaos that winter weather brought to their little school.

Registration was always a time of quiet in Jack's class,

where he insisted on absolute silence whilst reading. This, he felt, set the tone for the day, and gave a space when he could balance the attendance figures, and collect dinner money in relative peace. His sit-up-and-beg type of teacher desk, with its sloping eighteen inches square top, made matters difficult and wasn't really suitable for keeping even a small number of items from sliding on to the floor.

Every day, except for Thursdays, had Mr Moore performing his unmistakable but forgettable assemblies. Same format, same pattern – story, hymn, prayer, and notices. The first three items raced each other to be over first, with the hymn reaching a crescendo despite the efforts of the assembled choir of children. Miss Page's playing and the children's singing always seemed to be engaged in a duel up to the last bar, where she often threw in a few deliberately slower notes either to fool or to even up the tempo. The children were never fooled. They enjoyed a rousing sing song, and either didn't notice the tempo change or didn't care, carrying on regardless. The assembled throng always seemed to be as one throughout, enjoying the headlong chase to the finish line.

Large enough for the whole school, the hall was one of those ancient rooms with a huge vaulted ceiling which seemed to be held in place by umpteen ecclesiastical windows that would have been more at home in a church. Two wrist-thick iron bars stretched across the void at four feet over head height, piercing the walls at either side to the outside, and locked in place on the outer walls by enormous iron plates. Without this ugly, but effective contraption, the walls would have collapsed outwards long ago. I was obvious that Mr Harrison had been adhering to union directives about cleaning procedures, because to his meagre head height, the walls were clean. Above that line, the grime of years clung to the upright, as if an invisible dado rail had dictated thus far and no further.

Arrangements for the staff were divided. The women sat along the side of the hall nearest the Head's office, whilst the men stood in a knot by the staffroom door. What were the reasons for this self-imposed segregation? Tradition and protocol. Even in this enlightened era, it wouldn't have done for a man to have mingled with the women – except, that is, for Stanley Awad. He was a law unto himself. He even had his own regular seat, right at the end of the ladies' row, between the bookcase and the radiator. There he would sit, surveying the scene, with that fixed and almost benign beatific smile on his cherubic face, as if bestowing his blessings on all before his knee.

The denouement to all assemblies was eagerly anticipated by almost all the teachers, because the notices contained information that Mr Moore had always forgotten to mention in passing during the week. The low muttering undertone from Sparks never put the Head off his stride, and although he would never have taken exception with Sparks, Mr Moore would cast disapproving glances across at him as he continued. This, naturally, encouraged the Deputy Head to mutter all the more.

"Now then, boys and girls," he started, "you sang very well this morning," looking over to Miss Page who was shaking her head, "but not quite as well as I am sure you can. We must have a hymn practice someday soon."

"If he says that one more time," David hissed quietly at Jack, "I'll shove his national health glasses down his throat."

"Our second-year boys had a rugby match two days ago," Mr Moore continued, "against Cope Street Juniors at home, and won very nicely. Mr Aston tells me that we should be pleased with their performance. However, it's not their performance I want to talk to you about."

Here he paused, altering the position of his feet several

times, like a boxer skipping without a rope, straightening an imaginary pen in his non-existent top pocket.

"As the Cope Street players were entering the building to change," he continued to absolute silence in the hall, "there was a great deal of booing from our pupils. This just will not do. Pupils of Broughton Junior School must *always* behave properly at all times. You all need to remember not to do the three Bs – booing, bullying, and … er … pushing."

David and Jack coughed simultaneously and turned around as if to arrange the same poster on the wall behind them, so they didn't burst out laughing. The same fixed smile sat on Stanley's face, and the women didn't seem to have registered anything at all. Perhaps the friends were the only ones to have noticed?

A faint tap at the hall door prevented their discomfiture. The newcomer was a small boy, who was not too well dressed, with a head like a frowsy bush. Ian Lofthouse, a notorious late-comer to lessons and to school in general, arrived - after invariably having gotten himself up and ready - with a packet of biscuits for breakfast in his pocket. His mother refused to acknowledge his existence, and continued to work, leaving the boy, at eight years old, to fend for himself.

His situation wasn't a happy one, so he had become one of Jack's favourites, giving him help and encouragement when he could. This was one of the rare occasions when Miss Page, in whose class he languished, showed unfairness and discrimination. She didn't like Ian, simply because she couldn't stand lateness in any shape or form from anyone. To make matters worse, he didn't find the work in class very easy, and consequently he needed a lot of patience and time. Understanding his dilemma, Jack tried to compensate for the inadequacies of the other adults around him.

He knew very well that Ian would get into trouble for being late again, so he directed him to his room and gave him a job to do. Jack would cover for him later with Miss Page.

Jack went back in, just as Mr Moore was rounding off another memorable assembly. The children had already started to shuffle out of the hall when an almighty commotion erupted amongst the first year classes. A rugby scrum of a gathering had formed, with arms and legs wind milling the air, as if a fight had started. Pushing their way through the throng, teachers realised that one little boy had collapsed and passed out. The ones around him were ushered out quickly, and the boy carried by Mr Sparks into the Head's office.

"It's Tommy Paylor," Mrs Josephs' voice leap-frogged from the back of the group. "He's in my class. It'll be his diabetes. He always has sugary sweets to suck when he feels an attack coming on, so I wonder why he didn't have one today?"

"Because I told him to stop eating at the beginning of the assembly," came Sparks' short reply.

Mrs Josephs' look should have struck him down.

"Sugar dissolved in warm water I think," she went on, and proceeded to stir and spoon the mixture into his mouth. After a few moments, Tommy was sufficiently recovered to sit up, and mum was called to take him home, one limp little boy.

"It's all happening today," Jack said jauntily to Miss Page as they negotiated the obstacle course of 'educational' equipment in the corridor, "and we've only just started. What other exciting adventures will befall out heroes today? Wait for the next instalment …." he rattled on in mock Paul Temple style. Miss Page looked at him, puzzled by his strange behaviour and his comments. She didn't understand Jack's sense of humour because she didn't have one of her own. Jack's children spent the rest of the morning doing silent reading or finishing off work whilst he noted the things he wanted to say to parents the next evening.

At lunchtime the Head called an unusual staff meeting for one o'clock, to the surprise and amusement of most of the staff.

"What's the Old Man want now?" David puzzled at table in the canteen.

"Parents' evening, perhaps?" Jack answered through a mouthful of Mrs Dyer's apple pie.

"It's a nuisance, really," David observed. "Would you please pass the salt? I had something important to attend to."

"Oh, yes?" Jack continued, not really listening.

"Yep. I had two lovely pints of bitter lined up in the Ship across the road," he finished. "Still, I suppose we must forego our pleasures when duty calls."

–o–

"Thank goodness that's over," Jack gasped as they emerged from the canteen, sucking in great quantities of fresh air. "They've been at it in there like frenzied pigs with only a few hours to live. One of these days I'll pull out of dinner altogether, whether Moore likes it or not. I'm not up to such trough battles."

"You become inured to it after a while," David said. "Your first half year is the worst."

As they ambled to the steps leading to the back door, Miss Peterson rushed past them, white around the gills and looking definitely sickly.

"Brenda, what's…?" David shouted after her fleeing figure, but she either didn't hear or ignored his remark entirely. They looked at each other, shrugged their shoulders, and carried on into school. As they reached the staffroom door, which was now closed, they were able to hear her berating and deriding some child.

"The filthy little pig," she went on in a fury. "Sat there

feeling sick, and when it was too late, he threw up on the table, all over everything."

"Where was it?" David asked as they walked in, as Jack ambled over to make two mugs of tea.

"Of all places," she warmed to her subject, "right on *my* table, and to make matters worse, it was Gary Steeple in my class. The number of times I've drummed it into them not to dilly-dally if they feel sick. He is a bit dim I grant you, but … that." She gave a very real shudder and sat down.

"I didn't want any more of that curry needless to say," she went on, "so I left the dinner supervisor to clear up. I'll give him 'sick' when I get my hands on him."

"Been sick?" David added. "I shouldn't put my hands anywhere near him if I were you, Brenda. You never know where it's got to. Could have been all over him, and that's not to mention the smell. If I…"

"Enough!" she yelled as she made a dive for the door, hands firmly over her mouth.

Jack grinned, as the rest of the teachers drifted into the room. Mr Moore was there by himself, sipping his tea, waiting for them all to arrive and settle.

"Well, er, now," he started, rather hesitantly, "thank you for coming at such short notice, ladies and gentlemen. I have only a couple of things to bring to you, and one of them is a subject near to my heart. I have decided to retire at the end of the summer term."

The stunned silence was thick enough to touch and taste, but was dissipated to some extent by the untimely entry of Mr Sparks, noisy and uncouth and ill-timed to the last.

"Sorry I'm late, but I had something important to attend to," he hissed, emphasising his words which made his meaning abundantly clear. At one time this sort of behaviour would have upset Mr Moore, but now he had only a term and a half to endure Sparks' boorishness. He was already planning ways to enjoy his leisure time … a world with no Sparks to dog his every step and scar his every day. Sheer bliss.

"Yes," he went on, "it's time I moved over to allow a younger person to take the reins."

This was the first anyone, including his deputy, had heard of the matter. Most would be sorry to see him vacate his office for the last time, whereas others would be measuring his chair to fit their mean backsides, and hastening his personal D Day.

"My second point is one of considerable importance to us all," he continued, choosing his words very carefully. "I think we all need to be diligent in finding out the personal health issues our youngsters are facing in their everyday lives in school. Young Tommy Paylor's was a case in point. Had he been allowed to continue sucking his sweet when he was in need, none of that unpleasant business would have happened. It was all that I could do to placate Mr Paylor, and persuade him not to take further action. So, I would be obliged if we all could be careful. Thank you for your time."

His last point was obviously directed at Mr Sparks, whose face slowly turned a chameleon shade of crimson with rage. As Head, this was the one time Mr Moore enjoyed his position, dealing out veiled admonitions with Sparks as his implied target. With the staff meeting over, he retreated to his office. As soon as the door clicked shut, Sparks exploded.

"'Oo the bluddy 'ell does 'e think 'e is?" he said, dropping into his native vernacular. "Telling me where to get off. I'll give 'im 'Be careful'."

"Calm yourself down, Mr Sparks," Miss Page said, trying to soothe. "You'll do yourself no good like that. He's only a short while to go, so don't burst a vessel. You'll put in for the top job, won't you? You've always wanted to."

"Too true I will," he answered, regaining control. "That

job should have been mine by rights before 'e came."

Jack grinned at David as they neared the door, as David raised his eyebrows in answer. Nothing else needed to be said.

Throughout all this covert duelling between Moore and Sparks, the only thing on Jack's mind really was Lee. He had arranged to meet his cousin Irene after school at Lee's flat to check on her situation. He got there in good time, but when half an hour had crept past their rendezvous time, he wondered whether she had either forgotten and wasn't coming, or she had been unavoidably held up. Like an adventurer sneaking into a harem, he was about to pluck up the courage to enter that forbidden place, when a tap on the shoulder spun him around.

"Irene!" he gasped, surprised. "Where have you been? I had almost given you up for lost."

"Last minute appointment, I'm afraid," she panted. "Man with a dislocated big toe. Absolute agony. Anyway, let's go in, shall we?"

It was one of those enormous old Victorian detached houses that exuded solid indestructibility but which had become uneconomical to run as a family dwelling. Whilst the owners lived in the ground floor, each of the upstairs flats boasted its own entrance leading from a central stairway. Whilst the stone-carved mullions were undoubtedly original, newer more modern embellishments like leaded windows had been added.

Closed but unlocked, the door to the flats opened easily as Jack and Irene sought out Lee. A light brown leaf-patterned carpet covered the low flat treads to the first floor landing, which opened out unexpectedly after a kink of a corner, offering the choice of two opposite doors. Number

178

two was Lee's home.

Jack pressed the bell.

No answer.

He pressed the bell again. There was a slight rustling from inside, followed by a quietly gruff little voice which said, "Who is it?"

"Irene and Jack," they chorused. "We've come to see how you are."

"Just give me a minute," a weary wheezy whisper just managed to poke through the shuffling and lock latch clunking, "and then come in."

After a minute or so, the door gave way under Irene's insistent shoulder, to reveal a large living room which hid underneath subdued lighting. The nearer of two internal doors was slightly ajar, and indicated the whereabouts of their friend, leaving a gash of more intense yellow light to spill onto the otherwise uninteresting carpet.

"In here," the voice pointed the way again. "Please come in."

Wearing a pale blue dressing gown and a strained smile on her lips, her slight body was dwarfed by the enormous double bed - in which she tried to appear nonchalant.

"Lazing about again I see," Jack joked, only to feel Irene's sharp elbow in his ribs as a warning that this was no time to be flippant.

"Jeez … You and your British winters," Lee groaned. "These germs are potent enough to make inroads into the human race."

"How's it going then?" Jack asked tentatively.

"Not quickly enough," she snuffled, trying to regain something of her humour.

"How about food?" Irene began. "Have you been eating properly?"

"Not had much of an appetite, I'm afraid," Lee replied,

"but my landlady, Mrs Partridge, has been very good to me. I've had two hot meals today, and I don't think I could manage another.

For parents' evening tomorrow, Jack … I'd be grateful if you'd apologise to Mr Moore for me, but I won't be well enough to be there. The doctor says it will be another few days yet, at least."

"Don't worry about that," he cut her short. "They can wait."

"If you're sure you don't need any nursing," Irene smiled, "I must be away. I'm on call tonight, and I should get something to eat. See you both later."

"I'll stay another ten minutes, and then let you get some rest," Jack added as Irene closed the door behind her.

"Had a letter from James this morning," she snuffled, watching the reaction in Jack's eyes.

He gave a very non-committal "Oh, yes?" as if it were an everyday occurrence. "Is he well?"

"He's getting married next month," she uttered quite flatly. Jack was so taken off guard by his anticipation of her next words that his heart almost stopped.

"But I thought you…" he stammered, perplexed.

"So, I am now free," she carried on deliberately, a slight smile of triumph playing around the corners of her mouth. Jack's puzzlement gave way to a grin of happiness, as he reached out to take her hand and bending to kiss her fingers, never once taking his eyes from hers.

Chapter 15

Parents' discussion evening announced the half-way marker of the year, which, once rounded, gave a reasonably clear canter towards summer and that all-important six weeks break. The parents' evening, though, was an unnecessary imposition into staff lives – a great deal of time expended for very little return. Too much of a tradition to be discarded, it provided something of a platform to sound off about educational principles to an uncomprehending and disinterested audience.

The gathering of the clans usually started immediately after school, allowing the staff barely time to bolt a hurried sandwich or slake a parched throat. Mr Moore's one concession to the extra unpaid time put in was to ring the bell five minutes early to allow a super-speedy recharge of mental and physical batteries.

The staffroom seemed to have taken on a British Railways persona, with every teacher trying to gulp down sandwiches and tea. This was the only time apart from staff meetings that the whole staff gathered in one place at one time. Mr Moore, however, was already busy with parents in his office.

"Great stuff, these evenings," chuntered David sarcastically, through a mouthful of beef paste and pickled onion. "I make sure I get rid of 'em quickly with my '*eau de*

181

onion' breath, and then we can blow the froth off one or two at the Ship across the road."

"Sounds like a reasonable plan," Jack added, finishing off his third sausage roll in as many minutes.

"I think Lee must have caught that bug on purpose so she could miss this evening," joked David.

"I think you could be right," Jack took up the joke, winking at David, having noticed that Miss Page's ears were cocked in their direction. "She probably asked Irene's advice on the best ones to catch, her being a doctor and all."

Miss Page's nosiness got the better of her eventually, as she approached the pals, removing an imaginary crumb from her skirt as she did.

"I couldn't help overhearing you," she butted in, causing the last morsel of pickled onion to become stuck in his throat as he let out a huge guffaw which set him off on a violent bout of coughing. "But do you really think that's so about Miss Genet?"

"I should think so," Jack answered with a completely deadpan face, playing on her complete lack of humour.

She turned away, leaving the room with Sparks soon after, whispering to each other as they disappeared.

"Can't believe anyone could be so humourless," David gasped when he had dislodged the pickled onion and recovered from his fit of coughing.

"Serves her right for having such big ears," Jack went on, "and an even bigger nose."

Interviews held in classrooms at predetermined times, never worked well, because many parents often preferred to queue-jump. They never could see why Mrs Jones should go before Mr and Mrs Allen, or why the Smiths should be first and the Portmans had to be last. A better system could have been devised easily, but until the new Head Teacher took over, the old guard would have its way.

By the time he reached the second hall, Jack could see that almost all of his parents were already waiting despite the published list of interview times. As he approached his room, an enormous shape lifted itself from a child's chair, and veered towards the door where it blocked all ways through. Jack, who was not so small himself, was dwarfed and taken aback by this man mountain. His shoulders touched both door jambs and his close cropped hair scraped the top of the door frame.

"Ah wanted to si thi fust," he growled in the deep, broad West Riding accent that Jack knew so well. He bristled and stiffened, preparing for the next move.

"It's abaht mi lad, Jimmy Dooks," he went on, face stern and brows lowered. "Tha's 'is teacher, int tha?"

"I am. Pleased to meet you Mr Dooks," Jack returned, holding out his largish hand in greeting. The ham of a hand that Mr Dooks produced from behind his back would have served any boat as a paddle. Enormous and bristling with black hair, it completely engulfed Jack's, and held it in a vice grip whilst pumping his arm up and down. Jack was about to take off when he was released.

"Ah think tha's doin' a rayt grand job wi' yon little bugger," he carried on, as his face split into a huge grin to reveal two uneven rows of broken battlements where there should have been teeth.

"Ifn 'e iver giz thee lip", he went on in a gentler tone, "thy 'as my permission to catch 'im one be'ind t'earole, an' let me know anall."

Jack was relieved to hear such accolades from the likes of Dooks, because his Jimmy had never been an easy boy to get on with, and some measure of parental backing was very welcome. After that start, the rest was no problem at all.

By half six, having gone through much the same sort of thing in twenty or thirty different ways, there remained only two. One of these was Mr Brown, Jessie's father, who had decided to keep himself until last.

Jack welcomed the next-to-last parent, Mrs Wormley.

"Hello Mrs Wormley," Jack smiled, holding out his hand as a small thin woman shuffled towards him. "Do have a seat."

"No, I'll not stop," she said in a somewhat tremulous voice. "I only wanted to ask you if you know anything about Tim's coat. You see, it's a new one – second day on – and he came home without it. I wouldn't have bothered you really, but it was an expensive one, and I can't afford to lose it."

"Mrs Wormley," Jack butted in, "why didn't you come and see me earlier. You've been here all evening, and I could have told you straight away."

"Well, I could see you were busy," she apologised, "and I didn't want to be a bother, or to go out of turn. Do you know anything about it?"

"As a matter of fact, I do," Jack beamed in triumph, and strode across to the bookcase where he fished out a navy duffel coat with red braiding around the hood and cuffs. Mrs Wormley smiled in relief, gave him profuse thanks and wished him a good night.

Now for Mr Brown. He was already in the chair before Jack was able to regain his.

"Good evening Mr Brown," Jack said, offering his hand - a gesture Mr Brown ignored. As he sat down, Jack was about to launch into his usual opening remarks, when Mr Brown interrupted him.

"Don't give me the usual guff, lad," he started with a half-mocking smirk on his fat face. "I know the sorts of things you teachers trot out, and I don't want to hear it."

"Now just you hold on a minute," Jack butted in, anger rising in his throat.

"No. You hold on," Brown continued unabashed. "I'm not

afraid of you lot, and neither can you pull the wool over my eyes with your educational hogwash. I've been on a course, I'll have you know, so I know what's what. Why do you pick on my daughter in class? She tells me you accuse her of all sorts of crimes when in fact she's innocent."

"Not so," Jack butted in again quite aggressively. "Your daughter is one of the worst liars I have come across…"

"Now just…" Brown tried to interrupt, indignant at this accusation.

"No. You can listen to me," Jack growled, pulling himself up to his full size, and becoming even more aggressive. "Your daughter has been found out on many occasions, and I have the means to prove it. It's a pity some parents can't see further than their precious children's nose-end."

This outburst took Mr Brown aback more than somewhat, not expecting such a sustained and aggressive onslaught from a young teacher. He had been used to brow-beating the teachers of his other children, and he had no cause to expect anything different here. He was momentarily stunned into silence, and as Jack noticed this, he changed tack slightly.

"Had you come to me in a more reasonable frame of mind," he suggested more quietly, "you would have found out much more, much more pleasantly. Now, if you'll excuse me, I have another, more important engagement elsewhere. I wish you a good night. I think you know your way out."

With that, he left Mr Brown like a fish on a fishmonger's slab, mouth open and gasping for air. He was seen later, skulking his way across the playground, his tail between his legs, muttering dark threats against teachers, his daughter, and the world in general.

David had been sitting in the staffroom for about a quarter of an hour.

"Did I see Brown slinking out of the building a while

ago?" he asked of Jack, who was wearing his triumph like a medal.

"Yes," he grinned. "I'm afraid I went for his throat. Showed him he couldn't pick on *me* without a devastating fallout."

"Good for you," David retorted. "Your predecessor was well and truly put to flight by that bloated bully boy. It's good to see him in his place."

"Time for a pint or two?" Jack asked, raising his arm in drinking mime. "It's gone seven."

"I'm ahead of you, old boy," David chortled, making a dash for the door.

As they crossed the road to the Ship, the night air had a definite chill to it, reminding them of the cracking winter they had just had to endure. The door opened onto a thick bank of warm fog, which was heavy with blue cigarette smoke and the smell of newly stale beer. The snug was empty, so they decided to surround themselves with quiet whilst drifting into hazy merriness.

"How did you get rid of your vultures so quickly?" Jack asked, caressing his first pint of bitter. "Did the old onion trick work?"

"No. Not a bit of it," David said with a smile. "Do you know little Wayne Thicket?"

"Isn't he the smelly one in your class?" Jack asked, wrinkling his nose at the memory.

"Ah … So you *have* met him," David carried on. "Well, his father came into the queue soon after most of the other parents had settled down. Just imagine … a smell twice as potent as Wayne's, and there you have Tom Thicket, the local fishmonger. Cleared the room in double quick time, I can tell you. Fortunately for me, he had only popped in to collect his offspring's games gear. He said a quick "hello", then popped out again, leaving me with eyes watering and gasping with relief." He took a long gulp of his fast-diminishing pint, and, wiping the froth from his mouth, he added, "That was the closest I have come to death by smelling."

They chuckled heartily as they finished off their immediate drinks.

Another two pints saw the world taking on a distinctly rosy hue and the parents' evening consigned to where it belonged – history.

"Have to put off visit to Lakes for week after next's ha'f term, ol' boy," Jack slurred. "Fraid Lee not fit. Wait for Easter hols and then arrange."

"Agreed," David hiccupped, half way down his fifth pint. "Asked Irien ... Ineren ... cousin. Says sagoodidea."

"Same again, ol' man?" David carried on, brandishing his glass as it were a claymore. Jack got up rather unsteadily, felt in his pockets, and sat down again with a bump.

"How much you got?" he asked as David pulled out all his change, slapped it on the table, and proceeded to count rather slowly

"Tenpence ha'pny," he finally settled.

"An' all I got is sevenpence," Jack added. "Not enough for another pint. Must go now. Need fresh air."

They struggled to reach vertical, but when they did, they staggered out of the bar and into the night air once again. Meeting the cool freshness of outside was like a sledge hammer blow to the senses making them both reel as they crossed the forecourt. It also had a slightly sobering effect, clearing the head to some extent.

At eight thirty the school was in complete darkness, the last of the vultures having wheeled away with differing degrees of satisfaction. The streets were deserted, except for the occasional body scurrying to or from the pub or off-licence. Realising that apart from the beer swilling around in their gut, their stomachs were entirely ... empty. David shook his head and rubbed his eyes.

"Hey, Jack, how's your stomach?" he asked out of the blue.

"Drowning, slowly," was his short reply.

"Don't know about you, old chap," David went on, "but *my* stomach thinks I have forgotten *how* to eat. Let's go home and … eat. What do you say?"

Jack was staying the night with the Astons anyway, so it seemed like a good idea. David's mother always seemed to know when to cook delicious food for exactly the right time. Intuitively psychic David called her.

As they turned the street, a tantalising aroma floated towards them and assailed their senses, switching on their beer-diluted gastric juices.

"That's ma momma," David beamed, licking his lips, and feeling her food in his throat already.

–o–

Their three-day half term holiday was a welcome break from everything to do with school. It meant that all educational activities could be thrust onto the back burner, and the teachers would be able to indulge in dodgy activities like getting up at ten o'clock and dining late. The only problems Jack could see with half term holidays were that they were too short, and children were on holiday at the same time as him.

Lee's recovery and return to school the week before the break had prompted the two couples to resurrect their plan, and to spend some time in the Yorkshire Dales at Malham instead of The Lake District. They had decided to book into the Buck Inn for a couple of days and to drive the smell and fabric of school out of their systems by exploring and walking and eating and, of course, drinking.

"How long does it take to get there?" Jack asked once they were settled in David's cosy little car. Baggage had to be at an absolute minimum because of the severe lack of space in his boot, but apart from that, they would be comfortable.

"Don't know," David replied whilst trying to turn over the engine. "Never been before. Read a bit about it though and I know what's there to see. The Buck's supposed to be good, so I hear."

"How the hamlet are we supposed to get there, then, if you don't know the way?" Jack sighed.

"I didn't exactly say I didn't know the way," David said indignantly. "I did read it up this morning, and anyway, you'll make an excellent navigator. Here's the map."

"Woo hoo! A sign from the gods," Jack whooped as the car spat into life.

"To the road. To the road, my merry followers," cried David as he selected gear and let in the clutch. The car moved off in a very dignified if slow fashion – backwards.

"Are you sure you know how to drive this … thing?" Irene asked, suppressing a smile.

"Course I do!" David said indignantly. "Got the wrong gear, that's all. They *are* a bit close together in these little cars you know."

They moved forward at the second attempt, set for a ten o'clock start which would get them to the Dales in time for a pub lunch and a post prandial stroll. Although Lee had experienced much more spectacular scenery in her native Canada, she didn't realise the beauty of this corner of *their* universe.

"I've got to say," she uttered, lost in admiration "that I had no idea your county was so lovely."

"Best in the country," David boasted. "I always say…"

"Next road right, David," Jack advised.

"…in the whole of Britain…"

"We've just passed the next road right, David," Jack insisted. "Carry on along this road and we'll be spending the next couple of days in the Lake District after all."

"Oops! Sorry," he apologised. "Why didn't you tell me sooner? Hold on to your hair, everybody."

He braked sharply, slammed his protesting car into reverse, and immediately took off backwards. Fortunately, the road was empty, and they hadn't gone far past their turning. Within the space of a fifty yards or so again he braked and jammed it into first, catapulting them around the corner on two wheels.

"They ought to signpost these roads better you know," David muttered, as they passed a large arrow sign with the words '**Malham 2 miles**' in heavy black letters. Jack clawed his way back into his seat from under the parcel shelf, quickly re-folded the map, and hung on to his seat until they reached their destination. Still a very small village despite growing interest from tourist and general visitors, Malham retained its inherited character and charm very well, providing much from scant reserves. Little within the village had changed over many years, yet the indications were that the local council would have to rethink its attitude following the greatly increased interest from seasonal incomers.

Stone cottages by the roadside had remained unchanged for a hundred years or more, providing romantic and idyllic living for many of the folks residing here. Their problem was that modern internal sanitary facilities had been installed only slowly by landlords, and central heating hadn't caught on much either.

Sheep farming was obviously the main industry, if the numbers of sheep dotted about the hills thereabouts were anything to go by. A typical Dales village, it supported a cross at its centre, a pub opposite the church, a village hall by the side of the green – and not a lot else.

Eventually, David managed to find somewhere convenient to park, which shouldn't have been too difficult, as the real influx of visitors was some weeks away. Although still a little chilly, the sun poured out of a clear blue sky, making them glad they had chosen this spot now. Their digs for the night boasted also a rather good lunch menu, which Jack and David insisted they sample straight away.

"You two can't be hungry already," Irene complained with a smile. "You've only just had breakfast."

"But," the boys chorused, "we're … hungry!"

"And if we don't eat soon," David added, "we'll pass out, I'm sure. What do you say Jack?"

"Sorry, what was that?" he replied weakly, feigning a stagger. "I can't hear you very well. I'm feeling faint."

"All right. All right!" Lee said, laughing at their antics. "I think we'd better feed the brutes, Irene. Don't you?"

The inside of the Buck Inn had probably remained unchanged for a century or more, but that added to the charm of the building. The same couldn't be said for the bar, which was very much up to modern-day standards. It had to be, or the locals wouldn't have spent much time there.

They found a nice cosy little alcove where they wouldn't be disturbed - which wasn't too difficult as they were the only folks there.

"Drinks girls?" David asked, shuffling his way to the bar backwards as he waited for their answers.

"Nice place, this," Jack said, as he waited for the landlord to come to dispense their drinks. "How did you find it, David?"

"Ah well," he said, "you see, being a well-travelled man of the world…"

"…You guessed?" Jack smiled. "Or you looked it up in the gazetteer? Or…?"

"My mum and dad had their honeymoon here, truth be known," he admitted. "So it seemed logical, as I didn't know the place from Jerusalem."

"Good day landlord," said David very affably to the man behind the bar. "Do you serve snacks and luncheon here?"

"Aye, lad," came the low sharp reply. "Sit thissen down, we serve anybody."

That remark came without the slightest hint of amusement or jollity, leaving the two friends unsure as to any intent behind it. He offered a menu and a list of *Specials* whilst he prepared their ordered drinks.

"Funny one, that," Jack mused as they decided their choices of food.

"Quite a reasonable selection, really," Irene said. "I think I'll have cottage pie."

"Me too," Jack agreed. "I'm a simple soul, really."

"You? Simple? I don't think so," Irene laughed. "Your mother wouldn't have agreed with that ... one ...."

Jack fell silent. A wistful look overtaking his face, as tears began to well.

Irene shuffled over to him, a profound look of remorse covering her face as she witnessed his pain.

"Oh Jack," she said quietly, putting her arm round his shoulder and pulling his unprotesting body towards her. "I am so sorry. I didn't think."

"It's OK, Irene, really it is," he replied, a slight tremor in his voice. "Don't worry about it. Just that it's still a bit ... sharp. Now, that food ... David?"

Recognising and understanding his pain, David returned to his choosing.

"I think I'll have something more exotic," he mused. *"Poulet fricassée avec pommes de terre frites et salade."*

"Indeed," Lee offered, the slight hint of a smile at her mouth corners, "I think I'll have the roast chicken with chips and salad, too."

"Ah. I forgot you come from Canada – French-speaking Canada," David said, a look of resignation on his face.

Jack turned to shout the landlord to order their food, only to be greeted by him striding across the bar with an enormous tray of food. Before he had time to take breath or to speak, the lunch that each had decided to order was placed before them. Amazed looks bounced around the gathering, stunned that the landlord could have known what they were about to order.

"How on earth did he do that?" David gasped when the barman had disappeared to bring their drinks. "Smells good, which is all I'm bothered about really," he went on through a mouthful of chicken.

"What shall we do after lunch?" Jack asked eagerly, once his last morsel of cottage pie had been scraped from round the edge of his plate.

"Well," Lee suggested, "after we have unloaded and deposited our baggage in the rooms I would have liked a stroll around the area for a while, until…"

"…Afternoon tea?" Jack interrupted, prompting groans of pain from overflowing stomachs.

"How can you even think of such things?" Irene said.

"Easily," the boys chorused, to the laughs and guffaws from the girls.

"OK," Lee said. "How are we going to do this?"

"Girls together in one room," Jack burst in quickly, "and the lads in the other. That's the only way it could work."

Lee turned to look at this man, whom she had known relatively only a short while, with wonder and great respect in her eyes. Most men would have expected to sleep with their respective 'partners'. Not Jack. He was brought up to respect women, and never to take advantage of a situation. He firmly believed that men and women should sleep together *after* the marriage ceremony. *Before* was never an option. This couple of days was going to be good.

"I fancy nipping up to the tarn," David said, as they

staggered out of the bar "but we'd need to take the car as it's up hill most of the way."

"And I fancy skipping down to the cove," Jack was equally sure, patting his belly, "to walk off this lunch. Shall we meet here later?"

The girls had made their decisions, which, fortunately coincided with what the boys had suggested.

"See you back here in a couple of hours or so?" David shouted as the car engine rattled into life.

Lee and Jack started their trek up Cove Road towards their goal, whilst David and Irene screeched around the corner along Finkle Street, towards Gordale Scar, David's Morris Minor chugging along quite comfortably.

Lee and Jack had been walking for what seemed like only a few minutes when the houses fell away and the countryside started in earnest.

"Three hundred yards or so along the main road, the barman said?" Jack added, a puzzled look appearing on his face. "And then strike out across a field to the right?"

"Well, that's probably the way over there," Lee said, indicating a signpost which pointed to … 'Malham Cove ½ mile'.

"Doesn't seem to me like we've been walking for three hundred yards," Jack muttered as he turned to his companion. "Lee?"

"Do you think the signpost might be giving us a clue?" she said, smiling at her smart answer. She wasn't often so sharp, but when she was, she congratulated herself quietly.

"Smart arse," Jack muttered almost under his breath, his smile mirroring hers. "Ooh look. A signpost."

His attempt at mild sarcasm let her know that it was a self-deprecating ploy to boost her confidence in him. *She* knew he was having a poke at his own inept direction-finding ability, something she found endearing – endearing and attractive - in him as a man who didn't take himself too seriously.

"Shall we cross over, Jack?" she suggested. "There's a little gate thing in the stone wall. Say, what is that wall? Never seen anything like that before."

"It's what's commonly known as a 'dry stone wall'," Jack explained. "Farmers divide their fields by building walls, from flattish stones they find around or dig out of the ground, without using any binding material such as cement or mortar. They are very common in these parts. Very clever, because if you don't stack the stones properly, they *will* fall down."

"This is really neat," she enthused. "We don't have anything like this where I come from."

They crossed to the gate, which was a well-worn, well-used style. Surveying the scene around with one foot on the top rung and Jack's guiding and supporting hands around her waist, she drew a sharp intake of breath at the spectacular view.

"Jeez, what a fantastic view," she said. The fields at the other side of the wall ran gently down to the floor of a small valley through which a stream bubbled and chased on its winding way to the village. This water course seemed to have bored its way out from the base of the towering Cove itself; a curved limestone wall of perhaps three hundred yards long by eighty or so yards high.

Skeleton trees abounded within this little valley, marching up to the limestone wall itself, on either side of the well-used path that saved walkers' feet from the stream. They were skeletal only because of the time of year, the glorious time of rebirth was only a short way away for all the trees, when that pale green of fresh, newly painted leaves would begin its invasion of twig and branch.

Although formed by a cascade of rushing water after the

last ice age, there had been no waterfall over the Cove within living memory, leaving the enigma of the living, rushing stream.

"Come on," Jack said, helping Lee down after vaulting the wall himself. "Shall we make for the stream first? You'll probably need to mind your feet, unless you want to step in several pancakes."

"Pancakes?" she puzzled. "I don't see any…"

"Pancakes? Cows?" Jack tried to explain. "You know …"

"Oh, I get it," she said as the light bulb flashed on.

"I hope you don't," he replied. "Get it, that is."

They laughed at the funny picture Jack's words conjured, and the mime he played as if he had fallen in a cow pat.

"If there's one thing you don't need in a field," Jack added, with a hearty guffaw, "it's a pat on the head." The laugh was the only explanation Lee needed, as her grimace told him she understood.

Jack had wanted to be alone with her since the night they had straightened out their misunderstanding. Without really realising over the few weeks since, Jack had fallen for her, but had not had either the opportunity or the courage to tell her. Now, if the moment was right, he might summon the chance.

"Look!" he whispered, sliding his arm around her shoulders as he pointed to the sky. "A hovering kestrel. It's latched on to something it's going for. See?"

"Where?" she asked, eagerly looking where he was pointing.

"Over there, above that large oak," he explained. "It's diving at a little speck. Must be a sparrow."

"Poor little thing," she clucked in sympathy.

Jack left his arm around her shoulders, so he could hang on to the few seconds of contact he had. She could feel it firm and strong across her slender frame, as she turned to face him, eyes soft and welcoming.

"I love you Lee," he murmured softly. "Have done for quite a while now. It seems rather sudden, but I know I want you for keeps."

The weight of what he had said lay heavily upon her, with feelings of happiness and unrest fighting within.

"Let's not rush things, Jack," she said softly, taking his arm and linking it with hers. "I like you very much, but not for marriage. Not yet anyway. Besides, I've only just come out of one engagement, and I need to gather my bearings before I even think about another. Let's get to know each other a bit better first, shall we?"

She hadn't expected Jack to say any of this, so she was very slow and deliberate in her reply, seeming to be struggling within herself.

"I … I'm sorry for asking," he stammered quietly, looking down at the grass, a little embarrassed at his hastiness and her reply.

"Don't be," she said quietly, stroking his hand. "I'm very flattered, and I think you a dear person for asking. Let's work on it, eh?"

They strolled in silence, arms linked and hands clasped, luxuriating in each other's closeness as they reached the stream. An irregular line of stepping stones directed their path to the other side where they needed to pick up the path for the return journey to the village. Gentleman that he was, Jack crossed the stones to test for solid footing, and returned seconds later to guide his charge. The last stone proved to be their undoing as she placed her weight on its trailing edge. Losing her footing and balance, the stone threatened to pitch her into the icy water as she teetered on its brink. Realising what was about to happen, Jack launched himself past her into the water, catching her before she hit the surface. Their eyes met in tender understanding, as he kissed her gently on the lips, lost in each other for a few blissful moments.

He said nothing, but carried her to the further bank, her body held tightly against his.

He hadn't noticed that all this time he had been standing up to his knees in icy hill water, dismissing Lee's concern by saying he would dry out as he walked. Rounding a small knot of tall bushes, they noticed that several climbers clung to the face of the cove like burrs on a hog's hide. Their attention was drawn, however, by two people waving at the top of the Cove, as if trying desperately to catch their attention.

"Can't be us they want to attract," Jack assured her, "because there's nobody hereabouts that we know. Must be someone else they want."

"No," she insisted. "Just a moment … I think it's David and Irene. Yes, it is. I think they want us to go up, but that's impossible. We'd have to go the long way round, back to the village."

"No, we wouldn't," Jack said, pointing to a cleft in the rock face near the top. "Look up there. Those specks are people's heads emerging, so there must be a path to the top. Let's follow the path round to see. Shall we?"

They hurried on as fast as the path would allow, occasionally stubbing a foot against an unforgiving surfaced tree root, until they came within fifty feet or so of the limestone face. A small weather-worn and broken direction arrow advised them the route to take to the summit, which they followed without hesitation. Not very far as the squirrel climbs, the path suddenly became much steeper, forcing Lee to take more frequent breathing stops. Jack's helping from behind in single file through dense scrub and cloying shrub, allowed Lee to rest a bit as they moved - and to feel his strength and energy feeding hers. Suddenly, the undergrowth gave way as they burst through, along the cleft they had seen from the floor of the cove by the stream.

A strong hand and arm grasped hers and hauled her to flatter ground where she collapsed, gasping for air.

"Got to rest," she gasped. "Stay here … need to breath … just a minute … please."

"The car's just about ten yards away," Irene said. "You will be better sitting there, where it's more comfortable."

"Besides," David joined in, "it will be a more appropriate place for you to hear our news."

Jack noticed their use of the word 'our' and wondered what it might mean. The once-cramped Morris Minor 1000 now took on the proportions of a limousine, as Lee flopped into the near side back seat. Jack squeezed in beside her, offering her a broad shoulder to rest on as he slid his arm around her. David and Irene climbed into the front seats, closing the doors against the cool breeze that had sprung up, and turned to face them.

"Well, then," Jack started, "what's this news you think we ought to know about?"

"You tell them, David," Irene urged.

"OK," he agreed. "Obviously we want you two to be the first to know that I have asked Irene to marry me, and she has agreed."

A stunned silence gripped Lee and Jack, who struggled to grasp the important message, as they were still struggling to catch breath from the climb.

"Well?" David asked, nonplussed by their seeming reluctance to utter anything. "Does that meet with your approval?"

Lee threw her arms about Irene's neck, congratulating them both as tears began to flow down her cheeks.

"My goodness," Lee said at last. "You're a dark pair, and no mistake. Kept that close to your chests didn't you?"

"Jack, old man?" David prodded Jack. "Do we have your approval?"

"Not so sure, old boy," he demurred, after a moment's hesitation. "I mean, can you keep her in the manner to which she had become accustomed?"

His air of mock-seriousness fooled nobody, and very quickly he dissolved into a happy chuckle.

"Of course I'm delighted," he went on. "I couldn't think of a better partner for my favourite cousin."

"Well then," David said with obvious relief and satisfaction, "that's settled. We must get back to the pub and prepare for tonight's extravaganza of a celebration. Dinner's on me, although not the usual 'on me'.

Jack half-turned towards Lee who was gazing fully at him, a look of tender understanding in her eyes, and a slight smile on her lips.

Chapter 16

Three days to go.

The excitement generated by David's announcement had wafted the four friends along on a cloud of euphoria since their break away in Malham. It had now given way, briefly, to the anticipation and expectation of Prize Giving and Stanley's extravaganza.

The collective wisdom of Messrs Sparks and Moore had dictated that the two celebrations should be held on the same night, irrespective of the confusion that might ensue. There were camps of thought as to which part of the evening was the more important. Stanley and David felt the programming for the evening should reflect the importance of their play by giving it top billing – '*Scheherazade – 1001 Nights*' supported by Prize Giving. Mr Sparks and Miss Page held the opposite view, and so that's how the programme saw the evening panning out, much to Stanley's annoyance and irritation.

There had been the usual habitual arguments as to who should receive prizes and for what reason, but, as usual, Mr Sparks had his own way. The dissent in the staff ranks always focused upon 'show piece' presentations as opposed to 'deserving' presentations. In other words, youngsters who had ability in abundance and had not needed to work hard to succeed, always won out at the expense of those who *did* try hard, but *their* endeavours were never recognised. 'Sham' and 'fraud' were the words bandied around the staffroom, but not when Mr Sparks was present.

Beginning to feel his nerves jangling in case his little dears didn't perform to his exalted and exacting standards, Stanley had stepped up the frequency of his rehearsals so much that most of his time out of class was spent with his cast, attending to their needs as performers.

"We won't be ready," he growled, as he burst into the staffroom at break time. "I said there wouldn't be enough time to produce a play of the highest standard."

"Never ye worry, Stan," David said, as he tried to soothe him. "It'll come right on the night. Slow down or you'll give yourself a heart attack."

"And what about your scenery?" he snapped again. "Half of it's not ready, and we've only two more days after this one."

"Your scenery's almost complete," David assured him, trying to calm the storm. "Got my gang working on it right now. It *will* be ready for tomorrow lunch."

"But I need it now...."

They were interrupted by a rising female voice outside the door. "I saw you do it, Tommy James."

It was Mrs Josephs.

"I don't wear glasses because I can't see, laddie. I wear them so I *can* see," came her usual firm response to his protestations. "Now, if I see you doing that again, I will ruler you. You can now go back to classroom and write out your four times and five times tables."

There was a brief pause as she entered the room.

"That little creature will be the death of me," she went on. "He stood right in front of me and swore he hadn't flicked Miranda's ear with his ruler."

"They're getting cheekier every year," Miss Peterson added, taking a biscuit offered to her by Mrs Josephs. "We find it increasingly difficult and a much longer process to knock them into shape. I don't know what they do to them in the Infants."

Her last remark was directed to the offending building with a sneer and as much disgust as she could summon.

"Well, that's what you get paid for," Sparks ground out as he left the room. Miss Peterson's grimace of revulsion at him was strengthened by Mrs Joseph's words.

"Well of course," she put in coldly, "he wouldn't know much about education anyway. He *still* can't speak English properly."

"OK," David continued. "It'll be ready for this afternoon. Jack here has agreed to help."

"Much against my better judgement you understand," he insisted hastily. "I don't want you to assume you'll be getting free labour forever more."

"You are too kind," Stanley beamed, sarcastically, "but make sure you stick to your word. I need to rehearse *with* the scenery."

-o-

For the hordes of children involved with this piece, lessons were put on hold until normal service was resumed. Those youngsters in David and Stanley's classes not caught up in the production, were sentenced to hours of endless reading and … more reading. Stanley breathed a huge sigh of relief once the scenery had been erected in the hall to dry, although he wouldn't have let on to anyone else.

The fact that the remaining two days evaporated in a twinkling, preyed on Stanley's mind mercilessly, and turned him into an insufferable prima donna. The day of the performance disappeared in a puff of dust, and was taken up with the 'preparation of the theatre'. Final adjustments to props, scenery, costume, and the like, took an age, with a special dress rehearsal for the rest of the school in the afternoon. This passed without histrionic or problem, even though it was viewed with less than enthusiasm by some of the staff. The first year teachers Miss Peterson and Mrs Josephs had virtually ignored all existence of the play, either because they had no real part to play, or because they didn't subscribe to such a wanton waste of time. They seemed oblivious to all sighs, entreaties, and ravings of that madman Awad, and went about their daily routine as normal.

By the end of the normal school day, Stanley was virtually a nervous wreck, chain-smoking as if there was no tomorrow, dripping perspiration of exhaustion from every part of his body, and gasping with relief when the final bell sounded. He dragged himself into the staffroom, and collapsed into the most comfortable chair he could find, which happened to be that belonging to Miss Page.

"I don't care," he gasped, almost invisible behind a cloud of blue smoke, when it had been pointed out in whose chair he now languished. "She can go to … our house if she objects. I need this rest to recharge for tonight's performance. That wretched child with the curtains will have to be watched, you know. He nearly had the whole lot down at the end of the dress rehearsal."

"Give him a chance," Jack said as he tried to calm him. "He's trying his best; just a little nervous, that's all. He'll be fine tonight."

"Great Scott!" Stanley stoked up again. "How am I going to get through that ordeal? Never again will I produce a play in this school."

What he really meant was that he couldn't wait to get his teeth into another one, and he wanted everyone to persuade him to do so. David bustled in with a huge grin on his face, made straight for Stanley, who had struggled to his feet to refresh himself with a cup of tea, and slapped him on the back. This had a startling effect on him. He gulped very noisily, started to turn a deep shade of purple, and finally erupted like a half-cocked volcano, sending his mouthful of hot tea in a great parabolic cascade over the wall by the sink.

"Great show, Stan," enthused David.

"Is that your finale?" Jack asked, tongue in cheek. "Or is it by way of an encore?"

Before he could turn around and let fly at the two comedians, Lee came in, closely followed by Mr Moore.

"That should go down very well, Mr Awad," the head said politely, when in fact he felt it would go way over the heads of their usual type of parents. However, he didn't like to discourage endeavour or opportunity.

Stanley was feeling much more settled and relaxed by this time. Obviously his – their – performance would be successful. Mr Moore had just said so. The youngsters, of course, had taken it all in their collective stride, as they always did, and each performer knew not only their own part, but everyone else's as well.

"May I bring a book to read for when I'm not on?" one of the leading players asked quite simply. "You see, I get a bit bored when I've nothing to do, and I don't like sitting around doing nothing."

Although his request had been granted, reluctantly, the thought of his ploughing through another story and forgetting lines and cues, caused convulsions and a rising feeling of nausea in Stanley's throat.

Jack suggested to Lee that she might like to pop into town for tea before the night shift got under way. Everyone had decided voluntarily to become involved with this extravaganza, except for the two Year One teachers, who had decided not to attend on principle. They had felt for some considerable time that, although it was generally accepted that teachers did in and out of school what was 'necessary', and unpaid, for the good of the school, they wouldn't accept it. 'Used' and 'exploited' were the concepts they couldn't subscribe to any more. They had accepted that these were high principles which would bring them into conflict with successive senior staff members over time.

Lee and Jack left school together at the end of the day, as had become their usual pattern over the last few weeks, and by degrees they were growing closer without really noticing the change too much. Tongues in the neighbourhood had been wagging for some time that they had been seen leaving school together more often than not in Lee's Mini. *They* were oblivious to this, and wouldn't have cared even if they had known.

"Look, Jack," she started as they set off, "I don't feel much like tea out, if that's OK with you. How about coming round to mine for a bite?"

"Sounds great," he replied immediately. "But, are you sure?"

"Sure I'm sure," she smiled. "Besides, I feel like being away from … people … for a while anyway, and I'd like us to be able to talk some tonight before going back to this 'happening'."

Jack's heart raced. He had so wanted to be alone with her for since their time in Malham, as he had pressing questions of his own to ask.

"What about changing?" she asked, turning momentarily towards him as they slowed for the first set of traffic lights before town.

"And what would you like me to change into?" he quipped.

"Ha ha," she replied with mock humour. "Because I will need only about ten minutes, which will give us a goodly amount of time together."

"Shan't bother beyond a wash and brush," he said. "I'm

shifting scenery you see, and that can be a little messy."

The rest of their journey was spent quietly, both deep in thought, during which Jack was content to ride and sneak the occasional glance at her. She was a very attractive woman whom Jack would have been entirely happy to spend the rest of eternity with, but whose feeling he thought stopped just a little beyond liking him. Perhaps he might ask her again? No. That wouldn't be a wise move, for fear of a flat refusal. Should he sound her out at all?

"Jack?" her soft voice sneaked into his consciousness. "Are you all right? We're here."

"Pardon? Oh, yes. Sorry," he apologised. "I hadn't noticed. I was far away."

The air in the flat felt chilly and slightly damp, creeping around their ankles like an invisible ambusher. Once the gas fire burst into life, its warm fingers gathered the pockets of cold air and thrust them through the cracks in doors and windows.

"Tea first? Or shall we talk?" she asked as she stood with her back to the flames.

"Let's eat a bit later," Jack said. "Come and sit down here by me. There's something I want to ask you."

She sat down close to him, and automatically he slid his arm around her and pulled her closer to him. The initial slight resistance didn't deter him, as she relaxed into his strong body.

"Before you ask your question," she said quietly, "let me tell you my news, and then you can decide what you will. I've been a little distracted lately, as you might have noticed. Nothing against you, Jack, but my mom has been ill for some time, and seems to be getting worse. I had the latest letter from Dad, the poor dear, only yesterday, saying how things were deteriorating. I can sense his depression and growing feelings of futility and helplessness in his letters, and I'm stuck here not able to help him or be with her."

She turned towards Jack and buried her face in his chest, dissolving into floods of uncontrollable but cleansing tears. He pulled her closer, and lovingly began to stroke her head. He loved her, totally and unselfishly and unconditionally. She tried to control the tears at first, but feeling Jack's soothing and caressing hand on her hair and his strong supportive arm about her shoulders, she allowed herself to be carried along in its course until the crying wore itself out.

After a while, she became silent, as the sobbing ceased. Her tear-stained face emerged from Jack's chest with a deeply sad look around the eyes, but a more serene smile about her mouth. She lifted her face to his and kissed him on the mouth. He encircled her body completely with his arms, pulled her close to him and they sank into a deep and warming togetherness neither had experienced before. When they parted, loath even to be apart, Jack opened his mouth to speak, but she put her finger across his lips in a sign of quiet, and said softly,

"I love you, Jack."

This was the moment he had waited for his whole life it seemed. His questions had been answered in full.

"I'm sorry for burdening you with my troubles," she apologised, "but I feel a little better now."

"Sorry? For what?" he asked. "I want to share everything with you ... joys, problems, difficulties. I love you, Lee. Have for some time. I want to marry you, but that part I can wait for."

She looked at this man who had come into her life, and who was taking it over by degrees, and she smiled. Yes, she knew she would marry him, but not yet. Other things pressed, and she had her own mind to straighten out before she would agree to bind it to another.

"Shall we eat?" she said quietly.

"Yes please," he replied in a trice. "I'm starved, but are you sure you wouldn't rather go out for a meal? There's a good restaurant…"

"No," she said, quite firmly. "I feel much better now. I'd be grateful for a hand though."

The warm glow had by now spread around the room, giving them the comfort and cosiness they would find it hard to leave.

Once Lee had removed all traces of her upset, they prepared and ate well. Just as they were about to leave for school, Jack took her in his arms, looked into her eyes, and kissed her, a long lingering kiss meant to last an age.

"We must go," she said softly. "Time's moving on, and I am in mortal danger of staying."

Clouds had begun to thicken and threaten as they made for the car. The lovers, however, didn't notice as the drizzle wrapped them around like a fine lace curtain, being too occupied with each other and the life they were heading towards. Once inside the car, the first drops of a typical March shower striped the windscreen, awakening them to the real world of work and commitment.

-o-

The show was due to start at seven o'clock prompt, but Stanley hadn't been home between the end of school and curtain-up. He had managed to find something to occupy himself during that time, from looking over the play to fiddling with the scenery, to keep his nervous fingers and restless mind busy. Had it not been for David's returning early to tie up loose ends, Stanley could quite easily have become demented with the suspense.

The children weren't scheduled to return before six thirty and no later than six forty, but they had begun to sneak in by quarter past six. It was all that Stanley could do to contain their excitement until David arrived.

"Not long to blast-off now Stan," David said as he breezed into the hall, just as he was trying vainly to adjust the curtains. One of the leading actors needed to prove the leading actress couldn't fly from the edge of the stage. David managed to ground the would-be dove before she could attempt her maiden flight.

"Just one or two adjustments to make to that cluster of palm trees," Stanley muttered, as if having the conversation with himself.

"What? Again?" David moaned. "That's the sixth adjustment to that oasis you've had me make today. It's beginning to look more like a clump of elephant grass."

Six thirty, and there was half an hour to curtain.

Lee and Jack came into school, and promptly went their separate ways - Lee to the library to help with the catering, and Jack to attend to his job as stage-hand.

"You look pleased with yourself," David said as Jack ambled into the hall ready for his turn as scene shifter. "Had a ... er ... good evening?"

"Very, thank you," came his cheerful reply. "Now what about this scenery?"

"Oh, not you as well," David started up again. "Stan's already rearranged the whole of the Arabian Desert so much that no self-respecting camel would be seen dead in it. It gives me the hump."

"Not that old chestnut again," Jack grimaced. "I think you ought to be made to pay burial, resurrection and re-burial rights for that one."

"Ah, at last," came a hoarse wheeze from the slowly tiring Stanley, as he hurried across the auditorium. "I thought you would never get here. Where have you been? Don't answer that. You see this wretched curtain? It needs fixing. The cord-pull keeps sticking. So if you would shin up that step ladder, and see what's causing the problem, I should be grateful."

"Me? Up there?" gasped Jack in mock surprise. "You'll have to coax me. How grateful?"

"Oh for goodness' sake," Stanley spat out through a cough of exasperation. "We haven't the time for fooling about."

Six thirty-five.

Parents were gathering in the other hall ready to take their seats, as players were putting on costume and make-up in the adjacent classroom. Miss Peterson had relented at the last moment to help Miss Page with make-up, although Mrs Joseph hadn't.

Six fifty.

With the tape recorder and speaker synchronised to play music for his *Arabian Nights*, Stanley found the piece he wanted for the introduction.

Six fifty-three.

Parents started their seat-finding game, and settling in to the unusual position of not being able to find the off-button.

"For goodness' sake. Why don't they either hurry up, or go home?" Stanley tutted, tapping his feet, as impatient directors might do. "We're not going to start on time."

Six fifty-eight.

The last parents managed to negotiate umpteen pairs of knees, and had avoided just as many pairs of feet, with one or two exceptions, as the house lights began to dim and the spot-lights started to add depth.

Seven pm.

The enchantingly evocative opening bars to the intermezzo to *Cavalleria Rusticana* began to gain in volume as the remaining hall lights were extinguished. Stanley had very cleverly turned the disadvantage of the changing room being across the auditorium from the stage into a triumph of rear audience participation. The auditorium had in effect become part of the stage. A veritable theatre in the round a la Stanley Awad. The curtains rose slowly as the music reached its crescendo, and faded gradually when the first characters appeared – one already on the stage, and others were proceeding from the dressing room.

-o-

Stanley coaxed, prompted and cajoled his band of wandering players towards an entertaining evening's performance until the very end of the play. With the approach of the last moments, the curtains should have descended slowly on to a very poignant scene, but the curtain boy couldn't get them to move.

"They won't budge, sir," he hissed in panic, turning to David for help.

"They'll have to," David hissed in return. "It's time they were coming down."

"Please sir, they're stuck," the boy whispered again.

"For goodness' sake, boy, give them a tug," David added urgently.

The boy did as he was told, with catastrophic results. The dowelling rod supporting the rope couldn't take the strain any longer, and parted company with it. This brought the curtains down onto the entire cast in a blanket ending, leaving a writhing mass of tulle on the edge of the stage. Stunned at first, the audience dissolved into helpless fits of laughter.

Stanley stood, unable to move, in dumb amazement as he watched the finishing touches to what should have been his masterpiece. Once this unmitigated disaster had begun to sink in, he shook his head slowly from side to side, hands on hips, and turned to look at the little curtain boy, who, with a shocked and confused look on his little face, still held what was left of the curtain rope in his right hand.

Peace and order was restored after five minutes or so,

but not for Stanley. His priceless performance ruined, he slunk into the staffroom to let his ire and irritation subside gradually. He didn't consider that fifty-five minutes of a sixty-minute show had been an outrageous success. Oh, no. It had all to be perfect, or none of it was. Neither did he realise that that performance, excellent though it was, was simply a curtain raiser for the main event which was the prize-giving.

Mr Moore took the stage hurriedly, threading his way between lengths of curtain and rope, to introduce the dignitaries who would be presenting the prizes.

"Ladies and gentlemen," he started somewhat hesitantly, casting glances upwards and at the audience. This they took to be part of the 'act' and laughed uproariously again at his timely if unintentional piece of comedy.

"I hope you have enjoyed your evening so far," he went on. "This unfortunate accident with curtain and rope has in no way detracted from the excellence of the production. Mr Awad, I know, has…"

"Just starting on the accolades," Jack informed Stanley and David, who were sipping coffee laced with generous helpings of brandy from Stanley's hip flask in the staffroom.

"This is really excellent milk, Stanley," he went on, trying his coffee. "Local herd?"

The other two smiled. Stanley had recomposed himself, and had become his usual affable self. After all, it wasn't anything to do with him, and he couldn't have foreseen its happening.

"I suppose we will have all those interminably dull stories from Sparks about how many years he has done this excruciating prize-giving, and how … well, you know the rest," Stanley droned on, bored with the whole thing.

"Yes, I suppose so," David replied absently, his mind elsewhere. Having played his part, he could now indulge his thoughts about Irene without regret.

Jack also was elsewhere. His mind was occupied with his earlier episode at Lee's. She was under growing personal pressure concerning her folks, which would be alleviated only by a return to Canada. The closeness of Easter whispered to him that perhaps he ought to consider returning with her. He had a small amount of money he might use to help with fares and so on, in an emergency. The question was whether or not this qualified as enough of an emergency to warrant the outlay.

"She *will* go," he decided.

"What did you say?" Stanley asked, turning towards Jack.

"Pardon? Oh, sorry," Jack said, evading the question. "Just thinking out loud."

"Sounds like Spark's dulcet and gentle tones tuning up," David said with a wry smile. "I think we should go back in."

"…And this is the nineteenth time I've 'ad the honour of doing the score sheet," Sparks said as he grinned. The same polite laughter floated around the audience as had in previous years. Many of the parents themselves had heard all he had to offer several times in this same hall as children. They knew the speech almost as well as Sparks himself did.

By this time the stage had been cleared, to be repopulated by a row of seated solemn-faced men, the centre one of whom was enormously fat, and who carried huge black side whiskers, an equally large moustache, but … no hair! Every time he breathed out a thin reedy sigh whistled through his dense nasal undergrowth. This frequent intrusion did not, however, interrupt Mr Sparks' flow. He was oblivious to all around him as he ground out the same parrot-fashion speech as he had for the previous eighteen years.

"…If you would leave your clapping until the end of the presentations," he went on, "so that tail-end Charlie won't miss out."

The fat man seemed to have settled into a regular, even beat as his head nodded forward on to his chest. The steady rise and fall of his ample shoulders became even slower, until it was quite obvious he had found the proceedings rather tiring and tiresome, and had sought solace in slumber. A slight but barely hidden snigger surfaced and sprinted around the small group of youngsters nearest the stage, immediately to be taken up by one or two adults close by.

"…I call upon Mr Fletcher, worthy chairman, to present the prizes," Sparks concluded, turning to the side. Polite applause lapped around the auditorium, and was sustained while one of the flanking faces tried surreptitiously, to nudge the sleeping beauty back to consciousness.

He succeeded finally with hilarious effect. The large man staggered to his feet, eyes barely open and shouted in a raucous voice,

"Odd it there Jim, an' I'll gerr anammer!"

Suddenly realising too late what had happened, and covered in embarrassment, he tried to regain his composure.

"Oh, er, yes," he stammered, rifling through his saddle bag pockets for his notes. "Good evening ladies and gentlemen. I'm sure you will join me…"

By this time Jack, deciding that he had had enough, squeezed out of the hall on his way to see Lee in the library where refreshments were being served. She was standing at the far end of the room talking to some other woman who had her back to Jack, so he couldn't make out who she was.

All the refreshments had been laid out neatly, with tea tables down one side, biscuits and cakes across the top, and a table for empties down the other, making an elegant U shape. As Jack waved and moved over towards Lee, the other woman turned around.

"Irene," he said, grinning as he took hold of her arm. "How on earth did you get down here? I didn't know you were coming."

"I came to see Lee," she said pointedly, "and so far, we've had a lovely chat. I'm hoping we'll be able to continue it without too much interruption."

"OK, OK," he said. "I can take a hint. I know when three's a crowd. I'll just nip out and see you…"

"No, you won't," Lee interrupted. "We've just about finished anyway. You stay and have a cup of tea before the rabble comes in. I've been telling Irene about Mother and Canada…"

"Yes, and I say she must go back as soon as she can," Irene butted in.

"I had decided as much earlier today," Jack added, a little put out by her interference.

"But I can't afford to do that," Lee protested.

"Oh yes you can," Irene said quite sternly. "You can…"

"Please, Irene," Jack interrupted again, becoming a little cross at her insistence. "This is my affair. I've decided to use some of the money I have saved over the last couple of years or so to allow her to go back."

"And so I should think," came Irene's swift response.

"Hey! Just a minute," Lee put in. "Don't forget I'm here. Surely I have a say in what I am going to do? I cannot and will not accept money from either of you - money I couldn't afford to repay. I will not accept charity. So…"

"It's not charity," he insisted. "As my wife it would be yours anyway…"

Both women stood with their mouths slightly open, surprised by the suddenness of his statement.

"I'm sorry," he went on again quietly. "I've embarrassed you. I shouldn't have said that. You've already refused me once, and now it seems like I'm taking advantage."

Getting over her shock quickly, Lee slid her arm through his, and smiled warmly.

"There's no need to be sorry, my dear," she went on. "I've been waiting for what seems like an age for you to ask me again. I knew the last time I shouldn't have turned you down, and I had hoped you would try again."

"So, do I understand that you *want* to marry me?" Jack said, taken aback and winded by what he had heard.

"Yes, my love," she laughed. "I do."

"My goodness," Irene gushed. "That *is* something to celebrate. We could have a double wedding."

–o–

"They're just entering the final furlong," David's breezy voice butted in from the door. "Odds on who wins – Sparks or Fletcher. Old Moore is sitting ... Why are you three looking so happy? People will be thinking you actually enjoy these things."

"Close the door, silly, and come over here," Irene laughed. He did a pirouette, tried to vault two chairs, with noisy consequences ... and ended up collapsing at their feet.

"At your service, my lady," he said saluting.

"Be serious for once," she said in reply to his comedy. "You'll never guess what..."

"They're going to pull down this place and build a supermarket?" he guessed, obviously fooling. "Or you've won the pools? I could do with a few weeks in..."

"Jack and Lee are to be married," Irene interrupted, realising she wasn't going to get anywhere with him in this sort of a mood. It did silence him – for a few seconds, and then a great grin took over his face. He gripped Jack's hand and proceeded to try to pull his arm out of its socket.

"You old so-and-so," he grinned. "You *are* a dark one and no mistake."

He turned to Lee, put his arms around her and kissed her gently on the cheek.

217

"Congratulations you two," David added. "I'm glad to see you're taking him in hand at last. Celebration is due when the curtain has fallen finally on this magnificent show here at the Palladium."

Their jollity was cut short by the entrance of Mr Moore and the other dignitaries. He paved the way by sidling around the door, having a quick look in the room, and once he was satisfied, he ushered everyone else in to take refreshment.

The first in was, predictably, Stanley, beaming hugely. He was obviously pleased with himself, probably following the heaping of accolades on his very ample shoulders.

The rest of the evening drifted by, bolstered by inconsequential chit-chat and pauses to consume copious quantities of tea and cakes. One by one the dignitaries made their exits, eventually leaving the staff to clear up and lock up. Stanley had also departed – a prior engagement he insisted – before the cleaning parties set to work. Fortunately, this didn't take long, and by quarter past nine, the exodus to the Ship was well under way.

"Coming across for a drink, Mr Moore?" David asked as they closed the door behind them.

"Well, er, er, yes," he stammered in reply. "Just got a few things to see to here first. You go on over."

The others left the school, after wishing fond farewells to the caretaker and his enormous family of cleaners, and crossed to the pub.

"Old Moore's taking his time," David observed. "There's a pint here waiting for him."

"I should drink it if I were you," Sparks advised as he passed their alcove on his way to chat to his life-long friend behind the bar. "I just saw him leaving by the back way, heading for the bus, with his hat pulled low. He'll not be in tonight."

Chapter 17

"Sir?" a quiet and lilting little voice crept into Jack's right ear one morning as he was sitting at his desk marking. He started slightly and, lifting his head from his work, he noticed it was Tina Brady, a tiny pert but sharp creature with enormous blue eyes.

"Yes Tina?" Jack answered. "What can I do for you?"

"May I ask you a question?" she asked softly, big blue saucers gazing unblinkingly into his face.

"That all depends upon what the question is," he answered with a smile, putting down his pen to give her his full attention. "Anyhow, ask away."

"Is it true that you are going to marry Miss Genet?" she asked with disarming but disturbing candour. Jack had thought that this piece of rather important but private information had been a very close-guarded secret, and would remain so until the day. He coughed and spluttered a little whilst trying to catch his breath. He didn't want to lie, so he tried to hedge.

"Well, er, I don't…" he stammered.

"Oh good," she jumped in very quickly, with a knowing but relieved smile. "That's settled then."

"But … but…?" he continued.

"It's all right," she reassured him. "Now I know that you aren't, I can wait for you myself."

She turned on her heels to return to her place, as the colour invaded his cheeks and he had to suppress the giggle he felt bubbling up inside.

"Well I am very flattered young lady," he said with a smile of relief, "but I think we will have to wait a little while, don't you?"

She beamed in return and nodded enthusiastically.

–o–

Lunchtime that day was a very quiet affair. Lee spent most of the break in her room busying herself quietly so as not to think too much about Canada. As Jack felt she needed space to think and she would prefer her own company, he left her to herself.

After his post lunch cup of tea, he decided to join David on the field where he was putting the rugby team through its paces ready for the last game of the season. A win would place Broughton at the top of the league, but a loss would hand the victory to Singleton Junior, and with it the title and the shield. However, the match at the end of this day wouldn't be an easy one, because it was against the strongest team in the league – Singleton Junior School.

"Come on, Billy," shouted David at a sprinting figure on the left wing. "Put some steam into it. Tackle him Craig. Head down, shoulder in. Good boy. Excellent tackle. Play the ball …

"Hello Jack. How … No, not that way, Simon. Foot, boy, foot. … are you these days? Haven't seen you for a while."

"Well, you know," Jack answered. "So - so, I suppose. Lee's very much wrapped up in this business at home, so I don't see much of her."

"OK, boys," David shouted after blowing his whistle, "come round here. Like to muck in Jack?"

"Sure thing," he replied enthusiastically. "What do you

want me to do? You know how marvellous I am with games."

"Can't do much," David said, "because there's an extraordinary gathering at ten past one."

"Gathering?" Jack said, a puzzled frown growing on his face. "Why? I haven't been told about it."

"Miss Page's birthday," David smiled in anticipation. "Tradition dictates that she has to bring in cakes to celebrate. Nobody knows her exact age, but who cares when cakes are at stake? OK, lads. Time to pack away."

Miss Peterson and Mrs Josephs were already sitting in their usual corner, gossiping, knitting and generally wishing they were elsewhere. Mrs Josephs never joined in with such occasions, neither bringing cakes nor taking those on offer, because her principles wouldn't allow her to accept from those she would have nothing to do with. Her friend and colleague would have loved to share those same principles, but she was neither as highly principled nor as hard in attitude.

Miss Page was arranging her selection of cakes, as Jack and David ambled through the door.

"…And if we can contain them in the first half …" David went on. "My word that's a big spread. I wonder what's under that cover?"

He tried very carefully to lift the corner only to have his fingers slapped by Miss Page who was hovering close by.

"Miss Page is keeping us all in suspense," Mr Moore smiled, really meaning that he wished she would get a move on, so that he might home in on the one he had chosen mentally already.

"Now then," she drew the room to attention as she tapped the table. "I think you are all aware that it is my birthday today … and none of your jokes Mr Aston if you please."

The staffroom burst into guffaws at David's expense which he laughed off with the rest. She pulled away the cover to reveal two large trays laden with assorted cream cakes and plain fancies, which had been individually wrapped and set out.

"Please help yourselves," she added. "They all need to go before the end of lunchtime."

Mr Moore was the first to enter into the celebration, scooping up the one he had initially identified. The object of his gastronomic desire was a two-inch-thick cream-filled butterfly crisp, which he eyed with worshipful relish. Examining it from all angles, and after choosing carefully his point of entry, he sank his teeth into its delicious form. However, the crisp was a little harder and the cream much softer than he expected, causing the cream and pastry to part company rapidly and spectacularly. Under extreme pressure, the filling shot out of the sandwich, somersaulted perfectly, and landed - unseen by him - in his jacket top pocket, leaving only a little residue on his lapel. Quite unconcerned and oblivious to what had happened, he carried on eating his cake with obvious relish, licking his lips several times when he had seen it off.

"He's obviously saving that bit for later," Jack whispered to David, who nearly choked on a pastry flake from his vanilla slice.

"Well thank you very much, pal," David managed to croak through his coughs and splutters. "Remind me to repay the compliment one of these fine days."

"I must say Miss Page that that cake was absolutely delicious," Mr Moore said.

"Please feel free to take another. They must all go. Your birthday next eh, Mr Moore?" she said with a fixed smile of triumph on her face, her rhetorical question hitting the bulls eye.

"Well, er … Yes, er, I do believe you might be right, Miss Page," he stammered as he turned to leave for his office. "We mustn't, er, forget that one."

"Don't worry," she added quietly when he had gone, "we won't forget."

David and Jack were invited to polish off the buns that were left, and they duly obliged with relish. For once Stanley had had very little to say, and had stayed in the background. Wearing his second suit and fourth shirt that week, he was the picture of sartorial elegance – a picture that had been unsurpassed or even approached in that school for many years.

"Well," Jack said finally, minutes before the bell was due, "must be off to see that everything I need for this afternoon is ready."

"This afternoon?" David asked. "Why, what's going on?"

"You know very well," Stanley butted in sharply. "That inspector is coming to sign Jack off on his probationary year."

"Of course," David remembered with a half-smile. "I recall now. Miss Appletree, isn't it?"

"Appleby," Jack corrected. "I shouldn't say that to her face if I were you. I've heard she's a stickler."

"That she is," David replied. "Yet she never stays long. I bet you a tanner she's in and out within five minutes."

"I don't think so, old man," Jack sneered. "She must have a certain number of hours she has to put in, surely?"

"Of course she does," David agreed, "but her distribution of those hours is infinitely variable. I'll come down with you if you like, to give you the benefit of my greater experience."

Jack's grimace showed David what he thought of his suggestion as they negotiated the river of children washing against the walls of the corridor, until they heaved themselves ashore in his classroom.

The inspector was to observe a social studies lesson – part of the project he would have done had she *not* been coming. Jack was always true to the principle of honesty his mam had taught him from as far back as he could remember,

223

and so he would never put on a 'special' lesson just because he had a visitor.

Throughout registration and the early part of his lesson, he was aware that she might drop in unannounced at any time. He felt that it would have been better for her to watch this lesson with his own class, so she might get a good idea of the quality work he was doing. The second lesson of the afternoon was simply a cover reading session with a younger class, and as such would give no rein to his teaching skills.

With only ten minutes left of his lesson, a noise outside his door suggested there might be a military exercise in the making. With a loud knock on the door, it flew open violently, allowing a pair of brogues and a tweed two piece to bustle in, almost breaking Jack's hand in a navvy's grip of a handshake.

"Hello, Mr Ingles. Appleby's the name," she said with a deep, clipped public school accent, as she breezed in. "My word. I say. This stuff looks good. Social studies eh? Good. Well, mustn't keep you. Carry on."

She marched over to the display he had mounted, tapped some of the exhibits, did a double about-turn and mark-time which would have done any drill sergeant proud, and marched out of the room, skirts swishing and shoes squeaking. The door handle groaned under her grip as she wrenched it open.

Then, she was gone. It had taken three minutes exactly, and Jack was left with mouth gaping, his mind in a whirl, and his hand throbbing. He had just enough time to pack away, ready for his children's next lesson with David.

"OK, pack away," he ordered. "Reading books, general books, pens, pencils, dictionaries, trousers, knee caps, eyeballs and teeth, and line up in twos by the door. At the double. Mr Aston's waiting."

This brought the usual clatter and scuffling as they

sorted themselves out, and lined up for mobilisation.

"Away," he ordered when the lines were orderly and quiet.

-o-

On the whole Miss Peterson's class wasn't too much trouble, but because the children were incredibly small, they did seem to get under his feet somewhat. There were several youngsters in the class for whom normal classroom working was trying and difficult because of their special education needs. These youngsters were lovely children in themselves, but they needed expert handling from teachers experienced in such needs. Consequently, they were awaiting special school placements, where such expertise was readily available.

One such child was called Sharon. She was obviously extremely well looked after by her parents – clean, well turned out, nicely done hair – every day, but found difficulty grasping everyday situations and new concepts. In Jack's opinion she was not as bad as many folks made out, but just needed a little more patience than most.

When Jack worked with the class he allowed her to do things he wouldn't have contemplated with the others in the class. She would never have had any thoughts about playing up or taking advantage, because she didn't know any better. She had been accepted by the rest of the children in the class. They loved her, looked after her, and would have been heart-broken had she not been there.

During this reading lesson, Jack would either read to them or listen to them reading to him. He spent an inordinately long time with Sharon for the amount of constructive work he got out of her, but he felt he had to compensate in some way for the short-comings of the appropriate education she didn't receive.

In this particular lesson she was at his elbow before he

could beckon her. She knew very well that this was playtime, and that this Mista was nice.

"Like you," she said, turning on her large brown pools of colour to look at him.

"Oh, yes?" he replied. "And why is that?"

"Like drawing," she went on in her uninhibited fashion.

"Come on, then," he encouraged her. "Come and do me some drawings."

She was reluctant at first, but once she spied the huge painting pad on his desk, she was there in a flash.

"What are you going to draw for me today?" Jack asked.

"I draw dat moorieman," she said with glee.

Jack pushed the pad in front of her and gave her a pencil. After a long time sucking, biting, chewing, and using it for things other than drawing, she put pencil to paper to produce a matchstick man with a large hat on his head. This hat was tall, pointed, and had a backwards D printed on it.

"Very good indeed, Sharon," Jack said, praising her, all the while wanting to burst out laughing at her perception. "OK, back to your place now, and play with that doll I have put there."

Unconcerned and happy, she trotted back to the class, but not before turning a complete somersault on the floor by the door.

He heard a few more readers, but his mind wasn't really on the job. He couldn't help thinking about Lee and her – their – problems, and how to make sure she got back to Canada. He had said he would find the fare, and she had agreed, but she still had time to change her mind.

The minutes passed slowly until break time rolled around again. David was already in the staffroom when Jack got there. They were the only ones there.

"Tell you what," David said through wisps of steam growing from the cup of tea in his hands.

"Go on then," Jack replied, "make my day. What interesting snippet of invaluable information have you got to titillate my jaded palate today?"

"There's a new car in the parking area," he confided. "Well, not quite new – an oldish Morris Minor 1000 actually – but a new one nonetheless."

"Oh aye?" Jack said, eyebrows raised. "Who's the rich so-and-so who could afford such a luxury? Caretaker?"

"Wrong again," David shouted in triumph. "It's our much esteemed soon-to-be-retired headmaster."

"What? Old Moore? I didn't think he could ride a bike let alone drive a car," Jack gasped. "How did he manage to get a licence?"

"I asked him about that this morning," David explained, "and he said he learned how to drive in the army during the war – lorries and tanks and the like. Kept up his licence, but hasn't driven since. Said he thought it was right at his time of life that he had a shot again, and became independent of public transport. So, keep away – well away – from his inept gropings with the gear lever, at least until he has retired, and…"

"Hello, Mr Moore," Jack broke in, cutting David off as the head entered muttering to himself and looking worried. "How's the car? David tells me you have gone up in the world."

"Er, ah, well, yes," the old man replied, "quite well in the circumstances, really. I've never seen so much traffic. Never took too much notice of it before, when I was travelling on the buses. But now it's … it's all around."

He dropped off again into mutterings and mumblings, and shuffled over to the sink where the tea was steaming in the pot and picked up an empty cup. Still muttering to himself, he walked out of the room, stirring the imaginary contents as he went.

"Somehow, I don't think our Mr Moore is cut out for today's driving conditions," David observed.

Again, Lee didn't leave her classroom, but buried herself preparing and marking work, and generally keeping a level of occupation so as not to dwell too much on her parents' troubles. Jack was torn also between leaving her to herself and his immediate reaction to comfort her as best he could.

All these thoughts crowded his mind on his way home that evening. For once Lee had gone before him, and Jack was left to make his own way on the bus. He had had a reasonable lunch at school, and so he wasn't too bothered about tea, nor was he in any great hurry to get to his cold bedsit.

He realised that the seasons were changing rapidly as he noticed the almost imperceptible light green fuzz appearing on the trees, when he walked by the tennis courts at the bottom of North Park Avenue. The crocuses in their mauve, orange and saffron finery made a delightful carpet in the grass verges either side of paths by the courts. The first hardy tennis enthusiasts were working themselves into a lather, hammering balls everywhere other than where they should have been going. They were being watched too from the safety of encircling telegraph wires, by a gallery of sparrows and starlings.

His road was one of those great avenues of Victorian stone detached and semi-detached residences which had passed their prime, and in many cases had been converted to bedsits and flats. Huge plane trees marched down either side of the road, holding their massive crowns proudly as they came into leaf at the same time. Front gardens in the main were well-tended and neatly trimmed, usually protected by low stone walls and the inevitable close-clipped privet hedge. Occasionally, there stood out from the rest a privet-free garden, where a diversity of berried shrubs abounded, and the wonders of the stonework around the house could be admired in all their glory.

Forsythia was already in bloom in many places, thrusting its clusters of yellow flowers from leafless branches through many a beech hedge, adding a little life to its brittle brown deadness. Beautifully hanging racemes of laburnum also added a much-needed breath of spring.

Jack's bedsit was in one of those multi-storey semi-detached houses where the garden had been allowed to become overgrown and untamed. He hesitated by the hall table to see if anyone had written to him lately, sadly without success. The lock of his door wouldn't take the key, which puzzled him because it had functioned properly when he left that morning. He turned the handle and pushed slightly, finding the door was open. His immediate thoughts flew to burglars and thieves, which dissipated as soon as he stepped into the room because of the glowing light and fire.

"Hello Jack," came a soft voice from the easy chair by the fire. It was Lee.

"Hello Lee," he replied, gently understanding, almost not surprised to see her there. He closed and latched the door, taking off his outdoor clothes as he did.

"Been here long?" he asked. "Had I known, I wouldn't have dawdled. Spring's well and truly on the way. You…"

"Jack," she interrupted, quietly moving over to the sofa, "come and sit down. I want to talk to you."

He wasn't at all sure what he was going to hear, but he was glad she was there. Sitting next to her on the sofa he felt the room become distinctly more inviting and comfortable. Without persuasion, Lee shuffled closer to him and put her head on his shoulder. His arm slid easily round her, and he rested his cheek against her soft warm hair. They remained that way for several minutes staring into the fire, without movement or speech.

"I must go home," she said softly with conviction. "I don't want to leave you Jack, because I love you, but Father needs me now, and I owe so much to him. I know that he will be feeling lost, alone, and won't know what to do. You see, Mother has always been the driving force behind his success. Without her he wouldn't have done much at all; wouldn't have known how. We haven't any really close relatives nearby who could help, and so you see..."

"Steady, love," Jack said, trying to soothe, holding her closer. "You don't have to upset yourself. I will be here waiting for you. Term finishes day after tomorrow, then you can go the day after that. If you need me when you are out there, you only have to cable me, and I'll come."

"I love you for your understanding," she whispered, turning her head slightly to look in his face. "I shall have to book a crossing before long."

"No need," Jack added. "It's all taken care of."

"You mean...?" she gasped, looking puzzled.

"Yes," he went on. "I booked your flight some days ago. The return you can use at any time in the next two months. I'll get David to run us over to the airport."

"But how did you know I'd decided to go?" Lee asked, still not fully understanding.

"I had decided you *should* go," he answered without hesitation, "and so by booking the flight, I made sure you would accept."

She turned fully towards him, a look of tenderness and gratitude decorating her face, and tears welling in her eyes. The words she was groping for eluded her so she said nothing as she stretched to kiss him. They met gently at first, and then became lost in each other as he pulled her closer and kissed her passionately in return.

The wind began to whistle through the telephone wires, but the room was comfortable as the lovers were wrapped up in each other.

"Tackle, Billy, tackle," David shouted almost hoarse with the excitement. "Good one. Ball now, and out to the wing and..."

"What's the score?" came a voice to his left.

"Can't you...? Oh, hello Mr Moore," he said, changing his thrust deftly. "Glad to see you. Need the support. Six-three to Singleton, and there's only ten minutes ... Oh, come on ref. That was a bad tackle."

David ran on to the field to attend to his injured player whilst play was stopped. The little lad was obviously in some discomfort, and valiantly fighting back the tears as he hobbled to his feet.

"OK Tim?" David asked. "Like to come off?"

"No thanks, sir," he replied, regaining his self-control. "I'll manage."

Immediately on the restart, Broughton lost possession and were driven back almost to their own line. One last strong thrust from Singleton against a desperately tiring Broughton side would see them through for the crucial score. The home side's move on the right out-positioned and over-stretched the Broughton side, creating an overlap. It would be a certain try, David was sure, and the loss of the league and its gleaming trophy.

One man only to beat; a flying pass; a wildly loose ball – and Jamie Sutherland, the Broughton winger was on it in a flash. He was through the gap and away, haring up his wing. As almost all Singleton players had been thrown into attack, only their full back formed any credible line of defence. A great hulking West Indian lad who would normally have crushed Jamie, was left gasping by a deft sidestep, and a wiggle allowed him only the briefest touch of his flying shirt.

"Come on, Jamie. Come on. Nearly there." David croaked. "Watch out. Two behind."

Two very fast Singleton players converged on the

slowing Broughton winger. Ten yards to go and their pincer movement seemed like it was about to pay off. Two yards and Jamie, sensing his impending loss, took off in a spectacularly desperate flying leap for the line. The three players met in mid-air and rolled when they hit the ground – over the line. The referee, a fair-minded teacher from Singleton, had no hesitation in awarding the try. Broughton had done it. The crushed Jamie was hauled from the floor and shouldered back to his own half.

Six all.

The result depended on the final kick for conversion. Frankie Harper was their regular goal kicker, who hadn't yet kicked a goal. Still, he took his time, placing the ball as he had seen the internationals do, took six measured steps back, and said a silent prayer. He launched himself forward and, just before boot hit ball, he clamped his eyes tight shut. The thwack of leather on leather could be heard all over the ground. A second thwack a moment or two later echoed the first, as the ball hit the cross bar and ... bounced over. They had won. They had won. And nobody was more astounded than Frankie Harper, whose grin threatened to split his face in two.

The rest was a formality. Singleton had time only to restart the game when the final whistle signalled that it was all over. Broughton were the champions, and even Mr Moore was excited enough to stay almost to the end, probably so that he wouldn't have to give anyone a lift back to school. A happy but tired team, gaining strength from somewhere, chaired an equally happy David Aston from the field.

Chapter 18

The term ended as uneventfully as it had begun in school, but as far as the staff was concerned, there was considerable excitement. Mr Moore, last bastion of thrift in an increasingly spendthrift world, had made the unprecedented announcement that he intended to throw a retirement party, to which all past and present colleagues would be invited. It would be catered by an outside agency, and held in the school hall. This announcement was like a hammer blow to all staff who knew him, stunning them to disbelief. He announced also that his successor had already been chosen, and would be visiting the school in the summer term to meet the staff.

Jack finished school that Thursday with a feeling of misgiving, as Lee would be leaving for Canada within a couple of days. He wasn't looking forward to the two weeks he would be spending on his own.

Jack and Lee enjoyed their last full day together, walking, talking, and generally trying not to let their impending separation intrude too much. Inevitably they drifted into talking about their fears and pain following Lee's departure.

"We won't be able to share the Easter Festival in the park this year," Jack said as their day drew to its close. They ambled through that part of the park which was little frequented, giving them uninterrupted time without people surrounding them. Wildness in this area made it unattractive to the general public, which was the very reason Jack liked it so much. Deep tussocky grass rubbed shoulders with thicket and hedge, with sapling trees providing surrounding protection throughout. The park's new spring raiment was bright, alive, and breathed life into a previously dead area, allowing winter to snap shut its jaws for the last time this year.

They wandered aimlessly through waist-high shrubs and head-high interlocking branches, until they emerged at the other end of a safari of vegetation to glimpse the lake shimmering under the dying rays of an early spring sun. With scant cloud cover, it had to be content with the banks of beech, oak and birch to hide behind on the further side.

"Silly isn't it?" Jack said as they sat for a moment on a lakeside bench. "I'm talking as if this is our last spring together. We *will* have many other springs and Easter festivals together, because everything *will* turn out. You'll see."

He slid his arm around her shoulder and pulled her closer to him, as she gave an involuntary shudder from the cold. The sun had gone, dusk had slipped in, bringing with it a slight chill.

"Come on," he said. "We've been wandering about as if next year will do. You've a plane to catch tomorrow, and our staying out late won't help."

"It's fine, really," she assured him. "I've enjoyed myself today. You really are a wonderful person, Jack, taking me out of myself as you have done. Things *will* be fine, I'm sure you're right. It's just that I have this feeling gnawing at the back of my mind, and I have no idea what it means or why it's there. But you're right as usual. We need to get back. I *will* miss you, you know, but it won't be for long."

She wanted him to stay with her that night, but he

knew what that would mean, and he couldn't take the risk of diverting her from the path she had to take.

-o-

The journey across the Pennines was upsetting if uneventful, as was the return when they had seen Lee on to her flight. That parting was private, and nobody but Jack saw the pain that she bore as they said their goodbyes.

"I need a drink," David said suddenly as they passed through one of the Pennine hamlets on their way back into Yorkshire.

"Let's wait until we get back to our side of the hills, eh?" Jack suggested, "to find some proper beer? Can't stand that dishwater they serve over here."

Heavy rain the night before had made their tortuous road home dangerous - a road which a couple of weeks before had been six inches deep in snow. Downhill all the way from here, David could have selected neutral and coasted into Yorkshire with no trouble at all. In fact, he did that on more than one occasion, causing Jack a certain amount of disquiet.

"You really ought to maintain drive you know, old man," Jack said, a little worried that his fate was held in the balance by his friend's reliance on Morris brakes alone.

"You worry too much," David replied cheerily, turning to Jack. "I'm in full control. Saves petrol and wear and tear on the clutch. Do you know how much one of...?"

"Look out, damn you," Jack yelled as they came off the crown of another blind bend which was thickly covered by bush and tree. Just ten yards ahead of them, the road had been removed and a small lake put in its place. They could see nothing but water for a hundred yards or so, until the road emerged and climbed another hill at the other side of this mini inland sea.

"What the bloody...?" David cursed. He tried to push

235

his foot through the floor in an attempt to stop instantly, but with no response, largely because of his excessive riding of the brakes, and the wetness of the road. Hitting the water at thirty was a bit like running into a haystack. They shot into the water a few yards, then came to a juddering halt with the water just over the bottom of the doors. Jack was a little dazed from a bang he had taken to his head, whilst David was even more shaken to think he had parked his beloved car in a lake. Not really knowing what to do, they simply sat, looking at each other, puzzled looks on their faces.

"Well," David said after a while, "there's only one thing for it."

"Oh yes?" Jack replied, raising a quizzical eyebrow. "Come on then, what?"

"We need a push, obviously," David pointed out with an indulgent smile, "and being as you are only one here who can, I propose you."

"Ye … eh?" Jack stammered, not believing what he was hearing. "How do you make that one out? What about you? It's your car."

"Ah, well, you see," David tried to explain, "I can't really do the pushing, as I'm the only one who can drive."

"Wrong," Jack interrupted. "I passed my test last year."

"Well, er, ah," David wriggled again. "I'm the only one who knows how to drive *this* car, and besides, you're not insured to drive it under my policy. I mean, what would happen if we had an accident whilst you were in control and I was pushing? You can't be too careful with car insurance, you know."

Jack cast a disbelieving glance at David, but wasn't prepared to argue. He took off his shoes and rolled up his trousers. The icy water stopped short of his knees, but quickly struck through to his bones, sucking out the feeling in a short time.

"There's a pair of galoshes in the boot," David shouted from the car.

"I don't think ankle-length pumps are going to help in this ice, do you?" Jack shouted back, gasping for air at the back end of the car.

"No, I suppose not," David sighed. "Ah well, on with the job in hand. Could you give it a bit better push, old man?"

Jack crouched and put his ample shoulder to the off-side rear wing of the Morris, and, getting as good a purchase as the water would allow, he began to push. For the first few minutes, nothing happened. He strained and heaved until he felt a slight movement forward, making him strain even harder. The car's unexpected lurch forward caught Jack off guard and off balance, pitching him forward into the muddy water. He struggled to his feet, gasping for air, and soaked to the skin, with dirty water dripping from his nose end and everywhere else. The expletives directed at David would have made a navvy blanche.

"Oh come on, Jack," David shouted, dissolving into tear-jerking laughter. "This is no time either for a swim or a bath."

Jack, on the other hand, swished round to the driver's door, and, wrenching it open, he prepared to drag David into the cold muddy water.

"Now now, old chap," David tried to soothe, while holding on to the A-frame of the car. "A joke's a joke, and who would drive us back if I get soaked?"

Jack let go of the door handle, and, regaining his composure, he slammed the door, causing the water caught between the door and its frame to cascade over David. He too found the bottomless well of obscenities used by Jack earlier, and hurled them at both his pal and the water. Neither pal nor water took any notice.

"Shall we swim across?" Jack asked, suppressing a smile. "Or shall I summon the Gods of the Deep to send us their steeds to draw us back to yonder bank? Come O finned chariots and…"

"Oh shut up," David snapped, his mood somewhat dampened. "And get on with the pushing."

–o–

It was an hour later that two dripping and weary travellers splashed into the Drovers' Arms, the first Yorkshire inn they could find off the main road in a small picturesque village called Apptipply.

"Been swimmin', 'ave yer?" a terse question assaulted their soggy ears. All eyes fixed on their dripping clothes, and all ears strained to hear about their hapless experience.

"Well, actually, no," David replied in his best fashion. "We met with a little misfortune on the road about a couple of miles back. Someone seems to have forgotten to mark that lake on my map, and we ran straight into it. Is there somewhere we might dry out?"

"Aye, lad," the landlord answered. "It's back yonder." He nodded in the direction of a small partially open door. "There's a store in there and some towels behind the door. "Yer'll find a change o clothing 'anging on t'pegs. Three quarters of an hour to closing, so you'll 'ave to get a move on."

The two soggy travellers flapped their way into the room indicated, and proceeded to strip and dry off. They festooned the room with their own clothes, and put on the dry ones offered. After a few minutes they emerged, but not quite in the fashion they had entered. They shuffled out, rather uncomfortable in their new garb, and casting embarrassed glances at each other, and ambled over to the bar. The regulars turned away to suppress laughter and sniggers at what they saw.

The clothes Jack was given must have come out of the

early nineteen hundreds with plus fours, spats, a tailored tweed jacket with puff pockets and half belt, all of which was a size too small. David hadn't fared much better either. His super-wide Oxford Bags he found difficult to manage walking round corners and negotiating doors, and the tight Fair Isle sleeveless pullover was distinctly outré. They overcame their awkwardness, however, when they were confronted by a fully-stocked bar.

"Thirty minutes," David grinned. "Enough time to make sure our throats are well-lubricated. Set them up, landlord if you please! Two pints each for starters."

"And two of your delicious-looking pork pies," Jack added quickly, urged on by the noises his stomach was making.

The time left until closing wasn't enough, sadly, to allow them to drink to blissful oblivion, but they managed to reach that euphoric state of warm drowsiness in front of the blazing log fire. They barely heard the gentle bellow of "Time Genl'men if you purleaze!", and had to be nudged into mobility before being ushered into the outer 'dressing' room.

"Clothes are dry now, and if you please, I'd like to clear up," the landlord growled.

"Sorry, ol' chap," David slurred as he tried to catch the door knob which *would* persist in dodging around out of his reach. "A goo' man and a goo' pint of whatsit here. Don' you agree, my ol' fren'?"

"'Tis 'nall," agreed Jack, rocking back on his heels, fumbling with his buttons once back inside the errant room, and trying valiantly to focus on his ever-receding dry clothes.

It was a very happy pair that emerged from the warmth of the hostelry into the late afternoon chill, as a keen wind whistled around the ironclad gateposts of the inn's small car park. They had difficulty finding where they had parked the car at first, even though it was the only one there, as they managed to trip over each other in their attempts to walk. They rediscovered the old banger finally, by sheer accident. Jack stumbled and fell into it.

"Ah! Ah!" David cheered in triumph. "Tha's where you've been hiding, my beauty."

"You want to know wha' I think, Dave?" Jack said, keeping himself more or less upright by leaning on the car. "I think some blighter moved it to fool us. What're you loo … loo … looking for?"

"Keys – bloody keys," he answered, trying his best to find his pockets so he could fumble for the keys. "Mus' be here – somewhere. Ah! At last."

"Got 'em?" Jack asked, blinking very slowly.

"Not yet," David answered. "Found pockets though. Won't be long now … Tha's it. I knew they'd be around here … somewhere. You hold the car steady while I try to fit the key in the locks."

After several attempts at fitting the key through the quarter light, the window, and the windscreen wiper Jack managed to keep the car still enough for David to unlock the door and get in. Once inside, they set off, none too certainly, in the vague direction of home - which fortunately for them wasn't far away.

They didn't recall anything of the journey home, and didn't really know how they managed to get back without mishap. Jack stayed at David's that night and most of the following day, crawling home with something of a 'slight headache' later on.

Chapter 19

For David the Easter break was a time of happiness and planning, spending time with Irene as far as her duties at the hospital would allow, deciding on when they should marry. David had hoped for sooner, but because of her professional commitments, she prevailed, and they set the date for the end of August.

Jack saw them on several occasions, but feeling he would be intruding, he declined their invitation to spend more time with them. His thoughts often drifted out to Lee, and although he received only one letter from her, he felt he was with her in spirit.

Apart from the occasional chilly day, in the main, spring's nip was retreating gradually from the new season's advancing warmth. By the end of the holiday, the warmer days of approaching summer were more a promise than a maybe. Jack couldn't wait to share this time with Lee when she returned from Canada. This was the first holiday he had wanted to pass quickly, not because he wanted to return desperately to school, but because Lee would be back soon after its end.

–o–

The last Friday of the Easter holiday burst through his curtains in a blaze of brilliant sunshine. An early riser, Jack had been up for some time, ready to set out for a stroll in the fresh morning air. As he was about to leave, he was stopped by a thin high pitched voice from down stairs.

"Mr Ingles," it piped. "Telegram for Mr Ingles."

Jack's mind raced. He didn't know any... Could it be from...? He almost tore the door from its hinges in his haste to get down to the hall.

"Hello?" he said as he reached the front door. "Yes, that's me. Thank you."

The telegram boy bustled out of the house and revved up his motor cycle again as Jack tore open the flimsy envelope. It read simply

MOTHER DIED YESTERDAY STOP WONT BE BACK FOR A WHILE STOP BE BACK AS SOON AS I CAN STOP PLEASE INFORM SCHOOL STOP
LEE

Jack read the message several times before it sank in. Lee wouldn't be back for some time. He had never met her parents but he felt he had come to know them through her. He felt as sorry in that situation as anyone could be, and it was mainly for Lee that he felt the loss.

He stood in the hall for a short while, deep in thought. Clearly his place was with her, to offer what help he could, and support when most needed. His immediate reaction, therefore, was to pack a bag, and fly out.

"Impossible," he concluded to himself on mature and sober second thought. "School again in two days, and I can't now afford the fare."

Fortunately, the decision had been made for him. His giving the money for her to fly home had cleared him out, except for a few pounds he needed to tide him over. He would have to wait for her return, if return she ever did. She had told him that she loved him, and he believed that she would return as soon as she could. But, there was that little, almost imperceptible grain of doubt. Her 'won't be back for a while' could last an eternity. Her father needed her, she had told him that much, but were her father's needs more important that his? This was a question he wouldn't feel comfortable or confident asking.

"Of course she'll be back, stupid idiot." he muttered. "Just have to wait."

"I beg your pardon?" a thin quavery voice approached him tentatively. It was Miss Skanerly, a retired civil servant neighbour who had the flat on the floor above Jack. She walked about a lot, muttering to her enormous white Persian tom, Fleecykins. Jack had vowed on many an occasion that *that* creature was no more of a dumb animal than he was, and he was convinced he had seen those cunningly deep eyes somewhere before.

"Oh, nothing," he stammered, embarrassed he had been heard. "Just thinking out loud."

Miss Skanerly had made up his mind for him. He would take that walk after all so as not to waste such a beautiful day. So, with a cheery 'Good day' he bounded down the short flight of steps to the gate, and on to the park.

The bus shelters by the park's side railings were bustling with folks travelling to a multitude of jobs and places in the city centre. Jack was forever intrigued by the endless possibilities for destinations for these people he saw daily, often trying to fit appearance to possible jobs. He would be renewing his game about them in a few days, even though he had little chance of meeting the one *he* wanted any time soon.

He exchanged a few greetings with familiar faces before he strode on to the green and gilt main gates, the other side of which everything changed. This once stately home drew him into a different world; a world which didn't allow the chatter and bustle of everyday life to intrude into its multi-coloured natural sanctuary. The rich green still wore its early spring coat of mauves, oranges and yellows as the naturalised crocuses waved their cheeky greetings in the spring breeze.

More or less ready to take over this cheerful greeting, daffodils peek-a-booed their shy hello to those who would appreciate their presence, whilst shrubs had shaken out their new leaves to add a light green painted backdrop. Without the unabashed and unconcerned wild life, the scene wouldn't have been complete; from cheeky sparrows to the thrush with his strikingly elegant speckled waistcoat and his twice-sung song, to the jack-in-the-box squirrel newly roused from his restless winter sleep, his sparsely covered feather duster tail wafting in the spring breeze.

For Jack, as well as for many others, this was the time of rebirth and revitalisation, where many forms of life emerged from the long dark tunnel into the blinding brilliance of a new year. This realisation brought him back to himself again to thrust him into a new period of introspection, where he could think of nothing else but the sad and raw passing of his mam only twelve months before. He had suppressed all thoughts and feelings associated with this awful time, because there had been nobody to share them with, nobody who was interested in his feelings of loss, nobody to turn to who might be remotely bothered by how he might feel.

Lee leaped into his mind again, hijacking his sadness, and trying to dispel his gloom. He thought about this spring that they should have been sharing in all its excitement, and feelings of disquiet once again clawed at the back of his mind, sowing doubt and uncertainty about their relationship. Would she ever come back? Would this simple feeling ever be assuaged?

He was jolted back to reality by a small but firm hand

being threaded between his arm and his side.

"I could have taken your wallet as easily as breathing," a light voice said close by his left ear.

His arm involuntarily and quite automatically tightened, trapping the intruder irretrievably, and at the same time his head swivelled to find his cousin standing next to him.

"Hey! Not so tight if you don't mind," she complained, half smiling. "I didn't *really* mean to pick your pocket."

"Oh, sorry, cousin," he apologised, giving her an affectionate squeeze. "Why are you around at this time? No hospital?"

"Day off," she replied. "I came round to your place for you to offer me coffee, but found no welcoming sign on the door, and that it was barred to all comers. So I decided to walk a little, following your favourite haunts in the hope of finding you."

They turned towards the main gate, Irene's arm linked in Jack's, and made for his room.

Most of the way back was covered in silence, and it wasn't until they were within sight of Number 36 that the conversation was resumed.

"Thinking about Lee, weren't you?" she asked quietly.

"Yes," he returned slowly after a few moments' hesitation, still looking straight ahead. "I'm finding it difficult to believe she will come back, and if she does, things might not be the same as they were before."

With coffee on the perk and the door locked against the world, they settled to talk and to enjoy each other's company.

"You're worrying unduly, you know," Irene said as Jack was making coffee. "Lee will be true to her word. I know none of us has known her very long, but I think we know her well enough to realise her intentions. You wouldn't have asked her to marry you if you hadn't been sure - and besides, she loves you. You know that."

Jack's face was still impassive, even when Irene had finished her speech. He simply sat in the armchair opposite her sofa, sipping his coffee, munching on a digestive, and looking into the fireplace. It was some moments before he spoke, quietly, and very deliberately.

"I can't help the doubts," he went on slowly, "even though everything, I know, is fine. You see, this relationship with Lee isn't the first time in recent memory I've been serious about a girl. College was drawing to its close, exams were behind us, and everything else in front, with the path set for our happiness. The week before we went down, she took off to New Zealand with one of the Joint Course PE men, with no intimation about her feelings."

He looked across at Irene, who was gazing intently at him, with a half-smile of understanding on her lips.

"You have to understand and accept that not all women are like that," she added. "You must have confidence in her, or else your relationship will die. Lee I know is true to her word and her emotions - and the reason I know? I received a letter from her just the other day, telling me how painful it was to leave you, and how earnestly she is looking forward to being with you again. I wasn't going to tell you, because I thought you were sure in her love for you, but obviously I was wrong. It would cause her great suffering were she to know of your doubts."

She handed the letter to him as if to reinforce what she had been saying, and it was with a new light of hope in his eyes that he received it. When he had devoured its contents, there was a new depth of understanding in his heart.

"Lunchtime soon," she added after some moments of silence, dispelling any lingering atmosphere of gloom. "Shall we go out to eat, or shall we take a picnic?"

"It's warming up nicely out there," he replied, becoming animated at last. "Let's take a picnic into the park. You make the sandwiches and I'll do the drinks…"

-o-

"Damn that blasted alarm." Jack cursed, still half asleep as he emerged from the warm cocoon that was his bed. Mornings were still chilly and a little uninviting in the grey just before dawn, and school mornings were even less tempting than others. He raised a hand and thumped it down onto the offending instrument, in an attempt to cut off that interminably irritating noise. He succeeded the second time. He huddled down again, putting off the fateful moment when he would have to brave the chill of his unheated room, and hanging on to those last few moments of bliss.

"No good," he muttered, rubbing his stubbly chin ruefully. "Have to get a move on."

He spent the last few seconds screwing himself up ready to leap out of the sheets to light the fire, and perform his ablutions before a cup of tea and breakfast. Within ten minutes, ablutions completed, he was sitting close to a whimpering fire because he had run out of sixpences, a cup of tea in one hand and a slice of bread and butter in the other. This took him back to breakfast time when his father was on the early shift at the mine. The difference between them? Jack had no choice, as he couldn't afford anything else.

Unfortunately, time wasn't elastic. Buses had to be caught, the educational world had to be set to rights, and at five past eight he had to rush out still munching the remains of his bread as he hurried.

The air was anything but fresh and crisp, with wisps of the fog of the night before still drifting around the trees and lamp posts. He passed the postman on the drive, but there was nothing for him except for a cheery greeting. A good humoured and happy man, Jack often wondered how he could be so cheerful at that time in the morning, when all about him were having to reconnect with work. Apart from an early morning runner, a dog stroller, and two squirrels, Jack didn't meet any other bodies until he reached the bus shelter.

The bus was unusually busy for Monday morning, with standing room only into town. Commuter entertainment was assured on this particular run because their usual comedian was conducting the journey. A cross somewhere between Charlie Chaplin and Max Miller, his antics and witticisms sometimes barely stayed this side of vulgar, but his cockney badinage helped brighten an otherwise dull start to the week.

"Mind the doors pleez!" he chirruped. "Standing room only down in the stalls. Plenty of room in the gods. Fez pleez! Sixpenny sir? Certainly. You are assured of our best attention at all times. Henny more fez pleez?"

He tried unsuccessfully to negotiate a rather starchy lady in a fur hat and fox stole, but to no avail. She had planted herself in the centre of the aisle, grumbling loudly in a cut-glass accent about the ungentlemanly conduct of those lazy layabouts sitting while she was standing. After a few minutes jostling for place, the cockney piped up in a loud voice, "'Scuse me, my love. Any gentleman of worth willing to offer this lady the use of his lap? I'm sure we could fix you up. Marriages arranged by mutual consent, friendships started, and if it's marriage you *don't* want, I feel sure we could make some other arrangement. Henny more fez pleez?"

The Duchess turned a deep shade of purple, and looked as if she was ready to explode. Yet, the moment had passed, and so had the little conductor. Apart from the occasional diversion from this little minstrel in passing, the journey to town was an uncomfortable one. Jack was sandwiched between two boiler-suited manual workers who must have been coming off shift from somewhere close by. The one standing in front of Jack was very short but wide in girth, whereas the other one standing behind Jack was tall with a chest like a barrel, and shoulders to match. Caught in between an on-going conversation, Jack could only listen to their banter.

"Off aht tonite, 'Arry?" boomed the large one.

"Aye, I am that," replied an unexpectedly thin wheeze, like the air escaping from an old pair of bellows. "T'owd lady's off ter bingo, an' there's nowt on t'telly."

That small but very hard rucksack over the fat one's shoulder dug ever deeper into Jack's navel, and a nauseating odour of cold stale sweat delicately blended with the oil from his overalls caressed his nostrils. Between the Fat One's rucksack and the Big One's chest, Jack was forced into a very unnatural position.

"Si thi dahn at Crown then," the Big One drawled in his deep rolling rumble that most of the bus must have heard. It was with enormous relief that Jack got off for his connection to school.

–o–

"Good holiday, old man?" was David's cheery greeting as Jack set foot inside the staffroom. He had a grin on his face, one steaming cup of coffee under his nose and another one pointing at Jack, which he took with gratitude. There was nobody else in the room yet as it was still quite early.

"So-so you know," Jack replied, gulping his coffee in an attempt to compensate for his fraught journey. "Anything new, Oracle?"

The last reference was to David's uncanny skill in finding out unsought and unexpected snippets of information.

"Well," he replied, an unhealthy dose of glee invading his face, "as a matter of fact, now that you mention it, there is one thing. You know that Old Moore is retiring at the end of this term?"

"I had heard a little whisper," Jack said.

"His job was interviewed and appointed as we already knew," David went on, "but his replacement, an existing primary head, is due in today to give us the once over."

"Then why is he coming here, pray?" Jack's rhetorical question leaving a question mark in the air.

"Promotion, dear chap," David replied quietly; "that commodity most people want and only a few of the 'in' folks get. It's not what, but whom you know in this game. Small school to a larger one, I assume."

Jack stood there, cup poised beneath mouth, eyebrows raised through the steam in surprise and disbelief at the incredible Sherlock Holmesness of his friend.

"How on earth…?" he asked, swallowing a mouthful of coffee.

"Aha! Elementary, my dear Ingles," David replied in triumph with a twinkle in his eye, and touching the side of his nose with a paint-stained index finger. "The Oracle has spoken. Yours not to question, mere mortal. Anyway, he'll be here sometime this morning, so be on your guard, and keep a look-out posted at…"

He was cut short by the untimely entrance of Miss Page and Mr Sparks.

"…And that's how he found out," he confided to Miss Page. Turning to Jack and David, he grunted his gruff greeting, before disrobing. Jack never did discover who found out, and what it was they were intriguing about. "I need to prepare today's assembly, Miss Page, so I think I'll tell them about the time I spent in the navy."

"Oh my God. Not that again." David groaned as the two old stagers left the room. "We must have had that one three times last year alone. His war exploits really are enough to make a pig laugh. *He* doesn't know that *I* know an ex-colleague of his who dropped to me one day that he spent the entire war behind a desk in some navy office at the back o' beyond. The only action he saw was some typist knocking hell out of some old typewriter, and the occasional Saturday night brawl. There's more life on Miss Page's cat. You know also of course why he's taking today's assembly so cheerfully and without coercion?"

"No," Jack replied, losing the will to live with all this subterfuge. "Surprise me."

"Obviously because our new head will be in this morning. Haven't the heart to tell old Sparks that he's not coming until after break," he continued with a malicious chuckle.

"Not a pleasure to be back in the dungeon," moaned Mrs Josephs to her sidekick Miss Peterson as she 'cheerfully' removed her outer clothing and arranged it under its own polythene cover on the coat stand, to Jack's tuneless humming of 'The Stripper'. "I can't wait to get back to the excitement of another action-packed, palpitating, and completely unexpected term."

The sarcasm was totally lost on Stanley, who had followed the two ladies in.

"What's so exciting that's in store for us today, then?" he asked naively.

"Oh forget it," Mrs Josephs muttered, raising her eyes in unnoticed supplication to an unseen deity.

"What's the matter with that one?" Stanley asked as he approached the two soon-to-be-related-by-marriage friends.

"Well, she…" Jack started, but was cut short by David's interruption.

"Don't bother, Jack," David went on. "He wouldn't understand anyway."

"How's Lee?" Stanley asked politely. "I don't see her in yet."

"Oh shit!" Jack muttered under his breath, slapping a

hand across his mouth. "I'd forgotten. Must get in to see the old man, and tell him she won't be in."

With that he shot out of the room, almost knocking over Miss Page in his haste. The door followed in his wake, and slammed shut only three inches from her nose end.

"Well, I...," she gasped in amazement as she flowed through the doorway.

"First time *you've* been lost for a word, Miss Page," David smiled.

"He won't be popular," Stanley warned. "That means of course that Moore will have to take the class. If there's anything in school Old Moore doesn't like, it's teaching."

The staffroom buzzed with suppressed laughter at Stanley's astute observation. His assessment of Moore's character was unerringly accurate, and he would have gone so far even as to say that this applied to many head teachers. Old Moore would have done anything to evade being bogged down in front of a blackboard. Even the French teaching he was so accomplished at had begun to pall. He was only a term away from all that retirement had to offer, for goodness' sake.

Jack regained the staffroom, trailed by the dithering head, who was hopping from foot to foot, vainly trying to work out a solution to his banishment to the nether regions of Junior Three. Suddenly, as if a blinding ray of sunlight had pierced his personal gloom, a beaming smile spread across his face, and he stopped dancing.

"I'm afraid Miss Genet will not be with us for a little while," he started, "so I'm afraid I'll have to ask Mr Sparks to divide her class into groups for distribution among other classes for today at least. I would take them myself, but I'm afraid I can't. The new head's coming in you see, and he'll be wanting to talk to me for much of the time." For once in his life, he turned purposefully and walked slowly out of the throng, back to his office, and safety.

"You know the next step?" David uttered, giving barely enough time for the door to close behind the disappearing head. "I wouldn't mind betting a supply teacher from the Education Office will be taking Lee's class tomorrow."

-o-

"Tony, Peter, Stephen, put away the paints; Deborah, Lizzie, Sophie, the water; Tina, Beena, Suzie and Lucy, collect the papers and put them on the window table; Joe and Ivan stack the palettes, and follow me," David burst out near the end of the art lesson just before break. He left the classroom for a few minutes to return two large drums of paint to the store cupboard, seeing first that everyone in the classroom was busy clearing away. "I will be back in two minutes, so I expect everything to be clear and clean by the time I return."

The drums were extremely heavy, and there were far too many steps between his classroom and the main school. Although very bright and clear outdoors, the innards of the main school were like a badgers' set by contrast; dark, dank, and uninviting. The art cupboard was along the main corridor, affording little room at the best of times, but no leeway at all when hordes of fast-moving wildebeest were on the move. The only times to collect and return stock were a few minutes before the start or end of the lesson.

David had more or less finished putting away the equipment, when he happened to look up to his left. Even in the gloom, he caught sight of a small, dapper suit of a delicate shade of lovat floating along the corridor. Adorned by a similar-coloured tie, mirror-finished patent shoes, and a burgundy hankie in the top pocket, it looked as much out of place in those surroundings as a cocktail in a beer garden.

"Good morning. Would you be so kind as to direct me to the head teacher's office?" he asked. "I seem to be lost. The name's Barchester; Cecil P Barchester." The voice was soft, and underscored by a slight lisp. The thing which caught David's eye, however, was the strange way in which his head bounced slightly when he spoke, as if it were on a string.

"Certainly can," David replied, taken aback a little by the sudden appearance. "Follow me. It's something of a maze of tunnels in here. You are lucky not to have ended up somewhere much less … salubrious, like the boys' toilets, for example."

"Been there. Done that," Mr Barchester guffawed. "And I have no wish to revisit the experience, thank you very much."

Reaching the head's office, David banged on the door and ushered him in. As he took his leave, he noticed the end of a pink hankie sticking out from under Cecil P Barchester's shirt cuff. He also noticed the estimable Mr Moore had some files on his desk instead of the usual newspaper, magazine, or football pools coupon he usually tried to hide when caught off guard.

Chapter 20

Jack's outward façade to the world was, as always, jovial, friendly, and untroubled, but he wore this image like a shell; a shell that hid a depth of pain and growing unhappiness he had last felt when his mam died. It had been a fortnight since Lee's last telegram which told him she would be a little while before she returned. Now his worst fears seemed to have been confirmed. Each day he sought a word from her; each day he was disappointed. At night, he was gnawed by doubt that she wouldn't return.

That warm and comfortable time around Whitsuntide rushed in and left just as quickly. The short half term to the summer holidays left little time for meaningful school work, so it seemed sensible to use the time for sports days, fayres, galas, and other happy but meaningless activities. Yet ... Jack's first summer term as a teacher would insist on being his most unhappy. Most of his evenings were spent either listening to the radio, or walking his favourite haunts in the park.

For him this was a time of intense personal introspection, which was not altogether welcome. Weekends, once a source of endless pleasure as oases in a sea of unrest, were the worst time for him, being now periods when, with no other immediate occupation, he began to sink into his unhappiness. This unhappiness he hadn't felt since the death of his mother.

In such a short time, Lee had become so necessary to his life that her absence took away his drive, direction, and purpose.

During those pleasant warming weekends, he took increasing comfort in the nature he could watch in the park. He delighted in all wild life, from the endless antics of squirrels, the manoeuvrings of the many birds he recognised, and the escapades of the occasional rabbit or hare that had taken a wrong turning from the golf course close by. That the park was a marriage of contrasts pleased Jack particularly. The larger well-ordered section with its tarmac pathways, island flower beds, and row upon row of tailored shrubs, slid elegantly into the more natural - occasionally untidy - glady and shady patches of organised chaotic intermingling bushes and shrubs. He delighted in this area most in all the park, where he had a choice of favourite benches he was able to use in his desire to commune with the natural world. Fortunately for Jack, this was the time of year when most of his animals were at their busiest, and these 'golden acres', as he called them, were at their best.

The abrupt change from ordered to chaotic suggested to Jack that gardeners had had to abandon their restorative work for lack of time, but it suited him. He was able to slip from one to the other very easily; to take him into the tangle that welcomed his unruly and disorganised self as a corollary to his disciplined and obsessive nature.

The grassy areas were roughly trimmed at the edges where green met path, but there was neither paving nor tarmac to allow gently smooth walking. Here crunchy gravel heralded the approach of others, allowing an instant rapport with similar like-minded people. At first glance, in this part of the park, plants seemed to have been thrown down haphazardly, to take their chances in places they wouldn't necessarily have chosen for themselves. Yet on closer inspection, it was clear that soil types and companion plants had been chosen carefully to complement and enhance each other.

After the first twenty yards or so, the main gravel pathway rose gently and cut into a smoothly rolling hillside, which was covered by wild rhododendron and many specimens of birch, rowan, and lime trees. Other much smaller compacted earth paths dodged off into the undergrowth, allowing those who wished, to explore at their leisure what other secrets this park had to offer. At the summit of this slope a stream, like many of its brothers and sisters, started its life and rushed and chattered down the other side of the hill into a natural-looking lake. The main path ambled on for another fifty yards or so, rounding a gentle curve and mounting a small plateau, which boasted a large metal framed shelter, built to provide rest and respite from wind, rain and sun at times. Completely round and dome shaped, it was clad entirely in glass, giving an enviable vista across the whole park this side of the hill.

One doorway only, away from the prevailing wind, allowed entrance and exit for the tired walker to rest a while on the wooden slatted benches surrounding its inside. Jack often spent part of his walk here, and this Saturday was no exception, allowing him solitude and solace.

The shelter was empty, apart from one heavily muffled young woman who was standing close to the glass, gazing out across the undulating grass. Jack didn't feel much like talking, so he kept to the rear of the shelter so as not to disturb her. He stood there for probably half an hour or so, losing all concept of time as he had left his watch at home. Feeling it was time to move on back, he approached the young woman. The clothing she wore allowed him to tell only that she was short and slim, with well-booted legs, and that her neck, face and head were festooned by a large scarf.

"Excuse me, Miss," he asked, "but I seem to have forgotten my watch. I wonder if you would mind telling me the time?"

"Not at all," she answered, turning from her reverie. As she turned to face him, his countenance changed dramatically, his jaw dropped open, and his eyes widened considerably as he stood in utter amazement.

"But … but…" he stammered. "Lee?"

He lurched forward, and forgetting all decorum he picked her up like some weightless rag doll. He kissed her once, and then, gently setting her down, he kissed her again; a warm full blooded kiss, such as he hadn't felt for weeks. Giving themselves to this moment completely, they forgot all around them and all heartache to this point.

"How…?" he asked when they parted eventually. She put her finger gently to his lips in an effort to calm his surprise.

"Later, my darling," she said quietly. "I'm here now, and we won't be parted again."

The skin around his eyes wrinkled with pleasure as he allowed, for the first time in an age, a surge of joy to flow through his body. He slid an arm around her waist, and pulled her closer to him as they stood for some moments looking out across the park, the sweet warm smell of her hair infusing his senses as he rested his cheek against her head.

-o-

"You didn't write," Jack said quietly as they sat together in his room before a welcoming fire. There had begun to grow again a slight chill, as late afternoon drew on, and so they had decided to spend a cosy evening together talking over things.

"I did start to, once," she replied, "but I couldn't bring myself to finish it. Things haven't been easy. We both loved Mother dearly, and although we accepted it would come to this eventually, it was still a shock when it happened. Although Dad was heartbroken, he was a great support to me…" she broke off and looked wistfully into the fire.

With his petty grumbles and doubts cast aside, he put his arm around her shoulder again in a show of support and love. She turned and smiled at him through the tears which were trickling freely down her cheeks.

"Is it right to love someone so much that when they're gone, life loses its meaning?" she said, not really expecting an answer. "They were so inseparable throughout their life together that the one never did anything without the other. I really don't know how Dad is going to cope without her."

"That I can't answer," Jack said quietly, "because I don't have a model upon which to base any assumptions I might have. *My* parents weren't even remotely close. They *were*, once, but things sort of fell apart big style following my father's infidelity. Yet, I feel that ultimate trust and faith in the relationship will carry it through anything. I loved my mother unreservedly as she loved me, and I should have liked a *real* father to have done the same, both for me and for mi mam."

Jack stopped, tears filling his eyes, visibly upset at the thought of his mother's death, and at the idea that she never had a husband to feel about her like Lee's dad felt about *his* wife. Was he sure that he could provide for her as her dad had provided for *his* wife? He had a big act to follow, and he wasn't sure that he was up to it yet.

"I'm sorry, Jack," Lee soothed. "Here I am going on about my woes, not thinking that you lost your mum only a painfully few months ago, and you didn't even let on that you were suffering too."

"I didn't have anybody to share it with," Jack replied softly. "My brother lives a long way off, and Irene, who is the only other living relative close enough to me, lived in Australia. I have another – a second cousin called Kay – but she married very young and we never really got to spend any time together. I had to internalise my pain, really. Although

I spent a great deal of my earlier life with my grandparents, their grief was deeper than mine, because she was their second child they had to bury, and I have been away at college and in school for the last four years."

All the time Jack had been talking, Lee had been watching this man she loved, and was beginning to understand him and what made him the man he was.

"I love you, Jack," she said, reaching up to kiss his chin. "Promise we'll never be apart, because I couldn't bear another separation like this one."

"I promise, my sweet," he reassured her. "I think perhaps we need to set a date pretty soon, don't you think?"

"Sometime in August?" she said, beginning to brighten at the thought of being Mrs Ingles. "Dad retires at the end of June, and he said he would like to come over to visit with us for a few months, to get to know his future son-in-law, and to have a break. I think he would like to get away for a bit. Mother's presence is all around him at home, and it is still too raw and painful for him to be in the house all the time on his own. Don't mind, do you?"

"No, of course not," Jack said, "but it does mean we need to get somewhere to live big enough to hold three of us. I'm really looking forward to meeting him, as I don't even know what he looks like."

They hung on to each other making sure that neither would melt away somehow, leaving another gaping hole.

"Now, tell me about your journeys," he added, steering away from the subject. "How and when did you get back?"

"Well," she started, "it wasn't too bad really. My plane got in early this morning, allowing me to be home by lunch. I wanted a little time to readjust before I saw you, so I walked for a while in the park. Knowing that the old shelter was one of your favourite stopping places, I simply waited there until you arrived."

Jack drew her unprotesting body towards him, her lips slightly apart and her eyes half closed. Their mouths met and a warmth of anticipation spread through their quivering bodies, as Jack pulled her closer.

A loud banging at the door jerked them apart.

"Ignore it," Jack's whisper urged her, as he pulled her close to him again.

"You in there, Jack?" David's unmistakable bellow killed the mood. Mouthing a silent curse that nobody saw, Jack moved towards the door.

"Hang on a sec," he shouted, spreading his arms and shrugging his shoulders in resignation. Switching on the light and unsnecking the door, he opened it only a crack to answer his visitor.

"Hello, old man," he said briskly, "we haven't interrupted anything have we? Just thought we'd call by and … cheer … you up …?"

"Well, er, actually," Jack started, trying to indicate that he had someone in with him, hoping that at least Irene would take the hint.

"Hello, David," Lee joined in, "please come in. It's warmer in here. Is Irene with you?"

A look of puzzlement and surprise crossed both faces as they squeezed past Jack in the narrow doorway.

"Lee!" Irene squealed in glee as she threw her arms about her neck with unashamed warmth and love. "We hadn't expected you for some time yet, but we are over the moon to have you back."

Jack latched the door, and, resigned to missing his evening alone with his fiancée, joined the others by the fire.

"I hope we're not breaking anything up, are we?" David suddenly blurted out, thinking they might have had other plans before they burst in on them.

"Of course not," Lee assured them. "We're glad to see

you, aren't we Jack?"

"Wha …? Oh, yes," he replied emerging from his reverie about what might have been that evening. "Of course we are. Drink? You can have coffee with milk, coffee without milk, tea with…"

"He's only pulling your leg," Lee chided with a smile. "I think there's something a bit stronger in the sideboard over there."

"Well, actually," Irene said with a smile, "coffee would be fine for me."

"I *was* only joking," Jack interrupted, laughing.

"No, really," Irene went on, "the reason being that we've booked for a meal at the Mansion, and had rather hoped you might like to join us? A few drinks afterwards, and we could make an occasion of it. What do you say?"

Looking across at Lee who was nodding enthusiastically, Jack lost no time in agreeing. "That would be fantastic," he added. "A meal out is just what we need. Shall we walk up the Avenue, or shall I send for the Rolls?"

"The table's not reserved until half seven," David explained, "so we've time to sit and have coffee whilst we catch up a bit."

–o–

Jack couldn't remember a more entertaining and enjoyable evening since his brother's wedding when Val's dad fell off his chair and pulled a bowl of rose petal-infused water over himself. For the whole of Sunday Lee and Jack indulged themselves by doing very little other than spending no more than five minutes apart and being by each other's side for the rest of the time. Close, intimate, and very romantic, their time seemed to stand still, and it was only natural they should wake up to a new Monday morning, under the same roof, in Lee's flat.

Jack of course - pragmatic to the last - had set the alarm clock to fifteen minutes before his usual time for waking, so he could have his beautiful lady to himself for a little longer.

"You look a lot happier today," Stanley observed as Jack fairly danced through the staffroom door. "Won the pools or something?"

"More the 'or something', I think," Jack replied, shutting the door with his heel. "Although, I'm sure I have no idea what you mean, Mr Awad."

"Well," Stanley continued, "I thought there was something, er, *different* about you when I saw you vault over the side gate at the front of school this morning, and even more so when you petted that dratted cat that always sits on the front wall. But what finally convinced me was when you pulled the caretaker's new brush from under his leaning body, danced around the playground with it, and then *threw* it back to him."

"I'm sure you must have mistaken me for somebody else," Jack said, throwing his head back and letting out a loud guffaw. Mrs Josephs, following him into the room, raised her eyebrows as she turned to Miss Peterson.

"What's the matter with him?" she queried.

"Touch of the early spring sun perhaps?" Miss Peterson replied.

"You wouldn't understand," Jack explained. "It's a beautiful sunny morning, it's good to be alive, and…"

"…It's the open evening in two days' time," David butted in, bursting through and slamming the door after him. Most of the flaky paint had fallen finally from the wall above the door, leaving only one or two largish pieces ready to ambush the unsuspecting.

Jack clapped his hands to his head and gulped.

"Oh my god … fathers," he groaned. "I had forgotten *that* completely."

"Have to get a move on then," David taunted him good-humouredly. "You'll never get promotion like that, you know. Lack of organisation, that's what it is. You ought to be more efficient in your…"

Jack was no longer there. He had hared out of the room to make a start on rooting through his store of materials produced by his class.

"Good job I kept most of the stuff," he muttered as he flew along the corridor to his room.

"Do you think I ought to tell him that it's not this week but next?" David smiled.

"No, not really," Stanley replied, a wicked glint in his eye. "I shouldn't if I were you."

"You're hard, Stanley Awad," David chuckled. "Why not?"

"Because it *is* this week," Stanley added, drinking his coffee.

"That's right … eh? What's that you said?" David turned, taking hold of Stanley's sleeve. "You're having me on, aren't you?"

"Now, would I do a thing like that?" Stanley chortled. "Come over here to the notice board. Tell me, what do you see on the list of events under Week Commencing 13th May?"

He rushed over to the board and had a look at what Stan had said.

"Blast, blast, and double blast!" he cursed. "I could have sworn it was next week. You sure you've not altered it, Stan?"

"'Fraid not, old man," he said with a smile. "You ought to get a move on you know. Never get promotion at this rate - inefficiency and all that."

David mouthed something at Stanley, mumbled something else inaudibly, and hurried out of the room on the same fool's errand as Jack. His first call was to Jack's room, where he found his friend almost buried under an avalanche of paintings, models, and illustrations of work, all of which he had pulled out of the cupboards lining his walls.

"Having fun?" he asked.

"You might say that," Jack replied, sarcastically.

"Look," David started again, "dear Stanley has pointed out that I'm in the same boat as you. I thought the show was *next* week, and just meant to have a bit of fun at your expense. But in fact it *is* this week."

"Yes, I know," Jack added. "I knew all along."

"Well, why on earth didn't you tell *me*?" David burst out.

"I completely forgot, that's why," came Jack's reply from behind a pile of models.

"Anyway," David went on just as the bell was ringing for start of morning school, "I think it's time we taught old Stan a lesson or two. How about a practical joke? Are you game?"

"Yes," Jack grinned, emerging from his mound. "Anything for a laugh."

"Well then, this is what we'll do…"

–o–

The lightening tore a great gash in the night sky, and the cataclysmic crash of thunder spurred on the invaders to greater heights of effort to reach the summit. Two solitary figures could be seen at the top of the shattered pile of ashen boulders in their futile attempt to reach their goal. Within reach – within touching distance almost - they were carried away by a descending cloud, as all below were stunned and rendered deaf by a strident piercing bell. The Bell of…

Jack's voice cut through the noise and excitement, as the five minutes warning bell for the end of school clamoured.

"OK, let's stop there. We'll finish the story of Castor and Pollux later. Climb down from that pile of desks and chairs carefully, and then can we remove them to put the room back to normal, please? Home time soon, so we must make sure everything is ship shape, or Mr Harrison won't be best pleased. Hands up all those who want to help me sort out all this stuff for tomorrow's Open Evening."

Amongst the clatter and banging of the furniture being rearranged, a field of waving hands accompanied a chorus of 'Me, Sir'. It took only five minutes to put the room back to rights, and to pack children off to their eagerly awaiting parents.

Lee's night for washing her hair had already taken her off home, but not before Jack had told her he might drop by to say goodnight. David was waiting in the staffroom already to whisk his friend off to an exotic meal with his mum, the height of Jack's gastronomic week.

Dinner was muscling its way out of the oven as the intrepid munchers shouldered their way into the kitchen at the Astons, forcing them to salivate at the aroma of mouth-watering hot pasty.

"Good timing boys," Mrs Aston said. "Now upstairs to wash, and be back here in two minutes, please."

They didn't need telling a second time, as they were sitting at table as the main course was wheeled in to the dining room.

"I thought *my* mum was a good cook," Jack said as he helped the mountainous steak pie into his mouth gradually, "but I do believe I have never tasted anything quite like this, Mrs A … out of this world."

She smiled contentedly as she settled back to eat with these two hulking young men. For her there was nothing better or more satisfying than feeding her home-made food to appreciative men, and she couldn't have found any more appreciative than Jack and David.

"I'm going up to have a bath now, you two," she said, "and then Joan from the hairdressers will be coming round to wash and set my hair."

"OK, Mother," David answered. "In that case, I think we might just pop round to the Ship for a couple of pints, and to have a chin wag with the landlord."

The pub was quiet, being a Monday, but for a small knot of hardy and ardent drinkers who could not have done without their nightly pint no matter what. David slid into the corner seat next to Jack in the snug with a pint of Tetley's in each hand, and two packets of pork scratching held tightly between his teeth.

"You got a tape worm or something?" Jack laughed as he set the beer and nibbles on the tiny table. "You can't be hungry, surely?"

"No," David answered him, "but I prefer to have something to nibble with my pint. So, knowing you very well and the extent of your appetite, I thought I'd better bring you a bag as well."

"You done good, my boy," Jack smiled as he reached for his pint and the packet. "These aren't Castle crisps! What on earth *are* they? Not heard of … Scratchings before."

"Down the hatch my son," David urged, sucking the bitter nectar from the glass. "Just goes to show that millions of Yorkshiremen can't *all* be wrong."

"Not at all bad," Jack said after a handful of the nibbles. "More where they came from?"

"Now, I wonder if you might like a squint at this?" David said slowly, drawing a neatly folded piece of paper from his inside pocket which he passed to Jack. A wicked smile spread lowly across his face as he took in what lay on the paper.

"You sly old dog," Jack said. "You're not going to *send* this, are you?"

"Of course I am," David said. "Any reason why not, that you can justify?"

"Not really," Jack laughed, reading the paper a second time. "Stanley *will* be pleased. When will you let him have it?"

"Tomorrow, of course," David replied, rubbing his hands together with glee, "with the morning post. Do you think he'll fall for it?"

"*I* certainly would," Jack admitted. "How did you manage to get the official paper?"

"One of my many contacts," David replied, touching the side of his nose with his index finger, and winking over the rim of his glass. "Drink up old man, and nip off to get a couple of refills. It's your round."

-o-

It was a somewhat tipsy Jack Ingles who found his way eventually to Lee's flat around half past ten that night. He managed to find her door reasonably efficiently, but on bending down to peer through her keyhole to see if there was any light, he didn't see the large door knob which he whacked just above his eye. Sitting backwards with a bump, he saw several constellations floating around his head. Effects of an excess of alcohol apart, it was minutes before he was able to focus clearly enough to try to stand.

Fortunately, Lee was still up, reading, and hearing the bang, she shouted, "Who's there?"

"It's me ... Jack," he groaned.

"What on earth's the matter, Jack?" she gasped, opening the door to find him still on the floor. It was only when she helped him out of the shadows that she noticed the lump over his eye. "Have you been in a fight?"

"You're not going to believe this," he sighed from the sofa, "but I banged it on your door knob."

Puzzled, she was about to ask for the story when he began to explain.

"Well," he began, "you see, David and I went for a couple of pints after dinner at his, and, well, we *might* have had a

268

bit too much – we *did* in fact have a few too many. When I reached home eventually, I couldn't find my key, so I came round to you."

"But how did you grow that egg above your eye?" Lee asked still rather puzzled.

Jack felt the lump rather ruefully, wincing when he pressed it too hard.

"You'll have a black eye tomorrow," Lee warned, concerned he hadn't done himself damage.

"You see," he continued his explanation after taking a deep breath, "I couldn't see any light when I got here, so I bent down to look through the keyhole, and that's when I discovered you have a door knob just above the keyhole!"

"What would you have done had I been in bed?" she asked.

"Don't know really," he said, scratching his head. "Gone back home and slept outside my door, I suppose. There's a chair on the landing."

"You don't have to do that," she said quietly, as his face brightened somewhat. "You must stay here. I have a perfectly good sleeping bag you can have to sleep on the floor in here, if you can cope with that?"

"Of course," he agreed. "Where else."

"But first," she added disappearing into the kitchen, "I must see to that eye."

Jack settled back to wait for her ministrations, thinking about the time when they would be together all the time.

"Would you like a hot drink?" her tinkling voice rang from the kitchen.

"Yes please," he shouted back. "OK if I have a cup of tea? Night cap together all right for you too?"

The tray she brought back in contained stuff she would need for a cup or two – including his favourite chocolate digestives – and an ominous-looking jar with a large screw

269

top.

"Don't worry," she said, noticing his sideways glance at the jar. "It won't bite you. It's only ointment for that eye."

Jack was ready to jump in anticipation of the soreness she might cause him, but Lee's touch was very gentle and soothing.

"The swelling will go down to some extent with time," she advised, "but not altogether, I fear, and you'll have quite a shiner there by tomorrow. They'll never believe your story about the door knob."

Content to sit away what little of the evening remained, drinking tea and chatting about nothing much in particular, they had already turned down the lights, with a comfortable dimness from the fire softening the angular shapes in the room. The old mantle clock which had seen many scenes in its lifetime, chimed half past eleven softly.

"Time goes so quickly when we're together," Lee complained sleepily. "I think I might away to bed now, or I shall drop asleep here. I'll get that sleeping bag for you."

"I'll just…" Jack began, ready to get up.

"…Wait for me here," Lee finished as she was skirting the bedroom door frame. Back in a tick, she had a striped and zippered eiderdown under her arm. "You know where the bathroom is. Night night my sweet man."

She bent to kiss his face, but he pulled her down onto his knee, and, kissing her fully on the mouth, said simply, "I love you, Lee." Looking into his eyes, she understood that he meant what he said, and in that brief exchange she knew that this kind, gentle, and sincere man was the one she would build her life upon. As part of the foundation of her life had crumbled and fallen away, another had surfaced to fill the void.

Jack was content that night, and, despite the less than comfortable floor, he was happy just to be near her. His thoughts took him through many avenues, each time returning to the central point of his existence – the woman he loved. He wasn't aware exactly when, but slowly and comfortably he drifted off into that warm state of drowsiness that ushers in deep sleep.

–o–

"…And don't give me the old chestnut of having a fight with a door," David jibed, admiring Jack's shiner the next day. "Who did you manage to hack off, really?"

"Nobody," Jack protested. "Six youths attacked me last night as I got off the bus. It took me just five minutes to dispatch them all but not without the consequences you see before you. You'll probably see it in the Yorkshire Evening Post tonight."

"On your bike," David said, laughing at first, but seeing Jack's serious face he added, "Did you really?"

"No, actually," Jack replied with a smile. "I made that up."

"Well, how *did* it happen then?" David insisted, becoming more impatient.

"Had a fight with … a doorknob," he chuckled.

"I don't…" David was about proclaim Jack a 'bender of the truth', when the door crept open, and Stanley sidled rather nervously to the side table by the sink, unlike his usual flamboyant self.

"Morning Stan. Quiet today? Anything wrong?" Jack said, cutting David off in mid-speech.

"Well, er, not really," Stan replied, seeming embarrassed, and looking around to make sure he had his back to something solid. Very abruptly he perched on the edge of the table; something he would never have done in his wildest moment of delirium. Jack and David turned away, trying hard to suppress their mirth. Jack nudged David, and said very quietly, "There's something very wrong with your boy

271

there. He doesn't usually act this strangely. I wonder if…?"

Not comfortable at being the unwanted focus, Stanley interrupted their mirth.

"Look here," he whispered, looking round to make sure all the other teachers had gone off to class, "I have, er, a slight problem."

"Don't we all, my dear chap," David quipped. "Just keep on taking the tablets, and then go back to your doctor to ask for a second opinion."

Jack turned away to try to suppress the laughter he felt rising in his throat at David's lack of understanding.

"Oh, you're impossible!" Stanley burst out suddenly. Bethinking himself, he dropped to a whisper again, drawing the two buffoons even closer.

"I've…" he started, and looking furtively around, he continued, "I've … split my trousers." The last three words were mouthed voicelessly, and with them, the silence hung motionless in the air.

"Where?" David mouthed back, aping his embarrassment.

"Just outside my classroom," his almost inaudible reply slithered to a halt.

"No. No," David continued his mouthed conversation. "Where on your trousers?"

"Oh, sorry," Stanley replied, "right up the back."

"You'll be 'barely' able to walk around then," David quipped again in a flash. "Get it? Ha ha ha! I don't know where I get 'em."

All the time Jack was listening to this exchange with much suppressed mirth. At David's latest groaner, he was barely able to keep his heavily disguised merriment in check. Finally, last straw, he exploded, his huge guffaw taking them all by surprise.

"Well?" Stanley started again. "What am I going to do? I can't face my class like … this."

This made Jack even more helpless with laughter, the picture flashing across his mind of Stan 'facing' his class with his trousers in shreds, his credibility laid bare, and his embarrassment for all to see. By this time he was helpless in Miss Page's chair in the corner, unable to understand how David could keep such a straight face and jibe Stanley into action at the same time.

"There's only one thing for it," David offered finally.

"Oh yes?" Stanley leaned forward eagerly. "And what's that?"

"You'll have to take your trousers off," came David's solution, quite out of the blue.

"You must be out of your tiny mind," Stanley retorted indignantly, stung by David's abruptness. "I…"

"Hang on! Give me a chance," David interrupted again. "I *was* going to suggest your wearing my tracksuit trousers whilst one of our dear lady teachers, God rest their souls, might like to run a stitch or two through the offending rent in your rear end. It's all right. No need to worry yourself about, er, any indelicacy. They are all clean and laundered; perhaps not to your usual sartorially elegant standard, but a creditable standby nonetheless. However, seeing as you want no part of it, I'll be away to my classroom. Coming Jack? They'll be about ready to come in now."

The friends passed through the open door, and closed it gently behind them. After a few seconds, Stanley's shrill voice stopped them in their tracks.

"Hey! You two. Come back," he yelled, panic-stricken by now. Immediately, David and Jack immediately popped their head around the door, one above the other.

"Yes?" David uttered from above.

"You called, Sir?" came Jack's voice from below.

"Lead me – on second thoughts – bring me these trousers of yours," Stanley urged eagerly. "I'll make sure in future to have a spare pair in my store room."

"Pretty please?" David jibed, in a mock child's voice.

"Oh get along with you," Stanley returned impatiently. "I want to get over to my class."

David was out and back in two minutes, and, after handing him the trousers, he advised him to get changed quickly.

"We'll guard the door to stop any peeping toms or … *female* toms from entering," Jack added, and with that they stood, backs to the door with arms folded whilst the necessary alterations were attended to. They smiled at each other in anticipation of what was about to befall their unsuspecting and hapless friend and colleague.

"Oh. Oh," Jack warned in a low tone. "Just look who's on the way."

The imposing figure of Miss Page strode purposefully across the hall towards them. Children were due in at any moment, and she was the duty teacher for that day - her first job of the day being to ring the entry bell. *That* bell push lived just inside the staffroom door.

"Stand by to repel borders," David hissed as she approached.

One minute left to bell time.

The two looked at each other, not really knowing what to do to detain her.

"Well, hello, Miss Page," David added, standing in front of the door. "Fine morning I must say."

"Considering it's just started to rain, I would say that was a *false* statement," she said, matter of fact. While making to walk around David, who moved in the same direction to block her, she became blocked by Jack who had slid in next to his friend to add greater strength to their blockade.

"How are things with you today?" Jack took over, trying to add a casual air to the scene.

"They would be very much better, young man, if you would allow me to go through that door!" she uttered sternly, beginning to lose what little patience she possessed.

"What door?" he replied, looking at David, and shrugging his ample shoulders.

"The one you are so effectively blocking," she bellowed, as she barged between them to open the door. She half entered, threaded her arm between the door and the right-hand side of the frame, and pressed the bell button. A strident shrilling split the otherwise calm and tranquil school. Slapping their hands to their head in resigned failure, they were surprised to see her leaving muttering only about lunatics being allowed to teach these days. They peeked around the door expecting to see Stanley covered in embarrassment and little else, but he was nowhere to be seen. The room seemed to be empty.

"Where on earth…?" David asked scanning the room and shrugging his shoulders at Jack.

"Where else do you think, idiots?" a muffled voice crept out from behind a heavily laden coat stand. "That was a close shave, for goodness sake."

As he emerged into the light, Jack couldn't help an involuntary snigger growing from his midriff. The immaculate Stanley Awad, Duke of Broughton, dressed in his usual elegant way – mauve silk shirt, paisley tie, light grey suit jacket, and … baggy royal blue tracksuit trousers.

"Stanley," David started with a straight face, "I can honestly say that I've never seen you looking so … so … different."

–o–

Stanley's room was ready for that evening's invasion of the uninitiated and uninformed parental population of the neighbourhood. Usually they came to satisfy their offspring, insisting it was their duty to inspect the work they had done over the academic year to now. Many hadn't the first idea of how to appreciate anything other than their usual round of out-of-work pleasure. The intricacies of a Jimmy Smith portrait, the subtleties of glaze of a Tracy Pilkington pot - or the aesthetically pleasing lines of a Wayne Bottomley potato man - were totally lost on them. However, the school usually rang with many a *'In it luvly!'* or *'Oo, that's a nice picture!'*, which often left Stanley cringing in his highly-mirrored patent leather shoes.

The wall displays were immaculately arranged as usual, and there was usually more than one piece of his own work to add 'dignity and depth' to the arrangements. He had commandeered several of the tables for model displays (some of them made by his children), and had these suitably 'fenced off' at strategic points around the room. His desk had its usual bunch of flowers carefully arranged in a genuine Chinese vase, probably of the Smith dynasty, and nothing else but a pile of half-marked history books.

Everything was spotless and orderly, because he couldn't abide untidiness or mess, and he made sure that anything even slightly suspect was out of sight.

He had forbidden any child mentioning his 'new' trousers that morning, on pain of punishment. He had had quite enough of *that* sort of comment for one day, thank you very much.

He was putting the finishing touches to a magnificent mural his children had almost finished when he was disturbed by a polite cough behind him.

"Yes?" he asked rather abruptly. "What do you want, boy?" He hated being interrupted when in the middle of doing anything important.

"Please, sir," the little boy offered tremulously, "there's this."

Stanley snatched the offered piece of paper from the

little boy's fingers, proceeding to unfold it whilst waving the child away. It was an official Education Department memo concerning his classroom, which warned the occupant that, being a temporary prefabricated classroom, its walls were subject to occasional inspection by HM Inspector of School Buildings. That time for inspection was … NOW. Stanley began to turn purple with anger as he read on.

'…And so all walls must be cleared of all materials likely to cause obstruction to HM Inspector in the performance of his duties … so that inspection can commence at 10.30 prompt. This tenth day…' It was signed by the Chief Planning Officer, and counter initialled by the Head teacher, Mr Moore.

"But … but … that's now, today," Stanley exploded, unable to contain himself any longer. The class started, surprised to hear such an outburst. They had been used to Stanley's temperamental outbursts from time to time, but never anything like this. "This is utterly ludicrous. I've only just put them up."

He was about to storm over to Mr Moore to remonstrate, but he realised it would be pointless. He would still have to remove his display, and the quicker he did it, the quicker he would be able to replace it.

–o–

"Coffee Stan?" Jack chirruped as he stomped through into the staffroom at break.

"Had a good morning, Stan?" David asked jovially, over his coffee cup.

"Do you know," Stanley started, "that I'm about bloody well fed up…"

"Now, now," Jack interrupted, mildly taking the mickey, "no bad language, please."

"…With this situation," Stanley went on ignoring Jack's

remark. "I've had to strip…"

"…All of your walls, and move your tables for a wall inspection?" David carried on his conversation. "Anybody arrived yet? To do the inspection, I mean?"

"But how did you…?" Stanley asked, mouth agape, with a puzzled look on his face. At that moment, Miss Peterson entered, Stanley's trousers in hand, and, delivering one of her legendary withering looks to forestall any pending ribald comment, wrapped them over Stan's arm with a "There you are Mr Awad."

He mumbled his thanks and, looking at the two smiling faces in front of him, he realised who had been responsible for the 'official' memo.

"You … you … traitors," he exploded. "And I thought you were both my … Watch out from now on, because this means … war!"

He swished his trousers over his shoulder, catching a foot in one of his bracer's straps, and almost catapulted himself through the closed door. This folded Jack and David up completely, as Mrs Josephs and Miss Peterson looked on impassively from their corner, clucking at the juvenile antics of a pair of so-called grown men.

Chapter 21

End of school that day seemed like an eternity away; an eternity of perpetual motion in work. Jack's straightforward and pragmatic approach had brought his display to the best it could be, whereas David's was a little less effective but the volume and range were impressive. The fuming Stanley had managed, against all the odds, to remount, rearrange, and reorganise his to better effect, and, although he would never dream of admitting it to his arch enemies, was the better for its removal and re-siting. So far he had resisted the temptation to smile, accept the joke, and forgive, in favour of 'revenge'.

Everyone had mounted a display, from Jack's sophisticated programmed learning scheme, designed to test parents' geographical knowledge, to the simple-looking set of examples of children's work produced by Mrs Josephs and Miss Peterson. Their idea was to display work actually undertaken by their children 'uncluttered' by teachers' efforts at the same subject.

Even Mr Moore had knocked together an offering, in the main hall near to his room, so that he could keep an eye on the place (and slip into his easy chair unnoticed for a quick sit down and read of the paper). His stand consisted mostly of materials gathered on or about the visit he had taken the year before to Le Touquet with the youngsters;

information about the place, a few posters, and a pile of realia, like bus tickets, stamps and bottle tops. Condemned out of hand from its inception by Sparks as being educationally as worthwhile as a weekend in Blackpool, it still received rave reviews both from the youngsters themselves and from their parents.

Children had been tip-toeing about school for fear of knocking over any of the exhibits, and had been obliged to spend both break and lunchtimes in the yard out of the way, whilst teachers 'played' with their exhibits. The school's doors stayed locked until seven o'clock, until which time teachers remained inside to be on hand.

For once in his otherwise frugal life, Mr Moore had ordered in cakes for his staff, much to their pleasant surprise and profound shock, which were consumed eagerly with copious gallons of hot tea, after the sandwiches they all had brought.

They expected parents to start trickling in at around half seven as usual, and to stay for about an hour, giving them time to catch the last hour or so at the Ship. Although it was an event most parents would have loved to forget, it was the children who kept its concepts alive, because it gave them a band stand to show off their stuff.

"One thing about old Moore," David said, after a mouthful of cheese and chutney sandwich. "He may not be terribly well organised or strong, but he always seems to appreciate the efforts we make at this sort of event. He always remembers his manners when he says his 'Thank-you-one-and-alls'."

"I wonder if our new...?" Jack started, but was cut short by David's timely intervention. The door flew back onto its hinges, and in floated...

"...Mr Barchester," David said loudly. "We were just wondering if you might drop in to sample our parent event. To see what you're letting yourself in for."

"Good gracious," he lisped in that almost effeminate voice. "I wouldn't have missed this for the world. Between you and me, I find these soirees tedious, but necessary nonetheless. I've come straight from my present school and haven't had the foresight to bring food. Is there any where hereabouts where I might buy a sandwich or something?"

"Have some of mine," Jack offered, from his huge pile. Fortunately, he had been late starting and was still only part way through his stack of sandwiches.

"That's very kind of you," Barchester said, smiling as he took a bite. "Oo lovely; salmon spread."

With only four sandwiches left and two already consigned to the new head's seemingly bottomless stomach, a look of consternation started to spread across Jack's face. Was the greedy so-and-so going to filch the last of his tea? Desperate measures were called for.

"Have you got Mr Barchester a cup of tea, David?" Jack shouted across at his friend by the sink. As the new head turned towards David, Jack made a desperate lurch for the last sandwich in the pile. He didn't care whether he was going to be his new head teacher or not. There was no way he was going to do Jack Ingles out of his last sandwich.

During this feeding frenzy, the two corner ladies had left the room to take up station in their dens, leaving the three men on their own. Up to now, Lee had remained quietly in the background, wishing to be on her own for a while. As soon as she glided into the room, Mr Barchester shot to his feet.

"Jack – I can call you Jack can't I? – would you be so good as to introduce me to this delicious young lady?" he gushed.

"Yes indeed," Jack replied with a smile. "This is my fiancée, Lee Genet. Lee, meet our new head, Mr Barchester."

"Well, well," Barchester beamed amiably, taking her hand in both of his and looking round at Jack, who was by this time by his side, "you lucky man. I'm very pleased to meet you, my dear. How is Canada?"

"Blooming at the moment," she answered quietly, her hand still firmly locked in Barchester's. "I was there only a short while ago."

"You will be staying here at the end of your exchange, then, I assume?" he asked, genuinely interested.

"Yes, of course," she replied, having at last managed to disengage her hand, "but I'm afraid I shall be out of a job. Mr Simmons will be coming back to take up his post again."

"Oh, well, yes," he muttered, and then lapsed into thought for a short while. A sudden sparkle leaped back to his eyes and a beam to his face. "We shall have to see about that."

Lee glanced at Jack, slightly surprised at what he had said, but Jack simply threw a non-committal smile back at her.

"It's been an absolute pleasure talking to you all," Barchester added, "and I am very much looking forward to working with you all in September. I think I need to drop in to speak to Mr Moore before the hordes descend no doubt. I'll be here for a while, I think, circulating and generally rubbing shoulders with parents and youngsters."

Spinning on his shiny heels, he sailed through the door like a mini-cruiser in full steam.

By this time, the outer doors had been flung wide, allowing a reasonably continuous stream of small, eager bodies and a less than enthusiastic knot of larger ones to flow in. Once inside and presented with junior's hard work, most parents' chests puffed with pride to think that here was the product of their offspring's year for all to see. Almost all the teachers had been careful to display work from all their children which ensured that the classrooms were well visited throughout the school.

The one exception was Stanley F Awad. Unlike anyone

else on the staff, he didn't believe in that sort of clap trap, being interested in presenting a neat and tidy front only, from a seemingly well-behaved and intelligent class. His room was the only one in the whole school that didn't experience the parental footfall it should have received all evening.

Half past seven to eight o'clock was the busiest time, when many questions were asked and many explanations given, but very little was understood.

"…Well you see," Jack said to a very large bluff-looking red-faced man of whom a little boy in his class was the exact replica, "that's quite an easy process really. You layer as many different coloured wax crayon on top of each other successively on a piece of card as you want. You then carefully scrape away the colour levels to achieve your desired pattern effect…"

"…No, not really," David explained to Mr Thicket the fishmonger. "It's simply a matter of keeping a steady hand and eye. The rest's easy."

This time the fishy smell from Mr Thicket was nowhere near as strong as at the parents' evening, but it was strong enough to bring a tear to the eye. Occasionally David's nose wrinkled involuntarily in anticipation of the next waft of that blissful aroma. Yet, the people who had crowded into his small hut, in the main enjoyed their visit, whether they understood or not.

"Press that switch there," he continued, indicating a complicated-looking set of circuitry, "and follow…"

"…And of course, you realise, the French way of doing many things is totally different from ours," Mr Moore pointed out to a small group of parents that had gathered round his display. "Their road system is strange to us to say the least. And buses. If you were on the road…"

Mr Sparks and Miss Page were together, as ever, her sitting at her desk and him perched on it. Taking no interest in the proceedings, they ignored all the unwelcome bodies traipsing past them.

"Waste of bloody time, if you ask me," Sparks growled in a sufficiently low tone for nobody to hear. They seemed to have been left alone in general, with nobody venturing to ask about, discuss, or praise the work seen there. Passersby simply cast a cursory glance and passed on, mostly knowing the pair of old and preferring not to interrupt or intrude into their closed world.

Except for one bright interlude, the evening was an unqualified success. Mr Bortwhistle wasn't happy, becoming very frustrated and heated when he couldn't locate the piece of work his daughter had been faithfully promised would be on display. His daughter, Karen, was in Miss Page's class, and it wasn't until his ire had reached climax and threatened to become volcanic that she agreed to look for the errant piece. Once found and pinned to the appropriate board, Mr Bortwhistle - finally placated - about turned, and with a smile on his stubby face, marched out of the hall and into the pub across the road.

"Bloody trouble-causer," Sparks growled as he watched Birtwhistle's ample behind manage to squeeze through the half-closed outside door. "Wait till I see that girl of his tomorrow."

–o–

At eight thirty precisely, as if someone had pulled a giant bath plug, the school emptied of all parents, as well as Mr Moore who had last been seen half an hour before, hurrying across the back yard to his car, not wanting to be late home. Most of the teachers had drifted into their room after an exhausting day, to put feet up and have a brief chin-wag over a hot cuppa. Mr Barchester must have departed earlier than expected too, as he was nowhere to be seen.

"Well, Jack my lad," David piped up, "we're surely not about to stay here until tomorrow are we? The night is still young, and the Ship is beautiful. Fancy nipping over to caress a pint or two?"

"Yes please," Lee's voice rounded the coat rack. "I could just do with something a bit stronger than this ... tea."

"Make it a majority vote, old man, and we're half way across," David re-joined.

"Mine's a pint of Guinness," Jack said as he smiled across at David gleefully.

"OK. OK," he replied. "But let's get a move on shall we?"

The Ship was full almost to overflowing, the obvious attraction being a lively sing-along piano beating out some of the old time favourites, accompanied by a local choir. Strangely, *that* piano hadn't been played for many a long year.

"Not about to find a table in here, I fear," David observed as they squeezed, cajoled, and forced their way to the bar, where he caught the eye of the barman whom he had known since school.

"That's a welcome sound I've not heard for some time, Terry," he shouted as he paid for the drinks. "Who's the artiste? Anyone we know?"

"No, Dave, I don't think so," Terry replied. "It's an old teacher of mine from junior school days. Not seen him for an age, and then he just ups and drops in, unexpected like. He's a headmaster now I believe. Somewhere south of the city, I think. Dropped in for a swift half, and we got talking again. One thing led to another, and there he is now. Good isn't he?"

Many of the regulars were joining in, making the place come to life like never before. A few draughts of beer later, David could contain his curiosity no longer.

"Just popping round to the music room to see who this mysterious piano basher is," he said, leaving the other two.

"Be a few minutes, that's all. Guard my drink with your life, old boy."

Swimming against a rising tide of bodies, he threaded his path between tables, chairs, and hat-stands, to within a whisker of the music room screen. Managing to squeeze his head round its corner, he blinked. He blinked several times more, rubbed his eyes, and peered again through the thickening blue haze, remaining there for a few moments in utter amazement before returning to his friends. Thinking there must be a table and chairs free, they all made their way over to David, with Lee just behind Jack's protectively broad back.

"What is it, old chap?" Jack asked when they had cleared the last obstacle of a pair of booted legs stretched out across their path.

"Just take a look," David advised. "And no, you're not mistaken."

Taking his advice, they craned their necks round the partition and saw … Cecil P Barchester thumping away on the keyboard, a huge grin spreading across his face, thoroughly enjoying himself.

They remained in that cramped uncomfortable position for several minutes unable to believe what they saw. David even forgot to drink. Lee had noticed a vacant table round the corner in a small alcove, and made a rapid move to occupy it. Jack thrust his glass into David's hand, noticing a rival couple's move on *their* table. Although the couple was a little way ahead in racing terms, Jack's determination drove him through gaps between bodies he wouldn't usually have attempted. Sweating profusely, he 'occupied' the table with a grin of triumph and a commiserating shake of the head to the losers.

"Only two chairs, old man, I'm afraid," was Jack's greeting as they arrived to find him sitting on one of them.

"OK," David agreed as he about turned to forage for another, adding with a grin. "Back in a tick. You can get the drinks in."

"Hello there," a voice ambushed them from behind.

Jack spun around to give the rude intruder a piece of his mind, when he noticed through the haze that their pianist had joined them. They hadn't noticed that the music had stopped because of the loud buzz around them.

"Mr Barchester," Lee gasped, quite taken by surprise. "How nice to see you again. I think your piano performance was quite virtuoso."

"Oh my dear," Barchester beamed. "You say the nicest things. Couldn't resist it, don't you know. It's always been a weakness of mine…"

"Hello folks, again," came another familiar voice from behind. "I told you I wouldn't be long and…"

"For me, David?" Mr Barchester smiled relieving him of the chair he'd fought tooth and nail to acquire. "You're too kind."

He swung the chair under the table with a flourish, leaving David open-mouthed and quite nonplussed. There was nothing for it but to enter onto the chair trail again. Turning around without a word but with many mumbles and mutters under his breath, he disappeared into the undergrowth of sweating bodies on his quest again for the Lost Chair of the Ship…

"You know," Barchester continued unabashed, "I've always had a fascination for pub pianos. They seem to have a different tone from all the others; something deliciously … common about them. What will you two have?"

"It's all right," Jack interrupted. "It's my turn. Cider for Lee, Guinness for me, and for you Mr Barchester?"

"Oh, call me Cecil," Barchester broke in. "Can't stand formality with people I like … I'll have a lager and lime, thank you very much. Such thirsty work, don't you think? Do you play the piano, Lee? I can call you that…?"

"Yes, actually I do," she answered, "but not anywhere as well as you, I'm afraid."

"Oh, you're just saying that," Barchester said with a huge grin. "I don't play very well, really. It's just that I bang away and am not afraid to make mistakes. I shall take over quite a few of the assemblies and practices when I start in September…"

"Miss Page won't like that," David said as he put down his new-found chair which he sat on immediately.

"Well," Barchester went on, "I think a change is as good as a rest, and besides, it will give her chance to do other things as well."

The last words were said with a definite twinkle in his eyes, as if he had something, still secret, in his mind for the music mangler. Jack returned shortly after with a tray laden with liquid cheer and handed out the brimming nectar to each. Barchester took his with thanks, drained it at one go, and wiped his mouth with a dainty hankie afterwards.

"Well," he said when all traces of offending foam had been wiped from his mouth, "I'm afraid I must be toddling now; quite a lot to do for tomorrow yet. Thanks for the drink and the company."

With that, he was gone, through that invisible screen that allowed him to reach his other world.

"Man of many parts, our Mr Barchester," Jack observed.

"Yes, and most of them small," David added, draining the dregs from his glass. "Another?"

"I don't think so, really," Lee answered before Jack had time to open his mouth to say what he wanted.

"'Fraid not, old man," he said instead. "Think we ought to be getting back now. Work again tomorrow, you know."

He slipped his outdoor coat on and helped Lee with hers…

The journey back to Lee's flat in her mini was in the main a quiet one, for traffic and conversation. The days were lengthening, but the last vestiges of light by now had gone. Jack sensed a tension in the atmosphere as they sped past the park towards home.

"Nothing wrong is there Lee?" he asked quietly.

"No," she snapped, mouth set in a thin line and eyes staring. "Why should there be?"

"Yes, there is," she added quickly. "I don't see why I should keep it to myself. I didn't think it necessary to want to stay in that awful place any longer. I was beginning to wonder just how long you were intending stopping there if I hadn't spoken up when I did. You'll just have to think more about me and less about your boozy habits and…"

All the while throughout this tirade he sat still and quiet, taking in all she had to say, either looking straight ahead or at his lap, but never at her face.

"…and if you'd put me first a little more often, and not so much David Aston, you'd…" and here she stopped as she turned into the driveway to park the car in front of the garage doors. She simply sat for a few moments. Jack had been saddened by the unnecessary and unjust things she had said, and more than a little hurt by her jibes and unjustified anger against him. After five minutes or so, he began to speak.

"Lee … I…" he started quietly.

"I'm sorry, my dear," she interrupted, eyes filling with tears as she turned towards him. "I didn't mean those terrible things I said, but I've been feeling tense and strained lately, what with Mother, and then school…"

By this time, tears were streaming down her already pink cheeks.

"There's no need to…" Jack said as he tried very quietly

once again to reassure her.

"No, let me finish," she went on. "I shouldn't have taken things out on you…"

"No, no, my love," Jack said, putting his arm around her gently heaving shoulders, "there's no need to go on and no need to apologise. You're tired and over wrought, and I haven't taken any offence. I think we'd better go up and I'll make you something to drink."

She dried her face and wiped away all trace of make-up that had run as they made their way to her flat. It was quite dark and the air was alive with the buzzing of bunches of dancing midges forever vying for places in this ladder of life they wove with their incessant movement. Although it was reasonably warm, the two lovers shivered involuntarily as they parted the curtain of vibrating insects.

Once inside, Lee flung her coat onto a nearby chair, and Jack followed suit. She flopped into the other armchair, flicking on the fire to add focus to the room, as Jack emerged from the kitchen with two steaming mugs, a plate of biscuits and two glasses of brandy on his tray.

"You need something to warm you up and settle you down at the same time," he said, handing the glass to her. "Drink this, and sip your coffee."

"Jack … I…" Lee started.

"Not another word just yet," he said quietly.

Ten minutes passed before they spoke again. The only source of light in the room, the fire turned their faces into glowing pools. In that short time, they had visibly relaxed, and Lee was very much more composed. Raising herself slowly from her chair, and moving across to Jack, she sank into the sofa next to him and snuggled her head against his chest. She sighed contentedly as he slid his arm around her shoulder.

"I love you my darling," he whispered.

"Don't leave me tonight Jack," she sighed, face upturned to his.

"Not tonight, nor any other night," he answered softly.

He pulled her ever closer, bent his face to hers as their mouths met in an open, warm, inviting kiss of love. Their love overcame them, carrying them along on its waves of passion, stopping for nothing, and drifting deeper and deeper into an ecstasy of sensual sensation that would last forever…

Chapter 22

Monday returned as Mondays inevitably do, to find Jack very much happier than on previous Mondays. Lee had brought him in to school this particular day in her Mini, and both seemed well pleased with themselves.

The sky was cloudless and held a transparency which gave the promise of a lastingly bright day. The few trees that had survived successive council culls and annual bonfire chumping, had burst finally into full bright green leaf. Very late even for this year, folks hereabouts had given up hope of ever seeing them decorating their dour streets again. Everywhere wore that evocatively fresh scent of late spring to early summer - except, that is, for the immediate surrounds of the canteen, where that day's lunch was already half an hour old.

"Mornin' Squire, Miss," came a cheery voice from behind them as they left the car. It was the caretaker, for whom something must have changed in his humdrum round of cleaning in school, and his thirteen children at home. Greetings exchanged, they reached the school finally.

"What's the matter with him?" Jack muttered to Lee as they moved out of earshot. "Must be feeling under the weather, poor chap. Been overdoing it no doubt."

Lee giggled girlishly at the fun Jack poked at their beloved janitor. In the dim light at the end of the corridor they could make out the silhouettes of some of the other teachers. As they approached, Jack leaned close to her ear and whispered, "And remember, not yet" to which she nodded with a smile.

"'Ello, 'ello … What's this 'ere then?"

David's attempt at impersonating the caretaker wasn't very good, as Jack and Lee recognised him without turning round.

"Hello, David," they chorused. "How are things?"

"How did you know it was me?" he asked, surprised they had seen through his brilliant mimicry.

"Only you could make such a mess of an accent, old man," came Jack's reply. "Good weekend?"

"You mean apart from the fact that the car's in dock, that Irene and I had a quarrel on Sunday, that Mother's down with flu, that I've been stung for unpaid tax, and that the electricity was off yesterday for six hours? Yes, quite uneventful," he replied all in the same breath.

The group of teachers in the far hall doorway had shrunk, on their approach, to Mr Moore, who greeted them in the same cheery tones as all other days.

"Morning Miss Genet, Mr Ingles, Mr Aston," he trotted out as if turning on his tape recorder.

Lee looked at Jack and barely suppressed a giggle. David noticed and turned to say something to them but thought better of it. Mr Moore noticed nothing amiss at all. He always expected the simplest things from everyone he dealt with, and never noticed when it was anything otherwise.

The first half of the morning ran its course as normal, with break time seeing a gathering of the whole staff, unusually, in the staffroom. The duty teacher, Mrs Josephs, had managed to grab a cup of coffee before she was banished to a yard full of screaming steam-filled engines. David, Jack, and Lee, as usual, were standing together discussing nothing in particular, when Miss Page made her usual entry

– all bustle but little decorum. She sailed over to the row of steaming cups just off to Lee's right, and as she passed, she commented to Lee on the state of the weather.

"Fine enough today, Miss Genet?" Miss Page bantered.

"I beg your pardon?" Lee responded, looking across at Jack's smiling and nodding head. "But that's not *my* name."

She had chosen her moment with immaculate timing. The room fell silent for one of those rare moments, as her words rang through everyone's mind.

"Well – hey? What do you mean?" Miss Page asked, somewhat perplexed by this reply, not expecting anything other than an uncomplicated short response.

"As I said," Lee continued, "Genet is not my name – not any more. From now on it's Ingles … Mrs Ingles."

A stunned silence stole around the room. Everyone understood immediately - even Sparks, who was sitting in the corner trying to solve a crossword puzzle. David's mouth sagged, and it was a few moments before he was able to speak.

"You don't mean…?" he stammered with a knowing smile spreading slowly across his face.

"Yes," Jack beamed in reply. "We were married on Saturday; an impulsive move, but the right one we feel."

"You old so-and-so," David exploded, pumping Jack's arm and slapping him on the back. "Congratulations to you both. Hope you'll be very happy."

When the first flush of well-wishing had died down, David took them to one side and asked them about it, still with a degree of surprise.

"I thought you were going to wait until the summer hols," he puzzled. "Either we've finished early, and nobody's been told, or you two couldn't wait. How did you manage it? When…?"

"Hold on a bit," Jack laughed. "One at a time, please."

"Well," Lee interrupted, looking across at Jack with a smile on her lips, "we felt we had waited long enough, and so we took advantage of a cancellation at the registry office in town on Saturday morning. Fifteen minutes later, and that was it."

She slid her arm through Jack's in a first and last show of affection while in school, feeling she was allowed that one show of luxury in the circumstance.

"May I have your attention ladies and gentlemen, please!" Mr Moore's voice drew their attention from somewhere near the hat stand. The clatter and good humoured banter skidded to a slow sliding stop, which prompted him to hop from foot to foot – his one sign of annoyance. "If we might gather in here at one o'clock for a brief staff meeting I should be grateful. There are one or two items which need attention. Thank you."

He barely left himself enough time to beat his usual hasty retreat to sanctuary in his office. Retirement day couldn't come soon enough for him. A buzz of speculation bounced around the room as to Moore's intentions. Promotion for someone? Birthday? Sparks retiring? Nobody could even hazard a realistic guess.

"Must be bloody important," Sparks' hissed, his venom towards his head teacher no longer able to be hidden. "He's given a couple of hours' notice."

The sequel to Sparks' bile was sudden. The door almost sprang from its hinges, as a frothing, purple-faced Stanley Awad stomped in.

"Just look at me," he ranted, arms flapping like a demented seagull. "Look what she's done."

Nobody could at first see what his fuss was about, until David noticed with glee, a large wet patch spreading across the front of his immaculate pin-striped trousers, from waist to knees.

"A bit old for wetting yourself, eh, Stan?" David guffawed and Jack almost exploded. One of Stanley's famous icy stares cut them off immediately.

"Ruined! Absolutely ruined!" he shrieked. "My best suit, as well."

"Mr Awad," Miss Peterson asked, "what's happened? It was my class you were teaching last, wasn't it?"

"Yes," he went on, interrupted but unchecked. "Reading as usual. I had this little … child out at the front to hear her read – long fair hair with a fringe…"

"Lindsay Buckle," Miss Peterson replied.

"…And because she looked a little frightened," he continued at the same pitch, "I put her on my knee to reassure her, and this is what she did to me."

"Serves you right for being such an ogre," Jack jibed in mock seriousness.

"Well, I…" Stanley was about to explode again, when he was interrupted by the bell.

–o–

It was the second time that Stanley had had to borrow David's tracksuit trousers while urgent repairs were wrought upon his own. Mr Moore took over his class for half an hour whilst Stanley hot-footed it to the self-clean launderette down the road. This wasn't of course what he would have done normally, but it had to do in the circumstances. He couldn't be expected to wear stained and smelly clothing, a man of his standing, so he squeezed the cleaning costs out of Mr Moore.

The Head managed to cut the time spent with Stanley's class by half by various devious means, so he wouldn't have to spend any longer time with children than was absolutely necessary. It was with a deep sigh of relief he greeted Stanley's hugely beaming face, once he was again clean and dressed to the pinnacle of sartorial elegance.

The rest of the morning passed off uneventfully, except for an escaped gerbil from Lee's classroom, and a scruffy mongrel dog which managed to get in to school and camp in Sparks' room without anybody initially noticing, or being able to remove it when they did. Sparks, who was usually somewhat timid of all dogs, was brave enough to try to lead it from the room until it bared its teeth in silent defiance. He then left it alone at the front of the class, saying that it probably had more intelligence than most of the children anyway. It had been there just eighteen minutes when a very small stripling crept around the door.

"Sir … please sir?" came the faintly trembling voice.

"What do *you* want?" Sparks snarled in his own inimitable style. "What's your name, boy?"

"Sir, William Grey," was the reply.

"Been knighted, have you?" Sparks' poker-sharp reply shot back at the boy, raising guffaws from his class. "What do you want?"

"Sir, please sir … That's my dog, Gyp," the boy answered, feeling a little braver when he saw the dog stand up and begin to wag its tail, causing Sparks to back away slightly.

"Well? Come on then!" he shouted. "Take the blessed thing away!"

"Sir, can I take him home?" William answered.

"Yes. Anything," Sparks added hurriedly.

"Come on you stupid hound!" William hissed at the dog grabbing it by a loose handful of flesh by its left ear and giving it a hefty whack around the head. The dog whimpered submissively, and followed the boy out of the room, its tail between its legs.

–o–

The lunchtime's level of excitement reached almost breaking point, with speculation about the purpose of Mr Moore's hastily arranged staff meeting. Mesdames Josephs and Peterson were intrigued but would have come to school in the holidays rather than admit it.

More or less all the clan had gathered as the hands of the clock crept slowly towards the witching hour. Only two people were missing apart from Mr Moore, Stanley and Miss Page, both of whom liked to make an entrance.

The head came in with one minute to the deadline, to a buzz of excited whispering, and found an easy chair which he proceeded to place at the centre of the floor nearest the sink. With thirty seconds to go, and the door swung open to reveal the new party double act, Page and Awad, on the threshold, side by side.

"After you, Miss Page," Stanley offered, bowing low and appearing the perfect gentleman.

"No," she replied equally politely with a smile, "after *you*, Mr Awad."

Whereupon they both tried to enter the room at the same time, and, each being so ample in the beam, they wedged momentarily between the jambs to 'pop' into the room moments later like a split cork. Merriment over, they took their places to await the pontifications of Old Moore.

"Well, er, thank you all for coming," he began rather haltingly. His trouble had always been that he had never mastered the art of beginning a meeting, and quite often he had lost his audience long before he had reached the important bits. "Just a couple of points really. We have all known for quite a while now that two of our colleagues have signalled intentions towards each other, and that they would marry sooner or later. Well, we find today that it has been sooner, and so it is with great pleasure that I ask them to accept this small gift from the staff with our wishes for a happy married life. Mr and Mrs Ingles … Lee and Jack."

That was his only touch of informality in a forty-year

career, supported by a brief burst of applause from most of the teachers when he handed over the envelope. Totally unprepared and unrehearsed for this, the couple simply mumbled their thanks and sat down.

"Now, er, well, yes," Mr Moore stammered again. "My last little point concerns this school. It is to be pulled down."

His words fell like a clap of thunder on willing but unready ears.

"What did you say?" Sparks burst in. "Did I hear you right?"

"Yes Mr Sparks," Moore went on. "It has been felt for some time at the highest level, and not least by some of you..." here he paused to look across at David's grinning face "...that the school has outlasted its usefulness and should be replaced. So, the City Council has decided to replace this outdated building with a new one."

Gasps of disbelief and choruses of "About time too" rattled around the room.

"And when is this likely to happen?" Stanley asked quite unmoved.

"I'm afraid *I* shan't see it," came his reply. "The building starts three weeks before we finish for the summer holidays, and should be ready for Christmas."

"Impossible!" Sparks interrupted again. "Can't be done in that length of time."

"Yes it can, Mr Sparks," Mr Moore answered quickly. "You see, most of the building will be prefabricated and put together on site – I don't know the technicalities of the operation – and so shouldn't take long."

Stanley again raised a valid point. "How much say will we have in its design?"

"None, I'm afraid," Moore answered, becoming a little warm under his collar. "It's all finished and worked out, you see."

"How long has this been known?" he asked again quite pointedly.

"Well, er, you see," he tried to stammer his way out of the corner he found himself in. "Er, quite a long time. Anyway, I think we should end our meeting for now as the bell is about to go."

As he stood to leave, the dinner lady stretched her arm round the door to press the bell switch.

"Thank you all very much," he added, and beat a swift retreat to his room.

"The old toad," Stanley hissed when he was sure the head had re-entered the safety of his sanctuary. "I bet he's known about this little package for some time…"

"…And didn't let on to us," Sparks finished. "We should have been consulted and asked for advice. It'll be a right mess of a place; you mark my words."

"Got your exam question papers ready for our Fuehrer to mark?" David asked Jack and Lee on the way back to class.

"What exam papers?" they chorused.

"For this year's examinations - which start on Wednesday, the day after tomorrow," David said with a cheery grin. "Don't tell me you haven't done them yet?"

"Don't know anything about them," Jack replied, uninterested. "Suppose I'd better see Vanessa and sort something out."

"Vanessa?" David shook his head rather puzzled. "Who's that?"

"Miss Page to you," Jack replied, pleased he had gotten one over on his pal.

"Exams?" Lee asked incredulously. "You don't still use that outdated system in a school like this, do you?"

"'Fraid so," David replied. "Old Man's criterion for deciding intelligence and progress. Doesn't matter that young Paul might not be feeling well on the day, or Wendy might have had a poor night's sleep beforehand, if they don't come up to the mark, they are labelled as dim."

"That's very primitive and not fair on the children," Lee protested. "Don't you do anything with teacher assessments or anything else?"

"If you're worth your salt as a modern teacher, yes," David confided, "and I hope this new chap will do something about the situation. But for now, it's better to string along with the old guard, although Sparks is no great shakes."

This discussion came to a halt with the parting of their ways - David across to his prefab, and the others to their respective classrooms, with the prospect of an afternoon's slog ahead of them.

"No reason to fret," Miss Page said to Jack when he broached the question of exams after registration. "We'll use the same ones I've used for the last ten years. No reason to make work for the sake of it - and instead of starting at the appointed second on Wednesday, I suggest we start them tomorrow. Then, we can get them out of the way and marked by the end of the week. We can also give the oral ones – spelling, mental arithmetic and the like – to our two classes at the same time. You do the spelling and I'll do the mental arithmetic. We need only to have the joining door open to give the problems at the same time. He'll never know any different as he doesn't come down here much anyway. He's looked at my exams every year since he came and hasn't once noticed that they are the same from year to year."

She ambled over to her stand-up cupboard and pulled out a small folder secured with green ribbon and sticky tape. Unfastening it, she pulled out a sheaf of slightly faded papers covered by her impeccable copper plate writing.

"Pages get a bit faded after a few years, so I rewrite the ones that need it," she added. "No sense in *making* work, I always say."

Jack agreed, taking the bundle to make copies of his own in case Mr Moore asked to see his papers. All the time they had been talking, the noise from her class had risen steadily, which always happened when she was busy with anything else, and to which she seemed oblivious.

"Antonio Lall. Come here," Jack shouted sternly as he re-entered his room. The boy in question, who was rather tall for his age, dark-haired and wearing glasses, stood up slowly at the back of the room and made his way warily to the front, puzzled as to what he might have done wrong. He had arrived in Jack's class with a reputation for being naughty and mischievous, but Jack had found the opposite. With a little 'persuasion', he had turned out to be helpful and friendly, with the result that Jack had more than a sneaking liking for the lad. He loped out to the front like a giraffe among mice.

"Sir?" came the boy's rasping voice as he stood by Jack.

"Pop across to Mr Aston, would you please, and ask to borrow his large roller map of Europe?" he smiled, quickly relaxing his expression. Even though he liked the boy, he liked even more to keep him on his toes.

"Sir," came the lad's quick, relieved reply, and away he went, striding out like a circus clown on stilts.

"OK you lot," Jack said, as he turned to address his class, "we shall now have a little test, before our exams, to see what you know…"

Four o'clock couldn't come soon enough.

–o–

"We'll eat first," Lee said through a stifled yawn as they drove home, "and go to the supermarket later?"

"Tiring day, eh?" Jack replied.

"Tedious more than anything really," she sighed. "Children being silly, two taken home ill, that dratted ger-thing - or whatever it was called - escaping, and then I had to keep four of them in at afternoon recess to repeat work. Would have missed my cup of tea if you hadn't thought to bring it down to me. You're the dearest kindest most thoughtful person in the world."

"Who on earth's parked that great car in front of my garage?" she growled, rather annoyed, as she drew up to the block before the flats.

"Must be well off," Jack said. "It's a Mark 10 Jaguar."

Seeing them pulling into the drive, the man hurried towards them. Well-built and a little over six feet, he was perhaps around fifty-eight years old.

"Oh, my God," Lee gasped, shooting across to him and throwing herself into his arms. In turn, he let out a great guffaw, picking her from the floor as if she were a doll. Jack watched this pantomime with building surprise registering on his face as he ambled over to the laughing couple, who were now arm in arm.

"Don't be so surprised, Jack," she said. "I'd like you to meet my father."

-o-

"I still can't grasp that my baby is someone else's wife," Mr Genet mused with a faultless English accent as they were sitting down for a meal.

"Hope you don't mind, sir," Jack said, "that we married in a bit of a hurry."

"Heavens, Jack. Call me Ron," he replied. "I don't like all this formality stuff. You're part of *my* family now, so we must be friends. No, really, I'm very happy for you both. But you must promise me one thing Jack. Lee is all I have left in the world, so please take care of her." He broke off for a moment, eyes filling, looking across at her happy smiling face, and continued, "I've no need to worry, because I can see already how happy she is. This meal is excellent, my dear. You certainly inherited your skills in the kitchen from your mother."

Seeing the pained look drift across his face, Lee opened her mouth to speak, but he stopped her.

"You have no need to worry, my darling," he assured her. "All our life together … all our happiness and sadness are still alive in my memory. I've learned to spend my moments in careful but happy thought, leafing through our times together. She's never far from me."

These last words fell softly from his mouth, meant almost for himself, with a faint smile creasing his mouth corners and a distant look in his eyes.

"Nice flat," he continued, re-joining the gathering mentally, whilst looking around.

"It's OK for the time being," she agreed, "but we want something of our own as soon as we can afford it. Say … I forgot to ask. Where are you staying? And tell me you're staying longer than a couple of weeks."

"A week or two ago, I was given the option of retiring on full pension," he answered. "Not an offer anyone in his right mind would refuse, so I accepted and decided to spend the rest of my life in the old country."

"How on earth have you got such a perfect English accent," Jack wondered, "when Lee is so … so … Canadian?"

"You see, my boy," he started to explain, "Lee was born in Canada, but I started my life in Kent, England. My parents emigrated to Canada when I was ten, wanting a new and more prosperous life. I decided I wanted to safeguard my accent, even though eventually I spent close on fifty years over there, and married a native-born Canadian."

"Where are you living now?" Lee asked eagerly.

"It didn't take me long to decide to come back over here," he explained. "I already knew Lee would marry you at some stage, Jack, so it was a no-brainer really, and I've always carried a fondness for England. Finding a buyer at a good price was easy, but I *was* surprised to find I was better off, what with house values being much lower over here. I've a rented flat not far away, pending house hunting in the very near future. The Mark 10 has made me more than comfortably mobile, allowing me to find you easily. I like the area around here from what I've seen so far, particularly along – now what's its name – oh yes, Plains Drive."

"Did you say *Plains* Drive?" Jack asked not quite believing what he was hearing.

"Yes," Ron replied. "Why? Is that not good?"

"On the contrary," Jack answered, "it's only one of the most expensive and exclusive areas hereabouts. Houses cost a mere" … he paused as if summoning the courage to say the words … "twenty to thirty thousand pounds."

"Phew. That's all right, then," Ron said with a smile. "We'll have to see if there's one on the market."

Jack's very weak "Oh" came as a disappointing anti-climax.

Their conversation lulled for a while, as Lee's dad seemed to be in a rather pensive mood. They cleared the table, stacked pots, and joined Ron with a tray of coffee and brandy in front of the gas fire.

"I've been having a few thoughts on matters in general," Mr Genet finally broke the silence. "You say you want a house of your own?"

"Well, yes, of course," Lee agreed. "As soon as we can afford the type of house we want."

"I don't know what you think to this idea," he continued, but if we all pooled resources and bought something together worth having, how would that seem to you?"

"We rather wanted a house of our own," Jack said firmly, "not to lodge in someone else's, because with what little we could contribute it would effectively be *your* house."

"*Your* house, old chap," he corrected. "It will belong to you when I'm gone, and none of us is getting any younger. Besides, we would have a house big enough not to tread on each other's toes."

"That's an offer worth considering," Lee said, turning to her husband. "We have a little money put by, and obviously what Dad has suggested would be a sound investment. I think we all should at least consider it."

"When do you need to know?" Jack asked.

"I don't," her father replied quietly with a smile. "I shall buy the house, and you can go shares any time you decide. Is it a deal?"

They all agreed to sleep on it and arrive at a decision before too long.

"Good heavens," Ron exclaimed suddenly from his cosy chair by the fire. "That time already. I must go and leave you love birds together. Thank you for a most enjoyable evening, and I'm looking forward to seeing all the things you have to show me in this beautiful area of yours."

He sprang to his feet, kissed Lee on the cheek, and wrung Jack's hand in a warm gesture of friendship. As he was halfway through the door, he turned, and half over his shoulder he said as a parting shot, "I'm glad you two made it, I couldn't have wanted a better gift than your happiness."

And with that he was gone.

Chapter 23

The rest of that summer term was spent in blissful happiness – apart from having to go to school. Examinations had turned out to be a resounding waste of time, as everyone had pointed out. Teachers took little time over marking them, deciding ability levels far more effectively without them. Lists of class orders in all subjects magically appeared to satisfy the head, who filed each assiduously without so much as casting a perfunctory glance at them. There they would stay until some successor cleared them out, or the trump of Judgment Day began to blow.

Gloriously warm, sunny weather bustled its way in from around Whitsuntide - ideal weather for sunbathing with a class of readers surrounding you. Traditionally very little was achieved at this time of year by all the classes – with the exception of one. Stanley Awad's class *always* did something especially more advanced than any other group. The six weeks break towards the end of July set its stamp on everyone's thinking, affecting every teacher with tunnel vision, which became narrower as time crawled on. Diverse and 'different' activities proliferated during that last desperate drag to summer hols, where teachers invented strangely weird and wonderful pastimes to occupy their children outside when hot and inside when not.

Although Mr Moore had experienced this position forty

times already, he still felt the half term's grip on his collar as sweat, sometimes from trying to avoiding activities, ran in rivulets down his neck. Sports Day – the annual battle of the titans – was the first to re-awaken the Kraken, followed rapidly by the summer fayre-cum-jumble sale charged with raising a hundred pounds or so for school funds. For the staff this year, as a one-off, Mr Moore's celebration of his life in school would creep up on everyone. Everyone would tell each other how excited they were going to be and then boom - the day would dawn.

This was a particularly exciting and happy time for Lee and Jack, when their love began to grow and consume them. Her father was often heard to marvel that he'd never seen her looking happier or more radiant, sentiments her mother would have loved to share had she been around. During Whit they showed why millions of folks considered Yorkshire had the most beautiful countryside in the world.

York opened up its precious past to them, from their morning stroll around the walls to a dawdle through half-timbered tiny buildings in the Shambles to its fifteenth century Cathedral Minster, Ron couldn't believe that such a relatively small place could hold so many treasures of architecture and natural beauty, serenity and tranquillity as with St Mary's Abbey gardens.

In sharp contrast Harrogate shouldered its way in. At once open and bracing and fresh, with none of the close mustiness of ages past, its central position in the county allowed traditions of health, rest and relaxation to flourish. Its beautiful gardens welcomed the traveller who was unused to what it had to offer, and echoed its ancient name as the stunning enclosed park that it was. Harrogate was accepted not only as a glorious place in its own right, but as a centre for the many interests explorers might pursue around and beyond its boundaries.

Their encounter with the Ure Valley and the round trip from Harrogate to Jervaulx Abbey was one of their highlights that none of them had encountered before; along with the awe inspiring setting of that jewel of abbeys – Fountains. Very different in setting and nature, the two places appealed to different senses. Jervaulx's feeling of intimacy and closeness crept over them as they wandered through the ruins and on to the natural green carpet with its heady mix of of late-blooming cowslips – the only ones for miles around – and pale blue harebells mingling with dock and heath grass.

The narrowly winding and tortuous roads that had led them tantalisingly there had also whisked them through many pretty roadside villages where they had tarried a few moments, lost in the countryness of it all. They rejoiced in picturesque West Tanfield where they watched the rushing waters of the River Ure as they swirled mysteriously under its stone bridge, and soaked up the beauty of Aysgarth with its stunning waterfalls and billowy woodlands. Beyond Jervaulx they became captivated by East Witton crouching protectively around its village green.

They took lunch on the return journey at Ripon close to the river, before continuing their expedition to Fountains and Studley Park.

"I've never seen such wonderful countryside in such a small area," Ron Genet marvelled, as they cruised along the narrow winding snake of a lane on the approach to Studley Roger from Ripon, with Jack at the wheel of the Mark 10. His mouth gradually widened, however, as the road turned them through the East gate. Breath-takingly beautiful and majestic, the route before them squeezed them through a narrow bottleneck into the park. Trees of varying sizes and girths stood comfortably together with enough space for them to stretch out their limbs towards each other in gestures of friendship.

"Great Scott! Look over there," Ron exclaimed. "Aren't those animals ... deer?"

"Indeed they are," Jack smiled. "If we stay in the car, we'll be able to watch without frightening them away."

Although past the height of the day, the heat hung over the roadway in shimmering uncertainty, as if trying to bar the way in its desire to have them stay a little while longer. Not the slightest breeze disturbed the trees, providing no respite from the growing furnace outside the car as they passed. Deer languished, flicking away flies in what little shady corners they could find underneath sapling oaks. Heat in the car would have been unbearable had it not been for the draught through the open sunroof caused by their speed.

Rounding a knot of trees after a twisting series of hairpin bends, they were almost blinded by the intense flash of sun that ambushed them as they were confronted by the lake's unexpected appearance. Its cool-looking depths invited them to come, play, and rid themselves of the biting heat for a little while at least.

"There should be a reasonable amount of shade in here," Jack said as they headed to park under a galleon-like canopy of several huge oak trees. However, unfortunately for them, a large number of other day-outers had had the same idea that they might like to explore this treasure of a place.

Once inside the outer perimeter fence long, cool avenues of mature trees offered them rest and respite from the glaring heat, and even teased them with glimpses across the valley through living green windows. Ornamental lakes, lily ponds, waterfalls, and an army of classical statues beckoned them to come visit and spend time in their company. Shrubs and specimen trees abounded, offering the little and large of shorn banks of laurel, and the gargantuan height and girth of Norway spruce.

Out of the wooded walks, the long grassy approach to

the Abbey welcomed and soothed their tired feet with soft springy turf as the river chuckled and laughed along the open side. Although the most popular area in the park for picnics and for just sitting on the grass, there was scant space for many more people to walk let alone sit. Chequered multi-coloured picnic clothes covered the ground like so many legless tables around which to crouch and dine. Once folks had eaten their fill from now almost empty baskets, there was no immediate hurry to clear away, and so bodies simply sprawled where they were, to recover from their sumptuous meals, or simply … snoozed in the glorious sunshine.

Jack, Lee and her dad tarried long enough to cover the return journey homeward bound in the relative cool of the early evening. Jack's return route led them through miles of twisting but empty country lanes, allowing the cooler evening air to revitalise their heat-wearied bodies.

"Feel like a drink?" Jack asked as they approached one of the quaintest country inns in the district.

"Certainly do," was their excited return chorus, as they burst out laughing.

"Are we able to eat here?" Ron asked, feeling the need of something a little more comforting for his belly.

"Yes, of course," was Jack's immediate reply, pulling into the almost empty car park. "They serve one of the best chicken dinners-in-a-basket in Yorkshire. It's not very well known as an eating place, but those who do know, often return."

"Great," Ron added, as they walked towards the inn. "Now, you've given me a memorable time today - one of my happiest in fact. So, now it's my turn. The meal's on me."

"That's very generous of you," Jack replied. "I'll have the mixed grill, roast potatoes, asparag…"

"So that's chicken and chips all round then," Lee laughed.

The Turk's Head was a small but cosily appointed inn,

with copper-topped tables throughout. The eating area opened out from the bar, through a low square archway of oak beams and bare feature brick walls. Quite dim inside, it was lit by tasselled red lights hanging around the walls. Eaten in an atmosphere of tired contentedness, their meal certainly lived up to Jack's billing.

"You're not going to believe this," Ron sighed, fumbling through his pockets when he was about to summon the bill. "I can't find my wallet."

"Are you sure, Dad?" Lee asked, concerned. "Is it in your coat in the car?"

"I didn't bring a coat," he said, still with a puzzled look on his face. "No. I had it right here, in my hip pocket when we got back to the car park at Fountains."

"Well, the sum total of my fortune right now," Jack said, turning out his pockets, "is three and threepence, which won't, I'm afraid, cover the tip. I spent my last cash at the petrol station up the road. What about you, Lee?"

"I didn't bring any money at all, I'm afraid," she replied, looking rather worried. "What can we do?"

"Only one thing for it," Jack said, a smile creeping up on him. "You distract the waiter, Ron, and we'll make a bolt for the door. That should keep them locked in when you escape after us."

"Ha, ha," Lee said with a mock laugh.

"You stall the waiter here," Ron answered, getting up from his seat, "and I'll pop out to the car to see if I can turn up the wallet. The only thing we can do."

"…And what happens if you don't?" Lee asked.

"We'll cross that bridge when it's hatched," he said, winking as he left.

Sitting waiting for Ron to return, trying to make their coffee last, was something of a stretch, even for Jack. The barman eyed them suspiciously refusing to leave whilst they were still there. A quarter of an hour passed, and still no Ron, and the barman had decided he needed to investigate reasons for non-payment.

"Look out," Lee hissed. "He's coming across."

Built like a walking barn door, the barman decided he had waited long enough, eased himself through the service gate, and started his shamble across to see whether they might be prepared to fork out for what they had had. They tried to look unconcerned, but the half hour since they had finished their meal hadn't been easy.

"Can I get you anything else, – sir?" mumbled the walking mountain.

"Er, well, no, er, thanks, really," Jack replied, getting a little hot under the collar.

"Three dinners then," the barman continued, "will be one pound ten shillings and ninepence – if you please."

"Well, er, you see…" Jack began to stammer as the barman started to look menacing.

"There you are my man," a familiar voice tried to creep out from behind the human wall. "One pound fifteen shillings, and *do* keep the change."

Much to the eternal relief of all parties, Ron had returned at last.

"*You* took your time," Jack gasped, breathing an enormous sigh of relief as the barman retreated, satisfied with his haul.

"Had to turn the car over, you see," Ron explained, with a huge grin, "and that's difficult in daylight, let alone in the dark, but I found it eventually…"

"Where on earth was it?" Lee said. "Stuck in the seat?"

"…on the floor?" Jack interrupted.

"…in my coat pocket," Ron butted in again, finishing off his original sentence.

"But…?" the two chorused.

"I'd forgotten that I *had* brought it," he said, "and put it in the trunk because of the heat. That was the *last* place I looked."

They stared at each other, with looks of surprised relief lighting their faces, until they burst out laughing, much to the surprise and amusement of the other diners and drinkers.

–o–

Moore's retirement party was the last day but one of the current term, but the weather didn't match up to the occasion at first. Grey and uninteresting, over the previous few days it had threatened desperately needed rain to end the lengthy dry spell. The outriders of that particular storm had in fact swept in the night before, but were able only to dampen the pavements and tantalise the gasping grass and pleading plant life in general. Mr Moore was in quite a buoyant mood, for him, even though he had a good deal to do to organise the bash. Truth be known he had turned over that chore to the authority's catering services to provide a 'modest spread' after school, leaving him next to nothing to do.

Laying the foundations for the new school had been completed, just about, but the spread of workmen on to the school's field hadn't prevented children and staff alike from indulging their playing and sunbathing activities. Unusually for the council's works department, the project was well up to schedule, and apparently the shell itself would be erected by the company manufacturing its pre-cut sections in much less time than it had taken to lay the base. Making the place clean and habitable was up to others not employed by the clerk of works. All this exciting activity, however, hadn't stopped David trying to become a one-man demolition gang, as he bounced away more paint and plaster on a daily basis.

Many of Mr Moore's past colleagues had been invited to his sail away party - those who were still alive, that is.

314

One of the most exciting parts of his time in *this* school had been keeping folks guessing about the proceedings of this 'do', and keeping everyone away from the large area of the hall which he had had screened off. The comings and goings during the afternoon of strange folk carrying in untold numbers of mysterious packages and boxes, caused a great deal of clattering and scraping that nobody could even begin to guess at. Mr Moore's fixed and nervous smile seemed to have been painted on to his face throughout all of this.

Just before afternoon break, in a moment when there appeared to be nobody on guard at the perimeter fence, David mounted his attempt to peek, but Mr Moore appeared from nowhere and caught him. Mildly and good-humouredly chastising him, he sent him on his way with a metaphorical flea in his ear.

School finished at three as a one-off, allowing children to clear the premises and guests to arrive for the three thirty start. During that half hour, the staff enjoyed a lot of people watching, and guessing in which part of Mr Moore's professional life they belonged.

Three fifteen arrived; the time for unveiling the performance area, when screens would be removed to reveal...

...the most magnificent spread imaginable. Gasps from all echoed around the hall, everyone was astounded at the quality and variety of the fare that nobody would have associated with Mr Moore's natural parsimony.

Three long trestle tables groaned with large amounts and types of snack and finger food which almost defied description; vol au vents, sausage rolls, pies, open sandwiches, closed sandwiches, filled sandwich rolls, bun rolls, bread buns, tea bread, tea cakes currant and plain, fruit cake, marzipan fruit, cocktail cherries, nuts, crisps, and *five* different gateaux – the list was endless. Two catering attendants dispensed coffee and tea as overflowing plates were carried away to be gorged in some quiet corner before refills were sought, and there the merry-go-round would start again.

By three twenty-five, most of the guests had arrived from the far-flung corners of Yorkshire, and were standing about in knots of three or four to marvel at the party 'spread', urging it to begin.

"May I have your attention please, my friends?" Mr Moore shouted from a vantage point in the middle of the hall. "As you know, tomorrow is the last day of my 'term'" – loud guffaws – "and I have invited you all here today to help me celebrate my liberation. The food you see before you is, I can assure you, entirely edible and not left over from school dinners" – even louder laughter – "so I don't propose to bore you with long speeches. Consequently, I will ask you to help yourselves." Exceedingly loud cheers greeted the culmination of his entirely appropriate speech.

"An excellent speech," Jack said, turning to Lee and David.

"Too right," David agreed. "One of the best I have ever heard him give. Now come on, or we'll be left at the starting post."

The fare was exceedingly good; nothing second rate, even though it must have cost an arm and a leg. Still, it was Mr Moore's one and only act of extravagance in forty years of frugality. Everybody enjoyed the food, commenting on its quality and appropriateness. Everyone, that is, except Stanley Awad. He had been the only member of the school's staff to dissociate himself from the idea, insisting it was bound to be cheap and common, and would descend to a banal bun fight. Yet, despite his pre-party protestations, he had managed to force morsels between his lips many times whilst standing among admirers, a large plateful of goodies in his hand, that seemed to empty itself now and again to be magically refilled almost immediately after. This was a mark of respect, of course, for his friend and colleague, Mr Moore. David managed to eat enough for four, proclaiming afterwards that he hated to see good food go to waste. Jack would have followed suit but for Lee's steadying hand on his arm, although he did manage three large plates full of enticingly tasty goodies.

On the stroke of four, Cecil P Barchester made his entrance, right into the middle of a small group standing close to the door, who were extolling the virtues of their host. Two plates flew from two sets of surprised hands as Barchester found himself among them.

"I'm most awfully sorry," he gushed. "I didn't realise anyone might be behind the door. Here, let me…"

"No. It's quite all right, really," came the almost apologetic reply from two ageing ladies in grey two-piece suits. "It's our fault for being behind the door. Think no more about it."

"Well, at least let me retrieve and replenish your plates," he went on, gliding across to the food tables. Now everyone knew Cecil P Barchester was here. "Anything for two such charming ladies."

The ladies giggled and blushed in a girlish sort of a way, which took them back thirty-five years or more. They were his *first* new conquests. The first of many if Mr Barchester had anything to do with it. He intended fully to have both parents and staff eating out of his hand by the end of the year.

Time began to race, and Mr Moore could see that conversations were beginning to languish for want of something new to talk about. Being the good host, he tapped the table at precisely the right moment to begin to talk when an unexpected hush descended immediately, much to his surprise.

"Erm, well, ladies and gentlemen," he stammered, but quickly moved into his stride for the things he had practised.

317

"I am very glad to see so many of my former friends – when I say 'former' I don't mean of course you understand, that you are no longer my friends – and colleagues. Tomorrow may be the day I retire, but I have no intention of retiring from life. I will simply close one chapter and reopen another I have been meaning to reread for some years. I hope that you will not feel either that once away from school, you will never see me again, but will keep in touch.

"I have been in this game now more years than I care to remember, and have seen lots of changes – some good, some not so good. I am only sorry that I won't see started this area's newest venture, which will be led and directed by our guest today. Ladies and Gentlemen, may I introduce to you the new head teacher of Broughton Junior School, Mr Barchester."

Barchester stood up from his little table for four by the food trestles, slightly taken aback by this introduction. His surprise didn't, however, last for long. His self-confident yet boyish grin asserted itself as he accepted the acclaim offered by Mr Moore. He didn't make a speech to the gathering, but, taking over for a few moments, he had just a few words to say.

"Thank you very much, Mr Moore, both for your kind invitation and for those few words of introduction," he began. "I don't want to make speeches at someone else's party, but I should like to perform this one task instigated by the staff and parents of this wonderful school. As a mark of their esteem and gratitude to Mr Moore for his management over the years …"

He stopped for a moment and dipping his hands into a large holdall by his feet, he pulled out two packages and continued…

"Your staff and pupils wish you to accept these tokens of their respect and esteem, with every good wish for the future."

Both packages – one large and one small – were wrapped in brown gift paper and tied with the same red-coloured ribbon. Moore expected they might club together to get him something or other, he didn't expect that they would be *this* size! With fumbling and excited fingers, he broke his way into the larger parcel, and after much fiddling and ripping of paper, his hands emerged clutching a large ornately-bound tome about wildlife in the British Isles from the staff. The smaller one was from the children which they had collected the money at the rate of a penny or ha'penny each, and which they had turned into a rather nice ball pen.

Mr Moore was touched. His humanity struggled with his parsimony as it enjoyed the aesthetically pleasing presents and estimating their cost at the same time. His realism won by a short head. He was a good judge of value.

"I am very touched," he began, looking down at the presents in his hands. "I had thought to end on a note of thanks to my staff who, throughout my stay, have been a sterling help and support to me. However, I have now an even greater weight of thanks to press on them. In some ways I shall be glad to go but in others, sad. Whatever happens I shall think of Broughton with respect and gratitude, and hope I will be able to visit on occasion. What's that old saying? 'Don't lose your head when all about you are losing theirs…?' You are losing one Head but gaining another with whom, I feel, the traditions of the school will be safe. Thank you."

Obviously overcome by the occasion, he sat down abruptly next to his wife, who, smiling, had been a constant source of help and support throughout his career. They would now be able to enjoy many years of unencumbered freedom together when she retired the following year.

-o-

Last days of academic years are always somewhat tedious affairs which nobody really enjoys, except for the children, and even they tire from the lack of direction. Tidying up in the morning is usually followed by packing up, clearing out, and moving relevant stuff to the next class base. The afternoon traditionally is given over to playing games brought in by youngsters who are straining to start holidays. Flagging and tiring teachers are bolstered only by thoughts of tradition – the annual celebratory drink in the Ship at lunchtime, and the arrival of salary slips that can be drawn on immediately, much to the relief of most of them.

A great deal of to-ing and fro-ing allowed nobody any real peace and quiet, except for Mr Moore, who spent most of the time in his office leafing through his new book. Nobody thought anything of this even though he had indulged in the same activity for the last five years, feeling that he would have gotten under their feet anyway.

Lunchtime seemed to be another universe away. When it did arrive, the staffroom became littered quickly with exhausted bodies slumped almost comatose in easy chairs.

"Anyone for a pie and a pint?" David announced. "Or do you fancy school dinners instead? The first round is on … Jack."

"No chance of that," Jack replied indignantly. "You're paying today. I've no money."

"OK then," David agreed, "if you're coming you pay for yourself."

Everyone, including Mrs Josephs and Miss Peterson, decided to join the party; a matter which caused considerable surprise. Stanley, of course, had to be the odd one out as usual. His acceptance was conditional on not having to drink that awful beer. It just had to be wine for him. David replied that he couldn't care less what he drank as he was paying for himself anyway. The three old stagers were left to man the fort, as it wouldn't do to leave the school totally unmanned. Besides, it wasn't right for the officers to mingle with the other ranks.

The Ship wasn't noted for its exquisite cuisine, but it did provide a mean line in pies, pasties, pork sausage rolls – hot or cold – and sandwiches which on many occasions were infinitely preferable to the fare concocted by the school's canteen. Along with alcoholic stimulation and convivial company, lunchtimes grew into enjoyable oases in otherwise barren times.

Mrs Josephs and Miss Peterson turned out to be very good company, especially with a few glasses of cider under their belt, their dry sense of humour keeping the company in stitches throughout. Influenced by alcoholic vapours, they would have made a passable comedy double act, a matter suggested seriously by Jack. Expecting to be stamped upon for his presumptuousness, he was astounded that his suggestion was met by a hiccough and a giggle only.

"Well, I'm afraid we must away back to our nest," David said, trying to sound poetic as the bar clock stuttered its way around to twenty-five past one. "Unless, that is, you two beautiful ladies care to run away with me to some desert island in the middle of Scunthorpe?"

The last words he delivered with arms and mouth wide in a mock embrace. His answer was to have an extra strong mint dropped into his unsuspecting mouth from Lee, which had the effect of almost choking *him* and creasing everyone else. They all took their mints and sucked wildly in a vain attempt to remove all traces of their lunchtime excess from their breath before facing their last afternoon in school.

David and Jack had difficulty focusing throughout the afternoon, a matter exacerbated by insistent little children drawing them into their fiddly games with unreadable instructions. Jack's children cast him many a perturbed and puzzled look as he muddled through Monopoly, stuttered through Scrabble, and hadn't a clue in Cluedo. However, end of school saw them making their merry way home, glad to be liberated for another summer holiday break, leaving him sufficiently sober to stagger his unsteady way back to the staffroom to rehydrate his swollen and parched tongue and throat with mugs full of hot tea.

David was trying to focus on the last staffing bulletin of the year when Jack walked in.

"Now here's a job for you, my boy," David chirped. "You're going to have to move, you know, if you want to get on in this business. I'm sure you would be ideally qualified, what with your French and all."

"What's that, then?" Jack asked, quite absent-mindedly, as he drank his tea and waited for Lee. "Read it out."

"'Wanted for September next year, teacher i/c French, for Moor Secondary Modern School. Post will offer opportunities blah blah blah...'"

Jack didn't hear the rest. His mind was on that promotion possibility, and, of course, on the holidays just a few moments away. The door opened and his wife walked in, and as she did, a grin crept slowly across his face...

Author - Frank English

Born in 1946 in the West Riding of Yorkshire's coal fields around Wakefield, he attended grammar school, where he enjoyed sport rather more than academic work. After three years at teacher training college in Leeds, he became a teacher in 1967. He spent a lot of time during his teaching career entertaining children of all ages, a large part of which was through telling stories, and encouraging them to escape into a world of imagination and wonder.  Some of his most disturbed youngsters he found to be very talented poets, for example. He has always had a wicked sense of humour, which has blossomed only during the time he has spent with his wife, Denise. This sense of humour also allowed many youngsters to survive often difficult and brutalising home environments.

Recently, he retired after forty years working in schools with young people who had significantly disrupted lives because of behaviour disorders and poor social adjustment, generally brought about through circumstances beyond their control. At the same time as moving from leafy lane suburban middle class school teaching in Leeds to residential schooling for emotional and behavioural disturbance in the early 1990s, changed family circumstance provided the spur to achieve ambitions. Supported by his wife, Denise, he achieved a Master's degree in his mid-forties and a PhD at the age of fifty-six, because he had always wanted to do so.

Now enjoying glorious retirement, he spends as much time as life will allow writing, reading and travelling.